Maddalena and the Dark

Also by Julia Fine

The Upstairs House

What Should Be Wild

Maddalena
and the Dark

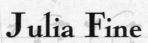

Julia Fine

FLATIRON
BOOKS
NEW YORK

This is a work of fiction. All of the characters, organizations, and events portrayed in this novel are either products of the author's imagination or are used fictitiously.

MADDALENA AND THE DARK. Copyright © 2023 by Julia Fine. All rights reserved. Printed in the United States of America. For information, address Flatiron Books, 120 Broadway, New York, NY 10271.

www.flatironbooks.com

Map design by Rhys Davies

Designed by Donna Sinisgalli Noetzel

Library of Congress Cataloging-in-Publication Data

Names: Fine, Julia, author.
Title: Maddalena and the dark / Julia Fine.
Description: First edition. | New York : Flatiron Books, 2023.
Identifiers: LCCN 2022045997 | ISBN 9781250867872 (hardcover) |
    ISBN 9781250867889 (ebook)
Subjects: LCGFT: Novels.
Classification: LCC PS3606.I53355 M33 2023 | DDC 813/.6—
    dc23/eng/20230112
LC record available at https://lccn.loc.gov/2022045997

Our books may be purchased in bulk for promotional, educational, or business use. Please contact your local bookseller or the Macmillan Corporate and Premium Sales Department at 1-800-221-7945, extension 5442, or by email at MacmillanSpecialMarkets@macmillan.com.

First Edition: 2023

10 9 8 7 6 5 4 3 2 1

This one's for Rick.

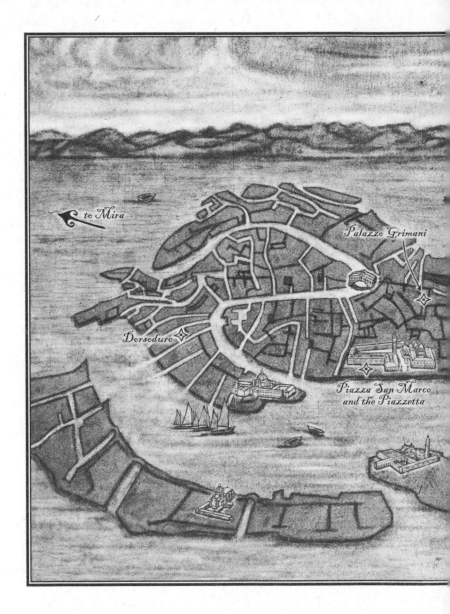

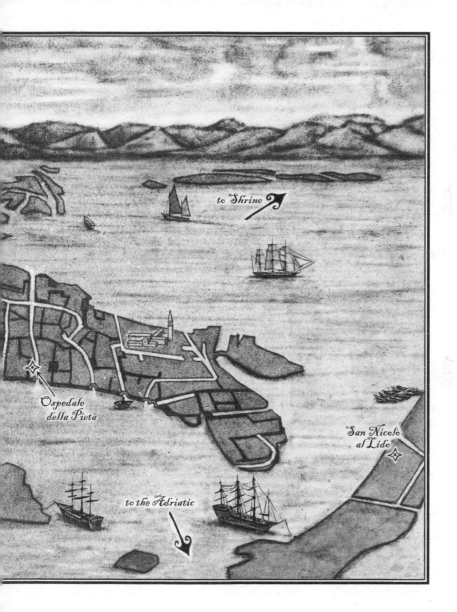

to Shrine

Ospedale
della Pietà

San Nicolò
al Lido

to the Adriatic

Maddalena *and the* Dark

Venice, 1717

There is so much that Luisa doesn't know. So much that Maddalena must tell her late at night, in whispers disguised as coughs when they hear the Priora stalk the hall. They lie together in a single bed in an airless dormitory in the Ospedale della Pietà, a home for foundlings since the fourteenth century, more recently a soil in which to cultivate the best young musicians in Venice. These musicians are girls, so they are told to play for God, rather than the many faces of La Serenissima, their Most Serene Republic. God excuses the fact that they are girls, that they play instrumental music, that sometime between the ages of eleven and fourteen they begin to desire and to bleed. They aren't meant to lie together, two to a cot, whispering. Before, Luisa didn't. Nights were spent asleep. All her dreams went unremembered.

They are newly fifteen. Luisa has always been here; Maddalena recently arrived from outside. To their left, Maddalena's bed is empty. To their right, one of the other girls wheezes rhythmically, head hidden by her pillow. Moonlight proves no match for two small, shuttered windows, the candles long doused. At dawn the bells will ring and the girls will rise for prayer, they'll eat and sew and take the air and play their music. Maddalena's big toe tickles the tender inner flesh of Luisa's foot.

"Every year for Festa della Sensa, the doge rows out to San Nicolò al Lido," Maddalena says. "He drops a ring into the water, and all the boats line up to watch him. And then he says a prayer and goes to Mass, and then we're married."

"Who is?" asks Luisa.

"All of us. The city and the sea."

"Why?" asks Luisa.

Maddalena presses a finger to Luisa's lips.

"Does the doge love the water, or is he afraid?"

"There is no *or*," says Maddalena. She curls her icy toes around Luisa's ankle. "Once he's tossed the ring, it's celebration. All feasting and music and games. We'll go together, when we're older."

They'll go together, tutti, a whole contained within the two of them. The girls press sole to sole, heel to heel. On Maddalena's, a ripening blister where her right foot has recently grown larger than her left. On Luisa's, the puckered *P* of the branding iron, claiming her for the Pietà.

"When I marry—" says Maddalena. Luisa waits, but Maddalena doesn't continue. Several beds down, somebody whimpers in her sleep.

When I marry, I'll wear pearls for a year, like every newlywed noblewoman, Maddalena might have said. She might have said: *When I marry, it will be to a youngest son, the only noble sons who marry in Venice.* She might have said: *When I marry, it is likely you'll stay here.* She might have said: *Will I marry?*

Maddalena says none of this. The unfinished sentence sits over them, a haze.

Maddalena's breathing slows and her eyes are shut, but Luisa can tell she's awake. A noise from the floor above. The dark coils of Maddalena's hair. Luisa rolls to her back and stretches her left hand flat across her stomach, lengthening each individual finger.

There has already been a bargain, and this is something else that Luisa does not know. A darkness takes its shape and fattens, coursing through the Ospedale della Pietà and its courtyards, past the gates, where the lagoon stretches out toward the sea. It rides down the canals in the whistling of the gondoliers, and it splashes the steps of the frescoed palazzi.

But before debts are collected, there are two girls breathing beside each other, legs entwined.

Luisa shuts her eyes. She pictures silty wedding rings, Maddalena's long hair weeping down her back. A deep-sea dirge and barefooted girls in soaked nightdresses, lips pursed around their post horns, reams of brackish water falling from barnacled cellos.

Spring

Maddalena

It begins with Maddalena at the edge of the gondola. Not alone, of course—her father's man to steer them, her eldest brother, Nicolò, leaning out from the cabin to watch the tail of the doge's bucintoro as it moves toward the Adriatic, flag jutting from the massive state barge to marshal the crowds, the winged Lion of Venice fierce upon red velvet. Somewhere on board her father, in his bright red robe, will be taking his duties very seriously, talking to many important men about important affairs. Her middle brothers, Beneto and Andrea, have already absconded, off to sample courtesans from safely behind their tied masks.

"A coward's choice, to wear the bauta for Festa della Sensa," Nicolò had said as they donned the black cloaks and tricorn hats and tied on the false faces that made them anonymous—thick white visors hiding all but the eyes and the occasional shadow of the chin. Maddalena imagines her brothers as turtles protecting soft meat under their papier-mâché bautas, their true selves impenetrable. For almost seven months a year, the Venetian elite go masked in all her public spaces. The rest of the republic at least pretending anonymity, with Nicolò here sunning himself, belly up, as prey.

He's removed his hat, and as they follow the bucintoro away from San Marco, his hair—his own—keeps plastering to his mouth. Their pace is slow across the vast lagoon, around the isle of Lido, which buffers Venice's main island from the Adriatic Sea. State gondoliers in their red velvet capes are too well dressed to do the actual work of rowing, so little boats filled with musicians tug the ambassadors' gilt gondolas, while more sleek black carriages follow behind. Then a parade of other boats—merchants and fishermen, pleasure crafts with pampered dogs and women drinking wine, boys with drums and pipes, men singing. Maddalena expects Nicolò to criticize the profligacy, the Venetian predilection for turning the spiritual into spectacle. *Surely we can show up Rome without these damned fireworks,* he should be saying, or *How much money did they spend to wrap that damask around those columns?* But Nicolò is silent. Planning something, bothered by something. He keeps looking at her sideways.

The gilded flotilla slows, its music dwindles. Maddalena turns her head to see the city behind them, an impossible stone kingdom rising from the water. Venice fancies herself man against the elements, although this is the calmest of spring mornings, and if the sky showed signs of rain, the senators would have rescheduled the ceremony. Still, the elements: the churn of the sea, which lilts the boats. The inconsiderate squalls of the birds. A mosquito at Maddalena's ear, humming.

All eyes are on the doge at the bow of his barge, his reedy Latin inaudible over the slap of water against the boat. Everyone knows what he is saying. "Desponsamus te, mare, in signum veri perpetique dominii." *We wed thee, sea, as a sign of true and perpetual domination.*

There are two churches in Venice, Rome's and the rule of the state. Maddalena reveres neither, though superficially she's forced to bow to both. Religion is like duty to her family: inevitable, uninterested in her personal opinion. And yet this ritual, the water, the requisite renewal of vows, the wedding band held overboard, the breath held quiet. If ever she believes in more than people's will to power, it is now, acting as witness to the love between a city and the sea.

Once the doge's ring is lost to the waves, artillery fires and the politesse is overrun by cheers. Horns sing out, drums resume. Nicolò turns to Maddalena. He squints.

"Well?" she says. "Come out with it."

"In light of . . . everything," Nicolò begins, which seems foreboding. Maddalena wants to press this *everything,* find out how and why it has conspired against them.

Instead she just says, "Yes?"

"In light of everything," Nicolò repeats, "we have decided you'll go to the Pietà."

She'll go to what?

"The Ospedale?" Maddalena laughs. He's joking, he must be. The Ospedale della Pietà, where orphaned and illegitimate Venetian daughters go to make celibate music? Abandoned girls come as nurslings, and mostly they stay. Maddalena's father is on the board of governors, which must be why they'd even consider her, as she is not an orphan, not a foundling in material need. Once Venice's four Ospedali Grandi were just hospices, but now they act as musical conservatories, their churches packed to the rafters on Sundays. A point of pride for her father to watch his girls at the Pietà outdo the Mendicanti or Incurabli with some haunting oratorio. For Nicolò, who'll one day take her father's place, to watch the neat economy of the concerts that pay for upkeep of the rest within the Pietà's walls.

Nicolò likes a balanced equation. All morning, Maddalena has wondered if another of his marital alliances fell through. Two years of promises and parlays, and they always come to nothing. How much longer will he try? It must be well past time to send her to a nunnery. She thought perhaps she'd take the veil at San Lorenzo, where for enough money girls of her ilk can have well-furnished apartments and social lives that, while confined to the grated parlatorio, might occasionally stir gossip. Maddalena remembers visiting a cousin at San Zaccaria as a child and seeing all the Sisters' gallants, the room delighting in displays of marionettes.

But this? The Pietà gives no puppet shows.

"You're finally disowning me, then?" She means it to be cutting, a jab at the rumors that have surrounded the Grimani family since her birth, rumors rekindled by her mother's disappearance three years ago. But Maddalena's voice cracks, and, embarrassed by her weakness, she hardens against Nicolò's look of sympathy.

The Ospedale della Pietà. Ridiculous. Impossible. He won't say how he's gotten her a place at the school, which is not really a school, no matter that it gives an education. Not a school, but a mill. A place to change Maddalena, to grind her.

"Why?"

"You're good at singing," says Nicolò. A stretch.

"Why?" Maddalena asks again, though they both know the answer. She is still being punished for her mother's sins. It doesn't matter how demure she is, how modestly they keep her. She can swallow her resentment, her frustration, she can curtsy at her father's table for her father's guests, and still they say, "Ah, but her mother." She can smile until her mouth is a puppet's slit, and still they say, "How can we trust what she'll become?"

"You think without this I won't find a husband." Maddalena stares out at the crowd, readying itself for the customary regatta, men goading one another between boats, flicking their oars. A vessel approaches, packed with pigeons protesting captivity, legs already weighted with the heavy paper that will keep them flying low and close to the crowd when they're released after Mass. Some puff their chests and sound pitiful coos, others stand frozen. Their ferryman tuts at them, laughing, lifting an oar to douse a particularly ornery bird.

"It isn't that you won't find a husband," Nicolò says over the drums, "but if we're gambling—"

"You're never gambling. It's why you're no fun."

"Well, I'm not going to play your future at a gaming table. We're going to give you an advantage. You'll cultivate a talent, and you'll prove that you're devout and take instruction, and if a husband doesn't come . . ." Nicolò coughs. "What would you prefer? To be a nun? To go immediately to a nunnery?" The tops of his ears are turning pink. People think Nicolò too sober for the casino, too clever. No, he has too many inborn tells.

"I would prefer for things to be the way they were," says Maddalena, although she knows the question is rhetorical, the desire impossible.

"Maddalena."

"I'm not going to do it. You've made the offer and I've listened, and I decline." She gives a pinched smile, to show him she does not need refinement. Then, to drive the point home, she says, "Thank you."

"Maddalena."

"You can't force me." Unspoken between them: that he can.

They sit, both looking out at the bucintoro, a gaudy golden pastry of a ship with its massive figurehead and rows of red oars, bobbing proudly at the center of the gathered crowd as it waits for the doge to finish hearing Mass. Finally his entourage emerges from the monastery, and Nicolò moves to the far side of the gondola to see the senators off to their celebratory feast. Maddalena uninvited, unmoving, as he waves to the passing barges.

She should have seen it coming. They rarely bring her out for Carnival or feast days, determined to keep the daughter from her mother's reputation. Nicolò views the world as an accountant's scale, and never offers pleasure without consequence.

The afternoon's perfection rankles her. The sky looks almost the same blue as the lagoon, spilling over with voluptuous clouds and that salted breeze sailing in from the Adriatic. Laughter escapes a nearby gondola, a voice raised over the rest: "Meet me at the Fiera, near the glass peddlers." A lone heron barking through the gentler birdsong; a woman pretending to be scandalized, her *ooh* and *ahhh*. The final two weeks of the Carnival season have begun, and all are giddy not because Jesus readies rooms for them in heaven, but because His Ascension brings them earthly delights.

This is the sort of day that Maddalena lives for—gentle, sun-dappled, significant. The city overflowing from the canals, from the lagoon out to the sea. Here is Venice, wedded to the water, still strong, despite the powers in the west, the newfound trade routes and the English shipbuilders and the money that Nicolò claims bleeds from the republic by the minute. Here is Venice as the rest of the world should remember her. The doge's oarsmen begin to sing, to row in rhythm. The bucintoro recedes.

Since her mother left, her life has gotten smaller. Gone are the visits from her former friends, her scandal too infectious. No more not-quite-secret trips with Andrea to the coffee shop, or picnics with Beneto's cohort, nothing that could be interpreted as flashy or untoward—only dull old Aunt Antonia to shuffle and chaperone. Once Maddalena enters the Pietà, there will be no political guests at the dinner table, no sunning on the roof of the palazzo, no leaning out over the canal at dawn to watch a drunken Andrea appear with the sun. It could be years before she's back at Lido, years before she sees the sea. The water, the narrow beaches, the distant trade ships that wait for inspection, mere toys in the distance, the misty view of the main island from afar. They want her to exchange it all for an old church school, with no gardens. An assortment of orphans, who eat plain foods and attend no balls and make boring conversation about violins and God.

She won't do it. She'll run away. She'll hide out in a bell tower. She'll lock herself in her room and refuse all food and water until Nicolò takes pity and sets aside his plan.

But then what? What will happen when Beneto is finally married, when there's no one to keep her and she has nothing to call her own? Maddalena would not prefer a nunnery. She sees Nicolò's logic, and she knows that if he's made the proposition, it's already been decided with their father, who will spoil her in the days before she goes, and act as if he has no say in the matter. As always, Nicolò has been left to do the difficult things. As he desires it, Maddalena thinks, because if he is the one doing the difficult things, he at least approves of how they're getting done. And there are many difficult things these days, with the nouveaux riches ascending, the noble families anemic, spread too thin. There are too many daughters and not enough sons, and there's no room for a girl with suspect parentage, Grimani name or no. Her father will never let her marry below her station, and within and above it are a smattering of youngest sons with the brightest of Venetian women to choose from, all with demure mothers and clean blood. Maddalena supposes she is desperate, that Marcantonio and Nicolò are desperate. Yet she herself has not felt actual desperation until now, being told she must go.

The Pietà musicians are rumored to be angels in their white dresses, standing in the choir loft above the church, behind their shadowed grate, anointing their audience. Who could refuse an angel? Or, concedes Maddalena, a pretty enough girl with a title, who has studied with the angels.

The vessels turn back to the Molo, a slow procession of giddy celebrants ready to feast. Nicolò finds someone to talk to in an adjacent boat, gesticulates such that one false step would send him toppling. Maddalena tries to hate him, but she doesn't. She doesn't envy Nicolò in the way that she does Beneto or Andrea. That he is a man, yes. That his peers seem to respect him, even like him. But he's so often at odds with himself, so often anxious and uncomfortable. Instead she hates herself, so ineffectual.

Maddalena turns from Nicolò, looks down at the now-empty place where the doge wed the waves, not twenty feet from where the Grimani boat rests. She finds no sign that the sea has sworn fealty to Venice, no manifestation of the awe she's just felt. The water is placid and formless, reflecting a perverse sketch of her own pinned hair, her dark dress. Her father has explained the Sensa ceremony as a mutual agreement rather than an ownership, a bond that supposedly benefits both parties, even as it appears to enrich only one. Venice asks of the sea its protection from invaders, its salt and its steady level, its proximity to trade. What does the sea want of Venice? What does the doge sign away with his yearly vow? *We wed thee, sea, as a sign of true and perpetual domination.* But who dominates? Do they dominate together? Maddalena has trouble believing that they do. Maddalena has trouble with that word, *together*. She is more like Nicolò than she cares to be, seeing the universe as transactional. Open to life, but never trusting it.

And what is there to trust? A mother who runs out on you? A brother who sells you like chattel and a father too busy to care? Whatever power the sea gives Venice doesn't extend to Maddalena, who can refuse with all the fury she can summon yet still find herself trapped in the Pietà compound on the Riva degli Schiavoni, as her family demands. She has no influence, no one who'll listen. Her only sovereignty over her body, and barely that. What would Nicolò do if he found her hanging from the glass chandelier in her bedroom? She pictures him racing toward her apartments, flinging open the door, seeing her. She could never go through with it. Besides, the chandelier would come down with her, too delicate to handle her weight. Could she jump into the lagoon? Maddalena imagines the inhalation, wonders if she has the will to submit. She leans down, trying to see herself clearly, but the light is wrong.

There, against the tide. Lapping, lapping, at the edge of the black gondola. If asked, Maddalena could not describe it, not its color or its size, the way it moves below the water, the way it glistens up at her.

She pulls back, looks around quickly. Does anyone else see? Surely someone should see, someone should help. Someone should row them away from this *thing*, the way it reaches and writhes, asking her to move closer, asking her to bend down and look. When she does, she sees a girl here with the darkness, or the semblance of a girl. About Maddalena's age, fully submerged, neither swimming nor drowning. Her hair floats up in fronds about her head, the white-gold color all the courtesans use bleach and sun to master. She wears white, and holds a violin aloft like a torch, its neck grasped so tightly Maddalena can almost feel the strings slicing the insides of her fingers. Can this girl see Maddalena? Her eyes are clouded over with what could be tears or cataracts or might just be the water, silty when the sea floor is disturbed. But she is looking in Maddalena's direction, she is turning toward Maddalena and opening her mouth, and as she opens it the water rushes in and she is sinking, heavy with the weight, until she has sunk past where Maddalena can see. The released violin drifts up to the surface. Maddalena leans farther, reaching out an arm to rescue it, but the f-holes are filling and it's lowering, too low, and then gone. Before she can raise her torso back onto the boat, that first shadow returns. Solidifies. It clasps her hands, its touch cold.

And the thing asks Maddalena, without speaking: *What do you want?*
And the thing asks: *What will you pay for it?*

Luisa

The new girl comes in May, in a black dress, during Latin. She stands in the doorway with Figlia Menegha, her eyes defiant.

"Are you sending her to class *now*?" asks Maestra Vittoria brusquely. "Bring her to her room and find her something to wear."

"Who is she?" asks Chiara. When the maestra glares: "Quis est?"

Maddalena Faustina Grimani, fifteen years old, the only daughter and fourth child of Marcantonio Grimani, who sits on the board of governors for the Ospedale della Pietà. She has a promising alto, a bit of talent with the viola de gamba, and enough family influence for the board to admit her despite her claim to at least one living parent.

"What this means," says Maestra Vittoria to her chittering class, "is that her family understands that the education we provide here is among the best in Venice. You will welcome her and treat her as you would one of our own."

Luisa tries to focus on her lesson, but behind her Orsetta is whispering. She can make out a muffled "chance" and a "bassoon" and then a giggle before "brother." When the maestra looks up, Orsetta's curly head dives down and Luisa is reminded of a bird seeking out food in the canals, Orsetta's meager meal not worms or fish but novelty. She thinks that Orsetta should be above such distraction. Repetition makes musicians, and at the Pietà, music is all that need be made.

But when Maestra Vittoria leaves the room, talk immediately turns to why Maddalena has been sent here, what it means. The girls have theories—she has come as a reward for her good work spying for the

Council of Ten, or else as a consequence for running away with a penniless gondolier. The Pietà takes foreign girls of noble birth, and it offers private lessons to the wealthy girls whose families can pay, but rarely does a Venetian of means enter their enclave so fully. Is Maddalena Grimani exceptional, or has she done something wrong? Having spent their lifetimes told that they are blessed to be sheltered here while watching out the window as the city sings without them, the Pietà girls can't come to a consensus.

While they chatter, Luisa's thumb rubs the calluses on her left fingertips, a childhood habit formed when the skin was first thickening. She considers that morning's rehearsal: how she froze when the maestra called her up, then the additional embarrassment of comparing what she'd done in the practice room to what she played for the group. The way Orsetta giggled from behind her double bass, and Adriana seemed genuinely distressed, as if her own value depended on Luisa's performance.

This has been happening to Luisa more often, this anxiety that creeps in to stiffen her fingers. She tells herself she's ready to accept a role as a lesser player, she doesn't need to be a star, but it's a lie. When she plays for herself—alone in the small sala, or during recreation hour while the other girls gather in the courtyard to roll hoops—she will think she's made a breakthrough, that at the next rehearsal the maestre will stand open-mouthed and say, *Luisa, how you've grown!* Then she's called to demonstrate in front of the group, and her heart pounds and she wonders if her palms will sweat and what she must look like, foolish and frozen and unable to begin. When she finally does begin, it's as if she is behind a sheet of glass while her body makes the motions without her. The notes are fine, but without feeling.

In the dormitory, wearing the red dress and white apron, Maddalena Grimani performs well, playing the part of a foundling despite the perfumed hair that escapes from her cap, and not a callus to be seen on her soft hands. She smiles at the girls flocking in after lessons, overly magnanimous in a way Luisa finds suspicious.

They gather around Maddalena, but Luisa stays apart. She practices her fingering against the edge of the mattress, marking the rhythm of the solo Anna Maria dal Violin played at Sunday's mass. *One*, one two three, and a *one*, one two three. This becomes the rhythm of girls' laughter, in bursts across the room as Maddalena speaks in her low voice. Should Luisa move to listen? Adriana has moved closer, standing awkwardly at the edge of the circle of girls, not quite excluded but by no means welcomed in. Luisa blushes on her behalf, keeps counting.

She's seen other musicians work through blocks, how girls lighten the pressure on the strings or purse the mouth or lower the reed and sound as if they have discovered a new instrument. She's watched girls catapult to soloist overnight, and be laid permanently low by a sprained finger.

The Pietà began Luisa with the oboe—at six she was taller for her age than most of her cohort, and the pipeline of oboists was depleted when Helia dal Oboe got married in the same year her initiate died of typhoid. Someone had to be groomed as a replacement, and Luisa's industrious disposition and relative height made her an ideal choice.

When played well, Luisa finds the oboe feline—a confident, bright sound that she prefers to its skulking sister, the clarinet. Unfortunately, Luisa didn't play the oboe well. After four months of little progress, she was given leave to abandon the endeavor and move to an instrument of her choice, the maestre having noticed her diligence and feeling generous despite her defeat. Of course Luisa chose the violin.

If the oboe is a trial of pure athleticism—having just the right amount of breath, pursing the lips just so—the violin is also psychological. It, too, requires physical discipline, but more so it demands total emotional devotion. To be great requires hours of the same fingered octaves, manipulating vibrato, the careful pressure from one string to the next.

Although she's known them all since they were small, Luisa hasn't bonded with the other girls in the way that she has with the violin. They don't dislike her, and for the most part she does not dislike them, but lately she wonders if this aloofness is why she can't play. She's never opened herself, doesn't know how to finesse feeling. Luisa watches Maddalena, act or no, conduct the dormitory so cleanly. A deferential nod of the head. An invitation to examine a silk shawl.

One, one two three, and a *one*.

By evening meal Maddalena has found her full court, gliding arm in arm through the passageways with Chiara and Orsetta, a wake of less enviable girls cresting behind.

"She's so *experienced*," says Adriana.

"We've had experiences," says Luisa to her soup.

"And she has *brothers*." Adriana sits poised and waiting, flush with the thought of opportunity.

"So? Only the youngest will marry, and he won't marry you."

"Marriage isn't everything." Adriana's gaze is fixed across the room, where Maddalena sets down her spoon. Adriana's tongue wet and pink, traveling her crooked teeth. Adriana's eyes restless.

Luisa looks, trying to see what the other girls see. When Maddalena rises, Adriana stands so quickly that her elbow knocks a tureen, slopping soup onto her skirt. She pats at the stain while Maddalena and her syco-phants make their way: coming closer, coming closer. Adriana smoothing and smoothing, that tongue seeking the crevice where a molar rotted several months ago, its removal an ordeal for the whole dormitory.

But Maddalena moves past Adriana to where Luisa sits, staring at her bowl, feeling two and then four and then six sets of eyes at her collar. If she doesn't look up, she won't have to face them, their twisted expressions, their curiosity as to why Maddalena has chosen her, and not someone else. What makes Luisa so interesting? Who is she? Truly, who is she? A second violinist. A quiet girl, who holds herself apart.

Maddalena is bold in her attention, unashamed. If Luisa breathes slowly, she thinks she might halt the blood that travels to her cheeks. She pictures frost coating the grates on her window, berms of ice on the canals. I will not, she thinks, break first.

What remains in her bowl sits oily and shining, reflecting the light.

Orsetta and Chiara, the newly anointed, seem unsure of their responsibilities to their mistress. They cough. They sniff. They glower at Adriana and Luisa.

Then Maddalena turns and smiles, her palms open: *Of course.* She follows Chiara and Orsetta, Adriana scurrying behind. Luisa looking after them, waiting for Maddalena to turn back. And Maddalena doesn't.

Maddalena

Maddalena recognizes Luisa immediately—the white-blond hair, the large doe eyes, a little scar below the right one, smallpox most likely, though if so she has gotten off easily. The Pietà ceilings suddenly seem higher, the air less stale, the constant bells demanding prayer less relentless.

"Are you sending her to class *now*?"

Maddalena must tear herself from the classroom to follow the figlia, looking back as she's led down an austere hall. She's either been chosen for something wonderful, or else she has gone mad. From any point of view, she has mismanaged things: too shocked to speak to the thing in the water, too frozen to reach out and take. After the Sensa, she resigned herself to the Pietá. She remembered the drowning violin, and she hoped. She didn't cry to leave her father's house, but now she feels she could, because here is the girl from the water, sinking into her seat.

The sea, ten days earlier. Maddalena would call it a dream, if not for the ineffable heat in her gut, set alight that afternoon, burning steadily since.

"Menstruation," said the maid, useless as Maddalena tried to explain.

Maddalena shook her head, just as she had shaken her head when she tried to describe that crucial moment to Nicolò, who'd looked across the gondola to see his sister leaning over the edge and scolded her for histrionics.

"If you'd rather drown than go have music lessons," he'd said, "that's your prerogative. But wait until I'm somewhere else so Father doesn't blame me."

"Didn't you—" Maddalena began. The water was calm, as it always was for the Sensa. Not a ripple. Not a sign that anything had passed between Maddalena and the sea, but for that burning. Still, she'd heard it, an echoing, a rasp in her own head, a thing that wasn't her thoughts, that came from everywhere and nowhere. It had asked, and she had not known what to answer.

What do you want?

What will you pay?

What did she want? A husband, safety, fame, a different life, her mother. A shawl against the sudden chill. A guarantee that she'd be happy. A partnership. She wanted to know, and she wanted to answer, but the gondola moved and the fog lifted and the moment was gone.

A quiet woman takes Maddalena through the kitchens, where one sister rolls dough, another cleans a copper pot, another stirs rice at the fire. A little dog nips at Maddalena's heels, and the woman holding her arm shoos it away. She smells something frying, the air heavy with grease and smoke. A bench is laid with salt-cured fish, and in the next room a girl lines a long table with artichokes and hums to herself. Through to the next, where an even younger girl sweeps the floor and another woman haggles with a man holding an octopus. Finally they reach the laundry, where more women are at work. A red dress for Maddalena, simple but soft. She steps out of her black one, ties on the obligatory white shawl, the white bonnet. When she looks down at her body she laughs, because here is a disguise just as potent as the cloaks her brothers wear, almost as anonymous as the bauta. A girl among girls. Unrecognizable.

Yet another woman brings Maddalena to her dormitory. As they walk the maze of halls, she takes note of the water gate, the alleys, any glimpse of a canal through a window, buckets in doorways, the sheen of recently mopped tile. The walls are bare but for the occasional niched shrine. Days at Venice's four Ospedali Grandi are spent at prayer, Beneto warned her. One of his friends had married a girl from the Incurabli, and she prayed upon waking, before eating, when she stepped onto a boat. Before the Sensa, Maddalena would have protested, but now this devotion will serve her. Now she has something to worry like a rosary: a desire to unravel, and a creature in the water to which she hopes to someday pray.

She's placed with the musicians, although her musical talent is middling, and by rights she should have a private room. Nicolò swears austerity will make her valuable—she'll gain character-building perspective, by mere proximity improve at domesticity, at deference, at the viola de gamba. The dormitory girls flock to her once they've finished with their lesson and devotion, each pausing to kneel in prayer while she sits on her new straw bed, watching them.

"Et semper, et in saecula saeculorum, am—are you staying here?" says Chiara, standing before her *amen*, eager to beat the rest to the new specimen.

"Of course she's staying here. Why would she be here if she wasn't staying?" Orsetta is almost as quick with her Gloria, but not quite.

Maddalena smiles her vaguest smile over their patter, surreptitiously seeking the blond girl from before, who kneels at her bedside, still whispering. Whispering to God? Or something else?

At Palazzo Grimani, Maddalena tried. To be mild. To accept her brothers' directives with grace, to smile at the guests and be the easiest version of herself. Every member of the family had a role, and hers was to negate the memory of her mother, quell talk of bastardy and cuckolds, staunching the rumors that have trickled down to stain both Maddalena and her brother Beneto. Never mind that she's a child, the youngest, the only girl. If she can marry well, society will smile at Beneto, and decide that he must also be legitimate, for why would a wealthy noble family welcome a bastard to its fold? How could the brother be tainted if the sister is pure? If Beneto can marry, then Andrea doesn't have to. Their branch of the Grimani name will flourish, and Andrea can focus on what he does best, which, Maddalena thinks, is drunken carousing. Anyway, he will be happy. Nicolò can pursue his political ambitions without fear of a scandal.

Too many people's happiness rides on Maddalena's marriage prospects, including her own. This she has known since her mother disappeared, since Aunt Antonia sat her down and said that life was never easy for a girl, and for everyone's sake she should do as she was told and stop bickering. There's no way to argue with someone who tells you to stop bickering, not without proving them right about you. So Maddalena tried to listen, and she tried to sit still, and over the past three years she thought she'd done a rather good job of disguising the fact that she is a person, with interests, with feelings, with taste.

She understands the Pietà to be Nicolò's final effort at extinguishment. A church school where girls are not supposed to speak idly, where days are regimented and individuality a curse. True, her dormmates flock to her because she is novel. Because they know that the nobility is powerful, and no one's told them that even a noble girl is just a woman once she's outside these walls. So she can stoke their little rivalries, command their little ship. Here, the girls admire her, but don't see her. At home, if her family sees her, they have chosen not to care.

You still might have influence. This Maddalena remembers as she shivers in her new bed the first night in the Pietà dormitory. She at her mother's feet, age five or six, fiddling with a broken doll. A cousin? A friend? The daughter of a friend? How many women must have come to her mother's rooms, bemoaning their fates? Some shadowed female figure on the chaise and her mother's hands stroking Maddalena's hair, her mother's slippered foot at Maddalena's bottom gently prodding, bouncing in time with her words.

For influence, what wouldn't you pay?

But this is wrong, this memory. It speaks too perfectly to Maddalena's current mind, and it smells of the marsh. Her mother's foot bouncing and bouncing and then suddenly a kick, the sort you'd give a little dog whose nearness smothers.

Be careful, Maddalena thinks as she falls into sleep, although unsure who she's addressing. *I'm not afraid of you.*

Luisa

The game has begun: who might look without herself being seen, who might catch the other out. The more exaggerated Maddalena's indifference, the more desperate Luisa becomes to hold her notice. With Maddalena nearby, Luisa trips over her shoes as she leaves the dinner table, tangles herself in the lace bobbin while at work. And Maddalena is always nearby, on the lips of every girl—the way she styles her hair, her husky solfeggio, her brothers, who come to see her when they can, despite the Pietà's rules and the Priora's disapproval.

"The youngest is handsome," says Chiara as they wait for the maestra during group music lessons, her chair dragged into the geometric swaths of sun that slant through the high windows. "But the oldest is clever."

"And the middle?" Adriana leans forward.

"The middle is a rogue."

Luisa pretends to busy herself with her bow, searching out dirty hairs.

"Tell more!" says Adriana, invigorated.

"Well—" Their two dark heads are bowed together, giggling, when Maestra Simona comes in. Luisa thinks she'll reprimand them, but even the maestre, even the Coro, have succumbed. Instead of arpeggios, they all spend the next fifteen minutes discussing the cut of Andrea Grimani's cloak. Luisa comes away from the group lesson with little new knowledge of either the maestro dei concerti's newest sonatas, or of

Maddalena herself, who sweeps in half an hour late, smelling of brine
and snuffed candle.

Where were you? No one asks, but as they put away the instruments
Luisa lingers, trying to glean answers from the dirt at Maddalena's hemline, the one escaping curl of hair at the nape of her neck. When Chiara
grabs her hand to leave, Maddalena shakes her head.

"My—" She makes a half-hearted gesture toward her sheet music.
Chiara's nostrils flare a moment before her face resumes a studied pla-
cidity. It's been a week since Maddalena's arrival, and though a tentative
hierarchy has been established, lines are not yet fully drawn. Right now,
Maddalena's good graces mean immediate social capital, make Chiara
remarkable—what every foundling girl at heart most hopes to be. To
walk with Maddalena means the other girls will look at her the way
they once looked only at soloists—a mix of reverence and jealousy that
earns the final roll at dinner, an extra blanket when the dormitory window creaks. But Chiara is pragmatic. Who is to say what next week will
bring, or the week after? She frowns and leaves the room, and here are
only Maddalena and Luisa. Neither girl speaking, neither girl looking
away.

Maddalena's eyes are dark, a black that in a certain light shines indigo.
She looks at Luisa and raises her fist to rest against her mouth. Luisa feels
anointed. She thinks she should do something momentous; something
grand must be expected. Still grasping her violin, she feels each muscle
in her hands and the back of her neck.

Luisa lightly twists the peg of her A string, a small movement at first,
barely enough to change the sound. But Maddalena is watching, is curious, and so Luisa turns the peg again, feels the string tighten, feels the
pressure of the string against the bridge. It is frayed; it could snap. Another
turn, and Luisa's like a tightrope walker actively choosing not to look
down while creeping out above a city square. Luisa's eyes on Maddalena's
eyes, Luisa's eyes stinging. And then Maddalena shakes her head slightly,
and lowers her fist from her chin. She almost laughs, a sound like a swallowed belch. It's too late for either girl to speak—they've passed the point
at which conversation would be comfortable. Maddalena smiles like a

spy encountering one of her own in the field. She opens her mouth, grins again, then shuts it.

When Maddalena leaves the room, Luisa collapses. Maddalena has taken all the air.

Luisa's mind often drifts during chapel. Weekdays, she thinks of the mistakes she has made at rehearsal, of that night's supper, of Don Antonio Vivaldi, who has recently been promoted to maestro dei concerti and might—these are her own private fantasies, so anything is possible— find her practicing and make her his muse, guaranteeing her a future with the Coro. The Ospedale della Pietà houses hundreds of girls and women, but only sixty are figlie di coro, daughters of the choir. While these elite few play solos written to their strengths, sleep in private rooms, and venture out to dine on softshell crab in the finest Venetian homes, the rest, the figlie di comun, who have not married and chose not to take vows, remain in the compound and make lace or embroidery, sweep the kitchens, wash the linens. Luisa doesn't yet know to which caste she'll belong.

On Saturdays and Sundays the Coro performs for Venice, and rows of rich-robed men and women can be observed from Luisa's place in the back loft with the rest of the uninitiated foundlings. The morning after their encounter in the music room, instead of studying the foreign dignitaries in the front pews, it's Maddalena that Luisa dissects. The new girl sits with Chiara, shifting her jaw, not bothering to hide her boredom. There's a tear at the hem of her skirt. A birthmark just below her left ear. She tilts her head to whisper something to Chiara, whose mouth tightens in a stifled smirk, though she continues to look down through the grate at the altar. Luisa tries to think of what Maddalena might have told her—a little joke about the way the priest's voice cracks as he intones, something outrageous about one of the noble families seated in the nave. She doesn't usually care about the other girls' closeness. She doesn't even believe that what's between Chiara and Maddalena is closeness, just proximity. Luisa has not seen Maddalena look at Chiara—has not seen her look at anyone—the way she looks at Luisa, really the way she pretends not to look at Luisa, miming indifference once Luisa meets her gaze, but certainly looking, every day since that first day.

Maddalena's head turns quickly now, her eyes finding Luisa's. Luisa's cheeks redden, Maddalena thumbs the hem of her sleeve. They're saved by the Coro, entering the large balcony near the chancel from a back staircase that connects the Ospedale to the church. The women fill the lengthy choir loft, a stream of bodies in white dresses with shadowy instruments, impossible to see clearly behind the ornate wooden grate that runs its full perimeter. If girls must play music, the church has decided they'll do so invisibly, though the sharp-eyed can still peer through the patterned wood to catch an elbow, the line of a cheekbone, the glow of a candle against the hollow of a throat.

Today Anna Maria, the Coro's darling, has the solo, which has been written specifically for her by Maestro Vivaldi. She stands near the front of the grate, her violin the bubbles in a glass of prosecco. Her violin the fireworks out over the lagoon. Her violin perfection.

Listening to Anna Maria makes obvious Luisa's lack. It doesn't matter how much Luisa wants the Coro, how much she cares. A love for an instrument, even a predisposition, means nothing at the Pietà, where not all girls are Anna Maria but many come close. Even the littlest girls in the novices' choir are as skilled as most professional Venetian musicians. It's not desire but talent and hard work that makes them elite, plus the death or the retirement of one of the older girls—now women, but Pietà girls forever, Pietà girls from the day they were left at the window in their Moses baskets, the day their parents peeled sticky fingers off threadbare skirts. They were marked at the heel when they arrived as infants, so that they would always be Pietà girls: the iron hissing, the wound blistering, slow to darken.

Luisa views that branding as a baptism. One morning the figlie found a baby where there had not been a baby before—Luisa might be the illegitimate daughter of a wealthy man's mistress, she might be a changeling, she might have been found wailing in a cradle next to a mother dead of fever, or she might have been a tenth and impossible mouth to feed. She cannot know. But she belongs now to the Pietà—no matter which tier she ends up in—and she belongs so transparently that no one can deny her.

They have a good life here, if cloistered. The Pietà girls are allowed to leave the compound only to be treated for sickness or, if they are lucky, to perform. In these rules the Pietà is no different than the nunneries speckling the city. Luisa thinks that hers is not so very different from the lives of other girls. It might even be better. After all, she has a home. She has been claimed, her scar a sign that she's wanted.

Maddalena, of course, has no brand. Maddalena has a surname. She has brothers who visit on Sundays. She has a family palazzo on the Grand Canal and a countryside villa in the Veneto. If Maddalena wants to whisper through Vespers or remark upon the smallpox scars that crater Betta dal Clarineto's cheeks or mimic Maestra Vittoria's slow mathematical recitations, she can and will do. For now, while her father lives and prospers and her brothers still dote, Maddalena can behave as she pleases. Luisa tries to convince herself that Maddalena's is not a better life, just different.

Luisa feels Maddalena's gaze, though she will not tear her own eyes from Anna Maria, the patterned grate in front of her, the orchestra behind. Whispered air at the back of Luisa's neck, although no one is whispering. The little hairs at her nape stand on end. Why, she wonders suddenly, should Maddalena have a rip in her skirt? They're all expected to be well turned out, especially at Mass, especially Maddalena, who they've been assured will be treated no differently despite her unusual status, although, of course, this has not proven true. If Luisa were to come to Mass with shredded skirts, she'd be sent to consider her sins in solitary confinement, or the figlie might make her skip a meal. Yet here is Maddalena, bold in her dishevelment, unpunished and unafraid.

The music ends in a virtuosic cadenza, and the congregants let out an appreciative exhale. The priest resumes, the incense thickens the aisles.

Maddalena

It seemed impossible to leave her family home—the massive mirrors, the long portegos looking out onto the water, her father's sala d'oro with his bound books and his art—to leave her life and come here and remain Maddalena, a girl who's known silk sheets and now sleeps, admittedly, on the softest of the dormitory cots, but a cot nonetheless. Who's had moleche and now is served porridge. If she holds herself apart from this new life, she'll reap none of its harvest. If she enters it too fully, she'll be lost.

She's always despised embroidery, sitting bent over a needle or a bobbin, back aching, mind restless. Though the foundlings are expected to work for a significant part of each week, Maddalena leaves lacemaking to the others. She follows her small cohort to the weaving room—after prayer, followed by prayer, interrupted at Nones for prayer—and spends the hours staring out the tiny window, trying to discern the comings and goings of boats on the canal. Adriana is chastised for working too slowly, Luisa for sticking her thumb and bleeding all over her lace. No one mentions Maddalena, who has nothing to show for the afternoon's work. The attending figlia shunts her off to the refectory with the rest of the girls.

So it continues that first week, some magic that frees Maddalena from the handwork, if not from her boredom and disdain. She uses the stillness, the silence, in the same way she does chapel: to consider the spirit in the water. While she practices viola, while she cleans her teeth, while Orsetta and Chiara whisper into her ear, Maddalena thinks about the shadow and that vision of Luisa.

Does the thing in the water want Luisa, or was Luisa its offering to

Maddalena? Most of the girls here are like the girls she knew at home, vapid or needy, trying much too hard to please. Luisa is different. Or is she? Is the attraction simply Maddalena's fantasy? Of course now Maddalena wants Luisa. How could she not, with such bait? To have seen something, someone, glittering in the water—like seeing someone in a dream and then encountering them, real, in the street. Maddalena keeps coming back to that moment of recognition, when she first saw Luisa among the other girls. A feeling utterly new. Delight and wonder, an understanding that hasn't yet arrived, but must be coming. A sense of possibility, the benevolence of coincidence that actually is fate. This is a gift to Maddalena from a world she'd thought incapable of any generosity. She feels that, because of the Sensa, she already knows Luisa.

Maddalena thinks she'd like to be known, that she, too, wants to be recognized. To cause in someone not merely envy or pity but excitement. Instead she sits, watching the other girls squint at their bobbins.

One day, after her individual music lesson—after prayer, followed by prayer—Maddalena skips the lacemaking entirely, walking past the room when the others turn in. The figlia looks at her, nods, and then closes the door. She stands stunned, alone in the stone hall. Four hours until Vespers. Four hours all her own. She's wasted three years on obedience with nothing to show for it, and now these first transgressions reap immediate reward. What will she do?

She tries the passage to the chapel, but it's locked, as is the door that opens out onto the calle. The Coro's stars—Betta dal Clarineto, Anna Maria dal Violin, the others who Maddalena doesn't yet know by name but who have been granted dispensation because they're musically talented—are resting somewhere in the private rooms above, and Don Antonio Vivaldi, their master, has gone to Vicenza. The rest of the Pietà at work or at prayer or at practice. There are no idle moments for these girls; they will have recreation hour, but this, too, is for improvement, to clear their humors with brisk air.

Not that Maddalena's recent recreation at Palazzo Grimani was much better. Sunbathing alone on the roof, looking down on the canal, mascaron faces glaring from the eaves, her father and brothers coming and going as they pleased. Leisure at the villa in the Veneto meant mostly the same, but in a garden even more ornate, and even more secluded. Before, there had been parties and games and other children to play with. But Maddalena was twelve when her mother left, nearing the end of girlhood, and with nothing to guide her adolescence but an older brother's fear, idle society disappeared.

"Once you're married," Nicolò said, "you will also come and go as you please." That *once* became more and more a fairy tale, not real life but a dangling promise of a life, as lovely and impossible as heaven. First one noble son, then another, then a barnabotto, then a merchant. Each presented as the ideal, each certain to accept her dowry, until he wasn't and he didn't. With each failure, the thought of a husband lost more of its thrill. He'd be just someone else to own her, to look past her. Maddalena the person is not desirable, which is why she is here, at the Pietà, acquiring talents.

She finds herself near the repair shop, the storerooms, the water gate that traders and deliverymen use to moor their boats. She tries to look as if she has important business, straightening her back and making her pace more deliberate. None of it matters, because no one else is near. Down here the Pietà, otherwise brimming with dour figlie, is empty. Maddalena stops at the water gate, peering through the iron grate at the canal, unnaturally green in the light. The steady lagoon traffic is muffled now, the bridges bare, the nearest boatman at the end of an alley several buildings over. A cursory glance reveals no children peering out windows, no maids sweeping stairs. Maddalena grasps the gate, pressing her forehead against the metal. She looks at herself in the water, the faintest reflection, just a red dress mottled purple and a muddy white veil. She wonders who she'd be without the costumes, all the artifice. Would she like herself? Does it matter?

"I want—" Maddalena whispers.

The canal ripples, one small concentric circle, spiraling out. Then, suddenly, the gondola. Silent and inky black, the ferro at its front depicting Venice—each district carved, the doge's hat above them forming a musical clef all its own. The passenger cabin holds one black velvet cushion, and behind it stands a man in livery Maddalena doesn't recognize, all black, a small golden crest at his collar. He's young, barely older than she is—perhaps seventeen, with all the gangly bravado of one recently a boy, dark curls and sun-darkened skin and eyes the muddy green of an afternoon storm. He's at ease on the stern of the gondola, steady with his long wooden oar, waiting for her. Not a sign that he's appeared out of nowhere, a boy and a boat where there was not before. The canal was empty. Maddalena knows.

Yet what is today but a series of impossibilities? The figlia nodding as Maddalena walked past the workroom, the silent halls. She's heard no bells since she began her exploration, although they should have rung for Nones. And now this boy, this boat.

Will he speak? *Do you speak?* At the Sensa, Maddalena hadn't spoken aloud to the thing in the water. *Are you here for me?*

"Yes," says the gondolier. He sounds like any other boy, voice newly deep, too sure of himself. "To both your questions."

The lock on the water gate is simple, just a latch to lift and then the door swings open, nothing between Maddalena and the canal. The gondolier holds out an arm to help her in, and she thinks this is the moment she cannot turn back, this stepping onto a boat made of bargains.

They travel down the canal—past boathouses and hanging laundry and the light dappling its secrets onto stone, past thick stripes of pearlescent barnacles that cling to embankments and chilly swaths of bridge-built shadow—out into the lagoon. The only sound is the dip of oar to water, the world still around them. Hazy clouds make a scrim across the sun and cast the green world into sharp relief, the marsh grass crisper and the white peaks of the rippling wavelets careful as Luisa's fresh lace. Maddalena isn't scared, although she thinks perhaps she should be. It was one thing to sit in her father's boat, oblivious brother at her side, and grasp at a shadow. The false memory of her mother, Luisa's ghost, the warmth in her gut—until now Maddalena could explain it all away as a fantasy. Yes, she told herself that it was magic, but how much did she really believe? How much did she actually think she deserved? And now this boat, the figlia pardoning Maddalena's misbehavior, the silenced bells, and this strange boy.

He navigates the lagoon with barely a glance at the bricole, tripods of oak posts forced into the mud to warn boatmen away from shallow water. Maddalena wants to ask him—she isn't sure what to ask, yet answers come in a barrage of sensation: the wind whipping her hair, blood on her tongue. They pass Murano, with its furnaces and fires. The tide-pools. The sandy flats teeming with gulls. They're deep in the marshes now, gliding toward a weathered shrine, a bit of wood atop old poles, a place where fishermen might stop and pray for their nets to hold firm. Many such are scattered throughout the lagoon, most with an icon of a saint or Mother Mary, but where there should be a relic or a portrait, this shrine has a mawing darkness.

The gondolier bows his head toward the lagoon, so Maddalena does the same. She expects the shadowed hand, the spectral vision of Luisa, but below her she sees only muddy water.

What do you want?

This time she has an answer. This time she knows, and she immediately speaks.

"To be recognized."

What is it worth to you? What will you pay?

What does she have? What does she have to lose? What is there for her if she doesn't make this bargain? More of the same, self-knowledge ever elusive, Maddalena a game piece pushed forward, then back.

"Gold. Pearls. Myself. My heart, carved from my chest."

And now to bind it, now to give. Maddalena edges toward the shrine, placing a palm against a thick wooden pole. She bites down hard on her tongue, then spits out blood, a bit of herself gone to the water.

"I wed thee, sea," she whispers, "as a sign of true and perpetual domination."

She returns in time for Vespers, her hem bleached from the salt flats, the smell of the marsh in her hair. She slides in next to Chiara, who brushes

Maddalena's hand with her own hand in welcome. On Thursdays, while the other girls do piecework, Chiara takes her private music lesson with Maestra Pulisena, so she has no way to know that Maddalena has been gone. Chiara's fingertips are rough from the pressure of the strings, inured to any sensation other than her instrument—Maddalena tells herself that this is why Chiara doesn't notice the dirt under Maddalena's nails, the small flap of skin on her palm where she slithered out a splinter of wood. Chiara smiles at Maddalena, and under her empty admiration Maddalena feels more the product of her family than ever, resigned to a fate in which beautiful things will only happen outside the frame of her public life, never changing the drab color of her painting.

No. She won't resign herself. Her bargain is newly made. She shakes her head through the hymn, realizing her own foolishness. How can she expect Chiara, unprompted, to set aside her own concerns, whatever imaginings she uses to numb herself against the endless hours in chapel, and notice that her new friend is now humming with discovery?

As they leave the church, Maddalena links her arm through Chiara's, pressing against Chiara's shoulder with her own.

"I—" says Maddalena. But speech sticks in her throat like unchewed meat. Her afternoon is impossible to conjure in language, not because she doesn't know the words, but because they won't come. Chiara smiles contentedly, pleased to have a friend of such significance.

"No, I—" Maddalena tries again, and now she doesn't know if it's a spell worked on her tongue or her own cowardice that stops her. She stands, letting girls in their red dresses stream past, the bells above them manic in their urgency. This is not the usual hour for bells, yet no one else seems bothered. Were she at home, Maddalena might assume she'd had too much wine, too much sun—but she is here, where there are no fine wines, no afternoons on rooftop gardens. Too much water, then. Too much open space, too much time spent alone in the presence of a man. Or maybe too much music, the voices of the Coro at prayer still echoing in her head.

"Is it strange—" Maddalena begins, but then swallows the question. Though it's been years since she has spent extended time with other girls, she understands the outsize value of confidence among them. "It's strange the way the bells go at all hours."

"You get used to it," says Chiara. "Soon you'll barely hear them."

"The same as any other church in Venice, I suppose," says Maddalena.

"Yes." Chiara seems impatient, trying not to be. She keeps twitching her ankle, like her shoes are too tight.

No one else looks up. No one else listens. The music has ended, so the listening has ended, as if there's only enough room for so much sound. They have the music as it's practiced in the girls' heads, and then the music as it's played. The music of the canals, the seabirds, the constant movement of the water—almost impossible to hear from inside these heavy walls. The music of the many spoons scraping bowls at the refectory, the Priora's voice droning through scripture. The music of the instruments tuning together, a mournful A, sounded by oboe then extended by the strings. The music of the littlest girls, playing their clapping games in the courtyard. The hush that falls over the Ospedale della Pietà in darkness, as the rest of Venice takes to the streets.

Each of these a carefully planned moment, music when there should be music, everything in order. The girls who live at the Pietà have been trained not just in sewing and musical theory, the rhythm of the bobbin and the rhythm of the score, but in the rhythm of their days. The minutes after chapel are a passing time, an in-between place where the order can collapse if the girls question it, where they are taught to move carefully away.

Yet here, perhaps one hundred feet from Maddalena, stands Luisa. Her head cocked, listening. Her cap is clean, and tightly covering her hair. Apron meticulous, her hands beneath it practicing some fingerwork so subtle that if Maddalena weren't watching her closely, she wouldn't know the other girl was lost in music of her own. Chiara stretches her wrist, lets it crack. She doesn't follow Maddalena's gaze, doesn't see Luisa look up to meet it.

Their eyes meet, and the bells stop. The sound becomes the usual flurry of travel, thinning as the chapel empties. Luisa blushes deeper than Maddalena thought a body could, until her thin skin bruises purple. She trips over another girl's foot in her haste, and Maddalena can see her neck tense with the knowledge she's been seen, that Maddalena is watching her. From a distance the Pietà girls are indistinguishable, a mass of red dresses and white aprons and caps, but Maddalena follows Luisa for as long as she can, until the waves of girls carry her over the threshold and back into ordered time.

More of the same. Waking before dawn to scurry to chapel. Gathering on long benches to eat quickly while the Priora reads liturgy. Smiling vaguely at Chiara and Orsetta as they share the latest gossip, putting on enough of a facade that they continue to share the latest gossip, want to link arms with Maddalena in the courtyard, to spend their free time asking questions about the Grimani brothers, Maddalena's own prospects for marriage, her experience with men. Maddalena says nothing of her mother or the burden of her marriage, instead sharing airy morsels—Andrea running away from his mistress, Beneto primping at the mirror—always laughing where she is expected to laugh, withholding where she is expected to withhold. Mornings aren't enviable, but they are manageable, and in the afternoons, every few days when her schedule allows, Maddalena absconds.

The gondolier. The water gate. The ride to that altar—she thinks they move in the direction of Burano, or sometimes toward Sant'Erasmo, or perhaps farther east. The sights are never the same, and she is heady with the freedom of it all: her own boat, her own Charon. Her own world, in which soon she'll be seen.

Luisa

The sound catches Luisa off guard, the crack like a bone, the awkward limp of missing notes before she realizes what's happened. A broken string, common enough. During one performance last month, Anna Maria's E broke twice, first on her own violin, then on the one the first chair surrendered. Anna Maria went on with her solo, barely missing a note, once and then again with her third instrument, finishing to an ovation, although in church such displays are not often allowed. Luisa has no such poise. The other string players continue around her as she lowers the violin, blinking as if she's just emerged from a dark room into daylight.

"Luisa! Pay attention." One of the older girls gives her a thwack on the back of the head, and Maestra Simona sends her down to ask Figlia Zanetta for a new string.

"Take this one, too." Maestra hands her a case that's been propped in a corner. "Tell her to look at the bridge."

Luisa nods. She carries the instruments past the rest of the girls in the practice room, cursing her bad luck. No one is kneeling to offer their own violin, to see Zanetta in her stead. Chiara gives a simpering smile, apologetic but cut thoroughly with glee, which Luisa tries to take as a compliment, because at least she's somewhat threatened. The music fades as Luisa moves farther from the practice room, trying not to think of how easily the others continue without her, how little her particular second violin actually matters, despite the maestre's constant assurance that there are no small parts.

Past the chapel, its door firmly shut. Luisa pauses at the end of the

hall, straining to hear the slick sound of a clarinet—perhaps Betta, one
of the Coro's stars, at practice. A murmur of deep voices and a rasping
cough mean that the maestro dei concerti is attendant, and awareness
of him turns Luisa's stomach. She imagines Don Antonio Vivaldi, the
Red Priest—his bright stubble and his prominent nose and the perma-
nent mark at his neck from his violin—appearing in the doorframe and
remarking on her carelessness. She quickens her pace.

Figlia Zanetta keeps her workshop on the lower level of the Pietà,
a temperature-controlled garden of old tubas and drumskins and amputated necks, gleaming shelves of rosin, hanging mallets for pounding
and tubes for unclogging and pliers that can as easily root out fingernails as twist a misshapen flute key. There are always boys cleaning and
cutting, and this, along with Figlia Zanetta's eternal disdain, is what
makes entering a punishment. Apparently in her youth, Figlia Zanetta
imagined herself mistress of a shop that built instruments, a luthier the
like of Stradivari or Amati, and petitioned the Priora and the board of
governors to let her craft the Pietà's new violins. The closest she has
gotten is this warehouse room with its stream of male apprentices, an
ever-flowing river of sullen girls insulting her skill with their minor
repairs.

"Give it here," Zanetta says. Luisa moves to hand over the violins, but
Zanetta tuts and cocks her head toward a boy at the workbench. Suddenly self-conscious, Luisa looks at her shoes and thrusts the instruments
toward him. When she glances up, she realizes he's hardly noticed her,
although Figlia Zanetta is rolling her eyes. "Go on, then," she says. "Back
to where you came from."

Replacing the string will take only a moment. Figlia Zanetta or one
of the boys could string a violin asleep, and if she hurries, Luisa can
make it in time to hear the maestra take the string section through the
final movement. But the boy is back to his carving, and Figlia Zanetta
stands waiting for Luisa to leave, a salty hand at her hip. Luisa could fix
the instrument herself. She knows how to thread the catgut, and could
make the proper tension to create the note she needs. She turns toward
the shelves, as if she'll find a cache of strings, as if she'll have the nerve

to take one, take the violin, take herself up to the orchestra room, and demand the maestra let her at the solo. "Go on." Figlia Zanetta swats the table with a polishing rag.

So she goes. Out of the repair shop, past the water gate that opens onto the canal, the Rio de la Pleta lapping thirstily at the stone steps. Through its shaded archway Luisa can see the sun-bleached brick of the building across the way, the iron prow of a moored gondola. She stands there, cursing ambition so unattainable it turns her to stone.

Someone is singing, not beautifully. Luisa makes out the dark legs of a gondolier in livery, the bulk of him obscured by the angle. The sun melts in pinks and yellows onto the stocky frames of the surrounding buildings, and she knows that the music lesson will be over soon, the girls rushed off to Vespers. So much for trying for the solo. So much for boldness. A tradesman transporting wooden poles passes between Luisa and the gondola, and the archway grows dark with stacked timber, piles floating close enough that if she dares she might reach out and touch them. Luisa lifts a hand, then drops it. Once the long flatboat has passed, the gondolier is gone.

No. He has not gone. Here he is, a breath away, peering at Luisa from his perch. He is about to speak.

"Are you ready?" he asks.

"Ready?" Luisa's voice comes out an ugly little whisper.

"No," the gondolier says. "No, not yet." He's younger than she'd expected from his singing voice, not much older than Luisa herself.

"Not yet?" she repeats.

He looks at her, assessing, until she can watch him looking no longer and backs up with some excuse about the hour and the bells. Who is this boy, and why is he loitering at the water gate? He stands in the prow of his gondola, whistling, examining his nail beds. Waiting for something.

Luisa stays just out of sight, the low sun offering shadows that hide her both from the people on the water—admittedly not many—and the few who pass the gate inside the Pietà.

When Maddalena comes tripping down the passage, it's inevitable. The final note that completes the harmony. The salt that elevates the meat. The gondolier makes a facetious bow, and Maddalena lets him help her into the boat without glancing back. If she had, she'd have seen Luisa, stepping forward. If she had, what would Luisa say?

Take me with you.

She shocks herself with the thought. There's nothing she desires less than a ride with a pert boy on a gondola. There is enough within the Pietà walls to please her, though the other girls are generally dull or impractical, though today her E string brought her low, and tomorrow is mostly for lacemaking and prayer. What she wants is to *be* Maddalena. To have some memory of outside, someone remembering her. This, too, surprises her.

She watches the boat pull away, turning toward the Grand Canal, disappearing under the bridge and then swallowed by the other traffic. Really, she should go tell the Priora. The figlie frown on tattling, but this is much more serious than a stolen hair ribbon or a botched Gloria. If she were Adriana or Chiara, she'd hold this over Maddalena, come upon her unsuspecting in the courtyard with some jibe about what she knows and what she wants for her silence. But Luisa, standing at the water gate, the canal empty, the bells for Vespers just beginning to chime, is not Adriana or Chiara. She pauses, trying to determine who she is, before scurrying off to chapel.

Maddalena

How does any friendship begin? A conversation. An affinity. A secret.

Luisa has been watching Maddalena. Maddalena will feel an itching at the back of her neck, and when she looks up she'll find Luisa enthralled in some task that is in no way enthralling: putting rosin on her bow, tugging a thread on her sleeve, looking sideways at a fingernail. She knows something. She suspects. She is curious.

"You're easily startled," Chiara says each time Maddalena jerks her head around to try and catch Luisa looking. "There's no need to be so jumpy." She's right, of course. As bizarre as it may seem, there's nothing here for Maddalena to fear. After her first day on the water, she saw judgment everywhere. The figlia walking toward her with the laundry, the little girls racing the loggia, the old woman with her cane of bone—all were coming to take her to the Priora's sitting room, where they'd force her into solitary confinement, or they'd starve her. But after two days of nothing—no slapped wrist, no knowing smiles, not even a remark about the tear in the hem of her skirt—Maddalena relaxed. She briefly entertained the thought that she might be hallucinating, but if she was, she reasoned no one else was harmed by her delusions. And which was more likely, that she was under an enchantment that let her escape the Pietà, or that she was in the hospital wing, prostrate with fever? The signs all point toward good fortune, toward some unconventional blessing, and away from malaria. Witchcraft? She's never believed in it—Venice is not England or Spain, constantly plagued by fear of heretics. There are things one must not speak of or examples will be

made, but Maddalena has always had the sense that such denounce-
ments are for show, more reassertion of natural order than an actual fear
of devilry. In any case, she is confident that were the Council of Ten
to bring her to trial, she could claim herself possessed and finger some
poor Pietà instrumentalist.

Whatever its explanation, the power is intoxicating, dangerous. Her
private gondola slides past merchants unloading their bounty, senators walking with their heads leaned together in intense conversation,
women hawking perfume and salt cod, fishermen and their nets. The
route changes, but the destination is always the shrine in the lagoon,
where Maddalena thanks her unknown patron for its favor: the open
water, the movement, the slow sway of the sky. She sometimes thinks
about her debt, of what might happen once her wish is fully granted,
of what else she might be called upon to give. Nothing's gained for
nothing, and she has promised the thing in the water the heart in her
chest. But doesn't the water already own Venice? She's been raised in a
gambling town, so Maddalena plays on.

She returns from these outings light-headed and giddy. When she
opens her mouth to sing her choral parts, she thinks she'll expel sea
glass or salt water. Instead, she sounds better than ever, which admittedly could be the result of being taught by some of the best musicians
in Venice, but which Maddalena attributes to her newfound freedom,
and her gondolier's esteem. The lagoon air is clearing her sinuses, her
soul. Even Maestra Michielina, Maddalena's private music teacher, notices improvement.

Michielina is tall and has thin nostrils, the blood so close to the
skin that they often appear blue. Michielina is concerned largely with
Michielina, especially since she developed some sort of throat condi-
tion last fall that requires frequent tinctures. She is thirty-eight years
old, with a glistening vibrato that the Priora calls scandalous; though
it might take her further from God's graces, it endears her to the board
of governors, who have often called on her to entertain their private
parties. Unless she solves this tincture situation, she'll be called upon no
more, and while instructing Maddalena is an honor, Michielina spends

much of their lesson testing her passaggio for weakness. If the other figlie have noticed, they say nothing. Michielina has long been a favorite of Maddalena's father.

"No Italian," Michielina will say. "We're not an opera." Pietà singers are only allowed Latin—never Italian, never folk songs or songs from the theater. But then she'll hum some aria of Cavalli's, one she'll swear no knowledge of if asked. Cavalli is also a favorite of Maddalena's father.

Yet even Michielina, with whom she spends the most time outside the girls in her dorm, who some days she will greet breathless from having run up from the water gate—her hair wet with impossible rain, her cheeks flushed with humidity—says nothing of Maddalena's frequent absences.

Only Luisa looks up. Only Luisa vibrates with the energy Maddalena associates with her gondolier, the water. Luisa of the ritual at Lido, Luisa of the white-gold hair, Luisa of the violin. Luisa who won't speak to her.

Does she sense the thing between them, the invisible bond that began that day at Lido? Or was the bond always there, did Lido simply confirm it? Perhaps Luisa was born from whichever courtesan or boatman's wife the very moment Maddalena slid out from her own mother. Perhaps centuries ago there was a prophecy that joined them. How does any friendship begin?

I think we'd get along, Maddalena wants to say. She practices, in her head, during prayer. During group music lessons she imagines that Luisa is sending her a secret message. Surely the other girl is better than that wrong note, that late entrance? Maddalena can't help but grin at the mistakes, and Chiara—who is proving both cold-blooded and competitive—will look at her as if together they're complicit in some late-night spew of gossip, a look that Maddalena worries Luisa will interpret as cruel. Maddalena imagines this is how it must feel to fall in love, struck dumb by the possibility of what a greater attachment might look like. Afraid to speak for awkwardness, simultaneously certain that the truth cannot live up to the ideal and certain that it will surpass it. If only Maddalena could find an opening—a moment in the rigid

structure of their days that would allow her to behave in such a way
that the bargain will vest and Luisa will finally see her, become equally
enthralled.

See how Luisa leans her cheek upon her hand. See how she visibly
swallows when the maestra stands behind her. See how she brushes her
hair in the evening, the dirt from her apron, her bow across the strings
of her violin. What would she say if Maddalena were to bring her to the
lagoon? What would she say if Maddalena were to tell her about the cold
piano nobile of Palazzo Grimani? What would she say if Maddalena were
to clip that stubborn hangnail with her teeth?

And then one afternoon, Luisa arrives at the water gate. It is the usual
time—though even if it weren't the usual time, Maddalena suspects
her gondolier would come for her, at her call. As usual she's walked past
the workroom, a nod to all the girls making their lace, not a word from
the figlie.

She is about to step into the boat, has grasped the arm of her gondolier, when she senses a commotion behind them. The quick patter
of feet, the force of a body through the hall. Maddalena turns back just
as Luisa stumbles, her foot caught in a dip in the stone. She goes down
hard on her hands, and releases a yelp of pain.

"You." Maddalena wishes she had something more insightful, but
in her shock at seeing Luisa, there is only this to say. She releases the
gondolier and moves back to the causeway, bending carefully down to
where Luisa shifts onto her haunches, regaining her balance in a quiet
crouch, examining her palms.

Luisa looks up, right at Maddalena. Weeks of stolen glances, weeks
of skirting and hiding and turning and now this, Luisa's large brown
eyes and Maddalena's black ones.

"Me." Luisa's bashful in the acknowledgment. The words release
her, cut a tether that had held her at remove from Maddalena. She looks
younger. She looks beautiful. Then her face changes suddenly, eyes wid-
ening and mouth making a little *o*. She says, "Your father."

"What?"

Luisa's breathing is still ragged from her run down to the water, from her fall. "He's here with the other governors to make their annual inspection, and I thought that if you weren't..." She takes her lower lip between her teeth.

"You knew where to find me?" This is obvious. Say something else. Luisa smiles a bit, she shrugs. Conceding what?

"I'd seen you here. I thought you wouldn't want anyone else to... if they called for you, if they noticed..." Again, a little lift of Luisa's shoulders, and now Maddalena sees the threads of blood moving down her wrist, the awkward way she holds her hand.

"You're hurt."

"You should go up now. You should go quickly. If you go now, they won't have missed you."

"They won't miss you." Both girls turn. The gondolier has spoken with his gravelly voice, his certainty. Luisa sputters. Maddalena wonders when she last spoke to a man, if she has ever. There's something so desperately pure about these Pietà girls, before they move into the nunnery or the choir. Not just untouched, but unseen. Unspoiled. Receptacles for a man's dreams not because he desires, but because he imagines. Luisa looks from Maddalena to the gondolier, confused.

"How? How could they not miss you?"

"They just won't." Maddalena says. "They just...don't." She takes a step toward Luisa, who is so close, so alive. "Only you've missed me."

Luisa stares at Maddalena. Then she nods. If she knows about the water gate, if she's seen Maddalena's boat, then she has also seen how Maddalena escapes punishment, how the Ospedale della Pietà continues its rhythms without her, closing like water around a skipped stone. Luisa reaches out a hand, and Maddalena isn't sure what she'd intended because all at once the color seeps from her face, and she hisses a breath. Luisa's right arm is angled strangely, the palm shredded and slowly seeping blood. She lifts her left hand to examine it, then shudders. Maddalena comes closer, holding her own hands in a gesture of surrender. Luisa nods.

It might be broken, it might be sprained. Maddalena doesn't have the medical knowledge to diagnose precisely, but it's clear that something is seriously wrong. It's clear that the figlie will remark upon Luisa's indiscretions, and that for a time she will be unable to play the violin.

"The water." This from the gondolier. Maddalena looks at him, and he cocks his head toward the canal.

"Do you trust me?" Maddalena asks Luisa. She's given Luisa no reason to trust her, and again she wants to pinch herself for the wrongness of her own self-presentation, and again she summons her confidence.

She's surprised when Luisa says, "Yes." More magic, though Maddalena doesn't know if it's the slippery enchantment of her bargain, or the beauty of an understanding, a joining of two minds.

On their knees, the girls lean down to the water, Maddalena buttressing Luisa so she can immerse her arms to the elbow, can hold them there in the murky canal, which rinses the blood from the palms, which soothes the sprain. Luisa's hands emerge pristine. She leans back on her heels, gasping, eyes large and unreadable.

"What is this?" she asks, circling her wrist.

"Us," says Maddalena. A gesture to the gondolier. "Him." Luisa is standing, looking at the boat, looking at the water. "A blessing." Then Maddalena can't help herself. She moves closer to Luisa. "I'm going out today. Are you coming?"

Luisa turns, her mouth open. Her two lower front teeth overlap—Maddalena hadn't known. The girls are so close to each other. The canal ever rippling. The gondolier still waiting.

It hurts to look at Luisa—the good kind of hurt: bleach at the scalp, a newborn lamb. Maddalena looks instead at the gondolier, now smiling as if he's won at the casino—a smile of luck and gratitude, a smile of having fallen into success without needing to execute a plan. If Maddalena weren't so caught up in Luisa—her smell (candle wax) and her calluses—she might notice the gondolier's smile, she might be curious. Yet there is only so much a girl can notice, only so much sensation a body can take. Luisa. Luisa, Luisa. *Are you coming?*

Luisa shakes her head, but what begins as emphatic turns questioning. Maddalena realizes that Luisa has not seriously considered leaving the Pietà, has not wondered what it would feel like to walk through this door. Maddalena realizes that Luisa's now wondering.

For a moment, Maddalena thinks to stay behind, but the gondolier is beckoning. And what would she do, go bow before her father? Bat her eyes at the governors? Make lace? She grips Luisa's hand hard, and then drops it. "Next time, then," she says. "When you're ready."

Luisa

At Vespers that evening, Maddalena ignores Chiara's beckoning, and slides instead into the pew next to Luisa, brushing her littlest finger against Luisa's skirt. Luisa's expression doesn't change—obedient awe as the priest takes the pulpit—but her hand finds Maddalena's, her own littlest finger linking to join them in their newfound symmetry. *Sicut erat in principio, et nunc et semper, et in saecula saeculorum.* They punctuate, like the rest, with the *amen.* To the lay observer there is no way to know that these two girls seek benediction from their own private spirit. That just a few hours ago Luisa's arm and hand were mangled, and now they are smooth. *As it was in the beginning, is now, and will be forever.*

Maddalena rode off in her gondola and Luisa stood there at the water gate, turning and turning her palm to the back of her hand. She'd thought that wonder was strictly the provenance of music. There is magic to be harnessed in the collective breath of the orchestra, just before they follow the conductor into the opening measures. Magic in the moment of reverberation that comes after the final note, when violins are still aloft and woodwinds vibrate with the last spent drafts of air. The way that Anna Maria communes with the music is a sort of magic, as are the stanzas that melt from Don Antonio's pen. What have the past weeks watching Maddalena been but that same sense of wonder? A titillation, an impossibility, the best kind of pain.

That Maddalena has some power, some bond with the canals, should be shocking. Luisa would have predicted herself shocked—scandalized and also frightened, because what she has seen is objectively frightening.

But the Lord Jesus walked on water. His body is bread, his blood is regularly wine. This afternoon feels like justification for Luisa's tendency to believe what the priests tell her, even when what she's believing seems nonsensical, even when a small part of her wonders if they are all played for fools.

That night, after the rest of the dormitory is asleep, Maddalena comes to Luisa's bed. This is forbidden, and Luisa should protest, but Maddalena slips in before Luisa can stop her, before Luisa can realize that she does not want to stop her. Maddalena humming with excitement, Luisa warm and pleased. They lie there, studying the wood-beamed ceiling as if for constellations, not touching, but feeling the heat between their two bodies.

"Where do you go?" Luisa asks, her voice so soft that at first she thinks Maddalena doesn't hear. "Where does he take you?" Both girls still looking up, afraid to disturb these first delicate threads.

"Nowhere, really. The lagoon."

"Are you frightened?"

"No."

Luisa believes her. After all, she herself is not frightened. What might once have been fear is now the underside of awe.

"If you could have anything," Maddalena asks, the dormitory very dark, oil lamps burned down and all the other girls so still they can't be dreaming, "and I mean anything at all, what would it be?" It's a simple question, almost childish. But the night and the intensity with which Maddalena asks, the certainty she seems to feel that such desire can be spoken, give it weight.

"Anything..." says Luisa. As if she's never asked herself, as if she's never imagined. Jewels. Palazzi. Parents. What she wants is this, this intimacy. Luisa chews on her lip, turning over her answer, examining all sides before she speaks. "I want first violin."

"We'll get it for you," Maddalena says, too quickly, her voice too loud. "It will happen."

Luisa smiles. "You aren't what I expected."

"No?"

"No," Luisa repeats, squeezing Maddalena's hand to show her this is good, this reimagining.

"You thought I'd be cruel?"

"Just harder. Shinier. Does that make sense?" Luisa knows it doesn't really, but Maddalena seems content to let it sit. "And you thought I'd be meek. Well, meeker," Luisa corrects herself. "You thought I'd want, oh, marriage to a clerk. Something small."

"There's nothing small about marriage."

"Not for you," Luisa says. "But for the rest of us."

"Well, some men are small," says Maddalena, "though I can't imagine you'd want them."

The laugh begins in Luisa's chest—she tries to swallow it, but with it comes a pocket of air that transforms into a hiccup. Meanwhile, Maddalena has hidden her smile beneath the blanket they share, stuffing her mouth with her fist when laughter bubbles. Luisa can't catch her breath. She sits up, an accidental hand on Maddalena's thigh to steady herself, and before either can react, they hear the rustling of sheets the next bed over. Luisa's grip tightens with the hope they haven't woken Adriana. She sits very still. Maddalena's hand creeps into her own.

When Adriana flops back over, muttering something about E minor, Luisa, too, lies back. She turns to Maddalena, both girls with eyes wide and hearts giddy. Another sigh from Adriana sends Maddalena back to her own bed, but her warmth remains until Luisa falls asleep.

Maddalena

She knows she should be careful. If she's wise, she'll woo these other girls along with Luisa, play two instruments, as Pietà students are all taught to do. There's no need to disturb the balance of the dormitory. But Maddalena is ecstatic at the difference between Orsetta and Chiara, and Luisa—the difference between moving through a garden maze, constantly butting up against the next hedge, and running through an open field. It makes her bold; it makes her reckless. She tries to hang back. Eggs in baskets, or whatever Nicolò would say. Yet she's emboldened by her bargain. Daily she slips her hand into Luisa's hand, nightly her body into Luisa's bed.

Maddalena has never felt more herself, and marvels at the ease with which she lets Luisa know her. A tap of shoulder against shoulder as they move through the courtyard, a hand on the arm, a flare of the nostrils, and a tilt of the eyebrow each its own full conversation. Maddalena straightening Luisa's sleeve, and Luisa retying Maddalena's apron. Maddalena's portion of rice to Luisa, who gives Maddalena the last of her meat.

This is luck, this discovery, and with it this chance to come in from another afternoon out on the marshes, take the back hallways, and slide into the pew next to Luisa just as the priest takes up his hymnal, to watch Luisa's fingers tap some complicated rhythm on the wood. Luisa swears she often doesn't pay attention to the priest and the preces, but to see her, one would never guess she's not exceptionally devout. Luisa looks toward the altar, mouths the Latin when she should. Maddalena is proud to know there's more to her, to be the only one who knows. Tonight, when the rest of the Pietà is asleep, they will whisper their desires—the particular

capon dish with the crackling herbed skin from the cook at Palazzo Grimani, the chance to play for Maestro Vivaldi, an outing to the opera, to
flirt with the boy who delivers the wine—or Maddalena will tell Luisa the
histories she's learned from her brother, or about Carnival, the drunken
carousing, the boat races, the city on display. Or they might lie together,
silent, just existing. Recognizing each other. Being seen.

If someone catches them together, they'll be punished. Maddalena
considers the blood she spat into the lagoon, the promise she made of
the heart in her chest. Will this be how payment comes due? She imagines herself sent to the cells that adjoin the Doge's Palace, crossing the
Bridge of Sighs and looking out at the lagoon to see that shadowy hand
rising from the water, clutching her own still-beating organ in triumph.
Maddalena's been told tales of the past Venice, the Venice known for
its creative forms of punishment. Finger screws for enemies of the republic, the dripping machine for Lutheran heretics, mutilation for men
engaged in sodomy.

What men do, women can do, if they're given opportunity. Surely
other girls in the long history of the Pietà have come together to whisper in the night. Surely some girls have done more than whisper, here
among only girls, girls with warm bodies and wet mouths.

Luisa angles herself to better see the altar. In doing so she slides
closer to Maddalena, so that their thighs press together.

At first, Maddalena was surprised at Luisa's nerve. Luisa's risks are
all weighed and considered—should she continue to play her violin
through back pain, would this stray hour be better spent on the final
cadenza or the run in the third measure? If Luisa spends her nights
with Maddalena, she's surely thought through the consequences. She
knows she might be punished—with solitary confinement, with lashes
or chores—and still she's chosen Maddalena. It feels good to be chosen.

Maddalena joins the priest in the *Magnificat* with gusto.

The next evening, Chiara finds Maddalena in the courtyard. The sun
still strong—the height of summer with its oppressive heat and wafted

rot is several months away, but the days are lengthening, and the light makes doilies of the arches in the loggia. Weeds shimmy between uneven stone tiles. The sudden shadow of a bird overhead darkens Chiara's white cap.

"I was waving before chapel. Yesterday, too. And this morning I tried to talk to you at breakfast. Haven't you noticed?" Chiara takes Maddalena's arm in her own, falling in step. Maddalena doesn't mean to recoil. Were Chiara not a musician, the movement might be explained away as a twitch or a tic, but like Luisa, Chiara is versed in the subtlety of the body, the way the shiver of a wrist can transform sound. She pulls back, studies Maddalena's face closely. After her bargain at the shrine, Maddalena looked at Chiara and thought, Why do I not seem new to you? When Maddalena sat beside her, Chiara saw nothing. It is only now that she turns to Maddalena and considers her—not just who she is in relation to the rest of the Pietà, but who she might be on her own. How Maddalena might break from her, and what that might mean.

Before Chiara can speak—if she even would speak—Orsetta is between them.

"The way Silvia coughed through the Our Father, I thought she'd spit bile at the altar. I wonder if they'll make her go to the infirmary? That would open up a place in the motet, and who would fill it? Not Catarina, I hope. She's—" And on like that, through the courtyard, into the main building, up the stairs to their dorm, until they see the matron glaring and Orsetta bites her tongue.

Until now, Maddalena has moved through the Pietà with the grace of Chiara and Orsetta, who are not necessarily well liked, but are well respected. Both present facades of confidence, which in the economy of the fifteen-year-old girl is more valuable than kindness.

Orsetta plays the double bass, which makes her appear both foolish and lovable—already a small girl, she is dwarfed by her instrument, though the sounds she's capable of conjuring give pause to even the cynics. Orsetta is bold because she doesn't know not to be. "That pimple!" Orsetta will say—Orsetta who has clear skin, though she limps due to an accident from childhood—"Do you think she even knows it's there?" Of course, the girl in question will now know, having heard Orsetta choose the most inopportune moment—generally a moment in which all else is silent, a moment in which they are required to be silent, but Orsetta cannot help herself, she simply must comment because how has no one mentioned whatever it is the person in question would prefer to let lie. Orsetta is often reprimanded with meals of bread and water. By now the figlie know she means no harm, and the consequence is meant to inspire self-control, rather than truly punish.

Chiara is different. Chiara's always calculating, which means that when she decides to strike, it hits true. They make a balanced pair—one a bird twittering, the other a fox lying in wait. When they play together— Chiara on the violin, Orsetta with her bass—Maddalena thinks it should be the other way around; the depth of Orsetta's sound makes more sense for Chiara, and Chiara's virtuosic high notes sound like Orsetta's chatter. But there they are, making music in the way they've been told to make music. When Maddalena was a child, her father asked, *What will you play?* and thus a tutor was found for the viola de gamba, which was chosen on a whim, but at least chosen. Here, the figlie say, *We're short a clarinet, we need more cellos.*

Since that first day when they came to sit on her cot and stroke the black silk dress that would rest folded in the chest at its foot, Orsetta and Chiara have been a buffer of sorts, filtering impressions of the figlie, teaching Maddalena which traditions are ridiculous and which should be revered. The girls have filled the roles of tour guides gladly, proud of the distinction it earns them. Orsetta's attitude: If you can't be the star, you might as well polish it. Chiara's: Soon, you'll be the star.

They show no sign of insurrection as they dress for bed that night, nor the next morning. Maddalena thinks she must have imagined the flash of understanding in Chiara's eyes. Chiara can't be so petty as to mind the subtle drifting of a barely formed friendship; Maddalena shouldn't presume herself more important than Chiara's truest love, the violin. Besides, what could she do? What does Maddalena have to be afraid of? A girl, locked away in a church, playing her music? It isn't as if Maddalena has turned on Chiara—she has simply turned away.

Meanwhile: Luisa. Once the night rustlings of the dormitory quiet, Maddalena lets out a stylized cough, looking around to see if any of the other girls respond. When they do not, she tiptoes the short distance to join Luisa, who lifts the sheet to welcome her.

She's never had this sort of friendship, and she knows the same is true of Luisa. Their proximity is dangerous, all-consuming. Headier than wine, the more exciting for its prohibition. Things that once frightened Maddalena no longer scare her, for what could stand against the two of them, together?

"When I marry—" she says, but doesn't know how to continue. She remembers the darkness at the shrine.

Maddalena often thinks about Luisa at Lido, Luisa coming up out of the water, her violin raised. She tells herself it was desire, or else fate, or else might not have been Luisa at all, just a girl with similar traits. The real Luisa's not the girl in the water. Luisa's loyalty is earned, and not just wished for.

The priests talk about the spiritual vessel, how God comes to make use of his representatives on earth. Maddalena must be Luisa's vessel, or else Luisa Maddalena's—the way they open to each other, the way Maddalena imagines opening, when they are older. When they are braver, or alone.

Luisa

She hadn't realized she was lonely. Now, it seems absurd. How could she not have known, having seen the friendships form among her cohort, having walked solo through the courtyard, and tossed and turned in her cot on her own? Now that the gap is filled, she can look back on its magnitude. When Maddalena curls her little finger around Luisa's, Luisa squeezes back. When she tells stories about Festa della Sensa or villeggiatura, Luisa listens, asks for more. She delights in Maddalena's body, here next to hers. Someone with whom to share her secret thoughts about the other girls, the Coro. Someone with whom to link arms when she's struck by the enormity of the world. Someone to love, and in doing so to help her understand what it means to be open. To trust.

This enthrallment is not true of everyone. As Luisa moves toward Maddalena, the other girls move away. What began as fascination curdles to resentment, and within four weeks of her arrival Maddalena's novelty fades.

"Her dress is always dirty," says Orsetta, "yet she never gets sent to isolation."

"She was late to confession," says Adriana, "and no one made her pay the fine."

"I heard she was caught sneaking her lover in through the alley," says Daniela. "He's planning to abduct her."

Luisa says nothing. Maddalena doesn't care about the gossip, so who is Luisa to intervene? Besides, what would she say? The girls are right; it is unjust that they are punished while Maddalena runs free.

Most Sundays after Mass, Maddalena's brothers come to visit. Shepherded with the rest of the girls, Luisa sees only their dark cloaks before the anteroom doors close. Back in the dormitory, girls will gossip about which foreign dignitaries were seen in attendance at church, how Michielina de Soprano fumbled her passaggio, how suave the priest was that morning at Mass. Maddalena might be gone for twenty minutes; she might be gone for two hours. Regardless, her absence is felt, and talk turns to the Grimani family: the women they are sure Andrea beds, the sums Beneto loses at the gaming table. All speculation, as Maddalena says nothing substantial of her life before the Pietà, and no one else could have access to the kind of information Daniela swears she's come by honestly.

"I heard from the boy coming in with the poultry," she will say, or "They were overheard last week, as Figlia Franceschina was stoking the fire." Daniela is known as a telltale: when Chiara spat in Adriana's porridge after the other girl laughed at her bowing technique, Daniela went to the Priora, and as punishment both had their hair cut off at the neck, Chiara for her retribution, Daniela for tattling. They were ten, then, but little has changed in the years since. Daniela's ears remain sharp, her tongue loose. "It's said the family are profligate even for Venice, that the brothers have all squandered years of wealth." Always *It's said.*

They are silent when Maddalena returns from her meetings, smiling vaguely and shaking off Chiara's attempts to take her in confidence, always polite, but firm enough that Luisa notices the slight, and worries for Maddalena.

"And were you with Beneto?" Chiara says today, a glance around the dormitory to be sure the other girls are watching and impressed with her knowledge.

"No." Maddalena goes to Luisa, who sits on her own bed with her head down, darning a tear in the sleeve of a dress. Luisa lightly knocks Maddalena's knee with her own. *Talk to her.* Chiara has always been bold, but lately her playing is improved such that Maestra talks of bringing her to Don Antonio, letting him see her new speed and precision and consider composing with her unique contribution in mind. This possibility has made Chiara insufferable. With her prospects so drastically improved, she has begun to reevaluate her role in the dormitory, becoming forceful where she was not before. Chiara as a loyal spaniel is annoying, but on guard she is dangerous. Much better to humor than cross her. Yet Maddalena says nothing more, just moves to hold Luisa's mending so the angle will be gentler, her back to Chiara's open mouth, the darting eyes of the other girls sweeping the room.

Luisa focuses on the thread, on the shirtsleeve. Next to her, Maddalena begins to hum a jaunty, unfamiliar tune. Luisa cannot read the mood, thinks that perhaps no one can read it. A week ago, Orsetta might have said something, Adriana might have hurried to Maddalena's defense when they saw Chiara narrowing her eyes. But as Maddalena's sheen wears thin, the Pietà girls rewrite their opinions. Maddalena has ruined the illusion that they are better off at their Ospedale, despite its rules and its seclusion. She returns from these meetings with her brothers and reminds them of the outside world, the canals and palazzi, the Ridotto and the operas, the men.

"Well," Chiara mutters, at first quiet and then louder, in invitation of judgment. "Well."

The girls tidy their dresses, lace their shoes. They repin their caps and close their drawing books and straighten their pillows, tie on aprons and ready themselves for the refectory. Maddalena tucks Luisa's arm inside her own, and as she does Chiara makes a sudden show of falling directly onto Luisa's bed, where her sewing lies folded. A piercing rip throughout the room as all the afternoon's work is undone.

"Oh," says Chiara, making little effort to appear apologetic. "Was that my fault?" She looks at Maddalena as she speaks, a dare. "What a shame."

Most of the girls are already in the hall, but those who remain hold their breath, look from one to the other. Maddalena shakes her head, scoffing, and leads Luisa through the door.

After supper and prayer, Maddalena takes Luisa's dress and repairs the sleeve, her even stitching erasing any trace of Chiara.

"Should I have said something to her?" Maddalena bites the thread to break it. "Is that what you would have wanted?" Luisa doesn't know.

"I can get you what you want," Maddalena has said to Luisa. But she will not say how, she won't say why. That day at the water gate, when Maddalena held her hand extended, Luisa didn't join her on the gondola, but didn't turn away. Luisa is bound to Maddalena—each time she looks at her own smooth palm she remembers the magic. Sometimes she thinks that when she touches Maddalena, the enchantment will rub off on her, a linked little finger as a small transfer of power.

"Next time, then," Maddalena had said. "When you're ready..."

Luisa wishes she were ready. She imagines herself in the gondola's cabin, moving down the canal, but can't picture herself taking that first step off the stairs. Therein lies the trouble she has always had—the desire to move, the capability, but none of the gumption.

"Connect to the music," Maestra will say. "Feel it." And Luisa will stiffen, her fingers banging the strings. "Less tension!" Maestra will say, which makes Luisa more tense.

When she watches Anna Maria play, or even Chiara, she envies the way they talk to their instruments—that intimacy between music and musician—the body in conversation with the violin, even as the violin appears part of the body. Anna Maria will often play with her eyes closed, while Chiara looks at her violin as if it's a lover. Luisa is too conscious of how she looks while playing, of what her mouth is doing.

"You're better than Chiara," says Maddalena. Luisa sits on the floor against her bed, stretching her wrist, Maddalena draped above her on the mattress.

"I wish I could be." Luisa shakes her head. "I don't have her—"

"No." Maddalena pulls a pin from Luisa's hair, combs through the platinum tresses with her fingers. "You are already, when you're playing alone in the practice room. You just have to do it like that in front of the maestre."

Easier said. Luisa leans into Maddalena's hand, Maddalena's fingers soft on her scalp. The slam of a door startles them both out of the moment.

"It's just my fourth finger, Maestra says." Chiara is presumably speaking to Orsetta, but her voice is so loud the whole dormitory hears. "Once I master it, she's certain I'll be ready. And"—voice rising, commanding even those girls who aren't already turned toward her—"when he returns next week, Don Antonio will sit in on the group lesson to see me."

"If it's the group lesson," says Maddalena, still twirling a strand of Luisa's hair, "isn't he sitting in to see all of us?"

Chiara's eyes glimmer. She has been waiting for this moment. She's spent weeks swallowing insult, weighing the relative strength of Maddalena's appeal, her own capacity for pain. To be a foundling and musician provides a broader tolerance for pushing oneself to the edge of what can be withstood: the emptiness of lineage, the thickening skin as the fingertips harden against strings, the awkwardness of holding up the arm hour after hour, nights spent imagining the look on the face of the woman who left you here, alone. Certain figlie are more serious than others about the board of governors' calls for silent contemplation, and there are days that the girls' inner thoughts are punctured only by music, days of spinning lace or practicing embroidery in a cold, windowless room while one of the stricter figlie slaps the knuckles of anyone who so much as whispers. Entire days spent first at prayer, then waiting in a hard-backed pew for your turn at confession, when you might admit to thinking of the new timpani instead of baby Jesus, to laughing silently at the expression on the old bassoon player's face when she inhales. The girls know better than to share their true sins: tripping a competitor with a boot as she files into church, coveting the finery of the foreigners who pay to hear the concerts, wishing to be someone else entirely. At ten, when Chiara revenged herself on Adriana, she wasn't acting on impulse; it was the consequence of long consideration. Even the most reckless of the Pietà girls are disciplined.

Chiara turns to Maddalena with a smile, and Luisa knows she will strike. Chiara walks toward where Maddalena sprawls on the cot, where Luisa is repinning her hair, scrambling to her feet in readiness.

"Well," says Chiara, savoring the word. "Maybe he'll want to see those who aren't trying to bribe our way into performance, those with more than just money and a patrician's last name."

Maddalena laughs, dismissive.

Then Chiara leans in so that Luisa can see the spit glistening on her canines, a popped blood vessel making a rivulet of red in the corner of one eye. "Those of us whose mothers left because they had no other choice."

What does she mean? A strange decision, to make motherlessness a weapon in a room full of girls without mothers. But Maddalena's olive skin is paling, her usual writ of amusement giving way to something Luisa can't read. She takes Maddalena's hand, which has gone limp. She opens her mouth for some defense of Maddalena but doesn't know what to say.

"Stop" is all she manages, and she knows it is pathetic against Chiara's triumphant glare, Maddalena's diminishment. Luisa squeezes Maddalena's hand, hoping to lend her strength, or at very least restore her pulse, which appears to have momentarily stopped.

"Ah," says Chiara, and if she were one of the other girls, she would now say out loud what only she and Maddalena seem to know. Instead, Chiara looks from Maddalena to Luisa with the knowledge that what she has withheld will do more damage if she's silent. Her smile a wedge between the two of them, Chiara meets Luisa's eyes and makes a face of mock apology. Perhaps Chiara has shifted the narrative in her own mind, has decided it was she, not Maddalena, who abandoned their bond. Luisa forever the second: in violin, in friendship. Maddalena, lost in her own thoughts, doesn't notice.

"I'll step on her fingers," Luisa whispers later, when they are alone in her bed, the other girls asleep around them. "I'll get up right now and find an anvil and drop it on her hands, and then we'll see what Don Antonio says when he watches her try to play." Seeing Maddalena rattled is like seeing the low-voiced priest open his mouth and suddenly sing first soprano. Wrong and somewhat pitiful, undeniably exciting.

"Chiara doesn't matter," says Maddalena, who has mostly now recovered her composure. "Let's not talk about her. She's just jealous."

"No, *I'm* jealous." Luisa sputters air through her lips, rolls onto her back. "Clearly."

"Of us, I mean. Of you with me." Maddalena says this plainly, no suggestion that Luisa could take this as an insult. Before Maddalena, Luisa faded into the Pietà like a sun-lightened tapestry, trailed behind the rest. Maddalena adds color. Maddalena makes other girls jealous. There is always the girl with the fire, and the girl warming her hands at the flame.

"She's good, though," says Luisa. "Almost as good as she says she is, and getting better."

"You could get better." Maddalena turns so she is facing Luisa's shoulder.

"Mmm." Luisa sighs.

"No, I mean it. You could get better." Maddalena speaking quickly now, with an urgency that makes Luisa look at her.

"I'm already missing Latin for extra practice," Luisa says. "I'm not sure what else I could do."

"You don't need more practice," Maddalena says. Luisa thinks she'll follow with "your confidence," or "relaxation," or one of the many other platitudes Maestra has bestowed upon her. Instead, she says, "Come with me, not tomorrow but the day after. We'll have enough time."

Come with me. This is the second invitation Maddalena has issued, the first at the water gate. *When you're ready.* Is Luisa ready? She knows that Maddalena goes, but not where. She knows that Maddalena doesn't worry about being found out, about being lost or abducted or drowned. She hasn't asked why.

Luisa doesn't say, *I do not understand.* She doesn't say, *Tell me.* She doesn't say, *What are you?*

Don Antonio is coming. He will listen to Chiara, he will choose his next protégée, and then it will be done. Luisa's playing will remain unremarkable, and instead of soloing she'll stand at the back of the ensemble, so far behind the grate that she sees none of the congregants, receives none of the praise. She'll teach the younger girls arpeggios and grow old and die within these walls, or worse, she'll lose what edge she has and join the figlie di comun, living in the draftiest rooms and cooking meals or beating cotton. No one courts the common girls, no one will marry her. And what would be different should she choose a nunnery, other than the need to begin everything anew? No, this is her chance to somehow conquer her shyness and become one of the angels of the choir, to play more perfectly and passionately than Chiara could dream, to dine with foreign dignitaries and perform at palazzi and earn her weight in gold. And if she returns home to the Pietà each night, if she's still chaperoned and sheltered, at least she will be sleeping on the warm side of the building. At least she will get the best food, the best care if she falls ill. At least Venice will speak her name—Luisa della Pietà, Luisa dal Violin—with wonder.

She'd be foolish to say yes, but even more foolish not to. She nods, her eyes closed in solemnity.

"What do you want?" Maddalena asks Luisa again. "What will you pay for it?"

The next day is spent on speculation. When will Vivaldi return? What will Chiara play for him? Chiara keeps flexing that fourth finger, telling anyone who'll listen that it's quicker than yesterday, that by tomorrow it will be quicker still. Out of the figlie's earshot, she tells the girls she thinks it is because she has prayed.

So Don Vivaldi will come. So Chiara will ascend to the Coro. Luisa will watch Chiara take the role they've both dreamed of since childhood, before they first held the solidity of varnished wood in hand. It will be awful. She isn't sure that she can bear it.

"It wouldn't be so bad to just teach the younger girls, for a while," Luisa says gamely. "Or to play second."

"It would be," insists Maddalena. "Because you're better than the rest of them. You've worked harder than the rest of them. You want it more."

"Everyone wants it. What else is there to want?" The sun is gone, but it's not truly evening, the sky a lulling, achromatic gray. Having left chapel, the girls are walking in the courtyard on their way back to the dormitory. Maddalena stops so suddenly Luisa almost trips.

"Come with me," Maddalena says. The third time. Threes are for fairy tales. Threes unlock what's forbidden. Luisa looks at Maddalena, so certain, so ready.

"I said I would, last night." She resumes walking, eyes on her shoes against the stones. She said she would last night, but then they fell asleep in Maddalena's bed, and it was lucky that Luisa sweated through her shift, the damp waking her just before the bells, in time to scurry to her own bed. Then the long day of prayer and music, with no room for conversation that isn't between girl and God and instrument. Not that Luisa would have mentioned the offer without Maddalena's prompting. Words spoken after dark belong to the night. Promises whispered once the candles have burned down aren't broken, per se, in the morning, but rather unbound—their thread unwoven. Boldness is unbecoming in the prying glare of sunrise, when crushing Chiara's fingers beneath a refectory bench seems absurd. Had Maddalena said nothing, Luisa wouldn't have pressed her. Luisa would have been content, even relieved, to put that slow nod of her nighttime head away. But here it is, a third time, and threes are for openings.

Maddalena

When she thinks she is secure, when she's found comfort, even pleasure, in the monotony of her days. Must things always be overturned just as Maddalena gets used to them? The light is dusty and the floors are bare and the food has less flavor, but she's determined to put up with it. She has a gondolier to do her bidding, she has a friend. She isn't a pariah—because who here could know the rumors of her mother? Though they've swept through the Veneto, surely this place is still safe. Then comes Chiara, thinking she's won.

Those of us whose mothers left because they had no other choice.

My mother didn't leave me, Maddalena wants to say. *She left my father. She didn't leave me.* She has said it before, in front of the mirror at Palazzo Grimani as she steeled herself to greet her father's guests—always the one who looks too closely, as if Maddalena is the code that can decipher her mother's misdeeds. As if Maddalena is nothing but Elisabetta's reflection.

Although Elisabetta's actions have impacted all the Grimanis, it is only Maddalena who's been blamed for them. When they were small, their mother preferred Beneto. The youngest children trotted in from the nursery to kiss their mother's cheek, and always the softer smile for her handsome little boy. Yet once she'd gone, no one accused him.

Did *he* think, in the night, in the dark, when thoughts find cracks in daylight's armor, that perhaps he could have stopped her? Did he think that if he were a better son—less headstrong, prettier, more special— that his mother might have stayed? Beneto and Maddalena had always spoken freely, even about their alleged parentage. When the Austrian soldier of rumor came back into town, and then when he was spotted with their mother, they'd spent an afternoon in strategy. What to say to Nicolò, how to comfort their father. Maddalena's memories of the day are almost fond—the lovely drama of what then seemed like a surmountable scandal, Beneto tossing a little porcelain maiden from one hand to the other, seeing how high she could fly. The stifled giggles and mock-serious expressions when Nicolò came through, Nicolò who quite certainly saw through them, who knew much more than they. They'd been children. Then Elisabetta had gone, and they were no longer children. What once flowed easily between them ran dry.

Neither of her youngest knew Elisabetta well, but Maddalena is the one who might have. She's the one who was approaching the age at which she'd leave behind the nursery, the childish things, the games of little consequence, to join her mother's gilded adult world. The one the rest of the family must protect, the one who would have been corrupted. She is the one most obviously left behind.

Of course she can say none of this, can barely formulate the thoughts without unearthing things best left buried, things that must be left buried, if she is to marry, if she is to go on. But Chiara has broken the scrim of protection, the mask of the Pietà and Maddalena's role within it. For that, thinks Maddalena, she will pay.

Maddalena has power now. At least access to power, which is more than her mother ever had, more than Chiara will ever have. More than all the rest, more and more rising up from the shores, over the cobblestone, into the square, limitless.

Luisa's breath is steady, her limbs splayed out in Maddalena's bed, her sweat darkening Maddalena's pillow. Very slowly, Maddalena edges her arm from under Luisa's shoulder, pausing when Luisa stirs, waiting until she's stretched herself and settled. She looks like a doll, flushed red, lips open. Maddalena goes barefoot through the dormitory, the tile against her soles surprisingly cool on such a warm night, the air dank and swampy. She's never left the ward after dark. Afternoons are for the gondolier, but nights are for Luisa—equally illicit, equally miraculous.

Luisa should profit from Chiara's demise.

Maddalena expects the violin room to be locked, but it isn't. Even the cupboard where the instruments are kept swings easily open, as does Chiara's violin case, scuffed at the handle, one clasp sticky with age. The sharp pine scent of rosin, the swan-bill of the nestled bow's head. This, too, feels like power. Standing over an instrument with the intention not to play but to ravage. Maddalena pictures her mother in the moment before flight—her Austrian loyal and warm, his boat waiting. Her own joy, waiting.

Luisa

Maddalena is scheduled to turn pages for the Coro in the morning, and Luisa's private lesson is midafternoon. Evening it will be, then, which is fitting. Each girl will begin in her own bed, and at the hour one would generally slip in with the other, they'll leave the dormitory instead. Hopefully no one will awaken; they are lucky that Chiara sleeps hard.

The plan sounds simple when Maddalena explains it, but Luisa knows that what appears effortless often requires the most work. There are so many ways this might go wrong—from someone's nightmare to the figlie's midnight whims to a rusted lock to a missing gondola. Luisa reminds herself that she and Maddalena are not the same. What Maddalena was born to, Luisa can barely imagine. For what Maddalena does freely, Luisa must pay. Still, beneath her dread, excitement.

The day begins at a glacial pace—the priest droning through his scripture at Lauds, the courtyard dense with early-morning fog, and the girls sluggish as they move through the loggia. As night approaches, the hours pass quickly—lessons and evening meal and Vespers a deluge, until Luisa is drowning in her seldom-used cloak, musty and creased from being folded up six months ago, when she last left the Pietà. Maddalena in front of her, carrying her shoes so her steps won't sound. Nevertheless, Luisa worries that she'll cough or jar a bed frame, that the thrum of her heart will escape through her throat. Maddalena pushes the door open, they tiptoe through the threshold, she shuts it. They are still in their bodies. They are still on their own.

Down, to the water gate at the Rio de la Pleta. Maddalena works the wooden shutters, undoes the latch on the grate. They can hear shouting from the bridge, an argument escalating, women's laughter. They walk through the archway and the water is a mirror, light from the Riva degli Schiavoni glazing it smooth. A torch flickers, dies. The stars seem close enough to eat. Will the gondola come? Before she can ask Maddalena, Luisa sees that it has, with that same boy, standing cocky at its stern. A lamp has been placed in the cabin, the felze's curtains pushed back so that once the girls sit, they are open to the eyes of anyone gazing through the refectory window, anyone looking down at the canal from a dark practice room. Maddalena nods, and the boy takes up his oar.

The silky dip of wood into water. The darkness is an unexpected ally, warmer and more generous than its indoor cousin. Luisa finds herself moved by the stillness of a city she has only known in frantic flocks of tradesmen hawking wares, as one in a swarm of girls hustled on foot once a season to attend Mass at a new church. Tonight is achingly precious in its privacy. Then a masked man lowers his trousers and urinates off the bridge, Luisa's romance spoiled by his friends' drunken guffaws.

Their gondolier, impassive, moves down the canal, away from the stream. Luisa turns to watch the Ospedale della Pietà disappear from view, but Maddalena faces forward.

"Oh!" Luisa says. "How will we pay our courier? I don't have coin—the figlie hold on to our pay for us, once—"

Maddalena holds up a hand to stop her. "Don't worry. I've taken care of it."

At the girls' feet the golden lamp, chained to a long pole, its flame housed in a complicated filigree of leaves and berries, casts an eerie light, setting Maddalena afire. Luisa can see only the bases of the buildings they pass—a glimpse of stone, a glint of iron-grilled window. They are traveling north on the Rio de Greci; Luisa marks their passage out of fear that their guide could turn on them, that they might be forced to find their own way home. But the gondola comes to a fork in the canal and she loses her bearings, and soon they are out on open water, nothing to guide them but bricole.

Luisa has never been off the main island. The salt marsh stings—she can taste it on her hair, coming free from its braid. Maddalena lifts the lantern. The shoals surround them, the pools that live dual lives, half their day spent as shore, the other half, when the tide flows, submerged and secret. Cordgrass splits itself, sprouting from shifting silt, the red-brown crisp of spent sea rush crumbling above the stagnant water. The Lazzaretto is somewhere nearby, Luisa knows—the isle of quarantine where plague victims are sent to die, where if you aren't dead from plague, you'll be killed by malaria.

The gondolier steers them around salt flats, through water so shallow Luisa imagines she can feel the hull scrape against mud. At one point she thinks she sees another traveler, but it's only a black-winged stilt beaking a crab, precarious on its twiggy legs. No moon tonight. Luisa wants to ask Maddalena if she's noticed, if it makes her feel equally unmoored, but to speak seems sacrilegious in a way flouting the forced Pietà silence never could. Maddalena looks out at the marsh, an empress eyeing her domain, more the ideal of nobility than Luisa's ever seen her. Her skin is luminescent, that flatness at the tip of her nose suddenly regal, her dark hair loose and salted. She sits so still that she might be the figurehead of the doge's state barge, golden Justice, her scale held aloft, her sword at the ready. Instead of lions or trumpeting angels, at her foot is Luisa.

The gondola stops at a bricola that at first looks the same as any other—thick wooden poles covered in barnacles, half petrified by salt water, forming a tripod drilled deep into the nebulous mud. Maddalena raises the lantern higher, and Luisa sees something perched atop: a little house, no larger than a postbox, with an angled roof and what appear to be two columns framing an archway. A shrine, she realizes—yet where the relic or Madonna should rest, she sees nothing. A yawning darkness.

Maddalena digs inside her cloak until she finds a small, carved object. A comb, Luisa thinks. Something Maddalena has kept hidden from the figlie, a reminder of home. But it is not a comb—it is a piece of wood, squat like a headless man with arms and legs spread wide, carved hands and feet, and at its center, like lungs, a small curled flower. It is the bridge of a Pietà violin.

"Chiara's," Maddalena whispers, beaming. She is again the girl Luisa knows, made flesh after a journey as an icon. She presses the bridge into Luisa's palm, where it feels heavy, significant.

Without the bridge, there is no music—the strings and body two entirely separate entities, no transfer of vibration, no true sound. Change the bridge, carve it out differently or vary the slope or shift it half a millimeter up or down the belly, and you've made a different instrument. For Maddalena to steal it is akin to carving out an organ from a body.

"This was your plan?" Luisa hisses. "What am I supposed to do with this?" Maestra will give Chiara a different bridge, another violin. This mutilation is for nothing. "Ruining her bridge doesn't make me any better."

Maddalena shakes her head, impatient, and directs Luisa to the shrine hovering above them.

"Tell it what we want," Maddalena instructs. "Be clear with it."

Luisa frowns. She expected something akin to a baptism—that she'd strip off her nightdress, enter the lagoon, and come away blessed. The shrine feels so predictable, so wishful. It reminds her of the girls who bring flowers to the Madonna outside of the church, asking for memories of their mothers or for a rich patrician to notice them.

"I'm not—" Luisa begins, and then falters. That place where there is nothing, that emptiness in lieu of the saint to which she'd pray, is beckoning her. Down toward the ferro, away from the unruffled gondolier, from Maddalena, pursed and waiting. It is dark against dark, and she can feel more than see it. What is it?

Even if Luisa stands on her tiptoes, she won't be able to reach the shrine—it's a full body's height above her, awkwardly angled.

Into the water. She doesn't hear the words so much as sense them. From behind, Maddalena grabs her hand.

"I want to be the Pietà's best violinist," says Luisa. She keeps her eyes open. The bridge hits the water with a silent splash, floats for just a moment, then disappears into the silt. Luisa fights the urge to go after it, to reach elbow-deep into the mud and dig until she has rescued the carving, clean the maple wood and slip it home and hope no one will notice. She clutches her own arms, holding herself, suddenly cold despite the June humidity.

Maddalena's at her side, sliding in to put a hand at her waist. The two girls stand together, looking down into the dark tide.

Summer

Luisa

"Keep the pressure, change the speed," he says. "Yes," he says, "that's it. Exactly." His breath is wet, and he seems constantly on the verge of coughing. Sweat drips down his nose, collects at his temples. As Luisa plays, his left leg keeps the rhythm while his fingers twitch. Occasionally his whole body will follow her spiccato, his weak chin bouncing along with her bow as he whispers something mystifying like, "The birds!" This is Il Prete Rosso, Don Antonio Vivaldi. The afternoon is too hot for a wig, so he has none. His own hair, of course, is red.

He is a priest, but he doesn't say Mass—not since he realized that the incense was a trigger to his asthma—and he doesn't move with the solemnity Luisa expects from the clergy. Of course she has seen him many times before. He was a teacher until his recent promotion to maestro dei concerti, and taught theory to the girls who then taught theory to Luisa. The governors do not like him, have even tried to dismiss him, but they like the money he brings to the Pietà with his oratorios and concertos, so here he is, standing in front of Luisa with the string section at her back, saying, "Slower vibrato, yes. Articulate, yes. Yes, yes. Exactly."

When he closes his eyes to listen, Luisa feels herself release. She imagines herself alone, or perhaps deep underwater, and only then can she give her full self to the music that he's given her, no thought to the movement of her eyebrows, or whether she looks wry (like Daniela) or bored (Adriana) or in pain (Fiordelise).

"You seemed sweet," Maddalena will say later. "You seemed like you'd drunk honey."

"That's terrible."

"Not for the larghetto. It felt right."

It feels right to Luisa as well, to be playing for Don Antonio Vivaldi, who wrote this concerto for four violins but has asked only to hear her. First, he heard Chiara, whose prowess he'd been promised. She was not deterred by her borrowed violin, its bridge intact. She began as beautifully as ever, her sound so pure that Luisa could have laughed at her own expectation, her faith in some phantom gondola, the water, and a wish. But Chiara played only a few measures before the Red Priest was shaking his head, wincing at what Luisa found faultless.

"You have it in your head a certain way," he told Chiara. "You'll have to relearn it. A mental shift. It will take time." Before Luisa had a chance to analyze Chiara's reaction—would she cry? Luisa herself would have cried, all that expectation smashed to pieces in the time it took to raise the bow—he was turning to Luisa, asking her to pick up the next part, show him what she could do.

And now here she is, doing it. Not suffering through the notes, not frozen, not stiff. When Don Antonio raises his violin, he becomes a different man—gone is the sickly priest, gone is the pedant. He will smile the sort of smile that only men can smile, an apologetic wince that neither winces nor apologizes, and calls attention in its faux humility to his own understanding of his brilliance. It would be infuriating, were what follows not actually brilliance—the sort of masterful performance, time and again, that makes you wonder not only that the violin can make such sounds, but what else it might do. His wrist is liquid, his bow flies. He is looking at his instrument, yet he is looking at you, his whole face opening to what he plays, his whole body opening. To close your eyes is still to hear a virtuoso, but to watch him play is to have a new understanding of what instrumental music can be. This little bit of wood, so light, so easily broken. Look what he's done for it.

Now he's nodding. Luisa can see him: the way his hands twitch, the way he mouths the *duh duh duh DUH duh*, one sleeve of his cassock coming loose from where he's rolled it as he marks the music's time. She can see him, but for the first time in her memory—certainly for the first time performing in front of the orchestra, with not only him but all the novice players watching her—seeing her audience doesn't change the fundamental truth: that she is playing, that she is turning fear and love and years of practice into music, and that her music has value. The entire solo lasts less than two minutes, at the end of which Vivaldi's mouth is scrunched, his eyes shut, his chin raised to the sky as if in prayer. He thanks her, tells Maestra Simona, "This one," and leaves, humming the allegro that Chiara apparently butchered, very low under his breath.

Maddalena lets out a squeal once he's gone, and one of the other viola players jostles her with an elbow.

"Back to rehearsal," says Maestra Simona. "From the beginning of that last allegro." Luisa slips back into place among the violins. A chair away, Chiara's face is stone. All the girls in this ensemble who hope for a promotion have mastered that particular look—disinterest, deflection. When they play in the church the girls are all in the balcony, behind the grille, and it doesn't matter what the face of a third violinist does during a clarinet concerto. But the Coro is hired out for private parties, and then, sometimes, that third violinist will be seen by the audience. The other girls will see if there is boredom, if there's jealousy. They have been told that God will see.

In bed that night—Adriana with the beginnings of a summer cold that has her sounding twice her size with every exhale, the night's humidity curling Maddalena's hair—Luisa marvels.

"That he even looked at me." She turns the moment over in her mind, searching all its facets for some flaw. "Me, among so many others."

"Everyone knows that after Chiara you're Maestra Simona's favorite," says Maddalena. "Of course you'd be the next, once he decided she's not right."

"If she'd had her own violin...," Luisa whispers.

"No, she played the same as always. He doesn't like her. He likes you." Maddalena kicks at the sheet, making a short, stale gust of air. "I'm going to miss the countryside this year," she mumbles.

"He likes me," Luisa repeats.

"Yes, silly. I told you he would."

"It was the water," says Luisa.

And Maddalena says, "It was you."

When Luisa walks into the practice room the next day, Fiordelise stops her. "You're to go see Pulisena," she says, with a shudder of what Luisa thinks at first is disdain but soon recognizes as reverence. There is a hierarchy among the initiates—the littlest girls are taught by the next littlest, who learn from the sotto maestre. Pulisena is maestra de violin, and doesn't see most girls outside of their group lessons or at orchestra. Luisa floats down the hall to Pulisena's private rooms, feeling outside herself, buoyant in the sense that she is filled with joy but also that she's easily transferred. To believe in the God of the Pietà is to submit fully; although Luisa tries to submit, she has never felt as passive as she does now, pushing open the door.

Pulisena sits at a desk in front of an empty fireplace, copying sheet music. Ink has freckled her right temple, just a few drops, but enough to lessen Luisa's anxiety. She is human, after all. The maestra must have begun where Luisa is now, a young girl awkwardly clutching her violin case, watching her own maestra de violin copy music.

"Luisa." Pulisena puts down her pen. "Come."

Luisa perches at the edge of her chair, trying not to sink into its plush cushion. She fiddles with the clasp of her case until she sees Pulisena frowning at the sound. A momentary flash of worry—that one of the girls has reported her nights in bed with Maddalena, that someone saw them step into the gondola or saw when they returned, that the theft of Chiara's bridge has been traced and will be punished—before she reminds herself that if she's singular, it's likely because Maestro Vivaldi was pleased when she played.

"You're going to shadow Anna Maria this afternoon," says Pulisena. "You'll turn her pages, get her water or wet towels for her brow, whatever she needs during rehearsal. If all goes well, you'll be her new assistant, and instead of the group lesson, you'll start working with the Coro."

"I'm to stop playing?"

"Of course not. This is an honor, girl. Your first promotion. A direct path to the Coro, though you'll eventually have to audition like everyone else."

"I'll stop lessons, then?"

Pulisena smiles, and Luisa can't tell what's behind it. Resignation, certainly. Some amusement. An inexplicable sadness seems to run through the rest like a thick streak of fat through meat, and Luisa feels a sudden chill against the damp heat of the study.

Then Pulisena says, "Don Antonio himself wants to teach you, while he's here these next few weeks," and Luisa forgets the cold, the sadness.

"Me?" she says aloud, because although she has asked this of herself, of Maddalena, of the gondolier on their boat ride home, of the statues of the Virgin in the courtyard, of Vivaldi himself when he called on her at rehearsal—although she has spoken to the water and has heard it answer yes—she still must ask. In her heart of hearts, at the core of her being, she knows that she is not a virtuoso. She is too insular, she cannot open herself to an audience. She doesn't know how to make listeners love her. "Wasn't Chiara..."

"Don Antonio doesn't feel that Chiara is appropriate for his newest concerto." Pulisena shakes her head as if she's getting water out of an ear, a small, unconscious movement. "So it will be you."

"It will be me."

And now Pulisena's feelings are transparent—she is annoyed at Luisa, who stills finds herself in awe of herself, the way a young girl looks in awe at her legs grown long, her hips taking shape, her thickening hair, and says "Who is this creature?" Luisa has that same attraction and repulsion, that same unacknowledged pride. Even when they hate themselves, girls see themselves at center. Even when they swear they aren't special, there is a buried seed of faith. Pulisena has known many girls, and even the most timid have this faith, no matter how the Pietà has tried to redirect belief in their own personal magnificence to gratefulness to God. They won't be the one to marry into nobility, *unless*... That solo could never be theirs, *except*... Who else is worthier? Not more deserving, no, not more hardworking or talented, but more innately made for a particular moment.

It isn't until they are older, and the sediment settles, that they abandon these destinies. They marry a fisherman who tracks guts through
the two-room house, take the veil to sit packed in the parlatorio of the
nunnery with simpering second daughters, or grow old at the Pietà,
copying music scores, watching teenage girls lose faith.

Luisa thinks that Pulisena's sadness must be because Chiara was her
favorite. How difficult it must be, to groom a violinist and to bring her
before the maestro, only to see your efforts stilled. Luisa decides she
will work doubly hard to win Pulisena's favor.

"Be careful," says Pulisena, and though Luisa hears the words,
she doesn't understand them. Backing out of the room, that loose
floorboard—be careful? Be careful of Chiara's wrath? Of becoming
too comfortable, dreaming too large? Or be careful of the thing in the
water, to which she gave a violin bridge and a wish?

"Yes," says Luisa, "of course."

Luisa

July in Venice is stifling. The heat boils the canals until their stench is inescapable, the normally bracing salt air rife with sewage. Maddalena tells her that this is when the monied families retreat to their country estates, to paddle countryside canals, to see the same people they'd see in the city, but near sheep. Maddalena's brothers are finished with their visits for the season, and she's cross with everyone, even Luisa.

"It will be what it will be," Maddalena says when Luisa wonders again about her private lessons, which are to begin that afternoon. They're in the refectory, just finished with their midday meal, and Luisa's stomach is sour.

"If my eyes go blurry and I can't read the music, what will he think?"

"That it's hot."

"I suppose." It is hot. The collar of Luisa's dress is lined in sweat; she can feel yesterday's grit between her breasts and at her hairline.

"It'll be fine," says Maddalena. "You'll be wonderful. Stop worrying."

And so when Maddalena goes to her gondolier, Luisa goes to be wonderful with Vivaldi in a practice room off the main rehearsal space. She is early—the bells haven't yet rung—but the maestro is already there, picking out a pizzicato and then scribbling over his sheet music. He has a nervous energy that speaks to Luisa, and she pauses in the entryway to watch him scratch out a measure. He then goes back to the violin, to play the tune to a motet Luisa recognizes, the key changed and a note or two off.

"Excuse me," she says when he sets down his bow to mark the music. He looks up, guilty, as if caught.

"Well," he says then, so she knows for sure, "I suppose that you've caught me." He winces. "It's just that they ask for so much." Luisa doesn't understand, but she nods. Vivaldi asks, "Luisa, can you keep a secret?"

Luisa considers. A month ago there'd be no question. And now? She and Maddalena share everything, but not the most important things. *I am so lucky to have you, I feel like I could tell you anything.* The operative word: *could.* Luisa doesn't know how Maddalena found that muddy shrine, that boat. She knows little of Maddalena's family life, or who she was before the Pietà. And yet she knows Maddalena, the smell of her breath, the way she makes her eyes wide and faux serious when the viola de gamba has the ostinato, how she tenses when she walks by Chiara. In this moment, both seem possible—a secret, and a friendship laid bare. Luisa swallows hard.

"I think I can."

He smiles at her, and now she is complicit. She feels suddenly quite grown-up and important. "This?" Vivaldi lifts his violin and plays a few bars. "Is rather easily changed to this." Another few bars, a different bowing technique, slightly higher, but fundamentally the same. Luisa frowns. This is the secret?

"That your concertos sound alike?"

"Ah, that I'm paid for them." His grin is boyish, and makes his small face almost handsome. "A bit of this one added to the other, and that's my quota of new work met for the month."

"You don't like writing, then?"

"I like writing too much. But I like writing what I want to write, not what they pay me two sequins to have you play for devotions." He turns to Luisa. "Are you appalled?"

She smiles. "You *are* a priest."

"And yet a mercenary." He lifts his instrument to his chin. "Shall we begin?"

When she leaves the practice room, violin case bumping her knees as she files away details to share with Maddalena, Luisa realizes that her lesson with Vivaldi marks the longest stretch of time she's ever spent with a man. Of course she goes to confession; Vivaldi *is* a priest. There are boys in other parts of the compound, and the board of governors might come to see the younger girls' progression, but mostly the Pietà is a female place, warm with women. When one girl bleeds, so do the rest. Vivaldi is foremost a man among women—teaching women, writing for women. Priests are celibate, Pietà women are chaste. This isn't scandalous in the sense Luisa has been taught the term; still, it thrills her.

"He makes me feel like what I'm doing is important," she tells Maddalena, who doesn't respond. They are in bed again, and Maddalena is looking at the ceiling, her eyes wide and dark, her lashes thick.

"Venice is most vulgar in its quiet ways," she says finally.

"Did you hear what I said? About how he pays attention?" Luisa raises herself onto an elbow to see Maddalena more clearly.

"Yes."

"It's..." Luisa can't describe the feeling—of being heard, of having a man stand so close, mimic her playing with his own, tell her, *Yes, that's it exactly.* "He wants to meet three times weekly, as long as he's here. Because, you know, he's back to Mantua soon."

"Mmm."

"He says the strangest things. Like, play a drunkard coming home from a dance. Play a rainstorm. Play a lamb."

"With the violin?" asks Maddalena, suddenly interested.

"What else would there be?"

Luisa is often late to dinner because she and Don Antonio do not hear the bells, such is their mutual hypnosis. She is scolded, but not punished, for she is becoming useful under Don Antonio's influence. Everyone knows she's being readied for the Coro. The sotto maestre have seen her improvement. While no official challenge has been set for first chair of the novice orchestra, they know it will come soon. Meanwhile, Luisa turns pages for Anna Maria dal Violin, who plays not just that but the mandolin prodigiously, and countless other instruments as needed. Don

Antonio has written twelve concertos just for Anna Maria and plans to write more; travelers flock from all over the continent to hear her play at Mass, and the most prominent patricians hire her out for private parties. She is twenty-one, and striking. Her cadenzas sound like birds taking flight, the way they gain momentum, then soar effortlessly. Luisa is lucky to assist her.

"Watch her closely," says Don Antonio. "Study her maniera. All those devotees who hear her from behind the grille have no idea what it's like to see her play. But they can sense it. How she holds herself. Look at her, then listen."

Perhaps it's Anna Maria, perhaps the wish in the lagoon, perhaps a newfound confidence from having been so drastically elevated, but Luisa's own maniera has changed. Maddalena watches from behind the timpani (by no means her strongest instrument, but the girl who usually plays has sprained her wrist and this concerto calls for timpani and someone must do it), and afterward approaches as if Luisa is a stranger.

"It went well?" Luisa asks, although she knows the answer.

"Very well," says Maddalena. She is distracted, frustrated in a way that Luisa has previously only associated with Maddalena's dealings with Chiara. But even Chiara shook Luisa's hand and said "Well done" when the last movement ended. Maddalena must just hate the timpani, Luisa decides. Although the foundlings are brought up from a young age to go where they are needed—be it the kitchens or the laundry or behind the kettledrums—Maddalena isn't used to direction. Anyway, Luisa doesn't have much time to dwell on Maddalena because the sotto maestra is coming to fawn over her and *Does Anna Maria really never sweat onto her instrument? When you saw him yesterday, what did Don Antonio say?*

Some nights, when Maddalena is back in her own bed, asleep, Luisa thinks about the bargain by the water. How her life had been, before, and what it now has become. It feels like another self, a dream self, who clutched that bridge so tightly that it scratched her palm, who whispered and gave. What did she give? Luisa isn't sure, and as of yet no one's come calling to collect.

When she prays, God asks only her devotion. Gone are the days of sacrificing one's best livestock at an altar, or bringing one's son to some high mountain to prove faith. God answers prayers because God loves her. Might His disciple in the water love her, too? She tells herself it must, that if she's living what has previously been beyond her reach, it is because she's finally acted, finally asked.

She puts aside all thought of payment. She is rising and rising, and here is her star. I just want to learn to play the violin, she thought as a child. I just want to play in the orchestra. I just want to be second chair. I just want one solo. To be first chair.

I want.

Maddalena

In the way of most wishes that are granted without any work but wishing—in the way of most luck—Maddalena's has backfired. This is not a republic that teaches its daughters how to ask for what they want. The priests insist that prayer is to give thanks for what's been granted, not to make personal requests of God. The noble families say prayer is for music—the church, of course, a home for all their unwed girls. Maddalena, caught between both, gets an education in specificity of language from neither.

Recognition. When given the opportunity for anything her heart desires, she has squandered it on the abstract. So much power has escaped through imprecision. The wastefulness embarrasses Maddalena. If you're going to sell your soul, at least know what you're getting in return.

Luisa asked for something tangible, to channel power in concrete ways that make themselves apparent as she's plucked from the second chair of the novice orchestra to take lessons with the head of the Coro. You are an idiot, Maddalena thinks as she watches Luisa skip off to her private room, to play her private songs. She has a maestro, and you have a boy paddling a boat. You could have had the sea, but all you've asked for are canals.

Maddalena hasn't set foot in the lace room since her first week at the Pietà, but in the time set for piecework she doesn't always prowl the lagoon in her gondola. When her brothers are in town she might meet them at the Ponte della Pietà and walk along the Riva degli Schiavoni— if Beneto and Andrea wonder how she's been able to slip out, they've kept their curiosity to themselves. Occasionally she walks farther, out of Castello and through San Marco, past the Doge's Palace, through San Polo, once even all the way into Dorsoduro. On her way home she finds herself at the Ponte dei Pugni and stands, looking down, waiting for some rival gangs to break the ban on street fights and start dueling, a taste of something flavorful to hold in her cheek until her next outing. Nobody comes, and eventually she hustles toward the Grand Canal, anonymous among the travelers boarding the traghetto.

Some days she wanders within the Pietà. She sits in the courtyard, counting clouds. She lies alone on her cot, looking down the empty row of other cots. She's considered exploring the secret spaces of the building—the private dwellings of the Coro, the Priora's office, the room at the lowest level where they keep instruments so broken they aren't worth the time or money for repair—but the thought of running into someone scares her. Maddalena wouldn't mind being caught. She isn't afraid of their punishments. It's when she imagines opening the door to a room in which a figlia is resting, or walking in on the Priora at her fire—watching them look up at her, acknowledge her, and then marking the glaze of their eyes as they return to their tasks as if she weren't there at all—that she is frightened. This is what happened on the fondamenta that runs alongside the canal when she walked headlong into a foreign dignitary, and what happened when her gondolier berated fellow boatmen trying to pass through too narrow a strait. Maddalena imagines this is what it's like during Carnival, when you move in your mask among anonymous throngs, and nothing is so shocking it won't be forgotten when heads turn away. When you are simultaneously you, and not you. A thrilling sensation, the utmost freedom, but not something she likes in what is slowly becoming her home.

Some afternoons, Maddalena goes by gondola. When she wants him, her gondolier comes to the water gate and offers his hand. She's tried to catch him waiting—she will lean out a second-floor window, hoping to spot him loitering, making his way down the Rio de Greci—but he anticipates her desires to such perfection that he doesn't show his face until she has use for him.

He will come and ask, "Are you ready?" to which she always answers yes, if not in words then by climbing aboard his boat and settling herself in the felze. Then he will take her out into the lagoon, always a different route, a different view of Venice to delight in—the painted women by the Ponte de Rialto, the glassblowers of Murano transporting their wares—and then the shrine.

Sometimes he'll serenade her in his raspy voice, not large and boastful like the other gondoliers, but its own tender ablution. He makes Maddalena nervous in an elegant way she thinks must mean she's reached adulthood. The physical fact of him is not as remarkable as that of Luisa—his body radiating cold where Luisa is warm—but he flirts with her, their conversation glancing across surfaces as the boat's hull skims the water.

A beautiful flower for a beautiful girl, when he hands her a burgundy rose. *Oh, sir, you flatter*. That sort of thing, empty banter. She doesn't know his name; knowing it would spoil the illusion. They never touch, apart from his arm helping her to and from the boat. He's young, handsome enough. Maddalena wonders if he goes home to a lover, if he goes home at all, if he exists outside her need for him.

When Maddalena returns from these afternoon forays, Luisa is no longer waiting for her. Physically, of course, she's there, as always. But instead of Maddalena, Luisa's mind is on the music, on her maestro. Maddalena didn't understand how much Luisa's attention meant to her until it was gone—how full she felt to have Luisa turn to her, that open face so ready to be taught. That face is still open, but it is not to Maddalena that she turns.

The girls gather to play through one of Maestro Vivaldi's concertos— this one a grosso with special parts for corni di caccia and bassoon. During the solos, Maddalena, stuck again behind the timpani with hardly anything to do, watches Vivaldi looking at Luisa. Here is Daniela, blowing her poor little heart out on bassoon, and instead of applauding her ability to look as if she doesn't need to breathe, Vivaldi stares at Luisa, trudging through the ostinato. He looks at her as if she has enchanted him. He looks at her as if she belongs to him.

Maddalena clears her throat, and accidentally knocks her kettle-drum. Vivaldi glances at her briefly, conductor's staff still in motion. Then he looks back at Luisa, although now it's just Daniela playing with the cellos, Luisa with her violin in her lap, facing forward in the awkward way of the orchestral musician at rest. Vivaldi smiles slightly when the violins resume, at which point Maddalena coughs again, leaning into the drums, this time on purpose. The resulting boom echoes through the practice room, startling Daniela, who flubs a slew of notes.

"What are you doing? Can't you read the music? You don't come in for several measures." This is Orsetta, hissing from behind her double bass. Maddalena looks at her with eyes deliberately blank, leans with her mallet, and lets out four hollow, syncopated sounds.

This time Daniela stops altogether and looks confusedly at the maestro, who says, "Play on, play on," with a shake of his red head. Did he not hear Maddalena? She clutches the mallets, heart beating quickly. Luisa's part is coming soon. Luisa lifts her violin to play the solo, and even Chiara, who leads the second violins so that Luisa can play first, is rapt to hear. Where the notes are sawing when played by the other novices, Luisa's sound is pure. Honey, thinks Maddalena, some sort of syrup, a nectar drunk by gods. Too lovely to interrupt with another misplaced drumbeat.

Vivaldi, too, is captivated.

"You are a *priest*," Maddalena whispers.

"What?" This is Orsetta again, voice far too loud.

"Nothing."

"Girls in the back!" Like all the others, Maestra Simona has heard Maddalena's interruptions. Unlike the rest, she suspects they are more than a misread score.

After they've finished, the sotto maestra stops Maddalena from leaving the practice room. "Do that again, and we'll remove you from the choir for *Juditha triumphans*. It doesn't do here to be jealous."

Maddalena almost spits back a denial. She stops herself both because quarreling won't serve her, and because she realizes it's true. This feeling, this hatred made up of both anger and desire, this resentment that wants not to erase but to own—what is it if not jealousy? The sensation is new to her—she knew a certain envy, yes, when she watched Andrea and Beneto come and go so freely from the house, or overheard the maid speak of her mother. Never anything so full-bodied and tangible as jealousy.

"You'll get your turn," says the sotto maestra, "if you deserve it. And if not, you'll do as all the girls here do." Looming unspoken over her words is Maddalena's father, his money, his influence. The sotto maestra wrinkles her nose. "Only so many allowances," she mutters as she leaves Maddalena standing in the doorway.

Luisa is just outside, pressed against the wall so that the maestra might pass without seeing her. She's breathless, still on the crest of the concerto.

"It went well?" She hovers, fingers rubbing against one another, as if wanting to reach out to Maddalena but waiting for some sign.

"Very well," says Maddalena, and with the acknowledgment Luisa relaxes. She takes Maddalena's arm in her own.

"It isn't new, you know," Luisa says, "he just revised it. The original had a cadenza instead of the cantilena, but I suppose I shouldn't complain."

"No," says Maddalena.

"He says the governors are mad at him. For revising old pieces when they've commissioned new. But he has to eat, you know."

"What?"

"He has to eat? It's an expression. It means he has to make money, to buy food." They are in the loggia now, looking out onto the courtyard, which is empty but for a single pigeon pecking the Virgin's plinth. The afternoon light makes its feathers iridescent, the black and green and purple far more lovely than they should be on a creature who eats trash.

"I know the expression, I just haven't heard you use it," says Maddalena.

"When would I have used it?" Luisa's laugh is tinny. "Who here has to worry about making a living but him?"

Maddalena doesn't rise to the remark, which she thinks Luisa hasn't intended as sardonic. Luisa's looking at Maddalena but not seeing her, imagining instead perhaps her violin, the little black music notes climbing the staff, Vivaldi's own little notes to the musicians: *the accent here, pizzicato, andante.*

"You like him," she says.

This time Luisa stops walking, says, "What?"

"Not just his music, or what he's done for you. You like *him.*"

"No." Luisa's blush rises quickly. "Absolutely not."

"It isn't bad," says Maddalena. "Just be careful. Just know it, that's all." Luisa's holding her breath, turning purpler. Maddalena repeats herself. "It isn't bad."

"He's old."

"He can't be more than forty."

"No, I don't like him. I don't dislike him, but I don't…" Luisa is still purple, and now she seems like she might cry. Maddalena feels sorry for her.

"It's fine. You're playing beautifully. He's obviously helping you."

"And the water," says Luisa.

"And the water." They walk silently, not touching. Where before they were one girl with two bodies, one heart with two heads, they now are separate. Before, Maddalena was master. May. June. It's now July.

Luisa

One afternoon at her lesson, Vivaldi tells Luisa that he has written a concerto just for her. No matter that she's not yet an active member of the Coro, or that she doesn't have seniority. He's been inspired by her, and inspiration won't wait. This is a concerto written to Luisa's strengths, and she will play it in concert in the church, in front of the congregants, for a debut complete with her name on the pamphlet as soloist.

"What, does she think she's at the opera?" Chiara grumbles when the news is announced.

"Indeed." This, surprisingly, from Maddalena, who continues to feel far away, even when they lie shoulder to shoulder. Something has changed between them, but Luisa cannot pin it down. It is this change—more than the audience's fawning, the smoothness of Luisa's legato, the toppled inner wall allowing her to play for others the way she's only ever played for herself—that makes her think of the shrine. Can a blessing be stolen? Likely not without consequence. Luisa's sad to remember how they'd been, how they might still be, had Maddalena not brought her to the water. But she's too busy for debating or wondering or regretting.

"It will mean extra practice," she says that night. "Even more than I've already had." She closes her eyes, just for a moment. Maddalena is saying something, but the heat makes her body repulsive. Luisa turns—to keep her limbs from touching Maddalena's limbs, a reprieve from clammy closeness. Maddalena is still mumbling, but Luisa's ears are buzzing with the continuo simple from that afternoon's rehearsal, the cadenza she is going to make her own.

"Don't you think?" says Maddalena, nudging her. Luisa doesn't ask her to repeat her previous question.

"I think I just need to sleep."

Her wrists ache, she can hear the bones touch bone. She grows so accustomed to the bruising on her shoulder and neck that she barely feels it. Vivaldi goes back to wherever it is that he goes—Mantua, Padua? Luisa isn't listening—and she spends the hours she'd spent with him alone with her violin and his music, which becomes her music. She has always played in tune; even at her most nervous, the notes sounded as they should sound, which is how she earned her place as second chair. Now her skill at intonation matches a newfound quickness, a fluidity through left-hand ascending pizzicato, an ease with double harmonics, with both up- and down-bow staccato. Every technical element that once required effort comes more easily, which lets her ease her mental guard so that her heart can surge through. That innate feeling only she can conjure, the sound—as Don Antonio says—of murmuring streams, of flower-strewn meadows.

When Luisa plays with the Coro, Anna Maria is delighted. "I'll be turning your pages soon."

Vivaldi won't be back in time for the debut, so the maestra will conduct. "But think," says Anna Maria, "of what he'll say when word spreads of our new star." She and Luisa descend the steps of the choir loft together. Tomorrow they will climb these same stairs, watch the congregation fill the pews. Luisa will stand at the front, and the lattice will make a variegated mural of the black-cloaked nobles, the tradesmen crowded at the doors. Anna Maria squeezes Luisa's hand as they separate—Anna Maria to her rooms, Luisa to her ward—and Luisa imagines a transfer of power, of skill, yes, but also allure. She is certain that tomorrow she will shine.

That night she goes to bed alone, and Maddalena doesn't come to her.

The next morning, she wakes to sheets soaked through. Her hands, which she has worked so hard to master, chatter and tremble. When she tries to stand for early-morning prayer, she collapses, the lights too bright, the bells too loud. A hammering in her head, like someone trying to break free.

"She won't be playing with the orchestra today," says the ward mistress when beckoned. "They'll have to choose a different piece."

Luisa could cry, but she doesn't. Instead she closes her eyes and sees that shrine, that dark water, that violin bridge buried in silt. This is what comes of stealing someone else's gift, of sabotaging Chiara. She feels like she herself will be buried in silt, like she is sinking, and then drowned.

Maddalena

Foreigners come to Venice to escape their lives, but few stay more than a few weeks. The freedoms that sound so appealing from London or Prague are only attractive in the realm of fantasy. Real life has its frustrations, of course—an inherited estate with debts to pay, a decided lack of courtesans—but is ultimately preferable to infinite phantasmagoria. This is why Carnival lasts just a season, albeit a long one, and why the Great Council has traditionally tried to curb the most outrageous of its gluttonies. Gone are the days when Venice acted as a military power, gone are the days when empires fell at her hand.

"Money draining, money draining," Nicolò will mumble, looking over his ledgers. There's no shame in the conflation of mercantilism and nobility, not here, in a republic built on wits and trade. But there is lately not much mercantilism, at least for the nobility, hence the choice to commit daughters to the nunnery and sons to the Ridotto. Even with the lack of suitors, Nicolò should not have had to worry about his sister, the only sister, with an old, respected name. And yet here she is, trying to build a lure.

What does a wellborn wife need in Venice? It doesn't matter if she cleans or cooks, servants will do all that for her. Is she pretty? Enough, and with the rest of the city to liaise with at leisure, looks are less of a concern. Can she bear children? She's from a family of four who survived into adulthood; she likely can. Is she a virgin? She has never been unchaperoned. Is she compliant? She hasn't proven otherwise. *Ah, but her mother* . . .

But she can play the viola de gamba, and she sings! Listen, she's an angel.

Listen, here is Maddalena standing in front of Maestra Michielina, stretching her jaw. Her soft palate lifts and she fills with vibration, with God. She is a good girl, with a pretty voice, and she is full of God.

"You're going to tell that to Nicolò?" she says to Beneto, who is in town on unelaborated business and dropping by to deliver their mother's moretta, as she'd requested in her letter. There's no explicit rule against smuggling, but Beneto's eyes dart as he angles the black velvet mask through the parlatorio's grate. Maddalena mouths her thanks, though they're effectively alone. Today's chaperone, Figlia Agata, droops on her better days, and has wilted magnificently in the heat, slumped in her chair, eyes closed, possibly snoring. "When you go back to Mira, you're going to tell Nicolò I've done well?"

"Of course," says Beneto. Even once the mask is through, he seems distracted. He keeps sniffing and glancing toward the door. Maddalena can see the sweat above his upper lip, the rising color of his cheeks in the humidity. Beneto is the best looking of her brothers, and the easiest. He has dimples in both chin and cheeks, a sharp jaw that makes up for thinner lips. The sort of face both men and women want to find behind the bauta, when he has them alone and unties its strap.

Nicolò intimidates with his power, Andrea his audacity. Beneto is the youngest son—the son who will marry—and as such submits to what his father and brothers have mapped out for him with genuine good nature. Maddalena thinks that if she were a man she'd be amenable, too. It is much easier to have your fate declared when it's a wealthy wife, a mistress or two, nights as you wish to spend them, maybe a seat on the board of a charity or theater.

Beneto's only concern is his mother's rumored infidelity, which if solidified from gossip to accepted social truth will change everyone's course. If he is seen as a bastard, Beneto will be shunted off to some outpost of the Veneto, and Andrea will take on the responsibility of continuing the family name. If he is known to be legitimate, Beneto's only real job is to make more Grimani children, and he can be comfortable in the knowledge that even if he fails, there are two other brothers.

Is this lingering uncertainty the reason that he now seems so uneven? It cannot be the mask, which burns its existence through Maddalena's layers of skirt like a brand to the skin but means little to Beneto beyond the game of its delivery. Something else is afoot, something he's hiding. Maddalena holds a hand to the grille, hooking two fingers into a square opening. Absentmindedly, Beneto raises his hand to link with hers.

"Is everything all right at home?" Maddalena whispers, so that if by some chance Figlia Agata has woken, she won't gossip.

"Of course," Beneto says again, surprised. "We miss you. We're lonely without you. But otherwise all right."

"Lonely," Maddalena scoffs.

"Without your company." One of the curls of Beneto's wig is lanker than the rest. He flicks it away as it creeps down his collar.

"Something is happening," Maddalena says. "Has happened?"

"Don't worry." Beneto's response is so rote that she knows she will worry. "It doesn't matter. Focus on . . . whatever it is you do here. Improving yourself." Is it a lovers' quarrel? A debt? Does it involve Beneto, alone, or the rest of the household? Is it her father? Maddalena suddenly feels very far from her family, very far from the self she'd once been.

"Why are you here when you could be at Mira?" she asks Beneto.

"Business." What a silly word, what a large umbrella for all kinds of indiscretions.

"You really won't say?" Beneto shrugs. "Why don't you leave, then?" Maddalena says, surprising herself. "If you've nothing else to give me, why are you still here?" Beneto steps back, burned by her unexpected vitriol.

"Maddalena . . ." But he isn't quick or clever or versed enough in young women to know what to say to her, and this serves to further provoke.

"It's hot," she says. "I have the mask. You should go." This isn't the first time Beneto has been told to go and been unsure of his next course of action, and it won't be the last. He looks again toward the exit, then back at his sister, who has set her jaw.

"I should—"

"You should go." Maddalena's voice is tight. "Give my best to the others."

He goes, and of course she regrets it immediately, now alone in a large, hot room with a forlorn Virgin hefting her poor son across multiple friezes. Figlia Agata sleeps on, and Maddalena is not inclined to wake her and return to the refectory. Instead she sits at the grate, passing her finger through and back. The same humid loll on either side, the same stagnancy. Beneto, the sweet brother who once fed her the family gossip, compatriot no more.

She is losing the girl she'd been, before the Pietà. Of course she had already lost her childhood. *My mother didn't leave me.* Silly to think that Maddalena could just wish for what her mother razed a whole life to earn. To think that the void left by abandonment could be filled, that she will ever be whole.

For a short time, Maddalena had Luisa. With Luisa, the loneliness was gone. She sees herself in bed with Luisa, swollen with possibility. She pictures Luisa now, always practicing, always dreaming beyond Maddalena's dreams, always speaking of Vivaldi.

She's lost herself. She's lost Beneto. She shouldn't have to lose Luisa, not yet.

Rain has threatened all day, and the weight of it continues into evening. Stepping onto her gondola, Maddalena anticipates a breeze off the water that does not come. Even the gondolier, always pristine, seems diminished, his hair a dark halo of humidity.

"To the shrine," she tells him, though he's already set out north, toward Torcello. The maze of Venice's calli and canals is still impenetrable, but Maddalena is developing a better understanding of the lagoon. She knows, now, that she is moving out of Castello, past Murano, into the long stretch of marsh between the bustling main island and what was once the heart of Venice, when Venice began. Before it was Venice, before the republic's power rose and then fell, there was a swamp, and there was silt, and there was salt marsh. Maddalena imagines the first settlers paddling toward Torcello, running from mainland invasions. They brought their churches here from where they'd first raised them, carried them stone by stone. They brought their priests. Over one thousand years, the people of Torcello bled out onto Murano, the main island; one hundred years ago plague exsanguinated the rest. Now Torcello is farms, laguna morta. It is ghosts.

At home, before the Pietà, Nicolò brought her into their father's study to teach her their history. These were the trade routes, these were barenas that used to be islands before being lost to the sea.

"If you go out here at low tide, it's a playground," he said, pointing. "At high tide, nothing. Just the water." Once, to be Venetian meant to cater to the tides, to know the water, to anticipate the floods. "Now, it means to waste your days on ineffectual politics, your nights at the Ridotto. Soon, we will all be losing prestige, losing money. We are being laid low."

Maddalena doesn't feel laid low. Maddalena never led crusades, never negotiated trade deals. Maddalena didn't go to war or build its ships. She is out here, on the water. She is watching her handsome young gondolier guide her through ghosts. One bird is awake, its cries slowed by the descending fog, long like taffy. Flies hover over a particular sandbank, unperturbed by the gondola. The lapping, lapping of the water and the oar.

Finally they reach their destination, and Maddalena slips out from the felze. The shrine seems larger than it did last month in the dark with Luisa, and at the same time less solid, as if its matter has stretched and thinned. A ghost, Maddalena thinks again. A ghost of a shrine. A bad omen.

She clears her throat and tries to laugh at her own superstition, because it's only fog. What does she stand in now, if not a wooden gondola? Who has brought her here, if not an actual gondolier?

Maddalena imagines Luisa waking in her cot, turning toward Maddalena's bed. Will Luisa sit up, will she toss off her blanket of sleep, will she worry? Or is she so exhausted that she'll blink a bit and ultimately turn the other way, falling back under the spell of the maestro and his work?

"Don't let him have her," Maddalena whispers to the shrine. "Bring her back to me." She reaches into her bodice and removes her mother's mask, the moretta from Beneto. Maddalena strokes the velvet, closes her eyes, and lets it sink down.

Luisa

Summer is the season for sickness. The Pietà's medico sees Luisa in the infirmary and confirms what she already knows: a fever, swelling in the extremities, perhaps also in the lungs, which would account for both the sense that she is drowning and the blood in her handkerchief. Everyone knows a bloody cough portends one thing—Luisa asks for confession, but the medico tells her she's being dramatic.

"The fever will break," he says, "and we'll let out the blood and fluid."

"Now?" asks Luisa. "Before the maestro's back from Mantua?" The medico tut-tuts, almost says out loud, *You foolish child*, but instead pats Luisa's sweat-darkened hair and tells her to rest.

She tries to rest. She shudders with the distinct cold of fever, the sense her bones have turned to water and are frozen and might very easily break. She imagines her arms shattering, first one and then the other. A single window lets in weak light, but her bed is too far from it for a view of anything but the occasional bird swooping out toward the lagoon, the shadow of a wing across a wall. She finds sleep waiting when she needs it, ready to cradle her for only a moment or sink her in deep. During the day she imagines Maddalena at her bedside, wearing the black dress of a noblewoman, her hair unbound and her eyes dark pits. She thinks she sees Maddalena's young gondolier in a chair by the door, cleaning his fingernails with a knife. One of the figlie comes to change her bedsheets. They bring her broth. Another girl takes ill and makes her hacking cough in the corner of the room.

At night, Luisa dreams of the sea. She closes her eyes to the twilit infirmary with its stench of sour bodies, and after a brief time in the dark opens them to the midday lagoon, where the salt marshes turn into sandy beaches and the Adriatic opens its vast mouth. Lido, she thinks, and she remembers Maddalena's lips against her ear, describing the Feast of the Ascension—the doge in his ceremonial red robes on his ceremonial red boat, tossing that ring into the waves, followed by cannon fire and music.

In her dream, Luisa is alone. She walks across the beach and into the water, which sparkles turquoise and mirror clear, unending. She wears a white dress, like the dress the Coro wears during performance, this one aproned with deep pockets. The pockets are full of what she thinks at first are stones, but upon examination appear to be instruments. They are much heavier than the instruments Luisa is familiar with—perhaps because there are so many of them, an unending stream of clarinets and cellos, bubbling up from somewhere in the seams. Luisa walks out into the sea, the instruments both in her and trailing behind her, and she feels herself sinking with the weight of them. The water rises, and she lowers, and when at last her head goes under, she opens her eyes with a gasp to find herself in the infirmary bed, sheets soaked with sweat.

Maddalena

Beneto returns at the worst time. Maddalena has forgone her afternoon on the canal in favor of stalking the hall outside the Pietà infirmary, listening at the door as the medico makes his prognosis. She knows that he is speaking, but not what he says, and when Figlia Menegha comes to tell her of her unexpected visitor, Maddalena is almost prostrate, her chin against the stone, trying to hear.

"What are you doing, girl?"

Maddalena doesn't know how to say she's repenting. Luisa woke yesterday morning feverish and swollen, and was whisked away before Lauds. The hem of Maddalena's dress stank of the salt marsh. She remembered the feel of the mask in her hand, the single concentric circle rippling out as it disappeared below the shrine. I take it back, she thought as she watched the dormitory girls bluster about in Luisa's wake. She should play for Vivaldi. She must.

She went to Mass and listened to the new, Luisa-less concerto, all the while planning her escape after Sext, when the others would go to their workrooms and she'd find her gondolier. But for the first time, when Maddalena reached the water gate, the boat was nowhere to be found. She sat in the shadows, watching the canal—a pair of noblewomen peeking from their felze, a boy in a red cap feeding a dog, a flock of birds about to land but thinking better of it—until the bell rang for Nones and, rudderless, she went back inside.

"The medico is with her," Maddalena was told when she asked after Luisa, first of the ward mother and then the Priora herself, whose initial irritation softened when she saw Maddalena's genuine distress. "You can see her as soon as it's safe." A sleepless night, the next bed bare. A somber morning. Finally this dirty floor, the certainty that Luisa will die and come to haunt her. Luisa will die, and Maddalena will be truly alone.

"Get up and get yourself together. You've a visitor." Figlia Menegha doesn't wait. "Come on, then."

When she sees it's Beneto, Maddalena is mostly annoyed. Did she think, perhaps, that her mysterious gondolier would be waiting behind the parlatorio screen? She dismisses the thought.

"You, again." She sits, unceremonious and unladylike, staring at Beneto.

"Me." His hands spread in the universal gesture of amiable culpability.

"Well?" Maddalena sucks her teeth. Beneto rubs the tip of his nose with the back of a hand.

"Can't a man visit his sister without being torn to pieces?"

"Apparently not." She knows it isn't fair to be so cross with him, but she can't help herself. "Do you have news or are you just here for the scenery?"

"I could have written," Beneto says. "I suppose."

"Yes. Well. Then you should write." Maddalena makes to stand, and he holds out a palm to stop her.

"Wait. I'm here on behalf of Nicolò. And Father."

"And before? This is why you were in town?" asks Maddalena. He nods.

"They want you to come home." Beneto is always careful of his words. *They* want you. I'm simply the messenger. "Not home forever. For a party Father's having at the villa. He wants to show you off to his guests."

"Well, I can't go. There's too much happening."

Beneto laughs. "Here? What happens here?"

Maddalena hates him again, that same fierce hatred she felt when he brought her the mask, new and startling. Because he is also a pawn.

Because he is, at heart, a good man—or he might be. Because Luisa is lying in a narrow bed, her lungs filling with water, and there is nothing Maddalena can do to make it right. She doesn't want to tell Beneto about Luisa, the one good thing that is her own.

"I'll consider it," she says. "You can tell them that."

She goes from the parlatorio to the water gate, brushing off Orsetta, who reminds her that she's supposed to be attending group rehearsal. Someone else can play the timpani, someone else can join the chorus—Maddalena finally has work to do, and if it doesn't correspond with the Pietà's hours, so be it.

"I'm ready for you," she says loudly to the canal. "I'm ready to give you whatever you want. Just make her better." No one answers, though an old gondolier gives her an odd look as he passes. "What?" says Maddalena to the water. "Are you scared of me?" She's had years to practice the bravado, to polish the mask. She knows how to fashion herself, but she needs someone to see her. The canal gives her a dirty reflection, the shadow of her humidity-mussed hair. Nothing stirring in the silt, no one rowing in from the lagoon.

She imagines what the thing at Lido would say: *You are a silly girl, mercurial. You don't know what you want.* But this would be inaccurate, unfair. It isn't that Maddalena doesn't know, it's that her desire has become impossibly large. She pictures Luisa in the infirmary bed, growing paler as the medico lets out her humors. What does he do with the contaminated blood, once it has left the body? Surely no one wants it. Can Maddalena return the sickness? Can she move it from one body to another? It seems worth trying. Anything is better than sitting here, screaming at the sky.

Maddalena already knows she can move through the Pietà unseen. She gives a last look out at the canal, a last chance for the gondolier to find her and offer redemption. He doesn't come, and so she slips back inside and to the second floor, where the medico keeps his office next to the infirmary.

The medico carries his bloodletting bowl in his bag, but it is up to the figlie to clean it. Luckily, the Pietà isn't a world in which one refuses domestic help. When Maddalena opens her hands to take the mess of fluid from the infirmary's attending figlia, it is proffered without question. The infirmary door shuts and Maddalena stands alone in the hall, holding a bowl of blood. She stops herself from gagging. This is penance. This is redemption, the blood of Christ turned to wine. She has to walk very slowly to keep from spilling it onto the stone.

Maddalena should be at chapel, but no one stops you when you're carrying a bowl of blood, even if you're flouting protocol. She goes to the water gate, where the canal has come to life with evening revelers. Still no sign of her own gondolier, so while she'd prefer to make her offering at the lagoon, she'll have to pray here, at the Rio de la Pletà.

"I'm returning what I took from you," Maddalena whispers as she tilts the dish and watches the blood spill into the canal. It spreads and spreads, weightless, and then nothing. She leaves the dish at the gate for the flies.

The next morning she waits for news from the infirmary, which has been promised her by the Priora. None comes, and she spends the whole hot day wondering if her entire world has been imagined. The bell tower insists that everything is only now, a steady throng of moment after moment after moment. Every day, the further erosion of shore. But there had been a violin bridge, and there had been a mask, and she can summon the memory of each in her palm, and the memory of Luisa in her bed. Perhaps it wasn't enough to offer what was already emptied. Perhaps she should have found a way out to the shrine on her own, and brought something more valuable. Maddalena travels the loggia with the rest of the girls from her dorm, turning over the idea of something larger. She thinks that if she had to, she could make an exchange: one of these interchangeable bodies for Luisa. A bit of something in a drink, a pressure point at the side of the neck.

"They want you upstairs." A little girl whose braid has fallen from her cap sidles next to Maddalena as she considers who would be the least missed among this group.

"Luisa?" she asks, but the girl is gone, and before she can hope, Maddalena tells herself it's probably Beneto, declaring himself her chaperone. I'll go, she thinks with desperation, if Luisa lives, I'll go.

The Priora stands at the window, looking out at some commotion on the Riva degli Schiavoni. She smiles at Maddalena's approach.

"Your friend is better."

Maddalena is surprised by the immediacy, no small talk or formalities first.

"My friend?"

"Luisa. Her fever broke last night. I thought you'd want to know."

"Yes." Maddalena's heart is beating so fast she imagines the Priora can see it in her chest.

"Auspicious timing," says the Priora, "don't you think?"

"What?" Luisa is alive. Luisa is a few stone walls, a few dirt floors, a few dirty windows away. Luisa has opened her eyes. Luisa is better.

Maddalena should feel joy—Luisa is alive. Instead, she feels relief that she herself is not a murderer, that she hasn't ruined her one good thing with her own selfishness, which in its way is another sort of selfishness.

"Just when your brother has come to collect you," says the Priora. From how her smile compresses, Maddalena can tell the Priora doesn't approve. The Ospedale della Pietà is a renowned musical institution, not a nursery at which noble families can leave and collect their children at will. But when you are a Grimani, apparently even the Ospedale della Pietà can be yours for the taking. "He's given word he'll come the day after tomorrow," the Priora says. "And wants you to be ready for him."

"But the motet. The pieces I've been working on with Maestra Michielina..." Maddalena knows it's futile, but she at least has to try. She does miss the country house. She does want to leave Venice, with its heat and summer sickness.

The Priora has a cup of tea on her desk, and she fondles the mug, looking at Maddalena with a sympathy that at once breeds Maddalena's resentment—who is she to feel sorry for nobility? She has no fine villa in Mira. She has no silk dresses, no gardens.

"He'll come the day after tomorrow," the Priora repeats. She lifts the mug to drink.

Maddalena says, "But what about Luisa?" and immediately she can tell something has changed, something is humming and humid and wrong in the room.

The Priora replaces the cup on the table, and Maddalena follows the sound of it, a lapping. The color very bright, for tea. She looks at the Priora, who seems confused, who is wiping blood from the corners of her mouth.

"She needs rest, doesn't she?" Maddalena forges ahead, ignoring her fear for Luisa's sake, to keep the two of them together. "She needs fresh air? And where better to get it? Orsetta said when she had smallpox she went to Mestre for the season. Luisa could act as my chaperone. She could help me continue my lessons. She could—"

"Yes," the Priora says. "Yes, of course. If the medico thinks that she's ready for travel, Luisa will go with you."

Maddalena knows better than to question her luck, but was expecting much more of a challenge. Her mouth, thinks Maddalena. Something is wrong with the Priora's mouth. That dripping redness. But Maddalena nods and gives an awkward sort of curtsy and turns to leave.

A figlia de comun has come to wash the floor outside the Priora's office, on her knees, humming to herself. She has a wet rag and is leaning into the stone, oblivious to Maddalena. Her bucket sits next to the wall, under a niche in which a little statue of the Virgin looks out over the corridor. Her bucket laps. It's full of blood.

The basins in the infirmary, which hold water to clean wounds and soak towels. The pitchers at the refectory table, the cups from which the figlie drink. The tubs that the girls use to take turns splashing water onto their faces and hands before bed. At sunset Maddalena looks out the window onto the canal, and even that seems to have taken on an impossible reddish hue. It feels like a warning, but also a welcoming.

Luisa is still in the infirmary, where she will remain until the girls travel to Mira. The day after tomorrow, Beneto will come at the second bells to bring them to the burchiello, the decorative barge that will carry them up the river Brenta. Maddalena considers going immediately up to Luisa, bypassing whichever nurse is on duty and lying down next to her. But Luisa is weak, and they travel soon. No one else notices the changes in the water. If Maddalena were to bring the basin over to find that Luisa, too, saw nothing amiss, she would have to reconceive herself and all that's happened since that day at Lido, when she first spoke to the water and heard it respond. There isn't time, not with her father and her brothers and the household at Mira to contend with. Maybe not ever. Easier to assume that the blood is a message, a reminder of her covenant.

The blankets are too heavy. The air is too stale. When Maddalena closes her eyes, she sees the red at the Priora's mouth, the way her saliva watered it to coat the tops of her teeth where they met the gum. Adriana, adenoidal as ever, mumbles in her sleep. If Luisa were here, splayed in the next bed, perhaps Maddalena would lie with her arms over her ears and hide her head under her pillow to block out the noise. But the next bed is empty, its blanket taken for disinfection and never returned. Maddalena swings her legs over her own mattress. She goes barefooted to the door, which opens silently into an empty hallway.

Her gondolier waits for her at the water gate, as she knew he would. His boat rests on a dark canal, but a canal that is still water. Oppressive heat has driven everyone inside, and so tonight there are no revelers, no midnight tradesmen or clandestine lovers meeting.

"I looked for you," Maddalena says.

"I know," he answers.

She wonders if she should tell him she's leaving. She wonders if he'll miss her. She wants to know how he found himself here, at her beckoning. At something's beckoning. What guides him? What does he seek at the shrine in the lagoon? What has made him and in making him made Maddalena? She won't go to the shrine tonight—she only wants to know if it was his doing, the blood in the bucket, the blood in the Priora's cup. His being here, his half-smile, the way he looks at her. Maddalena feels vindicated. Powerful.

The gondolier bows to her before he takes his craft to the lagoon, to wherever he will wait for her return.

"What are you?" she whispers before heading back to the dormitory, where she will toss in the heat until dawn.

Luisa

Once the fever's broken, Luisa is allowed to have visitors. Maddalena comes after Mass, standing for a moment in the doorway, itching an elbow. Luisa can imagine what she must see—her face pale, her hair lank, her body rusty with the remnants of the bloodletting. Maddalena is washed and rosy, glossy-haired and pink-cheeked and bright-eyed from the heat. Luisa's embarrassed, but tries not to be. Then Maddalena rushes forward and embraces her—a quick look back to make sure no figlie will scold them—and slides next to Luisa on the bed, taking her friend's hand and stroking her fingers.

"I was so worried," says Maddalena. "I was terrified. But it's all going to work out for the best."

Luisa doesn't mention the solo, the days that have passed since what was meant to be her debut became instead her endless hours with the medico, wincing as he sought her veins with his fleam. She lets Maddalena baby her—brushing hair from her face and tucking it behind her ears, fluffing her pillow, babbling on about the concert, and how awful it sounded without Luisa, which is certainly untrue. Then she mentions something about her brother coming to collect them, and Luisa shakes off her fatigue.

"What did you say?"

"Beneto, tomorrow morning. We'll go to my family's villa in Mira, and you'll get well. The medico agrees that you need to take the air."

"Leave Venice?" Luisa isn't sure if her light-headedness is the last of the fever, or something more. Until the midnight boat ride to the altar in the marsh, she'd rarely strayed out of Castello.

"You'll be happy there, I promise. You won't miss this." Maddalena surveys the room, wincing at the smell. "You'll like Beneto."

Luisa does like Beneto, right away. He comes in wigless, in a tricorn hat and the black jacket of the nobility, but removes both hat and coat as soon as they've walked out the Pietà door, a wink to Luisa and a squeeze of his sister's upper arm before he stretches his own to welcome the slight midsummer breeze. He helps both girls into a gondola that will take them to the burchiello that will take them to the Villa Grimani in Mira. Beneto looks like his sister—the same dark hair and eyes, the same sharp features—and as he directs the gondolier, he moves with the same ease that in Maddalena belies her innate watchfulness, but in Beneto appears genuine.

Despite having told Luisa that among all her living family, she's closest to Beneto, Maddalena is chilly with him, refusing to acknowledge him directly and disinclined to show gratitude. Luisa can't help but thank him in a manner that she hopes isn't obsequious. Beneto is, in a sense, rescuing her. She should be, and act, grateful.

"You'll wear yourself out licking his boots," says Maddalena.

"I thought you liked him," says Luisa.

"I do."

Luisa has no time to press her, because they've reached the burchiello. Luisa had imagined it as a larger traghetto, but it is little like the ferry that ushers both commoners and nobility back and forth across the Grand Canal. Both are boats, but there the similarity seems to end. The burchiello is in truth a floating palace, its cabin hung with mirrors and oil paintings, its little verandas adorned with fresh flowers. This is one of several similar vessels that brings the nobles from Venice to their properties along the Brenta, which winds through the small towns of the Veneto on its path to Padua. Maddalena takes Luisa onto one of the boat's several balconies to look out at the oarsmen who are steering them away from the city.

For all Maddalena's talk of Palazzo Grimani and its halls, her gardens and her brothers and their parties, this is the first time Luisa recognizes just how different their childhoods have been. She's seen women in their gondolas with their cavalieri, twirling long-stemmed flowers in their delicate fingers, and imagined herself knowledgeable. They all went home to bed, did they not? They all served the same God. But inside the burchiello, a girl polishes a silver-handled cup and gives it not to her Savior but to Beneto, who has drawn out a sheaf of papers he peruses as she serves him his wine. Luisa shivers.

"Forgive me," says Maddalena. "I'd forgotten you're still weak." She sounds like someone else, someone older, more regal.

"The air is good," Luisa says. "I'm feeling much better." This isn't enough to breach the distance between them. Luisa's hand twitches toward Maddalena, but she stops herself, unsure. They sit silently, watching the city recede.

Once they reach the Brenta, the oarsmen are replaced by horses that walk the banks, pulling the vessel between them. Maddalena wrinkles her nose at the smell, but Luisa leans out, watching. Horses are not allowed in Venice. Of course she has seen statues, she's seen paintings. Of course she knows that in most of the world people travel not by boat but by horse and carriage. That doesn't change the reality of them, their thick necks, the way they trudge along the towpath, their rippling haunches and the twitches as they shake off the flies. Maddalena grows bored with them, bored with Luisa. She goes into the cabin, pointedly sneezing.

Luisa remains. There are not simply horses to admire, but villas. Maddalena said "country house," and Luisa imagined a barn, a pump for water, perhaps an orchard or a field ripe with fruit. These are just palazzi picked up and placed in fields, stretching to take up what space they now can: white pillared, resplendent in the midday sun.

"That's an especially gaudy one." Luisa turns to see Beneto behind her. He comes to lean over the railing, pointing to a home easily the size of the entire Pietà. "The Contarinis," he says. "What can you expect?"

Luisa nods, as if she understands his reference. He sees through her and smiles. "Here," he says, handing her a blanket. "It's cooler in the shade."

"Thank you for bringing me. Us. Making the journey." Luisa keeps looking out at the Contarini villa, as if by focusing on landscaping she might escape her awkwardness.

"I was in Venice already, it's no trouble." Beneto turns into the breeze, which has swept suddenly, bringing whiffs of both horse and something floral.

"And to bring Maddalena. Away from... her education." Luisa falters, unsure what she's trying to say.

"Oh, we'd have come for her soon, anyway. My brother's hoping that this family penance has made up for certain previous bad behaviors. He's going to try to 'show her off to best advantage.'" The last he says raising his brow, only the slightest challenge to his brother, but enough to give Luisa a sense of his loyalties. She wonders if Maddalena knows that Beneto's on her side. On their side. She leans forward, to see what Beneto sees, but when her head spins, she sits back.

"Do you need water?" he asks.

She shakes her head. "Show her off?" she says, realizing. "Will there be many people with us?"

"Oh, everyone comes to the Riviera del Brenta in summer," says Beneto. "Don't worry, we'll keep you mainly to ourselves. We all know you've been ill. Mostly it's just the household and Nicolò and Andrea. Me, of course." He chews his lip, and Luisa has the sense that there is something he's not telling her. "Don't worry," he repeats. "You're pretty enough that Nicolò will want to keep you relatively quiet. Pretty and, I'm told, quite good at violin." Luisa isn't sure how to respond. She can feel her face heating. "Be careful with both of them," Beneto says softly. "Nicolò and Andrea."

The burchiello passes under an outstretched weeping willow that casts a dramatic maze of shade over Beneto's face. Seeing him, somber and shadowed, Luisa decides she will be careful. She considers Maddalena's warnings about Maestro Vivaldi, considers Maddalena's experiences with men, and feels a sudden burst of pity for her friend. Luisa will spend the next few weeks in the fresh air, listening to the birds, to the goats, to the country, and when she returns to Venice she will be able to play all these new sounds on her violin. Maddalena has no such refuge.

Luisa finally stands, leaving Beneto on the balcony, and goes shakily into the cabin to find Maddalena. She sets herself in a cushioned chair next to where Maddalena sits napping, and reaches for her hand. Thin eyelids, fluttering open. And nothing to disguise Maddalena's pleasure when she wakes, the warmth as her hand returns the energy Luisa expends, joining the girls once more.

Maddalena

The heat is drier than it's been. Maddalena looks at Luisa as they board the burchiello, imagining Luisa searches the docks for some sign of her maestro, that she listens for—what did he call it?—"the music of the flower-strewn meadow."

Where was he while you were sick? Where was he while I was bargaining? Merely to think this—let alone speak it aloud—is to admit both her guilt and her jealousy. She will never tell Luisa about the mask at the shrine. There have, of course, been other things that Maddalena hasn't told Luisa. She lived a whole life at Palazzo Grimani, and her mother lived a whole life before Maddalena was born. Yet for a girl without a history the past is immaterial; Luisa has never pressed Maddalena for details, and Maddalena has never felt deliberately withholding. They find each other between the bells of Compline and Lauds, suspended together in time. At least they did, before Vivaldi and his music took precedence.

Now, thanks to the shrine, Luisa is in the world next to her, bony wrists and golden hair and that unconscious half-smile when she sees something she thinks shouldn't delight her. Maddalena has to sit on her hands to keep from reaching out, has to bite her lip to keep from asking—what, for Luisa's affection? For her gratitude? She's angry with herself for her need, and with Luisa for withholding, with the horses who plod along the banks of the canal, flicking their tails. She pushes back from the burchiello's railing, hoping Luisa won't follow her inside. Of course, she is upset Luisa doesn't.

In the cabin, Beneto perches on the arm of a chair, his boots muddying the cushion. He's taken the last bite of a plum, and Maddalena glares at him, eager to direct her irritation at something so obvious as open-mouthed chewing.

"Do you want me to prepare you for Mira?" Beneto asks once he has swallowed. "Or would you rather let Nicolò surprise you?"

"I'm prepared enough," says Maddalena. "You think I haven't realized what they're doing? What you're doing?"

"What am I doing?" Beneto reaches down into a bowl of salted nuts, pops an almond into his mouth.

"You're disgusting."

"I'm just as much in it as you are," says Beneto. "There will be several girls trotted out for me, or at very least several of their fathers."

"The stakes are lower," says Maddalena despite herself, turning to look him in the eye. "If you ruin your chance with so-and-so, you'll always have another behind her."

"So will you." Beneto slips from the arm of the chair to its velvet seat, oblivious of the dirt. "In spite of everything, you have the Grimani name."

"For now," says Maddalena. "Maybe."

"For as long as I have it." Beneto tugs at his dark hair, the perfect match to her own. "If we're bastards, it's together."

"Don't." Maddalena looks out, toward Luisa's shadow.

"It isn't true, what they say about our mother." Beneto sits very straight, unblinking.

"You only know as much as I do," Maddalena says softly. "Don't pretend to know more." And although for her entire life it's been Beneto who best knows her, she feels as far from him now as she does from their mother. As far as she feels from Luisa, who she was supposed to immediately resume loving, who was supposed to immediately resume loving her.

Luisa

The Villa Grimani sits back from the river at an angle, and when the burchiello rounds the bend, the house faces Luisa head-on. It's a behemoth. Commanding and solid, its facade is built like a Greek temple, with Ionic columns and a roof styled like a pediment, steps winding from the sweeping lawn over the ground-floor servants' entrance to a door that's twice the height of Beneto.

Luisa hasn't thought herself a stranger to splendor. The Chiesa di Santa Maria della Pietà—the church in which the girls have Mass—is gilded and painted, and it fills with gilded, painted patrons every time the Coro plays. But Luisa never imagined the sort of luxury that hides behind the masks of the Venetian patricians, whose family names go back to the closing of the Great Council in the thirteenth century, who refuse to speak to foreigners and wear solemn black in public, who only move among themselves. "At my father's parties," Maddalena would say, or "At my father's house," and Luisa imagined a more expensive version of what she knows: softer sheets, richer foods, less of a draft in the winter. This is a whole different existence. What has Luisa's life in common with the painted ceilings in the piano nobile, the hedge maze and the frescoes, the fountains, the cathedral of an entryway magnifying the setting sun's light for no cause but the Grimanis' own? Luisa looks at Maddalena anew for what feels like the hundredth time today. How did a girl like her go from this decadence to such a spartan existence? And how will the two of them go back there?

It isn't especially late, but as Luisa has been ill, Beneto decides it isn't time to meet the other Grimani brothers. Instead, Maddalena and Luisa have dinner brought to Maddalena's rooms, and it is all Luisa can do to swallow down a few bites before crawling into Maddalena's bed—four times the size of the beds at the Pietà, made up with silk and damask. She goes under immediately, gratefully. At some point she feels Maddalena slide in next to her, winding their legs, pressing her chin into Luisa's shoulder. The ceilings are too high, the bed its own ocean, and Luisa is glad to have an anchor.

When she wakes, Maddalena is gone and the windows are open, daylight illuminating a fresco of a naked winged child eating fruit. The walls have been painted to look carved, and Luisa's dizzy with the illusion. The burrowed sheets still warm beside her mean Maddalena can't have gone far, and Luisa sits for several minutes, waiting for her friend's return, before she's curious enough to slip out of bed. The frame is gilt, like almost everything else in the room, and ornate to the point of distraction. Luisa's Pietà uniform seems shabbier than ever as she slips on the red dress, ties on the apron.

Still no sign of Maddalena, and Luisa's appetite has returned. She looks around for the remains of last night's dinner, but as expected they've been cleared away. Through the large windows the garden sits dew-kissed and empty. From somewhere in the house comes the faint sound of dishes clattering, a poorly whistled tune. Luisa's here, isn't she? They've invited her. She might as well leave the room.

She follows the sounds through the central hall—a large colorful dome of further trompe l'oeil, its walls painted into pillars, shadowed nooks adorned with two-dimensional statues, contorted bodies stretched across the ceiling, scantily clothed in the classical style—and into a smaller room off its nave. First Luisa notices the table, laid with assorted meats and pastries; second, the young man seated with his back to the door.

"Don't just stand there," he says, without looking at Luisa. "Come join me." She is frozen. This must be a brother. The tall one—is there a tall one, or are they all mostly the same? "The cream puffs are quite good. I'd avoid those little tarts, unless you like tripe."

"Um..." Luisa puts a pastry on a delicate white plate.

"You don't need to be nervous, no matter what my sister's said." He finally turns toward her. Definitely a brother: his coloring lighter than Beneto's and Maddalena's, but with the same strong chin, those inky eyes that mark him a Grimani. "Come," he says. "Sit."

Luisa sits, waiting for him to introduce himself, wondering if she should be the first to speak. Finally she can hold off no longer, and she eats.

"Beneto's right," the brother says, tone conversational. He licks powdered sugar from the corner of his mouth, his tongue long and darting, playful. "Nicolò's going to want to hide that hair away."

Luisa touches the knot at the nape of her neck. She is unschooled in flirtation, in patricians, in almost everything but God and violin. She's embarrassed to ask him to explain, really to say anything at all to this brother, whom she now knows to be Andrea, the rogue. She's blushing—always blushing—but Andrea pretends not to notice.

"I'm a musician myself, you know," he says. "Well, we all are, who isn't?" Luisa's not sure what to say. "I do appreciate the Pietà, though I'm partial to the singers at the Mendicanti." Luisa is down to a single bite, and she picks at it slowly, avoiding his eyes. Something about him sets her on edge, a manliness that was lacking in Beneto, no matter how close their bodies, how strong his cologne. Andrea is less put together, less put on—his short hair mussed, his jacket unbuttoned, the faintest trace of sugar still dusting his lip—yet still seems suaver, oily and seal-slick.

Luisa considers explaining that Silvia dei Mendicanti, the Ospedale of that same name's current star, uses too much vibrato on her high notes and sounds like she's calling to the goats. But if Andrea's a musician, surely he'll have noticed already. She says nothing.

"Well." Andrea pushes back from the table. "This has been scintillating." Luisa isn't sure if she's ashamed of her deficiencies, or relieved that he seems to be leaving her alone. Before she can decide, a commotion comes from the central hall—quick footsteps, what sounds like a pair of boots being tossed aside, unintelligible grumbling. Then the door opens and the final Grimani brother steps inside.

This is Nicolò, whom Luisa saw once in the parlatorio, but as with Andrea it is Nicolò unvarnished, at home. No wig, shirtsleeves rolled. Where Andrea is disheveled but still obviously expensive, Nicolò's clothes are almost as plain as Luisa's; he seems almost as incongruous here in this ornate room. His hair is longer than Andrea's, and he's cleaner shaven. Thin, not muscular. None of Beneto's easy charm.

Nicolò barely glances at Luisa, turning instead to Andrea. "She says tomorrow is too soon, she isn't ready." Nicolò clenches his hands into a fist. He's standing close enough that Luisa can see his fingernails dig into his palm.

"So?" says Andrea. "Will you wait for her?"

"It isn't up to me. Father invited him. He's coming."

"Well, there you are, then," says Andrea.

"Why don't you talk to her?"

"Me?" Andrea laughs. "What would I say?"

"That she should behave herself. That this is her best chance. That she should listen to me." Nicolò closes his eyes at the last, clearly wishing himself elsewhere. Wishing himself a second son? A second self? Luisa sits very still, hoping to escape their notice.

"Rich, coming from me," Andrea says.

"Help me make sure she's at least dressed the part." Nicolò opens his eyes, and their expression is determined. "And try to help her be less...obstinate."

Andrea gives a grinning salute as he goes, and Nicolò watches after him before turning toward Luisa, who makes herself as small as possible.

"And you," Nicolò says, eyes boring into her, "you'll help me. Maddalena will sing, and you will play."

Maddalena

Maddalena wakes up in her own bed at Mira, and for a moment she forgets the past three months, her world again reduced to this row of trees—carefully pruned soldiers lined up in the garden—this same slice of white-blue sky. But here is Luisa, sleeping next to her. Luisa looks peaceful, her hair spread across the pillow, her lips fluttering ever so slightly with each exhalation. Maddalena reaches out, trailing her finger across the length of Luisa's jaw. Her thumb hovers over the pulse point in Luisa's neck, the bruise from her violin. Maddalena isn't doing anything wrong; still, this feels dangerous. The way the light surrounds Luisa's hair, turning each strand phosphorescent, turning her skin deliciously pink. Maddalena leaves her asleep and slips through the halls, out to the villa's large back terrace.

Outside, the wind is gentling the trees so that the shadows of their leaves dance across the open arches of the loggia. Birds chitter away in many voices, most of them lovely. The sun is still low and the day not yet thick with summer, and Maddalena can imagine how one might want to make this moment into music. A little white puff of some feathered flower floats lazily across the sky, and Maddalena looks up and out to track it.

She feels she's somehow disappointing the Priora and the figlie by lingering here, dancing a foot in and out of a silk slipper as she stares at the canal. But when has she not disappointed them? Likely they talk about her at their table in the refectory, after the younger girls are gone. Likely they sit with the board of governors and complain about Marcantonio

Grimani and his idle daughter, who imagines herself invisible when really she is spoiled. Better to be spoiled than locked in a workroom, spinning bobbins. If she cared about the gossips, she would die.

"You aren't dressed." Nicolò's voice comes from the bottom of the garden, where large stone columns hide him from immediate view. Maddalena's in her nightdress. She walks the steps down to her oldest brother.

"A pleasure to see you, too." She doesn't smile, and neither does Nicolò. Despite the month spent in the countryside, he looks worse than when she last saw him—his eyes deeper set, his cheeks more sallow.

"We might have had company," he says.

"It's early."

"It's past nine."

That breeze, again, ruffling the bottom of her nightdress. She kicks off a slipper to draw a circle in the parched grass with her toe. Andrea and Beneto visited the Pietà regularly when they were in the city, but Nicolò only came once, at the beginning, after a crowded Sunday mass when the parlatorio was filled with visitors, the Coro lined up for a second act, taking refreshments with their patrons from behind the iron grille. Nicolò had asked gruffly about how Maddalena was settling, if she was comfortable. As soon as he could leave, he had left, and that was mid-May, and now it's early August. Doors have closed and then opened, closed again.

"Don't you have anything to say to me?" Maddalena asks finally. Nicolò opens his mouth, shuts it. Apparently he does not. She sighs. "When is this party? Who's coming, and what do you want me to do?"

Nicolò runs a hand through his hair, leaving it on end and ridiculous. "Tomorrow night, Maffeo Celsi, and you'll sing for him." Maddalena digs a toe into loam, trying and failing to find roots. A part of her hoped Nicolò would name some old man with a gut and maybe ten years left to live, who would fill her with seed and then retire to his library until a good death left behind a few small children and his fortune. Or maybe a known rogue and scoundrel, who'd leave an easily traced trail of bastards, his debts and the money to pay them, and Maddalena mostly alone. Nicolò might have named no one. He might have called her for the pleasure of her company.

But Maffeo Celsi is a catch, although his family's name is only newly noble and he has red hair, which chance might pass on to his children. Veritably surrounded by red-haired men, thinks Maddalena. What are the odds that there'd be two of them in such quick succession? Though surrounded is the wrong word, when Maffeo Celsi is the target and she, herself, the arrow. Maddalena is under no illusion about the nature of the hunt.

She has been groomed for Maffeo Celsi—and for his uncle Bastiano, who heads the Celsi family, and loves music. The Celsis have recently bought their way into the nobility, and sit low enough in the hierarchy to throw away the usual cautions. The nature of the Senate makes true power a closed twelve-family loop—it's not as if a Celsi will ever be doge. These are the sort to overlook rumors of bastardy. They have money enough that a dowry doesn't have to be obscene, and they'll get a feather in their cap from a connection to the Grimanis, however uncouth the whispers about Elisabetta.

Furthermore, if Maddalena is to marry a man and have a chance at actual happiness, that man might be Maffeo Celsi, who once handed her a wildflower on a group picnic at Sant'Erasmo. She was eight, he was sixteen. His fingernails were smooth but bitten, and he told her the name of the flower, but she immediately forgot.

Maffeo is now in his midtwenties, and by all accounts he's kind. His father will be looking for a family with a well-respected name, if not deep pockets. Maddalena's the wrong choice to usher in respectability, but if negotiations have gotten him here to Mira, to an evening at the villa with Maddalena in attendance, for him the rumors of her parentage must hold less weight. She should be thrilled at this chance. She should be racing to her room to run through the exercises Michielina taught her, practicing vocalise and curling her hair and airing out her best skirts.

Instead she thinks of Luisa, the way the coverlet sighed with her as

she slept. That bruise at her neck, the chafed skin that's already soften-
ing now that she's away from her violin. Their time has always been an
illusion, the idea that they could ever have more than stolen nights in
the dormitory cot. That they could be more than they are to each other.
What are they to each other?

Mira is supposed to be different. Luisa will recover here, and Maddalena will tend to her. She doesn't have time for high-stakes games.

"Tomorrow, perhaps, but if so, not Maffeo Celsi. Maffeo Celsi, perhaps, but not tomorrow." Maddalena looks Nicolò in his bleary, sunken
eyes, willing him to understand the gravity of the situation, how it is in
everyone's best interest to abort this plan.

"I'm not asking," he says. "You know that I'm not asking. I'm telling
you, it's happening." Nicolò closes his eyes, he looks so tired, too tired.
Is he also ill? More likely just the burden of his role as oldest son, a
burden he himself has welcomed. Maddalena won't feel sorry for him.

Why is it like this with Nicolò? Always his demands, her refusals.
His pressure, her concession. When she was small he'd been a sweet
brother, attentive. He'd helped her learn to read, and shown her maps
of the Adriatic, explained the tangled politics of the inner chambers of
the Council. When had things soured between them? Was it as she grew
older, and less pliable? As their father grew older, more interested in
affairs of state and less in his own home? When Elisabetta left, and the
vultures descended? She can see them all looking at her and seeing her
mother, searching out her father's features and failing to find them.

It was better at the Pietà, when they all stopped watching her.

Luisa

Before she can stop herself, Luisa is agreeing to perform. She listens as Nicolò hashes out details—how long they'll play, where they'll stand, how they might highlight Maddalena's voice to best advantage. In the back of her mind she knows she should have deferred, waiting to see how they would choose to feel together, Luisa and Maddalena united. Luisa, Maddalena's only ally, has immediately consorted with the enemy.

And Luisa does want to play, she would love nothing better. Her fingers stretch subconsciously, her eyes well imagining these high-ceilinged rooms—with their vast windows looking out upon brilliant green lawns, their frescoed angels and gold-filigreed settees and intricate glass sculptures—filled with music.

"Maddalena will come around," Nicolò says. "You can tell her that I tricked you into it. I could trick you into it, if you'd rather." Luisa can't get a read on Nicolò, although he wears himself openly. He's not as handsome as Beneto and Andrea—his hair is muddy, and he lacks the chiseled features of his siblings. He talks to her as if she is a person, not a de facto nun or a musical savant. "Would you rather?"

Luisa considers. The past few weeks have changed what's between herself and Maddalena. What was once nothing became clear glass that is now dirtied, and Luisa doesn't have the heart to make it even more opaque.

"No," she says to Nicolò. "I'll tell her I said yes without thinking it through."

"And did you?" Nicolò looks at her as he might art on his walls. This makes it difficult to answer him, alongside the fact that he's twenty-five years old and powerful, and she is Luisa, until recently barely able to address the maestra during group rehearsal. She stands there, awkward and silent. He stands with her, waiting.

"Yes," Luisa says finally.

"So you don't want to perform?" Nicolò asks. "You aren't up to it? I should have asked that first, I'm sorry. I know you've been ill."

"I want to play," Luisa says quickly. "I always want to play."

"Is it my sister?"

"I don't—" Luisa says, then stops herself. Something about Nicolò is opening her, in a way his sister never opened her. Luisa feels that same nervous energy, that vibration between their two bodies, but this time accompanied by a gentleness that simultaneously feels easier and more frightening. "I'm feeling fine," she says to her fingernails. "Well, better. I just don't want to . . . I don't want to abandon her."

Nicolò winces, then glances sideways around the room, which is empty but for the two of them and Prometheus, who swirls across the ceiling with his fire. He tries at first to pretend away this initial reaction, then breathes deeply and moves to sit in a chair by the open window, inviting Luisa to join him with a tilt of his head. She has nowhere else to be, and she is no longer hungry. She sits.

"I imagine you two must have talked about the rumors." Nicolò leans on his laced hands for a moment, then quickly stretches back, agitated and incapable of stillness. Luisa suddenly remembers Beneto's warning not to trust him. Or perhaps it was not to listen to him. Not to be alone with him? Luisa has been ill. It was hot. She can't remember.

If she admits to knowing nothing, will Nicolò end their conversation? Luisa finds she doesn't want to stop talking to him, to stop looking at him. She says, "A bit."

Nicolò runs his hands through his hair, leaving it on end, unpolished and frantic. He is the third man with whom Luisa has had close sustained contact, and though one of the others was his brother, she finds Nicolò reminds her more of Vivaldi. He has that same streak of earnest, if self-serving, principle, and though she suspects Nicolò hasn't written any music, she can see that something in him, too, marks him as a man in the wrong time. Luisa realizes that this is what intrigues her about Nicolò, this difference. Don Antonio has the music to allow for its release, but Nicolò's passion simmers within him, just below the skin, looking for escape. Maddalena never mentioned that her brother was alive like this. Luisa can't help but stare.

"They can't prove anything. We've made sure of that." Nicolò has dropped his hands to his sides, but keeps squeezing his thumb into a fist, and then unsqueezing. "Of course you can see why it's so important that she turn out well tomorrow."

"Of course." She should be curious about the history that's so scandalous it could determine her dearest friend's future. But Luisa has never been one for gossip, and she's never been so interested in the way a man's lips flatten and then purse. He seems alone. In this vast house, with these servants and this family, Nicolò seems as alone as she was, before she had the violin, and Maddalena. "Whatever I can do," Luisa says to him, "I will do."

Nicolò nods, though it's clear he's still distracted. He isn't seeing her the way that she sees him. To him she is a child, his sister's friend who'll serve a purpose. Pretty, yes, but very young, and Maddalena's. She wonders if he'll think differently after he's heard her play.

Maddalena stands out in the garden, wearing her white nightdress among a row of carefully pruned trees. Luisa approaches her with caution, as if she is the one who's been ill. Through the hedges she can see the river Brenta, clearer than the canals in the city.

"You let me sleep," Luisa says, once within earshot. Maddalena turns to her, and at once Luisa feels her own full-body betrayal—for agreeing to conspire with Nicolò, for even speaking to Nicolò. "I spoke to Nicolò," she blurts out.

Maddalena rolls her eyes, but it's an act, and Luisa can see what it costs her. "I'd hoped he'd leave you alone for at least your first few hours. Alas." She grimaces. "I spoke to him, too."

"He doesn't seem awful," Luisa offers. "The situation's not ideal.... I mean, I know you've ... But he seems like he means well."

"Does he?" Maddalena looks past Luisa to where the house looms, sunlit and threatening. It's unfair that Maddalena could enter Luisa's world so easily—how quickly she fell into place among the hierarchy of girls, understood the loves, the rivalries, decided who and what was worthwhile. At Villa Grimani there are far fewer players, but the game seems more complex.

"If we give a little concert," Luisa begins, "what can it hurt?"

Maddalena looks ancient. "It won't hurt you," she says. Luisa feels this like a slap. The sun is brighter now, so bright her vision's swimming, and Maddalena seems to grow, a dark blot against the light.

"Luisa?" A hand at her elbow, a hip against her own. Maddalena guides her down so they are both seated against a narrow tree trunk, the solidity of ground and grass a balm.

"I didn't mean it," Maddalena says, her head bending down to rest on Luisa's shoulder. "It's not your fault that this has ended up the way it is."

Luisa isn't sure she understands how exactly it is, but as she's done so often lately, she nods in a quick gesture of forgiveness. She does forgive Maddalena, she'll always forgive Maddalena. She doesn't envy her friend's choices, which aren't actually choices but fun-house illusions. She pats at Maddalena's hair.

"I told him yes before I'd thought about it," Luisa says, looking not at Maddalena but at the long stretch of grass in front of them. At the lip of the garden stands a statue of two youths, mostly naked, in the midst of what Luisa thinks at first to be some sort of dance, but on reflection realizes is a darker tableau. The woman twists away, her mouth mid-scream. Luisa can't tell what's happening to her hands—they seem to be sprouting, perhaps flowering. Leaves and branches, but no fingers. The man holding his hand to her waist is serene, utterly oblivious to the woman's distress. "I suppose I just wanted to play," Luisa says. "Here. Outside the Pietà. This once."

It's not uncommon for members of the Coro to be rented out for private parties. If she ascends, Luisa might come once every few months to a palazzo or a villa much like this one, eat a rich meal, and play a cantata for the Pietà's patrons and their guests. But she would dress in the Pietà's Coro uniform, be one among a mass of women and girls. This, though. To be just the two of them, resounding through the villa, not "della Pietà" but as themselves. Even if they'll be performing for a crowd, it will be intimate. They'll be thickening their bond.

Luisa doesn't know how to explain things this way to Maddalena. To be honest, she's not yet sure that she's explained it to herself. She wants to play the violin in a pretty room that is not a church, in front of a pretty man who is not a priest. Is that so terrible?

She can tell that Maddalena is looking at her—the itch of skin, the gaze like a fly crawling over her neck. Luisa stares out at the statue, careful not to turn her head. She presses her left thumb against her fingertips, rubbing each callus like a talisman.

"We'll play," says Maddalena. "If Nicolò says we have to do it, we'll certainly play."

"He gets what he wants?" Luisa asks.

"He only asks for what he knows he'll get."

Still looking out across the lawn, Luisa finds Maddalena's hand and squeezes. "We'll make you sound wonderful."

Maddalena sighs. "It's just moving faster than it should be. I thought there'd be, I don't know, time to practice? I thought there'd be more time."

Luisa thinks back on their nights together, Maddalena's assertion: *When I am married.*

"What's happening there?" Luisa asks. "To those two people?" She tilts her head toward the statue.

"It's after Bernini," says Maddalena. "A poor reproduction, but my father had to have it."

"After who?"

"They really haven't taught you anything." Maddalena pulls her hand away and turns to face Luisa. "He's a sculptor. It's a story, from the Romans."

This isn't the time to ask Maddalena about her mother's story, about the rumors, about Nicolò's fear. Luisa looks down at her skirt. Maddalena sighs again, and it feels more like what Luisa's used to, a sound put on for its effect, as opposed to an involuntary reaction. The change makes Luisa feel tender toward her friend, and she offers what she hopes is an expression of the right amount of sympathy. She has to be careful: too little, and Maddalena won't see it, too much, she'll be put off. Luisa furrows her brow, widens her eyes, pretends she's looking at a poor hurt puppy, its hurt slight, an inward hurt. The dog has been shooed from the hearth. The dog has tried to catch a rabbit and hasn't been fast enough. Stretch the mouth a bit more, so you're not pouting. Maybe blink.

"What are you doing to your face?" Maddalena asks. "Do you need to lie down?"

In the Villa Grimani, the family are planets revolving around the sun of the vast central hall, timing their entrances and exits so each exists in their own separate season. Andrea waits until Nicolò has passed before returning to the breakfast room. Maddalena holds Luisa back at the portico steps until Beneto has disappeared out the front door. The game makes Luisa even more grateful for the rhythms of the Pietà, which, while often dull, never feel dangerous.

"Let me just put something on, and then we'll go back to the gardens." Maddalena is already tugging at her shift. In the dormitory the girls dress quickly, with just enough time between waking prayers and chapel to tidy their hair and help one another with their stays. Luisa has seen Maddalena's body—the mole at the base of her left shoulder blade, the foreign saucers of her breasts—but always in the half-light, rushed and practical. Now Maddalena stands framed in the window, fully naked as she sorts through fancy dresses. Luisa averts her eyes, fingering her own dress, which is not even her own, but one of dozens in the same size sewn and washed and assigned by the Pietà. Watching the ease with which Maddalena flicks through fabric, her dimpled buttocks and slick hips and the sun on her skin, Luisa feels the material lack of her life at the Pietà.

"Rosa?" Maddalena speaks at a practical volume, too soft, Luisa thinks, for anyone but the two of them to hear. Yet here is a maid, come immediately from the ether with a clean shift and garters. Luisa steps back awkwardly, and Maddalena, now shimmied into the first layer of six, grabs her elbow. "You're smaller than me, but I think something from the last few years will fit you. Rosa, see what you can find. In blue." Luisa opens her mouth to protest, but before she can speak Maddalena says, "It's best that we're the same."

But we're not the same, thinks Luisa.

"Besides," says Maddalena, "your sleeve has a stain."

Luisa lets herself be laced into blue. Then she follows Maddalena to a private portico off the apartment, the realization dawning that everything at Villa Grimani is less private than it ought to be, the emptiness of the large house an illusion. Someone is here to scrub the floors, to serve the breakfast. Someone plants the flowers and powders the wigs and pins the stomachers and ties the silk skirts. At the Pietà, there are no servants, only figlie. A social order, of course, with the musicians at the top, but still a sense of community, fostered by the time they spend together in chapel and the shared lack of family name. Tomorrow night, the Villa Grimani will give a lavish dinner, and while the Grimani family will host, it is the servants who will do the work of welcoming.

A gardener whistles to himself while pruning bushes. Maddalena passes him without acknowledgment and, when Luisa slows to hear his tune, yanks her away. "Hurry! If Nicolò catches us he's going to make us practice for the concert."

"Shouldn't we practice?"

"Not yet."

They're traveling away from the canal, down a stone path lined with trees. The barchessa, the outbuilding where the work of the villa is done—the managing of grain, the plucking of chickens, the feeding of horses—stands squat ahead of them, its courtyard a flurry of preparation. Here, the mood is jovial. Two women polish silver while a man stands behind them, arranging massive bouquets of flowers, pausing every so often to flick the tip of the younger woman's ear, at which she giggles and swats him. A little boy runs after a cat. Someone shouts over a clanking in the kitchen. It's hard to believe that just one hundred yards away, the brothers Grimani face the morning in silence, alone.

Maddalena ignores the barchessa altogether, turning into a copse of trees that opens out onto another hidden garden, this one with stone archways braided with vines, a little fountain at its back, a sculpture of the open-mouthed Lion of Venice standing guard upon a faded stucco wall.

"If I write down and feed it rumors, will your father have to arrest us?" Luisa teases, nodding toward the lion. But Maddalena stands at the edge of the path, staring at the fountain, fearful.

Maddalena shuts her eyes, reopens them. She swallows. Finally she turns to Luisa and says, "Did you see?"

The heat has edged in slowly, dryer and sweeter than what Luisa knows in the city. "See what?" she asks, moving toward the fountain and dipping her fingers, trailing them wet along the stone. Maddalena winces, half gags. For a moment Luisa thinks that her fever has moved on to its next victim. She rests a damp hand on Maddalena's wrist. Maddalena flinches. Then she is shaking her head, fixing her expression, smiling a forced smile that Luisa has seen directed at others, but never herself.

"I'm fine," Maddalena says. "It's nothing. I'm fine." She's clearly not fine. Her leg jitters under her skirts. Is now the time to ask, *Who was your mother? Why is Nicolò so nervous?* Maddalena has been shaken off her axis, and if Luisa pushes, she thinks she can turn the conversation her way. But does she want to? In trying to look casual, Maddalena appears very young. She braces herself against a tree, clearly hoping that Luisa won't notice.

"Maybe we both should rest," Luisa says kindly. "The heat…"

"Oh, but not at the house," says Maddalena. "Stay here with me." She pulls Luisa through a final hedge maze to a small space at the bank of the canal, under the trees. Luisa could have sworn they'd been moving away from the water. She isn't sure where they are in relation to the barchessa or the villa. Of course she'll stay with Maddalena; she'd be lost on her own.

Maddalena lies down on the grass, leans back, and stares up through the trees. Luisa sits, making room on her lap for Maddalena's head. Her hands are still very pale, and one of her violin calluses is flaking. She puts that finger to her mouth. The glen is quiet, not even birdsong, not even the rustle of leaves.

"This is what I wanted." Maddalena's voice is almost obscured by Luisa's skirts. "Just us. Just this." Her lids are heavy. They sit for what feels to Luisa like hours, until Maddalena's breathing slows. She is asleep.

Maddalena

One ever-present memory of her mother: early spring, the air heavy with pollen. Laughter, the tug of Maddalena's arm as they ran through a grove of trees. She remembers the flit of a rabbit darting ahead, the low whoop of a swan. Maddalena must have been five or six, tripping over her shoes, slipping in the wet grass. She sees her mother holding her side, smiling, putting a hand on the lip of a fountain. Behind her gapes the lion's mouth, with its tufty brows and pointed nose, less lion than the winged ones of St. Mark's, less human than the bocche di leone where, in Maddalena's grandfather's time, the state collected secrets. This lion's mouth once spurted water, but no longer. Now it stares out from the wall, silent and dry. In Maddalena's memory, her mother turns to her and speaks. She has spent hours trying to trick herself into the words, straining for the sound of them, sifting for meaning. But all she has is this, the image and the smile and the feeling of being, if not cared for exactly, then invited. It's only right that this once-fountain is where Maddalena will bring Luisa, once they've talked around the issue of tomorrow night's concert.

First they go back to the house, so they can dress. Maddalena stands with the sun warm on her bare backside as she rifles through the wardrobe, feeling Luisa's studying eyes and their own covetous heat. A perfect, crystallizing moment: the kiss of the light, the bated inhalation of a movement about to begin. Then the maid clinks in the hall and Luisa lowers her gaze and the girls see their tune deferred, though not forgotten.

Soon they're bored with these rooms, itching for air. Maddalena tugs

Luisa toward the hidden lion fountain, a perfect mirror of that morning years ago, the quickening pace, the innocent trailing the knowing. When they get to the clearing, Maddalena stops abruptly. Luisa moves ahead, toward the lion, and Maddalena wants to call out, but the words stick in her throat. The lion, whose mouth has been empty for decades, now spews down into the basin—not water that streams from its fanged mouth, but blood.

Maddalena inhales sharply. Stupid to think she'd left the bargain in Venice. When you sell your soul, the money that you gain is worth as much in the Veneto as in the city itself. It was easy to accept the gondolier, the salt marsh, the sacrifices to the shrine, because the Pietà is not her real life. The Pietà has always been a stopgap, a means to an end. This is her home. This is her mother's fountain. What in Venice was good luck, here is corruption.

Maddalena feels herself shaky on her feet. Luisa asks if they should go back to the house to rest, but Maddalena says no.

"Stay here with me."

She's tired. She's imagining things. She's overwhelmed by Nicolò's announcement, much as she's tried to pretend that she isn't. She looks back at the fountain and sees that of course it is water. Her father or her brothers or some resourceful member of the household has unstopped the pipes and got the fountain running, and now water is pouring from the mouth to the pool. In the light it looked red, but see, it's clear. Luisa has her hands in the water; Luisa touches Maddalena with hands that have been dipped in the water.

They lie down. Luisa close, Luisa wet and still smelling of flowers and iron. Luisa listening, still here, and concerned.

She wants to take Luisa's mouth to her own mouth, to straddle her and have her and wear her skin around Luisa's body, Luisa protected and safe inside Maddalena. This could be the blood. It could be their blood, intermingling. Maddalena grasps at Luisa's hand, trying to send all of this through her body to Luisa's body. What are words when there are bodies? Know me, Maddalena thinks. Please.

She falls asleep in the grass. When she awakes, Luisa's gone.

Luisa

Luisa shifts her skirts, angling out from under Maddalena, careful not to twist her neck.

She isn't used to idleness. She's feeling better, thanks to a long night's sleep and a relatively lazy morning, and now that the sun is high she's restless. Ideally she'd go back and find a violin, brush off the dust of the last few weeks, and plan for tomorrow. She doesn't trust herself to find her way back to the villa, and she doesn't want to imagine Maddalena waking up alone. Still, she can't just sit here. She brushes grass off her dress and ducks back under the hedges.

The villa's gardens are mostly greenery—bushes and ornamental trees—and, of course, statues. Two children in marble holding harps, a young woman holding a baby, a man holding a hunting bow. Some are fountains, others hung with vines. Luisa tries to keep track but is beginning to worry about how she'll find her way back to Maddalena when she hears the impossible. Through those two trees, a violin.

A man stands, playing out toward the water. Someone from the barchessa, she supposes at first, but quickly notices the fine cut of the shirt, the abandoned hat that rests atop the violin case. Beneto, she hopes. Andrea, she prays. It's Nicolò.

His back is to her, and she waits a moment, listening to him play. He's technically proficient, but not good. His notes are slightly flat, and his vibrato could be stronger. But he feels the music. She can tell he feels the music. She's reminded of how she used to play, alone in the practice room, before Maddalena, before the shrine and its gift. As much as Luisa appreciates accompanying musicians, there's nothing like the reverence of playing alone. She stands still, listening.

After several minutes she's struck by the horror of how she will feel if he turns to see she hasn't announced herself. She sniffs loudly, then coughs a bit, and when none of that catches his attention, says, "Hello?"

Nicolò turns. His hair, which she had thought a light brown, appears struck through with gold, a sweat-curled forelock falling down toward his eyes. She has startled him. He drops his arms so that the violin and bow hang at his sides.

"I'm sorry to sneak up like this. I heard you, and I couldn't..." The words feel insincere. His eyes are lighter than his siblings', a warm brown. Why does Luisa's chest feel so expansive, looking into them?

"If you shift your fingers on your bow hand, it would sound—" she starts. "I don't mean to intrude." Will he hate her now? He is older, she's a friend of his sister's, she's no one. To Luisa's surprise, Nicolò laughs. He offers her the violin.

"Show me."

Any weakness Luisa still felt, any lingering cough or fever, vanishes when she lifts the violin. She brings it to her chin, tests it. He has a gorgeous instrument, old and expensive, with a lovely, deep sound. It's richer than the one she plays at the Pietà. A man's violin, she thinks, before shaking her head at the ridiculousness of the thought. There's no such thing as a man's or woman's violin. In the choir loft or the orchestra room, all are the same.

"Like this," Luisa says, and plays a quick arpeggio, angling herself so he can see the way she moves the bow. "It will be easier. You'll be able to move faster." She blushes, swallows it back. He might be a patrician, he might know politics and money and fine art, but she has known the violin since she was six. She's been trained by Don Antonio Vivaldi. She has the power of the thing in the lagoon, and she can play.

Nicolò watches her. He takes the bow. "Like this?"

"More like..." She mimes it with her fingers.

"Show me with your hand." And then his hand is over hers, smaller than she'd expect, leaner and stronger. The emotion that sparks when she plays music is kindling, strengthening. She tries not to gasp. She molds his fingers, pulls away.

Here is her heart, a basso continuo. He stands holding the bow. She has his violin, but she is frozen. What is this in his smile? An incredulity, to be sure, but full of gentleness, all kindness. *What luck*, his face seems to say, *that we are here together*. He feels it, too.

Part of her knows it's the music. Whatever power she'd taken from the lagoon is expressed when she plays. This morning in the breakfast room he barely saw her, but now a slew of notes, a sole arpeggio, has transformed her in his eyes. But maybe it's more. Don Antonio never looked at her like this, like he can taste her. And if it was just the spell, just the shrine, would Nicolò now be shaking his forelock, trying to cast off this haze?

Nicolò makes his face very serious, but can't seem to hold off for long. The smile returns, and stronger. Luisa passes him the violin. He plays a few notes, then says, "Thank you."

"You're welcome." Luisa's also smiling. Here they are, just smiling at each other. How ridiculous. How beautiful. The canal lies empty and quiet and the villa rises in the distance, sun-drenched and transformed. What will they do? What is there to do? She clenches a fist to keep from reaching for his hand.

They are still standing, facing each other, when feet come crunching up the path, trampling the leaves. Nicolò looks away from Luisa's eyes, finally, and over her shoulder.

"There you are," says Maddalena. "I've been looking for you."

Maddalena

Maddalena finds Luisa on the bank of the Brenta, having followed the brief sound of an arpeggio, made at first by someone else but then quite clearly by Luisa. As she approaches, Nicolò is lowering his bow, having begun again to play, and then abandoned the attempt. He's looking at Luisa as if this is the first time he has actually seen her. His lips are pouted into a ridiculous closemouthed grin, and he seems almost as if he might laugh out of utter delight. Maddalena can't remember ever seeing Nicolò delighted. It suits him much better than his usual angst. It is not only inconvenient, but infuriating.

Maddalena wishes Andrea were with her, to surreptitiously impart some dry commentary that would break the tension of her arrival. She shouldn't think she's interrupting—Nicolò is the stone in her shoe. But she feels clumsy and overdressed and awkward, and when Luisa turns and takes her hand, Maddalena can't help but read disappointment under her smile.

"I didn't realize you had picked that up again," Maddalena nods toward the violin, which Nicolò now returns to its case. "I mean, I thought you'd stopped playing."

"Oh, well. Yes." He swallows. Blushes. Is she embarrassing him? That hadn't been her intention, but Maddalena must admit she's pleased.

"He plays well," Luisa offers.

Maddalena looks from Luisa to Nicolò. "We should go in and practice so we can say the same of ourselves tomorrow night."

If Luisa notices Maddalena's about-face, she says nothing. The three walk back to the house together, the girls arm in arm and Nicolò behind them. Maddalena can feel the effort Luisa makes not to turn back.

"I'm sorry if he made you uncomfortable," she says, not bothering to keep her voice low, though not deliberately goading her brother. "He doesn't care much for tact."

"Oh no," Luisa says. "Not at all."

They walk on.

At the house, Beneto and Andrea sit together, playing faro at a small table in the loggia, each with a glass of red wine, although it can't be much past two. A light meal has been spread on a sideboard, and Maddalena can see where Beneto has been at the prosciutto, leaving only a few lank slices next to crystallizing cheese. Bunches of grapes, fat and waxy. A napkin sops up droplets of some pinkish punch, a bee circling the spill.

Andrea slides over to make room on the banquette, patting the place next to him and gesturing to Nicolò.

"We'll deal you in," he says. "It's nothing serious." But Nicolò doesn't play cards, and nothing serious to Andrea means much more to soberer men.

"The girls are going to get ready for tomorrow," Nicolò says. "I have to help them set up."

"Do you?" Beneto asks.

"Ah, tomorrow." Andrea ignores Beneto, straightening his cards against his palm. One beat, another. "Tomorrow, when the—what is it, the hens? the chickens? When the Celsis come to roost." He's drunk, or partway to it, or at very least bored with the country house. "The hour is upon us. The moment is—"

"Shut up," Beneto says. "We have company."

Maddalena shrugs. "Don't stop on my account." Her whole life she has collected these moments of abandon. Details about both her past and future are beads on necklaces long broken and scattered; they turn up in odd places, at unexpected times. She often must crouch to reach her conquests, pocket them surreptitiously. "I always want to hear about the moment and the hour."

"Not you," Beneto says.

"By all means, have her practice her music." Andrea is speaking to Nicolò, not a glance at the others. For the second time in as many hours, Maddalena feels like an intruder. "That's been the point of the whole charade, hasn't it? Respectability. Lost, what did you say, dignity? Maddalena Grimani will bring back Venice's golden age of politics! They'll want her for the papacy! She'll win Dalmatia. Not a global power will stir without asking for her sage advice. But only if she marries." Maddalena can't tell if Andrea's rancor toward Nicolò extends to her, or if in some roundabout way he's defending her.

No one says anything. Beneto is clearly ashamed, Nicolò's face uncharacteristically blank. Maddalena smells the blood again. That wineglass in Andrea's hand sloshes with each gesticulation, one dark droplet rising up over the lip of the cup and dribbling down his wrist. He brings his skin to mouth and cleans it with a lewd, wet sound.

"She performs well," Luisa says finally, an echo of herself just moments earlier.

"She had better. Nicolò's whole life is riding on her." With that, Andrea sits forward. He fans his cards, considering, and then places one faceup on the table. "Your turn."

"You're nowhere near as charming as you make yourself out to be," Beneto says, letting the playing card sit. Nicolò says nothing. Maddalena's surprised by how stoic he's remained.

"Run along, little birds! Run along to make your music." Andrea waves a dismissive hand. He belches, then laughs.

"This act is unattractive," Maddalena says, her best impression of the nurse who used to swat him for putting pebbles in her shoes, who was at least sixty years old, and ineffectual.

"Ah, how she turns!" Andrea now speaks to the garden at large, an audience of cypresses. "A fickle woman, already. And yet here he is," a nod at Nicolò, "trusting her to clear our name."

"It's just a concert," says Maddalena, who knows that it isn't.

"Just a concert." Andrea laughs without humor and reaches over to pat her hand, spilling more of his wine. "My dear, your whole career will peak tomorrow night. We'd better hope those lessons worked, yes?"

"Enough." Nicolò is tired but firm. "This isn't her fault. So you've pointed out the obvious. Was it worth it? Was it fun?"

Nicolò is only two years older than Andrea, but he speaks as if to a child. Maddalena stands frozen, her eyes darting. She feels Luisa next to her, lungs still not quite cleared, so that each breath is a wheezing announcement of her presence—not a Grimani, not comfortable. Not that Maddalena's comfortable. Beneto looks positively ill.

Andrea's outburst is unusual. There's no hot blood in this branch of the Grimanis, no long-set family rivalries that lead to fistfights over bridges, not even fisticuffs as children. These patricians of Venice are practical, notorious equivocators, leaders of a nation-state that's known for wait and see. Not that the two younger Grimani sons will ever see the inside of the Senate Hall. Nicolò is the one groomed for state service, but even he might lose his standing if the matter of his two youngest siblings isn't appropriately resolved. Maddalena is a pawn in the truest sense, an opening gambit that clears the way for her father's rise, her brother's beginning.

Funny, how a man can be a cad and all will laugh at him, but a woman's indiscretion is an undertow. A choice her mother made—a series of choices, perhaps in the throes of lust, perhaps in love, perhaps so meager that they had no consequence other than rumor, which, when fed, can grow as powerful as any truth. Rumor a tick gorging on the whispers, a bite at Vespers, now at the theater, now in the Piazzetta, growing fat with blood. If Maddalena marries well, the abdomen will burst. She pictures her own heel stomping and smearing, her meager rise as a meager noble wife.

If Nicolò can pull this off, it will be quite the coup.

If Maddalena can. If she chooses to.

Luisa digs into Maddalena's side with an elbow. "Do you?" she whispers.

They're all looking at her: Nicolò, exhausted. Beneto, sympathetic but still harboring the sting of their previous interactions. Andrea—without the capacity for shame—swirls his wineglass. She should ask whoever's questioned her to repeat himself, but looking from brother to brother, Maddalena can't tell which one spoke.

"Yes," she says, then looks to Luisa for confirmation. "Yes?"

"Well, then this conversation is over," Andrea says. "You do realize I'm trying to help you?"

"Don't say the conversation is over and then keep going on about it." Beneto's tone is pleasant, despite the bite of his words. He plays his next card with a quick glance and an apologetic smile at Maddalena, who grows suspicious. She gives them all an ironic little curtsy and tugs Luisa's hand, moving into the house to find out what she's just agreed to.

"Only that you'll do your best," Luisa whispers. "It's not ideal, but we'll figure something out. You'll get your husband." Her cheek pressed next to Maddalena's, to reassure and to hide from the others who look in from the porch. Nicolò says something to Andrea. Does he owe the Celsis money? That has to be it. What else could have prompted this vitriol? The elder Grimani brothers have never been close, but this seems to surpass their usual sniping. The pressure mounts, the clock ticks, the horses chafe at their bits.

"You're lost again," says Luisa. Maddalena feels the heat of her breath, the prickling of her own neck and chest from their nearness, the fact that Luisa is here at the villa, she's recovering, she's going to play her perfect violin and save them all from infamy.

Nicolò finds the instruments, presenting them as if he's readying his sister for battle.

"If we had more time, we would sound better," Maddalena says. "More time and more players."

"We have what we have," says Nicolò. "And you'll sound wonderful." Nicolò's an awful liar, but at least he tries.

If she were anyone else, Maddalena might worry about Luisa's recent days without practice. But when Luisa lifts the violin, it's clear that her near decade of experience overwhelms any rust. Luisa, at least, will sound wonderful. Maddalena will do her best. They'll play an aria

Maddalena learned with Michielina, something simple from one of the Coro's oratorios that Luisa and the hired musicians can easily accompany. Then a movement of a concerto for violin and viola. They'll end with a barcarole, one of the traditional songs of the gondoliers, which they are told is one of Uncle Celsi's favorites. This will sound best with just the two of them—Maddalena's voice, Luisa's accompaniment.

Will it work? Some spell will be cast, as is the way of music, even poorly practiced. If Maddalena is lucky, it'll be the right one. The notes a net to ensnare Maffeo Celsi, to cut the rest of her family free.

Luisa

A day of bathing and dressing and being dressed. A maid attends Luisa's hair, first washing and then combing it, curling and pinning and powdering, until she feels like a pheasant stuffed for supper. Maddalena orders chocolate on the terrace, a long sunlit hour of silence. They go to the family chapel for a brief mass, and Luisa is surprised by how little she's missed the liturgy of the hours here in Mira—she hasn't prayed in earnest since leaving Venice, but the fir trees and the grassy lawns, the willows leaning out over the water, are their own sort of worship. Beneto sits at the back of the chapel, Andrea nowhere to be seen.

"He probably went to some fete last night," Maddalena whispers, "and will sleep until midafternoon." Maybe drinking off the discomfort of yesterday's conversation, when his knife went too deep and hit bone. Or else he's forgotten it all, whether through drunkenness or the simple fact of his manhood, his privilege, the money and the birthright that close over any ugliness like the smoothest of the medico's stitches, leaving no scar.

"Does Nicolò not come? Was he out, too?" Luisa asks. Before Maddalena can answer, the priest has begun mumbling through the Latin, just as eager to be finished with this ritual as those in attendance. They kneel and stand, and sit, and kneel and stand. After one of the many changes in position, Luisa feels a tickle at the back of her neck, which she attributes at first to her new hairstyle. But moving the offending curl does nothing to assuage the sensation, and when she glances back, she sees the seat behind her is now filled.

Luisa shivers, and because it is hot Maddalena puts a hand on her knee, as if to ask if she's well. Luisa's hand atop Maddalena's gives a pat in reassurance. Nicolò clears his throat. Her nape prickles.

He is older than you, he is titled, he is never going to marry, you are his sister's silly friend. She repeats this in place of her Hail Mary, and by the time Mass is over she has almost convinced herself she's finished reliving those few moments during which he leaned toward her, the silly half-smile, the boyish curl of his hair. He has his wig on now, and his coat, and a distracted expression that makes it clear he is thinking not of Luisa but of the evening ahead, all that he stands to lose if Maddalena's not successful. Luisa couldn't specifically say what it is he'll lose, though by the strict line of his mouth and the bags under his eyes, she can assume it's something valuable. She hasn't asked Maddalena to detail the stakes. The goal is obvious enough, and the beam they walk so narrow that it seems silly to derail her friend with anything that might increase anxiety.

To win a husband on a single performance, after a day of practice, on an instrument that isn't even yours, seems like the height of folly. It isn't that Maddalena's unpleasant to listen to, but her wit and charm seem much more likely than her music to attract the sort of attention that would lead to a proposal. Still, if music it must be, music it will be. The guests arrive. Luisa can hear them on the lawn as she and Maddalena are laced into their gowns.

First there are candied fruits, then malmsey. The sky fades white as the group—what Luisa has come to think of as the Celsi delegation, an older uncle who seems to head the family, three women, and the night's prize, the auburn-haired son; Andrea and a few of his own guests, bachelors all; Beneto and a friend he says paints landscapes; a senator who strolls in with Maddalena's father just as the first dish is served—dines on multiple courses, is poured further fine wine. The wax candles are lit, then the sap. More guests arrive, apparently unexpected by Nicolò, acting as host, and additional places are set for the giggling young wives with their beauty spots and jewels, the cavalieri serventi who've accompanied them. Luisa notices that none of the others are marriageable women, not even Andrea's surprises.

"Am I going to meet your father?" Luisa asks.

Maddalena shrugs. "If he comes over." Luisa thinks this is no in-sult, but she can't be sure. The servants change the table, replacing car-casses and empty shells with pastries and spun sugar, the wine from dinner with the wine for dessert. "We don't want to interrupt him while he's talking to Senator Memmo. It looks important." It does look important—the two patricians in close conversation, heads leaned in to block out the rest.

Surely Maddalena, too, is important, on this night that she's been told will be the crux of the Grimani family's future. Luisa wonders if it isn't perhaps easier to be fatherless. Maddalena looks over, plaintive, less the bold girl who corralled the Pietà than a lost child, large-eyed and dark and wanting. Luisa tries to engage her in conversation—about the woman whose breasts seem ready to burst out of her stomacher, or the man who looks as if he's eaten bad shellfish, or even the pieces they'll be playing for the assembled group within the next few hours. Maddalena responds, but her eyes never stray far from her father. Finally, he catches her glance. He smiles and beckons, and without a word to Luisa, Maddalena is gone to his side.

The chairs around Luisa all sit empty, but she isn't sure where she'll go once she stands. The wine has gone to her head. She takes another gulp and pushes back from the table, steadying herself as she rises, grate-ful for the excuse of recent illness.

"Are you all right?" It's Nicolò. "Step out to catch your breath. The sunset's marvelous."

Luisa follows him outside. Lanterns bob on the boats the guests have docked, and the sky froths with low clouds lit orange and violet from below by a fast-descending sun that even in its last moments is blinding. Half of Nicolò's face is swathed in shadow, and Luisa stands looking out at the water, but also sideways at him. Her throat feels thick with what she eventually decides must be contentment. "Is this better?" he asks, and she suspects he looks deliberately out and away from her, keeping his distance. Avoiding that shimmer between them.

"Much."

"I'm glad."

It's companionable, this sunset and this silence. She imagines his hand in her own. The night descends and lanterns twinkle in the trees, across the loggia.

"We'll have the concert soon?" she says. Nicolò nods.

Another gondola drifts up the canal. It is black, like those in the city, and it seems empty but for its spry gondolier. In the dark Luisa sees the shadow of the man as he moors his boat and tucks away his oar, then straightens his jacket and walks the path from dock to villa. Odd, for a guest to bring himself. Luisa looks to Nicolò for his reaction, but he's turned back toward the house.

"Are you ready?" he asks, which Luisa takes to mean: Is Maddalena ready? The answer is that she's as ready as she can be, if they're going to play this evening, which they are. The aria's decent. The split concerto mostly shows Luisa's skill. The barcarole is sweet, but seems childish in its simplicity. It is a folk song, a tune all gondoliers and their passengers know. When they rehearsed, Luisa felt like a little girl playacting, calling her father home with the imitation of his livelihood. Beneto liked it, though—he'd whistled through the open window, blowing the girls kisses.

The guests are mostly drunk by now, which will work in their favor. The acoustics will be marvelous, with the villa's high, round ceilings. The candles aflicker and the girls in their finery, their hair littered with flowers. Luisa light and Maddalena dark. Old, rich instruments and a sweet breeze off the canal. An enchantment.

It comes off beautifully. The eager slide of her wrist, the pressure of the strings against her fingers. The hired half orchestra behind them is surprisingly spry, and the audience holds them in a tender, breathless bubble of attention, lips slightly open, eyes wide.

They finish their final song to rapturous applause, the Celsi uncle pounding the marble floor with his walking stick, enthralled by the duet. Before they can put away the instruments, Maddalena has been swept off by the women in the Celsi party, which Luisa takes to mean she's passed at least their first test. Luisa can't quite place the expression on her face, the widened eyes, the flush that blooms across her neck and chest. Wouldn't anyone be overwhelmed, on the night of her conquest? The night her life would change, after having changed, before changing again. Luisa slackens the hair on both bows, kneels to pack first the violin, then the viola da gamba, into their cases. A man's boot approaches, and then a man is crouching down, helping her with the clasps. Maffeo Celsi.

"Oh," says Luisa, surprised. She could have sworn he'd made off with the rest of his party, to the garden or the ballroom, or wherever the swarm has settled. A few of Andrea's friends remain in a corner, but the other guests of honor have gone.

"The Pietà, yes?" He's of Beneto's build and height, likely about Beneto's age. From the smoothness of his fingers, she knows immediately that he does not play.

"Where I'm from?" Luisa nods.

"You have a lovely clarinetist." He carries both cases to a waiting footman, and then offers his elbow. Luisa's gaze darts around the room—servants clearing the buffet, those drunken friends of Andrea's in intense conversation, a little dog lapping at spilled cream. She's fairly certain that the evening's prize is best left alone until the Grimanis can have at him, but she has nowhere else to go and no one else to talk to, and she isn't sure how to decline without being rude.

"You must mean Betta," she murmurs, letting her arm rest lightly atop his jacket. "She is quite good." Funny how it feels to claim Betta, as if the Pietà is family in the same way that Maffeo and his uncle are family. The women do call one another daughter.

"Though not as beautiful, they say, as some of the other musicians." He leads her out onto the portico, and she tilts her head to try to parse his words. Is he flirting? With only lantern light it's hard to tell if his cheeks color, and without knowing him she can't read his tone. Her face must reveal her discomfort, because he immediately apologizes. "That was tactless of me, wasn't it?" he says. "Let me make it up to you with a stroll through the garden."

It's not a question, though Luisa thinks he wouldn't press her if she declined the invitation. Maffeo seems put on, compared to Nicolò. It is suddenly impossible for Luisa not to compare him to Nicolò. She thinks she will forever be comparing men to Nicolò—if and when she meets them—and the thought makes her sad enough to nod at Maffeo and gesture for him to lead the way down the villa steps, lined with fairy lanterns and garlands of white rose, into the garden.

Torches have been placed at strategic locations, and with the raw gibbous moon there's enough light that nothing feels improper. Maffeo guides Luisa with his arm through hers, and though their bodies brush, she feels none of the excitement of linking hands with Maddalena, the exquisite terror of standing next to Nicolò, anticipating his breath. The relative serenity of her body makes her lower her guard, and though this is a man in the dark—this is her dearest friend's man, or it might be—she dispenses with most caution. Four men in fewer days. Who would have guessed that Luisa, who rolled her eyes at the other girls' daydreams, would be the one to walk the gardens of a nobleman's villa with a man who stops to save the hem of her dress from the mud?

"They have wonderful statues here," says Maffeo. "The elder Grimani is quite the collector."

They're approaching the statue of the man grasping the woman as she escapes into literal greenery. "This one is after Bernini," Luisa says, feeling a fraud but unsure what else to tell him. "A poor reproduction."

Maffeo grins. "Taste across all the arts, I see." He has a kind smile. He will be kind to Maddalena, Luisa decides. Like all Venetian husbands he'll go off with his mistresses and leave her to her cicisbei, the men who'll take her to the theater, the opera, Carnival and the Ridotto and church. Still, when he is home and at her table, and when he is in her bed, Luisa thinks that Maffeo will be gentle. He is good-looking enough. He's willing to waste time perusing statues with a foundling, to tuck the falling flower back into her hair with timid yet capable hands, to talk quietly about this dancing cupid and that fountain. He speaks quietly, Luisa realizes, not because he's trying to seduce her or hide their association, but because he is a soft-spoken man. She likes him for Maddalena. He might soften her.

"We should get back to the house, shouldn't we?" They've seen the topiaries and the bow and arrow and the boy with the harp. Maffeo has talked about his favorite coffee shop and the British art dealer he befriended and the salons he likes to frequent. He's dissected the best of Monteverdi, surprised at Luisa's limited knowledge of opera. One of the hired musicians is playing a gavotte, and through the windows they can see figures dancing. In their absence another boat of revelers has arrived, ushered in by a jubilant Andrea, and they careen about the central hall in their feathers and their jewels. Luisa thinks she catches Maddalena dancing with some man, before the pair is out of sight, replaced by another laughing set. Shouldn't she be with Maffeo? Luisa tries to find a subtle way to force the two to meet.

"Do you dance?" asks Maffeo. "I assume you wouldn't have much opportunity in Venice, but I would love to be proven wrong."

Before Luisa can answer that he's correct—of course she does not dance, when and where would she?—Maffeo's uncle, looking rosy and delighted, accosts him.

"Luisa dal Violin!" The older man bows, which startles her into a smile. "A beautiful concert. Inspired. One might say touched." A split second of panic, as she tries to figure out what the old Celsi might know of her talent. But he's patting Maffeo on the back and kissing her hand and in all ways seems unaware of shrines and promises. Then Maddalena's father has joined them, Nicolò not far behind, and Luisa takes the opportunity to go alone into the ballroom. Let the men talk dowries and country homes and whatever else it is they'll need to shore up. Luisa will have wine and stand in the corner of the central hall and feel the swoosh of passing skirts and tap her foot to the cello.

The tables and settees have all been cleared and the sconces are lit, dancers reflected in large mirrors, their skirts and cloaks ashimmer. Beneto swoops by with a partner. Andrea gesticulates over by the spread

of snacks. And here comes Maddalena, indeed in the arms of a man Luisa thinks she might know but can't quite see head-on. He's dark-haired,
wearing black velvet. He spins, and Maddalena's eyes meet Luisa's, and
there's something foreign there, though Maddalena is always foreign, a
magician's scarf that continues to come forth, color after color, never
fully unspooled. Luisa lifts her glass in greeting, and she could swear
that Maddalena's eyes well such that she might cry, but it's unclear if
they'd be joyous tears or tragic, and then there's only her back, as she is
danced off into a different part of the room.

Candles everywhere, flames infinite and flickering, multiplied by the
many mirrors and the ladies' polished jewels. A pair of lovers in a corner
are only half shielded by a brocade curtain, his wig askew. Luisa can't tell
if they know she can see them, and can't tell if they care. The man presses
the woman against a table, her skirt knocking a plate with the remains of
some brown sauce onto the floor with a splash that makes a stained lace of
its hem. Luisa can't help but think of the other spills and stains, the mess
that will be left at whatever hour the guests leave and the Grimanis retire.

"There you are." Nicolò is at her side. She senses him before he
speaks, a tension in the air, a sweet, musky scent.

"Here I am." He's tall enough that she has to look up at him, the tilt
of her chin an invitation, though to what she's not yet sure. He's wearing
green, which makes his eyes look darker. His lips are pressed together,
again swallowing a smile. Hers is wide in response; she reaches up to
touch the flower in her hair. An uproar in the corner, which appears to be
someone choking and then making a quick recovery, redirects her attention to the Celsis, and the goal of the evening, and her role.

"And?" she says.

"And what?"

"The proposal. Did we play well enough? Did the Celsis ask for
Maddalena's hand?" She thought she cared because Maddalena cared—
Maddalena's fate determined by those forty minutes spent in the niche
between the windows at the end of the central hall, Luisa plucking and
bowing and making Maddalena sound magical, Maddalena whom she
loves. Yet now she finds it's for Nicolò, who looks so serious in those times

that he's providing for his family, who has a sweet, crooked smile and a responsibility that seems far too heavy to carry alone.

"They won't commit tonight, but they said that the music was lovely. Heavenly, I think Bastiano Celsi called you two."

"So you feel good about it?" Luisa looks him in the eye. "You feel better?" He nods, and she loosens with relief because she wants him to feel better. She wants him to always be the young man with his violin at the banks of the Brenta, warm with joyful surprise as he held her hand over his bow. He isn't who Maddalena described, those nights in bed at the Pietà. Perhaps it's because she's fifteen and suddenly in love, but Luisa is sure Nicolò isn't who anyone would describe, she's sure that only she can know him. What a cruel God that would make him a nobleman's eldest son, that would make her a foundling. They can have nothing; she knows this. But here he is, nodding with amusement in the direction of the couple who knocked over the dishes, who are now cooing at each other, mouths wet. She stifles a laugh.

Suddenly Nicolò takes Luisa's hand in his. His touch is just as potent here in the jostling ballroom as it was upon the Brenta, at once warm and tingling. The sun.

"Dance with me," he says, pulling her toward him. And though she's just told Maffeo she could never, she agrees.

Maddalena

They're halfway through the barcarole when she sees him. Maddalena can feel her voice break, and looks to Luisa, who gives the smallest nod. *Keep going.* There's not much Luisa can do to save Maddalena if she falters—this piece isn't like the concerto, or even the aria, which allow the violinist some degree of improvisation. This is just Luisa keeping 12/8 time under Maddalena's voice, the water rocking the gondola. They've deliberately put the barcarole last, in hopes Luisa's brilliance will be dulled by her switch to basso. Maybe the audience won't remember the sweetness, the speed, the triumph as her fingers climbed and the violin sang higher. They could have left off the concerto altogether, but even Nicolò couldn't resist the glory of the Pietà's new star. And Maddalena held her own— she saw her brother nodding from the middle of the crowd, and though she felt like an amateur at the viola, her aria was quite good thanks to all Michielina's work. Bastiano Celsi looks pleased, and Maffeo has remained interested, and Maddalena feels exceptionally triumphant until *he* walks in the door. His steady movements imply that he's deliberately chosen this moment to make his entrance, this moment when her voice is at the forefront, this moment when she sings the folk tune of the gondoliers.

Maddalena is proud of how she regains her composure, and thinks that only Luisa and the accompanists and maybe the most studied of the guests will even know she lost her way. Her father certainly hasn't noticed— whispering to Senator Memmo, as he's been whispering all evening. She had a moment with him, a sweet moment while the senator relieved his bladder or refilled his glass, in which he asked after her studies, her health, if she would like a new dress to replace the one she's given to Luisa. No mention of the pressures of the evening, or how his good name rides on her achievements. No mention of her mother. And then the senator returned and Marcantonio gave her a pat on the arm in dismissal. At least he's never been unkind.

Once the two older men were deep in conversation, Andrea approached her, remorseful.

"It can't be easy," he said, which she took to mean that he was sorry for his spectacle the previous afternoon. By that point in the evening, she'd lost Luisa. The lack of her made Maddalena feel naked, moving with a smile among her brothers' guests, but constantly aware of something missing. A relief, then, when Luisa returned, the sun spent and the lanterns lit out in the gardens, the instruments tuned. Before they went out to perform, Luisa gave Maddalena a peck on the cheek, and the memory of her lips burned through the aria, as if all her skill had transferred to Maddalena, the lagoon spirit doubling its gift to accommodate two.

It was Maddalena's voice attacking the melisma, but not only Maddalena's. Now she has accidentally called him from wherever he hides when he's not at the water gate. He has followed the burchiello and followed the blood. Her gondolier, here, in her family villa, watching her. Waiting for her.

The final note she sings is followed by the last orchestral upbeat, then enthusiastic applause. Beneto, near the front, has his fingers in his mouth for a wolf whistle. It's hard to stay mad at him, especially when she knows that she was never actually mad at him. She turns her head to hide the gondolier. Beneto raises his brow, and Maddalena nods at him. A truce.

Luisa curtsies, and nudges Maddalena to take her own larger bow. When she rises, the guests are on their feet, both in praise of the performance and in search of the evening's next pleasure. Maddalena has been to the opera and seen even the great castrati lose the crowd before the curtain; not every venue can be Chiesa di Santa Maria della Pietà, not every voice can hold a room in stasis. Maddalena might not be Luisa, but she'll count this as a win.

"How lovely." A woman in heavy perfume approaches, fingering the simple pearl necklace that marks her as recently married. "It's clear you've studied with the best. Although I really can't imagine how you live there, day after day."

The woman next to her laughs shrilly and nudges a third. "It's like a nunnery—but without the intrigue." This is Maffeo Celsi's sister, the others cousins of some sort. They overwhelm the space with chatter, sweeping Maddalena off toward a side chamber where someone has set up a game of cards. The younger one fans herself, then folds and points in an elaborate language that catches the eye of a young man across the room. There are at least a dozen men in here, none of them the gondolier. Maddalena can't focus. She nods and smiles and hopes her panic will remain below the surface. The sister strokes her hand like a little pet, and Maddalena's perfectly happy not to catch what she is saying over the chatter of the others, a great wave of women in rustling skirts, materializing from every corner. *A small gathering*, Nicolò had said. *An introduction.* The Riviera del Brenta, at least this part of it, is small enough that no gathering remains small once word has spread. Andrea must have told his companions at whatever fete he'd attended last night, and taken care to staff this evening with more footmen. Not that the surprise boost in attendance means much to Maddalena—if she'd known before her performance, nothing really would have changed; it would still be the Celsis, those two particular Celsis, for whom she would play. All this deluge of guests has done is make it easier for her gondolier to slip in unnoticed, to hide and bide his time.

Maddalena sips her wine. She was ravenous just before the performance—too irritable to do much more than pick at her dinner—but now her appetite is gone. The hired orchestra tunes in the next room, some of the accompanists who'd played with Maddalena and Luisa, and an assortment of others brought in for the dances. At the sound, the Celsi cousins squeal and fluff their wigs and check each others' beauty marks. One of the cousins downs the contents of her goblet in one long gulp, a bit of wine dripping onto her bosom. She giggles as her sister wipes the spill with a spit-wet thumb. Then Maddalena is swept with the gaggle into the next tier of the night.

As soon as she enters the central hall—decked out now as a ball-room with hung chandeliers and preposterous flower arrangements and a quartet of Andrea's friends beginning to dance a gavotte—he is next to her. He smells like the salt marsh, and newly snuffed candles, and the heady sweet cloy of turned wine. He bows and offers her his hand.

A part of her imagines that to touch him will be eating the fruit of the dead, a choice to bond them inextricably. But she is bound already; she has steadied herself on his arm so many times that surely once more won't matter. She lets him lead her in the dance.

The longer he waits to speak, the more he owns her. She's a fly in his web, dangling, watching him spin lazily, watching him shake the hair from his eyes, watching him smile. Can anyone else see him? He's wear-ing livery, but no one seems to notice. *Whose livery is it?* she wants to ask, but her voice is caught in her throat. Besides, they are weaving through the dancers, joined together, then apart, their movements the rhythms of a boat on the water, the lilt of Luisa's accompaniment throughout the barcarole. She wants to grab his hand, to pull him from the pattern of the dance. Forward and back. Another jump. Another turn. And then she does.

She thinks she spots Luisa—that white-gold hair impossible to miss, even in the darkened ballroom—but she can't stop because she has her gondolier's wrist, and he is following her. She wants him far away from Luisa, who never asked for this. Somewhere are the Celsis, and Madda-lena's father, and she'd better get the gondolier away from them as well. Best to get him out of the villa entirely.

She bites the inside of her cheek so hard that she draws blood, curs-ing herself for her foolishness. How had she imagined this would end? Did she think she could move freely without consequence? To live among others is a balancing act, stepping lightly on your left foot so your brother can come down harder on his right. Telling your mother that she still looks young, your father that the color of that jacket suits him, timing your escape for the crucial moments the maestra's back is turned, deciding to stay because the girl you love needs you. Nothing in isolation, nothing insignificant. Even in Venice, where half the year is given away to anonymity and its cousin, the ephemeral, the gauze of society remains. You cannot make a deal with an unknown power and expect it will not seep into the few lovely, clean moments of your life. The deal created those lovely, clean moments. You, yourself, are now the darkness.

Maddalena pulls the gondolier out onto the portico, then down the steps to the garden, aware that she's not strong enough to actually be pulling him, yet also aware of her gumption, the frantic beating of her heart. The sculpture garden is empty, but so well lit that Maddalena fears someone will see and join them. She yanks him farther, faster, through the hedge maze and past the barchessa, to the lion fountain, which hasn't stopped sputtering. Here it is truly dark, no torches flickering, no lanterns bobbing on moored boats. Her breath comes fast and heavy. She releases him.

"What are you doing here?"

He touches a hand to his wrist, stretching and wincing, though she knows she can't have hurt him. She waits. He drops the act. He smiles.

"You sang for me."

"I didn't," she says. He hums a few bars of the barcarole, again that gravel to his sound. Michielina would balk at the technique, but Maddalena doesn't mind. It sounds truer, somehow, than the castrati with their voices clear as water. Maddalena shakes her head. "That wasn't for you."

"For her, then," says the gondolier. "La Serenissima. La Donna."

This doesn't make sense. La Serenissima is Venice—the republic herself, her canals and her councils, her fleet, her history.

"What?" says Maddalena. "A representative?" She looks at him, shadow against shadow, leaning on the fountain. The water plays its constant tune behind him. The moon shines like a bruise. "Who are you?"

Maddalena doesn't expect an answer, not really. She is surprised when he says, "We serve the same."

"Who?"

"When you needed her, she came to you, yes?" He speaks quietly, leaning in so she can hear him. His breath is cold. "When you asked, she heard and answered." Maddalena wishes for the light now, so she could better see his eyes. "A city in a lagoon," he says. "A city made of water. Impossible."

Maddalena frowns. "What do you mean?"

"We're at her mercy. We have been always at her mercy."

The mosquitoes are hovering, drawn to the fountain. The party is a distant blur of light and sound. Maddalena's not one for sidestepping. Her family life has always been a study in the cryptic, and she doesn't have the patience for this boy and his portentous philosophies. "What do you want from me? What are you trying to say?"

"When she calls for you," he says simply, "come."

"I don't understand." Maddalena moves back, and he moves with her. Even here they are dancing, though she's lost the steps.

"It doesn't have to be difficult. Just continue to give of yourself."

"And she'll give back?" Maddalena asks. Her gondolier—and she knows now that he is not a gondolier, that she knows nothing about him and less of his mistress—nods. "And if I don't? If I'm done taking? If I don't need her anymore?" Marriages in Venice are annulled all the time, more often than in any other Catholic state, much to the pope's chagrin.

He shakes his head. "It doesn't work that way. You can go willing, or unwilling. Believe me, the first is easier."

"I owe her, then?" The inside of Maddalena's cheek still bleeds, salty and pooling. She wants to spit, but she's afraid to give of herself.

"Always," the gondolier says.

She wants to scream. She wants to rip the ribbons from her hair, the ruffles from her skirts, she wants to run and keep running. To avoid being sold to a convent, she has sold herself to the sea. Maddalena thinks of her mother—a rising voice at the end of a hall, a sapphire ring on a slim finger, the tug of an arm through the trees—and for the first time isn't angry when she imagines the man who is rumored to have taken her away. If Maddalena had an escape, wouldn't she take it? Hasn't she tried?

She cannot cry in front of her gondolier, he whom she has always treated as her plaything. All the time they bantered under bridges, rode down canals and through the salt marsh, he must have been thinking about what the trip would cost her. Each time he took her to the shrine, was he imagining her veins turning black with the bargain? Does he imagine her like him, lifeless and smooth? And Luisa...

Luisa at Lido that first morning, an echo of Maddalena's desire. Was there even a Luisa before Maddalena wished her into being? Does it matter?

"It isn't bad," the gondolier says. "It doesn't hurt."

Oh, but it does hurt. To know herself a fool, smiling and smiling at Bastiano Celsi, following Nicolò's instruction, batting her eyes and looking demure and going to Mass and learning music and trying not to be her mother. For a girl, there's only following. Even at the Pietà, when she led her merry cohort, when Chiara and Orsetta knelt before her, she was playing notes written for her, on an instrument she'll never own.

Maddalena thinks of Maffeo Celsi, where he must be, if he is looking for her. She hopes that he is looking for her.

The gondolier kisses her hand, and his lips burn with cold. He bows to her, and she can't tell if it's in jest. One small tap of his finger against the lion fountain and it slows to a trickle, then ceases to flow.

"Wait!" The word wrenches itself from Maddalena's lips, but it, too, is apparently inconsequential. The gondolier walks away down the pruned alley of trees, his shape receding in the dark until she isn't sure if he's gone to his gondola or simply dissolved. She stands in the dark, where her mother once stood, her heart pounding.

The rest of the party is a display of drunken fools. One of Andrea's friends knocks over a candle, and a curtain catches fire. The flame is quickly stifled, but the resulting confusion clears the dancers out into the gardens to rib the offender, who does not appear bashful. Someone gets sick in a shrubbery. A group suggests going to see what the Pisanis are up to at Stra; another wants to go into the village.

Emerging from her hidden grotto, Maddalena almost trips over a woman on the ground who is sobbing because she's broken her shoe. Some of the lanterns have burned out, and the paths seem lit in indecipherable code. Maddalena searches for a familiar face. A particular face. There is Beneto, talking to an older gentlewoman, stifling a yawn. Andrea heads an expedition down to the boats, his laughter carrying. It's dark enough that Maddalena must approach each small cluster of guests, peering at them through the gloom, to find Luisa.

She's on the portico, standing with Nicolò. She looks exhausted, and Maddalena is grateful to see that her brother has offered his arm, on which Luisa leans with gratitude. She's wan, but not unhappy. Glassy-eyed. Maddalena bounds up the stairs to remove her from Nicolò and bring her to bed.

"There will be fireworks," Luisa murmurs. "Let's stay just a moment." Maddalena turns to Nicolò, who nods, Luisa still clutching his arm, although Maddalena has offered her own.

A hiss and a crackle as the sky explodes with light, and a whoop comes from the party on the water. Maddalena reaches for Luisa's hand, and Luisa squeezes with pleasure. She's seen fireworks from the Pietà— during Carnival they're everywhere, the girls can look out windows nightly to see color. But Luisa has never stood on a hot night in the countryside, wine-drunk and dressed like a princess, and had a show of her own. Maddalena doesn't especially like fireworks—they last too long and scream too loud—and tonight her mind churns with the gondolier and his coaxed promise. She does, however, like watching Luisa. She turns from the display to see her friend's face aglow, and finds Nicolò also looking. Their eyes meet.

Luisa is too tired to hear about Maddalena's encounter, besides which Maddalena doesn't know what she would say. She's embarrassed by her own need. She's ashamed that she drew Luisa into a contract with paperwork she hadn't read. So when Luisa asks after her evening, Maddalena chatters about the Celsi cousins' dresses, the praise heaped on their concerto, the meal. She half expects Luisa to see through her, but Luisa just nods and yawns and nuzzles into her neck, soon asleep. Maddalena spends the night staring at the shad-owed ceiling, the cupids menacing with their dark curls and open mouths that might sprout teeth, the sharpness of the catgut on their harp strings, the luck of their wings.

Luisa

No proposal arrives the morning after the performance. No proposal the next morning, nor the morning after that. Luisa and Maddalena take a rowboat out onto the canal; they picnic on the banks of the Brenta, have coffee on the terrace, and nap in the gardens. Luisa grows stronger, her skin freckles and her gold hair bleaches white, and still there is no word from the Celsis, though Nicolò won't give up hope.

"It was a strong performance," he promises Maddalena. "All is going according to plan. Maffeo's young, you are young. Father's still talking to his uncle, and there's no need to worry. It's not like he's been matched with someone else."

Luisa can tell Nicolò's patience is thin. He avoids the girls when he can, breakfasting early, going off alone on horseback, finding small tasks at the barchessa that require his attention. Maddalena's the opposite— always beside Luisa, more attentive by the hour, although Luisa's health has obviously improved. When they walk along the water, Maddalena clenches her hand so tight the blood runs out of it, and Luisa asks in jest if she's afraid of falling in.

"No," Maddalena says, relaxing her grip only slightly. Luisa attributes the caution and the nervousness, the dark circles under Maddalena's eyes, to anxiety about the state of her marriage. Luisa likes to be able to anticipate what's coming, to move into each phase of her life with a plan. She thinks this is what makes her such a good violinist, able to settle in the current phrase while readying herself for the next measure. She understands why Maddalena would be worried, why her appetite would lessen, why, if Luisa wakes in the night, she finds Maddalena is also not asleep.

After two weeks, the country doctor declares Luisa ready to return to the Pietà. She expects that Maddalena will put up a fight over whether to go with her, opposing whatever it is that Nicolò suggests simply because he has suggested it. But Maddalena just nods in agreement. Where else is she to go while waiting? The Pietà is home now. What would she do, here at Mira, without Luisa?

It will be weeks before the Grimani household returns to its palazzo in the city, so the maidservants have only the girls' belongings to prepare. Their Pietà dresses are washed and pressed. A picnic basket is filled with enough to get them through the journey on the Brenta. Beneto will again act as chaperone—he has no business in town, but Luisa gets the distinct impression he'd like to avoid some of the families who come to call at the villa with their daughters, or talk of their daughters.

On the morning of their departure, a knock comes at the entrance to Maddalena's quarters. It's just Luisa here, Maddalena taking one last long soak in the tub before the return to Pietà hygiene. The serving maid has gone to ready her clothes, and Luisa is perched on the settee, looking out at the statue garden, memorizing the slant of the sun, the sweet heat. Nicolò enters, and she jumps to her feet, tucking her hair behind her ears and smoothing her skirts.

"I hoped you'd be alone," he says. What will she say to this? That she hoped he would come when she was alone? For the past week she's been waiting for him, and now she is leaving and he is too late. "I brought you something." Nicolò holds out a violin case, and gestures for Luisa to unclasp it. She draws a breath when she sees what's inside—the instrument he played by the water, old and rich, almost weightless when she lifts it. "To bring with you," he says. "To be yours."

Luisa gasps. This must cost at least five hundred sequins. Even more than the expense is the rarity of such an instrument—a violin takes decades to age, and no matter what price he offers, Nicolò will have trouble purchasing another of this quality.

"I couldn't," she says. "I can't."

"You'll do it more justice than I've done." Nicolò's bashful, tugging at both his hair and collar. Luisa looks repeatedly from the violin to his red face to the mosaic-tiled floor. Then his hand comes forward in a slow, almost ethereal motion. He stares at his arm as if it doesn't belong to him, swallows, and steps closer. The choice is hers now. She, too, could step closer, so that his fingers graze her cheek. When he speaks, it is almost a whisper. "And when you play it, you'll remember me."

She can't help herself, she's toward him, and his hand cups her cheek. "Luisa." So quiet, so gentle. He says her name like it's spun sugar, liable to melt or break. Her eyes fill with tears, and she laughs.

"Nicolò."

Luisa hears the rush of water as Maddalena steps out of the bath. She puts her hand on top of Nicolò's and moves it from her cheek to her lips. Shivering with her own temerity, she pulls away from him just as Maddalena comes through the door.

Maddalena's hair is wet, and water pools down her shift. Luisa would have balked at an intruder, but Maddalena has never been modest.

"What are you doing here?" Maddalena asks Nicolò as she pulls on her skirts, shaking away the maid who's come to do her stays. At the Pietà, the girls dress themselves. With her exit from the bath, Maddalena has transformed from nobildonna to student, not that Luisa sees much difference between the two.

Nicolò coughs. "I've come to see you off," he finally manages.

"No news, then?" Maddalena twists the water from her hair and begins pinning it. Luisa automatically moves to her side. Nicolò shakes his head, backing up slowly and awkwardly. "Well?" says Maddalena.

"Well, what?"

"You're seeing us off?" She kneels for her shoes.

"Oh," he says. "Yes. Wishing you ... safe travels." He turns to Luisa, but there's nothing he can say that won't rouse Maddalena's suspicion. What's between them is too delicate, too new. Nicolò bows, and then he's gone.

Maddalena

Luisa seems to have come through Maddalena's impulsive late-night visit to the shrine mostly unscathed. Not so Maddalena, suddenly missing her mother's moretta, which she hadn't known she held close to her heart until it was gone. Elisabetta's mask was a reminder that it all had been a mask, that the mother Maddalena had known was simply surface. Not that she hadn't realized, as a child, that the glimpses of her mother—slipping into the nursery in full Carnival finery for a distracted kiss, smiling when she caught Maddalena's eye over a gaggle of picnickers—said nothing of who the woman really was. The Grimani children had been raised mostly by nurses, and Elisabetta had been mostly with revolving cicisbei, performing the usual role of a Venetian noblewoman, until all at once she wasn't. All at once that role was left to Maddalena, with the picnic blanket pulled, wineglasses scattered.

Once they put you in the role, you can abandon or explode it. You can betray your children, you can leave your husband bereft. Or you can strike a bargain to find something new in the depths, something beautiful and yours: a friend to love, a secret to keep. That it comes with a price—doesn't everything?

Maddalena tries to tell herself she isn't afraid of the water. She wasn't when this began, when the thing and its shrine were a game and she was comfortable gambling. She had challenged the spirit, asked more of it. Even now, with an insidious gondolier, with never-ending blood and shadows, Maddalena thinks she would feel more aroused than frightened if not for Luisa. In giving the water Luisa's blood, what has she done?

The losses and gains here are difficult to calculate. If Maddalena hadn't made Luisa sick, she'd be alone with her brothers, would have performed alone, would spend each night alone in the large four-poster bed. Luisa would be at the Pietà, her every day like any other. If Maddalena hadn't led Luisa to the shrine, Luisa would still be an exceptional violinist, but she'd be playing alone in a practice room. Maddalena tries to convince herself she's done Luisa a service.

At Mira they braid flowers into each other's hair. They skip stones. Maddalena watches Luisa play the violin, and there's an intimacy to her practice that could never exist under the watchful eye of the Pietà, even within the private music rooms. When Luisa plays the violin, Maddalena finds proof that their love is mutual. Her eyes grow wet and large, her appoggiatura is an obvious invitation, her cadenzas are meandering in an adorable, lost sort of way that makes Maddalena smile. To be young and in love and in the countryside, to turn in the night and find the one you want there next to you. At midday, with the sun high and white on the canal, the heat baking them into terra-cotta, the sky wide and brilliant, she can forget about the gondolier, or what the Venetian lagoon looks like at night, the way the loons cry low and the mosquitoes thrum.

There is no more blood in the fountain. Maddalena watches every serving dish, peers into every cup. She clings to Luisa during their outings and allows herself momentary relief when the Brenta is just water, strewn with leaves. Once, Luisa starts to play that same barcarole.

"Don't." Maddalena has to stop herself from lunging for the bow and is glad when the sharpness of her tone is enough to give pause.

"You'll hear from him," Luisa says, putting down the violin and coming to sit by Maddalena in the window seat. Her hand atop Maddalena's hand is soft but for the calluses, and her eyes look pained when she feels Maddalena flinch, because how could she know? Maddalena has been careful to hide her meeting with the gondolier, has stuffed her fist into her mouth when she wakes frightened in the middle of the night. She relaxes when Luisa says, "You sounded wonderful. If Celsi doesn't propose, he's an idiot and somebody else will." Luisa blushes at her own choice of words, which makes Maddalena laugh.

"I'll miss you," she says to Luisa. It will be true no matter the outcome of that ridiculous recital, no matter if Maddalena marries and Luisa's in the Coro, or if Maddalena takes the veil and Luisa takes up with a boatman. Even if they could be here at the villa for the whole hot season, for the entire year, Maddalena would still miss Luisa because what they have is fleeting. There is no future for two girls such as they, no world in which they'll be able to meet in the way that Maddalena wants to meet Luisa. They have now, they have the next few months. They'll have the knowledge that they had a bond that can't be replicated, will never be matched by an arrangement with a wealthy widower or a contract with God. That Luisa feels this, too—that her eyes scan the veranda when she comes down late to breakfast, that her music aches with wanting— sustains Maddalena through the presage of the future.

She doesn't worry about Maffeo Celsi, or her brothers, although the thought of them is there, a buzzing gnat at her jaw, irritating but inconsequential. She'll know the gondolier's darkness even if she weds Celsi. She is already married to the sea.

Luisa is why Maddalena doesn't protest when her brothers send her back to the Pietà after a fortnight of leisure—rather, her father and Nicolò send her back, with Beneto again acting as spaniel who will do the actual travel. Luisa has been given to the Villa Grimani on loan, and it's time to return her. Until Maddalena has a proposal—no, until she has a ring—she, too, will continue her education at the Pietà.

Nicolò seems surprised when Maddalena takes his instruction without argument. He comes to bid her farewell on the day of their departure and is lost for words, awkward and bumbling while watching her prepare to leave. A footman carries Maddalena's single bag to the burchiello—Luisa has only the violin the Grimanis have given her in thanks for her service, and the outfit in which she arrived—and Nicolò and Andrea wave them off from the portico. Her father, of course, is attending to business. Maddalena wouldn't be surprised if it is business with a courtesan.

"Bring back the paperwork from the second study," Nicolò tells Beneto. "Locked in the—"

"Black box, I know." Beneto hops onto the boat, holding a hand out for Luisa. The girls watch the house disappear. Maddalena tries to capture the way Luisa leans on the railing, the way light hits her when not filtered by the Pietà loggia. She thinks she can use this, return to this memory when Venice rises from the lagoon in all its blinding rose marble, its sun shards of glass on the canals. She will remember this when she spies the gondolier lurking behind the columns of the Piazzetta, when the thing beneath the water makes its reach.

Beneto sits with them in amiable silence, and Maddalena is grateful that he doesn't press the issue of the Celsis. She has forgiven him his earlier deception. He, too, is an instrument. He'll be expected to breed, just as she will, if she marries, if her acceptance in society announces their legitimacy. Why is it that a girl must always lead the way into unpleasantness? Beneto learned to hunt, to swim, to read, before they thought to teach her, but because she's a girl, Maddalena is thrust into marriage a good decade ahead. So many of the girls she grew up with have already been given to old widowers—no one says a word if a husband is sixty and his new bride is sixteen. So many of the girls she grew up with will die in childbirth, to be replaced by fresh blood, ad infinitum, until the old man finally dies.

If Maffeo Celsi doesn't marry her, will Maddalena be sent to some septuagenarian patrician? Will one have her? Will the hand in the water provide? What will it mean to be bound twice in unhappy marriage? The burchiello docks, and they move into a gondola and closer, ever closer, to the future.

Luisa

The girls at the Pietà crowd around Luisa, asking questions about Mira. Was Andrea there? How many noble families did you meet? Did you drink prosecco? Did you picnic all afternoon? Were the chamber pots made of gold?

"We heard you gave a concert," says Daniela, who somehow hears everything. "With a hired orchestra. Is it true?"

"Just for the senator," Luisa says, unsure of her obligation to either the Grimanis or the Ospedale della Pietà. Once girls leave here, they are not allowed to perform—any Coro girl who marries forfeits her right to an audience—but surely there's no law against a concert for your host and a few guests during a sojourn to the countryside. Surely no one is going to lock her away for doing what they asked of her. Still, she's tight-lipped. When they press her for details of her two weeks, she says simply, "I recovered."

Maddalena, they do not press. If news of Maffeo Celsi's courtship has reached the girls in the dormitory, they've chosen to keep quiet.

"You look tired," Chiara says, raising her eyebrows, when they all dress together for bed. Maddalena doesn't look at her. Luisa tries to find Maddalena's eyes, but Maddalena's murmuring her prayers. Luisa, too, gets in her own bed. She waits until the room is full of heavy, slumbered breathing, then tiptoes to the next cot. Maddalena's eyes are open. She makes room for Luisa next to her, and when Luisa burrows in, Maddalena clutches her arm as if they're sinking. Luisa tries to think of how she might help, but there was nothing to say last night at Mira and there's nothing to say now. She lets Maddalena hold her until her body unclenches, and she wonders at how quickly they have gone from sharing everything to nothing. She thinks of Nicolò; she trembles.

Maddalena's nostrils flare in sleep—she's no less fierce, she looks no younger. Luisa fingers a strand of her hair, which still smells like the orange blossoms of the perfumed baths at Mira. Finally, she extricates herself very slowly so as not to disturb Maddalena's already troubled slumber. When she stands to return to her own bed, she sees that another girl is sitting up several beds down, her coverlet crumpled at the foot of her cot, her body turned toward Maddalena and Luisa. A strip of moonlight edges through the window, illuminating the angles of the other girl's face. Chiara is watching them.

Luisa swallows. She lies down immediately, ready to pretend sleep-walking or nightmares. Chiara doesn't approach, which doesn't surprise Luisa. It's enough that Luisa has seen her, knows she knows. Maddalena's been certain that the Pietà's charmed indifference extends to these nights with Luisa, that if the other girls see, they will look past the cot, remember these two girls together as a dream. But that was before Mira. They'd been protected by the smallness of their world, the limits of Luisa's own imagination. Now there's no pretending away the other foundlings' curiosity—the question of what one of their own, and one who never will be one of them, might do outside these walls. What they might bring back inside with them, and how it might spread.

Could Chiara understand? Luisa thinks it more likely that Chiara will use this against them. Chiara's friendships are like Luisa's before Maddalena came, circumstantial and utilitarian. A girl to gossip with (Orsetta), a girl to roll her eyes at (Adriana), a girl to tolerate (Luisa). Maddalena, herself, a girl to what—to despise? To adore? To emulate?

Luisa forces herself to lie still, counting down the time until enough has passed that she feels comfortable leaning up on a surreptitious elbow. Chiara lies with her back to Luisa, sheets still pooled at her feet. She might be asleep. She has certainly filed away the information, though what she thinks of this new knowledge—whether it is in fact new knowledge or simply confirmation—Luisa doesn't know. What are they to each other, she and Maddalena, these girls with their hearts in their throats and their affection and their secrets, and the sinuous jealousy that motivates each muscle, all that sweet venom in the blood?

Maddalena

Maddalena's mattress feels especially hard after her weeks at the villa. She sleeps fitfully, and in the morning is absorbed into rehearsals and chapel and refectory lectures. While her cohort does piecework, she's given extra music lessons, making up for lost work on her motet. There is no time for the gondolier or the water gate.

Again, she sleeps poorly. Gauzy dreams that feel half fantasy: her mother standing at the end of a dock, the moon coming unpinned from the sky. Blue-green barnacles crawl up Maddalena's ankle, higher with the rising tide, the skin of her calf still tingling when she jolts herself awake. That barcarole teases her, a siren. Again her day is scheduled so precisely that she cannot slip away. Again she dreams. Finally, on the fourth night, after the dormitory is asleep—after Luisa is asleep, her lashes still against her cheek and the blue veins of her eyelids patterned in gentle movement, her clenched fist finally unfurled—Maddalena carries her shoes through the hall and goes down to the canal.

The sky sits heavy, clouds moving to blot out the stars in an announcement of the kind of summer storm Venice is known for. Deep, purring thunder and lightning that cracks steeples. Frightened waves that pound against locked doors and overturn unmoored boats. Even seasoned seamen—some still left in Venice by the dawn of the eighteenth century, despite Nicolò's claims—won't try their luck against this weather's portents. Maddalena steps out into the wind.

The gondolier is waiting, and it's only when she sees him that Maddalena allows herself to consider what she'd have done if he hadn't been idling, balanced in the stern of his black boat, despite how the canal already knocks it toward the causeway. She knows from the way he stands so straight amid the frothing water that there's something not quite human about him. He doesn't flicker like she imagines a spirit would; instead, it's his solidity that marks him as other. Maddalena feels that when she steps into his boat, she, too, will be cloaked in that protection that allows him to be standing here, unfazed. She steps into his boat.

They move more slowly than Maddalena is accustomed to in this gondola, the choppy waters urging them back. She should say something, but doesn't know what she should say. If she's too shy to speak to him—this boy she's spoken to dozens of times, this boy who wears a lazy grin like her brother Andrea's and rolls his sleeves like her brother Nicolò—how can she speak to the darkness at the shrine, of which she knows nothing? What would Luisa say to the gondolier? she wonders. Think of that, then do the opposite—Maddalena loves Luisa dearly but would never look to her in matters of audacity. Be bold.

"Is this what you meant when you told me she'd call for me? That I'd toss and turn and think of . . . her? Is it because of you that I can't sleep?" She doesn't mean to sound so uncertain, and feels lucky that the volume of her voice is excused by the wind.

"Me?" The gondolier turns to her.

"Well . . . any of you."

"Any of us?" Must he make her questions circular? He has a wry look on his face, as if he's teasing her.

Before he saw Maddalena at Mira, the gondolier seemed to move entirely at her will. He appeared—mostly—when she called him, and he flirted without being too forward. He was a risk that still felt fundamentally safe. Not so since Luisa's illness, since his infiltration of her country home. She wonders about the power of the barcarole—is it a net she can use to tow him in when needed, or, as she suspects, an anchor? When you whisper the name of the devil, he wakes from fiery depths to listen, but mostly to take.

The gondolier is fully in control now, steering them out into the lagoon, where the rain has begun in a mist that kisses like eyelashes on Maddalena's cheek. She tucks farther into the felze, ending any immediate conversation, and he paddles them faster, careful to avoid the shoals that stir in the rain, releasing secrets from silt. The raindrops fatten, and the gondolier's hair is soon plastered to his forehead, his livery soaked through. It isn't until the force of the downpour lashes his neck that he pulls in his oar and joins Maddalena under the canopy.

He drips onto her dress, which isn't dry but at least does its job as barrier between her body and the elements. The rain sounds like millions of hard-shelled insects, chittering. The gondola rocks nauseously, the only boat of its size out on the lagoon, the only boat of any size within sight. The two of them the only bodies. There is no way around the intimacy, the fact that it's them against nature, in more ways than just the obvious. Pressed against him in the gondola's cabin, she's able to look at him. He's olive-skinned, tanned in the way of an adventurer. He has a scar on his top lip, almost invisibly thin. Green eyes, a dark green that looks black in certain lights. In this, the light of a lantern over which they hover, hoping the shield of their bodies will keep it lit against the wind, they are the color of the evergreens that border her family's palazzo. She asks him, "Who are you?"

The gondolier is wringing out his shirt, trying to flick the wet out toward the lagoon so it doesn't pool under the felze. She leans in for his story, but none comes. He shakes his head, this time an obvious dismissal, not just a way to dry his hair. So she asks instead, "Where are you taking me?"

"Where do you want to go?" The way he turns the question seems flippant, but his face is as serious as Maddalena has seen it, so she answers him seriously.

"To speak to the thing in the water. To buy myself back." Until she says it, she doesn't understand that's what she's after, but it seems obvious now. "Can you do it? Can you take me?"

The gondolier's impossible to read. "The Piazzetta will flood tonight," he says. She waits him out. "There are certain things you sell and can't buy back. Other things you shouldn't want to."

"And you would know, would you? You, barely more than a boy?" Maddalena puts on her most imperious expression. The rain intensifies. The gondola should be filling with water. They should be using buckets to scoop water from the sole. Maddalena's hair and dress are wet. The boat is empty. "How?" she asks.

"Would you believe me? I, barely more than a boy?" His eyes sparkle. "How?"

"Imagine that you lose your maidenhead. Imagine that you lose your faith in Rome's God."

"The two aren't the same," says Maddalena.

"No. They aren't. But no matter how you miss your innocence, it's gone. There's nothing to buy back, because even if you had it, you still wouldn't have what you had before. Do you understand?"

"No."

"You will understand," he says. "And realize you're better for it."

Maddalena pushes her hair behind her ears. "Why can't I sleep?"

"I can take you to the water," he continues. "I'll row you out to Lido, or the shrine. But what you see and what you speak to won't be different. It will offer, and you will accept. How much do you think you've changed in these past few months? You can't sleep because there's something that you want, and you know you'll ultimately turn to the water to get it. What do you want?"

What she wants now is Luisa. Maddalena pictures her, drowning that day at Lido. She saw Luisa before she knew it was Luisa, Luisa as a dream of what was possible. Maddalena thinks that she'll pay anything— the marriage to Celsi, her nobility, her family's honor—to hold on to what's between them, to lie at night in the little cot with Luisa and bury her face in Luisa's loose hair, to listen to Luisa play her violin, to feel Luisa's knee knock against hers at chapel. That Luisa truly saw her is, of course, part of the bargain with the water. But she wants Luisa's feelings to be real, not an enchantment.

"What is it?" Maddalena asks. "The thing in the water?"

Their breath under the felze in the damp is a strange, oily fug that makes Maddalena feel dirty, like she wants to peel her skin. They are alone in the middle of the Venetian lagoon, lightning bending itself around their gondola, spared the worst of the rain. The gondolier leans closer, and she mirrors him. It's like leaning toward fire, the stifling nearness of the air warning danger—but the flame. The flame is tantalizing, dancing. The waves and his green eyes and her own heart beating time with the rain as it drums against the boat. His lips smooth and close and pink, so different from the lips she's longed for, so much colder. The bellows of his breath.

What she wants is Luisa, but what's here is the gondolier, the bargain. His cold mouth, his slippery tongue, his perfect rows of teeth. She imagines those lips moving down the line of her jaw, his curls dripping rain, his body taut and lean against hers. She imagines his breath at her ear, and the black canopy above her when she arches her neck.

She pulls away. The rain has stopped. All at once she's tired, aching for sleep.

"Do you still want to sail to Lido?" the gondolier asks. Maddalena shakes her head, and he begins to row her home.

Autumn

Luisa

Life at the Pietà goes back to much as it had been before her illness. Prayer and practice, plain meals and community work. After the villa, falling into these rhythms feels partly like punishment, but mostly relief. Luisa takes Nicolò's violin to the practice room and the others *ooh* and *ahh* at its construction. When she plays it, their silence is reverent. If she was a good violinist already, and exceptional after the shrine, with such an instrument Luisa is transcendent. Chiara watches her with a mix of admiration and suspicion, and when they are given a concerto for two violins, practice becomes a competition. Since returning from Mantua, Vivaldi has warmed to Chiara, but Luisa doesn't mind. She wants someone to race against, someone to push her, an escape for the deep wells of feeling that have emerged since her stay in the countryside. And if this is a competition, how could Luisa lose? She has the promise from the lagoon, the memory of Nicolò. Chiara has only her talent and ambition.

When they are alone in the practice room, Luisa expects Chiara to remark upon her nights with Maddalena—perhaps not outright, but at least some subtle dig. Yet Chiara says nothing of what she has seen, and Luisa is left wondering how much or how little she knows, if she has followed Maddalena to the water gate, if she understands why her bridge went missing months ago. She is polite, but cold. While they play, Chiara opens herself just enough to let Luisa's violin become a partner. As soon as the last note sounds, she closes off again, as if a screen has dropped behind her eyes, replacing the passion—the bleeding emotion she's been known for since the girls picked up their instruments, age six—with a calculated blankness. They were never friends, Luisa and Chiara, but until this year Luisa never thought Chiara was an enemy. They've been taught that each instrument matters, each role is vital to the success of the whole, and that their Ospedale won renown because, unlike at the theater, they haven't any divas. Now, even in duet, they are against each other. Luisa must defer to Chiara or beat her.

They make their joint debut in front of the congregation at Sunday vespers. They wear white dresses and pomegranate flowers in their hair, and they stand behind the filigreed grate, candles fore and aft, the incense thick enough to see. The orchestra buoys them, and afterward the crowd seems awed, a few foreign attendees holding out their hands as if to touch the hems of the girls' skirts. Luisa feels like a saint's relic, a precious bit of bone or fingernail that men will travel miles to worship, if only to say they were there, that they stood close and they heard.

The piece goes off flawlessly, and as reward the maestra allows them to go into the parlatorio to greet their admirers from behind another grate. Pocketbooks might open if they stand just a bit closer to the openings, if she perhaps cracks the door.

Neither is a good conversationalist. Luisa wrings her hands, anxious despite her brief experience at Mira. Chiara attempts an occasional smile, but mostly stares nervously out at the people—mostly men—who've come to fawn. They look to the older members of the Coro as examples. Betta the clarinetist, twenty-five and well versed in the language of her admirers, laughs with two men in dark cloaks and tricorn hats, the quality and simplicity of their clothing marking them as noblemen. Anna Maria talks animatedly to a woman who speaks accented Italian, and the Priora herself converses with another older gentleman whose face Luisa can't make out.

Luisa looks for Nicolò. She'd been worried she wouldn't be able to help seeking him out in the church, and that such action would distract her. But from above, the audience was a blur of silks and wigs and whispers, and the moment the orchestra opened she was swept up in the music. It was a silly thought, to begin with. His household won't return to Venice until October. Yet even if he wasn't in the audience, he was with her. She played his violin.

He's absolutely still in the countryside—if he'd come back to the city, Maddalena would know. And why would he come back to the humidity, the stagnant social scene, the diseases that spread in swampy heat? Still, she looks for him. A particular set to the shoulders. An expression of polite interest that doesn't quite mask its wearer's impatience. A bitten fingernail. A bead of sweat.

"Luisa!" She looks up, expectant. She is surprised. Not Nicolò, but another man she knows: Maffeo Celsi. He must be here for Maddalena, she thinks, and the fact sinks in her chest. This is what Maddalena has been waiting for—Maffeo's proposal, her new life—and all Luisa feels is loss: soon her friend will be gone. Chiara's eyes widen as Maffeo approaches, and Luisa imagines what she must be thinking, imagines what she might say to Orsetta, who'll spread gossip to the farthest reaches of the Pietà. What she sees: a young man with a good figure and fine clothes, speaking directly to Luisa with her given name, waving a hand in joyful greeting, nudging aside a group of ladies to get close to where they stand at the grate. It is no matter. Soon he'll be engaged to Maddalena and all rumors will be worthless, unless they are about Maddalena's wedding trousseau or what they'll serve at her feast.

"Even better than before," Maffeo gushes when he reaches them. His enthusiasm is endearing, like a slobbering dog eager to demonstrate affection.

Chiara stands, not quite gawking but clearly put off by his informality. Maffeo notices and flashes her an apologetic smile. He makes a quick bow, and reaches out as if to kiss Chiara's hand, but is stymied by the forgotten grate, which doesn't allow for it naturally.

"You were lovely as well," he says to Chiara, saving himself with a slight genuflection. "Maffeo Celsi. At your service." If Maddalena were here, she would scoff at his platitudes. But Maddalena is not here, and Luisa takes them as an omen: he will try.

Chiara gives a thin-lipped smile and nods her head in acknowledgment.

She looks to Luisa, as uncomfortable as Luisa's ever seen her, and Luisa feels a stitch of pride at her own success with Maffeo and the Grimani brothers several weeks ago. She hadn't been loquacious, but she'd been with them alone and come off well enough that here Maffeo is, coming to greet her.

"Have you been in Venice long?" Luisa asks. "I hadn't realized you intended to leave the Riviera." It's small talk—*for small minds*, says Maddalena—but perhaps the Priora will see and applaud her for wooing a potential donor. Perhaps he'll ask Luisa and a sampling of the Coro to his house for a concert, and she'll get to play the best parts.

"Just for the past few days," he says. "The heat, you know." It's good that Maddalena isn't here, if talk is turning to the weather. Chiara's eyes dart back and forth; Luisa hasn't a clue what's behind them.

"Yes," says Luisa. "The heat."

"And you seem to have recovered? I'd imagine they wouldn't let you perform if you were still feeling ill?" Dull, and getting duller. Luisa nods. At least he's kind. It's kind that he's asking.

"Oh, I've recovered fully," she says. Then they both speak at once:

"Are you—"

"If I could—"

"Go ahead," says Maffeo.

"Are you here on business, then?" Because a proposal is business. A marriage is business, when it's between a wealthy family who has recently purchased their nobility and a centuries-old name looking to hold off scandal. Anything arranged, with calculations to be made on either side, with weights and measures and analysis and planning. If money is exchanged, it is business. What else is a dowry?

"You could say." Maffeo grins. "You could very well say."

Luisa is about to answer him when her eye catches a movement in the corner of the parlatorio, and her chest tightens and she freezes and she feels like she might vomit. It couldn't be. It is.

Nicolò is in the room, looking befuddled, as if he also can't believe he's back in Venice. He's holding his hat, running his fingers over and around its brim, and nodding along to some fellow patrician who apparently feels strongly about whatever they're discussing. Does he see her? Is he looking for her? He must have heard her play.

As always, Luisa is surprised by her need for him. When she plays music, she is aware of herself in her body. Her elbow will ache, her chin will bruise. Part of the joy is the transcendence—the moment she can hold both the knowledge of discomfort and the fact of the music's escape. The pursuit of perfection demands pain, and who better than a foundling to harness it? What she feels for Nicolò is a different sort of being in a body. A folded paper, opening and opening. A bird in the chest. A flower in the mouth.

"Yes," says Luisa to Maffeo, because Chiara is looking at her strangely, because she must say something or risk Chiara following her line of sight, deducing, roping the knowledge of Maddalena in the night and Luisa in the day into a noose. "Well."

Maffeo winks. Luisa coughs, then has the sense to look embarrassed when he asks her again, "Are you well?"

"The incense," she says. He's made his polite conversation, and she isn't sure why he's still standing here. Neither she nor Chiara make for fascinating partnership. As if he's read her thoughts, Maffeo bows and makes his farewells. That's Uncle Celsi talking to the Priora, Luisa realizes. Nicolò is near him—this must be why Nicolò has returned. As the eldest son and with his father either busy with affairs of the state or remarkably absentminded—Luisa can't tell which, but thinks perhaps it is both—Nicolò has taken on most familial duties. Will this be Luisa's last night with Maddalena? Surely they'll give her some time to prepare herself before sending her out, but on the occasion of a Pietà girl marrying, she is generally given her own room while the details are secured. It doesn't do to flaunt a marriage. There's no upside to getting the other girls' hopes up, no spiritual profit in jealousy.

The parlatorio empties—the crowd is slow, but they do leave. Luisa worries that a figlia will come to take her and Chiara back to their room before she's had the chance to speak to Nicolò, though she doesn't know what she'd say if he approached. The Priora eyes the girls, surely aware of their deficiencies. At least Chiara looks pretty, with the coral-colored blossom against her dark hair and her eyes big with the occasion. Pretty girls count for something—another lesson Luisa's had from Maddalena. Here comes Figlia Menegha to retrieve them. It's been a long day. The hour is late.

And then, by magic, Nicolò is coming over. He's still talking to the energetic man, or rather being talked at, while attempting to appear interested. As always with Nicolò, the attempt is obvious and endearing. Chiara turns to follow the figlia, but Luisa puts a hand to the grate, grasping with her fingers, unwilling or unable to go. Here he is. His hand brushing her hand. He has a note, folded small, and as she takes it, she marvels at how cool he is, how calm he appears when she feels his hand tremble. Luisa slips the note into her sleeve and hurries after Chiara, her whole self a pounding pulse. She'll have to wait until tonight to look at it. What she has with Nicolò is private, to be kept even from—especially from—Maddalena. She can wait.

Luisa hums a few bars from the evening's concerto, scurrying to keep pace.

"Luisa—" A voice from the parlatorio's anteroom, one of the sotto maestre. "The Priora wants to see you."

Has she been found out so quickly? It seems impossible, but really it's inevitable—at the Pietà, someone is always watching. Luisa follows the sotto maestra down a hall to the Priora's office. Candles flicker in sconces. The littlest girls are already abed. The Priora stands in her doorway, looking tired but triumphant. She thanks the sotto maestra and leads Luisa inside.

"You showed yourself well today," the Priora says. "You represented us well." Luisa supposes she should thank her for the compliment, but Nicolò's note itches against her arm, and the adrenaline of the day has begun to dissipate.

She yawns. "I'm sorry."

"No." The Priora smiles. "It's late. I'm sorry for calling you in. I suppose this could have waited, but it seemed the perfect ending to what I'm sure has been a rather eventful day." Not a punishment then.

Nothing to do with Nicolò, because there's no world in which the Priora would call what they've begun together perfect.

Or is it to do with Nicolò?

"You've received an offer of marriage," the Priora says. Luisa has been standing, but at this she drops onto the nearest chair in an unflattering, perhaps dangerous, certainly disrespectful flounce of skirt.

"I'm sorry," Luisa whispers again, though the Priora is smiling. "I'm sorry...it's just...very unexpected."

"The timing is right," the Priora says. "You'll be sixteen soon. Once you're a member of the Coro, you'll owe us ten years of service. If you go with him now, you'll have a fine life. The choice is yours, of course, and we'll be very sorry to lose your violin, but we do see what he can give you."

"He," says Luisa. Nicolò? It is a dream. It is impossible. "But...how?" Nicolò. It couldn't be. It isn't.

Very softly, Luisa says, "Who?"

The Priora's mouth quirks.

"Maffeo Celsi."

Luisa

She doesn't read Nicolò's note until the middle of the night. She walks back to the dormitory from the Priora's office as if trying to guide a needle through thick cloth, every step effortful. She thinks that if she pauses here by the entrance to the practice rooms, here in the loggia, she might unspool the evening until there is no possibility of Maffeo Celsi. How can she go to bed and wake up and play arpeggios and shuffle to and from the chapel and wait for the maestro dei concerti to pat her on the head and say, *Well done*? How can she stay the path when it is branching? If she does nothing, she's made inertia a choice. And if she marries Maffeo Celsi . . .

Maddalena asks after Luisa's time in the parlatorio under her breath as they remove their outer clothes and kneel for prayer. The dormitory warden still stands in the room, one arm holding the other at the elbow. Usually by now she's with the little girls. Luisa wonders if she's been sent as a spy. The Priora instructed Luisa not to tell anyone—not even her closest friends—until she's made her decision. As if this is a choice that can be made in isolation, as if Luisa on her own is capable of choosing wisely. The other girls would be disrupted, the Priora said. The news would cause a stir. There's no use adding fuel to fire, by which she means a gaggle of teenage girls is difficult enough without an errant proposal. And what will Maddalena say? Will she be angry? Will the news break her heart?

Luisa tells Maddalena that the parlatorio was fine, which it was. "Overwhelming," she whispers. "Too many people, and none of them easy."

Maddalena crosses herself, turns down her bedsheets. "All fawning, I imagine?"

Luisa shrugs. She isn't going to mention Maffeo, and she isn't going to mention Nicolò. She's always been an awful liar, almost as bad at obfuscation. She climbs into bed, turns her back to Maddalena, and pretends sleep.

Best be practical. At this point, there is a place for her in the Coro, if she wants it. She's already soloed, Vivaldi has taken an obvious interest, and there's the promise from the lagoon, whatever blessing bestowed that has smoothed her rough edges. Yet this last is an argument against staying, for if she takes her place as an active member of the Coro, she will never know how much of her accomplishments are actually her own. She'll always wonder if what she hears as she plays is what her audience hears. She'll always think about the lagoon, the gift she stole with Maddalena.

If she marries Maffeo Celsi, she will not play at all.

Oh, she'll be able to give him private concerts, and she can have an instrument on which to dally. But no one will write music with her bow in mind. She won't have admirers, she won't wear a white dress and pomegranate blossoms in her hair and send some visitor from France or England home with stories about the spirits who serenade Venice. If she tries to take the stage, her new family will be fined and disgraced. She herself could be banished. If she marries Maffeo, she'll be giving up everything.

What will she gain? Rich food. Fine dresses. Freedom. She'll gain the city and the countryside. The Ridotto, where she might join a gaming table. The opera, where she can hear the divas sing. Likely a cicisbeo to take her to coffee shops and concerts while her husband is occupied. She'll no longer be waiting for Chiara's betrayal, anticipating how her rival will use nights with Maddalena against them. And Nicolò...

In the shock she has forgotten his note. Now she tangles the sheets to get to it, still in the sleeve of her shift, having crawled to the elbow. She's reluctant to open it. What if she has imagined the heat between them, what if the smiles and the gifts are just his way? Adriana is always pointing out some congregant, swearing he's mad for some girl. Orsetta was in love with the medico's apprentice, and made a fool of herself scampering after him. If Luisa's misread Nicolò, she doesn't know how she can trust herself to choose between music and marriage. If she hasn't misread him, her choice becomes less of a choice. Luisa lives, for a moment, in both possible futures. Then she unfolds the note.

How can I see you?

She has an answer. By some providence, Luisa has an answer. She can marry Maffeo Celsi and leave these walls, and find a way to see Nicolò. Does desiring something make it worthwhile? She knows that it doesn't, but the solution is so elegant. The timing is impeccable. It all would be impeccable, if not for Maddalena.

As is, she doesn't have a logistical answer to Nicolò's question, or even a way to respond. She doesn't know if he'll be angry that she's stolen his sister's proposal, his family's chance at legitimacy. But she feels that same heady desperation she can sense from his scrawled words. She's drawn to him. She wants him.

Before Mira, she wanted to be the world's best violinist. She was a child, then, and thought that there was such a thing as *best* without a price. There had been only one way forward, so she'd clung to that way, told herself she loved it. Now there is a different way, a better one. If the Avogarìa di Comun confirms the marriage, it must be a better way, as the role of that council is to sit in judgment over what is best for Venice. The Celsis are newly ennobled. There's always the chance that a connection with a foundling will be laughed out of the *Libro d'Oro*, but Bastiano Celsi seems a prudent sort. Luisa can't imagine that he'd let Maffeo offer without first tidying his house and making sure that the request will not disgrace his family's name. She imagines it must be en vogue, to have a little songbird. Luisa's easy-mannered, she'll represent well.

She could do worse for a husband than Maffeo Celsi. She could hardly do better. Still, the choice is not between Maffeo and the violin. That choice is simple. One she loves, the other she merely respects. Nicolò and the violin, though . . .

Luisa imagines herself in his rooms—at the villa, at his palazzo, in a hovel on the mainland—with him, with his instrument. She pictures herself as his beloved. Surely she can have both things, the man and the music, the luxury and the fame? A different sort of fame than she's imagined, but more lasting, because it will be in the eyes of a man who adores her.

It is late. She can't know what she gives up until she makes a decision. She tosses and wonders and sweats in the stale dormitory air until at last she falls asleep.

The bells wake her, the dormitory still dark. Luisa shakes off sleep, tidies her bed, and finds her stomacher. Next to her, Maddalena does the same, then stops.

"What is this?" She has knelt to lace a shoe and found a folded piece of paper. Luisa shudders involuntarily, weighing her choices, all of them bad.

She swallows the panic. "Maffeo Celsi has asked me to marry him."

Maddalena's wrist goes slack. She was going to know eventually. It's not like Luisa can keep something so massive from the person who'll be done the most harm. Maddalena examines the scrap of paper, holding it away from her body and turning it first one way, then the next. Her eyes are calculating. Luisa hopes she doesn't know her brother's handwriting.

"I haven't said anything," she says quickly, trying to explain as much as she can before they're silenced for prayer. "It was a shock. I only found out last night. I'm sorry I didn't tell you, I didn't know what to say."

Maddalena licks her lips. She doesn't seem upset, so much as thoughtful.

"Do you love him?"

Luisa laughs out loud, and receives a glare from Figlia Giustiniana for her indiscretion. She trails Maddalena down the dormitory and out into the hall. "Of course not." She wants to do more to assure Maddalena that this hasn't been some scheme, that she never tried to undermine the Grimanis. Figlia Giustiniana's eyes are at her back. She sidles up so that

Maddalena can feel Luisa's breath on her neck, walking so close that if Maddalena stopped suddenly, they'd topple. "I barely spoke to him," Luisa whispers.

Maddalena keeps walking, though the tide of girls is walking, and she doesn't have much choice in the matter. She can't respond without turning around to break the line, and Luisa uses this to her advantage. "If you don't want me to, of course I won't." She doesn't really mean this. Luisa can't believe that Maddalena would actually forbid her from marrying Maffeo—it's not as if he'd move down the list and inevitably ask her instead—though on the chance that she did, matters might be made easier. Luisa's used to being told what to do, where to go, when (if ever) to give an opinion. Either way she will lose. Either way she will win. Let Maddalena decide.

In her heart, Luisa's already decided.

"I'd never tell you not to," Maddalena says once they have made the long walk from bed to chapel and are filing into pews. "Not on my behalf. I'm just surprised, is all."

"As was I."

"It does make sense," says Maddalena. "Given your skill. The way you look. The way you are." It could be taken as an insult, Maddalena's tone matter-of-fact to the point of condescension, but Luisa knows better.

"Be quiet!" Adriana sits behind them, and she swats Luisa's shoulder. "The figlie."

Punishment varies if they're caught talking at prayer, but Figlia Giustiniana, who has seated herself a negligible distance away, is known for her lack of understanding. It isn't until they've finished Prime and are heading to the refectory for breakfast that Maddalena continues.

"It makes sense, and it's an elegant solution," she says under the drone of the Priora reading scripture. Girls throughout the room are whispering to one another, and the occasional voice rises in disbelief or laughter. Recreation isn't until late afternoon, and the Priora has tacitly agreed to give her girls the morning meal.

"Elegant how?" Luisa asks. She picks at her porridge, which seems heavier and blander since the hot chocolate and pastry that was offered every morning at Mira. Since returning, she admires Maddalena more. She understands how Nicolò might think that time at the Pietà would serve as redemption.

"Well, if I left, and you didn't, how would I see you? They'd never let a woman join the board, and there are only so many times I could request you for a concert. This way we both can leave."

"You'll leave, too?" asks Luisa.

"I don't know why they'd keep me here. It's expensive, and I've had my run. Surely there's some less fashionable old man to pawn me off on." Maddalena seems much calmer than Luisa would have expected, discussing her future. Perhaps she plans to go back to the water and ask its assistance. If Luisa can be made into a prodigy, the work of keeping Maddalena from the nunnery can't be all that difficult.

"You think I should agree?" Luisa turns her back so that she and Maddalena are their own private planet, the bustle of breakfast revolving around them.

"There are benefits. We'd be able to see each other freely." Maddalena is stirring her porridge, stirring, stirring. Luisa hasn't seen her take a single bite. "My family won't be thrilled, but they won't blame you. They liked you. Every day could be like Mira, more or less."

Every day like Mira: the anticipation of Nicolò around a corner, at the table, standing in the doorway while she played. Long mornings in lazy sunbeams, nights at masked balls. The only sacrifice, her music. It's only cutting off a limb. It's only closing a window so that the air grows stale and dormant, the room thick with unspent desire. The clouds and the sky and the sea bright and blazing while inside she does, what? Coifs her hair?

And yet Luisa's always played in private. Before the lagoon, she could only truly play in the privacy of one of the practice rooms, after the others had gone. What sacrifice is it, truly, to return to what should always have been? Every time she plays in public, she will know it isn't actually her. The audience doesn't actually adore her but an idea of her, a mirage formed by the pact made with the water. It makes her feel further from herself, it makes her lonelier. Fame, says Anna Maria, is difficult enough. The tourists come with an idea of what you'll be, and when they see the actual you, with your overbite and awkwardness and your strings that snap like any other player's, they recoil. They hear you, of course, and they're enraptured. But though they leave with stories of your prowess that will spread throughout Europe, you will know that, in your way, you've disappointed them.

Wouldn't it be better to play for one man, who will not be disappointed? Wouldn't it be better to play just for Nicolò?

"And you would help me?" Luisa lets herself imagine leaving. Collecting her few belongings—an extra dress? a pair of shoes? Nicolò's violin—and walking out the Pietà doors. She pictures a home full of light. A city of dark corners, in which to meet Nicolò.

"We'd be together constantly," says Maddalena. "Once I sort out my own situation. I'll find a way. We'll both be married and move freely through the city. This will be good." Luisa doesn't ask how Maddalena is so sure she'll be able to, as she puts it, sort out her own situation. But if she's confident, there's no use in questioning her. She knows so much that Luisa doesn't. She trusts herself in ways Luisa will never understand.

"So I should say yes," Luisa presses. "I should marry him?"

"I can't decide for you." Maddalena pushes back from the table, almost haughty. "You have to figure out what you want, and then choose."

Luisa thought she wanted the violin. She thought she wanted the Coro and the fame and the way it feels to master difficult fingering, to fly her bow across the strings, edging closer to the moment in which her idea of the music will match the way she's made it sound. She thought she wanted the way it feels to join with an orchestra, the forgetting of the self in service of the larger goal. Luisa had never felt closer to another human being, more necessary.

But that was before Maddalena. That was before Mira, and Nicolò.

Luisa spends the day strategizing how she'll reach Nicolò. Her only lifeline is a solo performance that is so astounding the figlie are forced to trot her out in front of her admirers. Unless she commits to the marriage now, before talking to him, before finding out if he will hate her for ruining his plans for Maddalena. If Luisa goes to the Priora and accepts Maffeo's proposal, she can ask for time in the parlatorio to meet with the Celsis, she can admit to being overwhelmed and request that they meet among others, in the socialization hour after mass, so she can maintain her modesty. She'll prepare a note for Nicolò. She'll have to wait a week for his reaction, but at least then, he will know.

Instead of going to the courtyard with the other girls during their recreation hour, Luisa walks the endless corridor, dread a stone in her chest. The Priora's unsurprised. She doesn't offer Luisa motherly advice or reassure her that she's made the right decision.

"We'll tell them today, and we'll begin negotiations." Pen to ink, a letter to Celsi, another to the board of governors, another to a lawyer who will help them with the Avogarìa di Comun who must approve the marriage contracts. Luisa backs out of the room, fighting an urge to put her thumb in her mouth, a habit she broke over a decade ago. She can't help but feel she's chosen incorrectly; she needs to know that Nicolò will approve.

She finds Maddalena in the courtyard, alone on a bench, staring out at the littlest girls rolling their hoops.

"I accepted," Luisa says, settling next to her.

"I thought you would." Maddalena doesn't look at her. A little one has tripped, scraping a knee on the stone. Her friends circle her, stroking her hair and looping elbows, their sense of camaraderie never stronger than when outside ill befalls one of their own.

"You aren't mad?" Luisa blurts out, despite herself. "Or disappointed?"

Now Maddalena turns and takes Luisa's hands in her own, which are smooth and dry despite the afternoon heat.

"You're looking out for yourself," Maddalena says, her eyes on Luisa's eyes, their beam so intense that their surroundings blur and soften and there is only the two of them, here on a bench, holding and looking at each other. "You're looking out for us. I'm proud of you."

Luisa squeezes Maddalena's hands white.

"And your family?" And Nicolò? Nicolò, who'd plotted and paid; Nicolò, whose indifference or disdain would destroy her.

"They'll be fine," says Maddalena, soothing. "It will be fine. I'm going to settle it all on my own. We won't owe them anything."

Luisa is so caught in her own relief and hope that she doesn't question how or what Maddalena plans to settle.

The Celsis are delighted with Luisa's acceptance. Bastiano Celsi presses a hand to the grate when they meet in the parlatorio after Saturday mass, as if Luisa is the sun and he's absorbing her heat. Maffeo blushes and stutters, and Luisa takes this as a sign he's just as awkward as she is, which she sees as a good omen for their marriage. Better to bob along together, to be equals. She thinks Maffeo will not force her, she knows that he'll encourage her private musical development. In many ways he's a perfect match, but Luisa has eyes only for the rest of the room, for the moment the Celsis in their great mass of bodies leave the grate and she can take stock of the parlatorio.

People filter through the doors, past the grates, making casual conversation with the Coro. Luisa twists a lock of hair, tucking her pomegranate blossom more firmly behind her right ear. She bites her lips to give them color, and fights the urge to pinch her cheeks. She'd been sure he would be here—what else could he do after that note?—but now she remembers he's a man, the de facto head of an important family, with business to attend to across the Veneto. She turns to make her exit. Then she sees him.

He loiters by the side door, hat in hands, running its brim through his fingers. He looks out of place and obvious, and she knows at once that this is why she loves him. Nicolò doesn't want to be anything other than himself, and in a city of disguise this is a rarity and also a danger. The danger makes him beautiful, and she likes to think it means he needs her. He comes over, seeing that she's seen him.

"You were talking to Celsi," he murmurs.

"I've—" She can't say it. Surely someone else can tell him?

"I know. I heard."

"Are you angry?" She keeps her voice as steady as she can, eyes darting to be sure no one is giving them undue attention.

"Of course not."

The relief is so intense that she's sure she'll burst out crying. Barely a sound as she whispers, "It's for you."

Maddalena

Maffeo Celsi is both a boon and a burden, certainly a recalculation. Even before Luisa has officially made up her mind, Maddalena writes a letter to her father, thinking it better that he hear the news from her rather than as gossip at one of his cafés or in the doge's palace halls. It's hard to know how he'll react—Marcantonio the sort who one day rails against the fates that gave him such a frustrating daughter, and the next sends to Paris for her new shoes. Maddalena spends a long time considering what she should say, only to come right out and tell him: *Maffeo Celsi has proposed to Luisa, who will likely accept.* She sits with pen in hand, trying to decide if she should own this as a failure. In a roundabout way, Maddalena is responsible: if she hadn't made Luisa sick, Luisa never would have come to the country to recover. She never would have played for Maffeo Celsi or walked with him in the garden. There are many available girls in Venice. Many are like Maddalena, but none like Luisa. Maddalena suspects that the Celsis would have found Luisa some other way, heard her in church or seen her in the parlatorio. If they wanted an angel, they did not want Maddalena. She apologizes for the wasted time and money, the favors her father called in to get her here that ultimately served him no end. She doesn't apologize for herself, or for her mother. She ends the letter, *yours with love.*

On Saturday afternoon, Maddalena is taken from rehearsal—again they've given her the timpani, an afterthought that appears only in a single set of measures at the end of the piece, see how already she has fallen—and brought to a small room in the Priora's quarters, where a marble-topped table has legs engraved to look like rams. Their horns elaborately curl to make the base, tapering out into hooves, and at the center is some sort of deity. It belongs in a palazzo or casino and is how Maddalena knows she's in the part of the Pietà where they entertain the governors. A pitcher of wine sits on a side table, and the figlia di comun stutters, trying to decide whether to offer Maddalena a glass.

When the door opens, she sees Beneto ushered in, and not her father. He accepts his wine and removes his cloak and stares pointedly at the figlia until she mumbles something about the kitchens and backs out of the room. Then he sits, gestures for Maddalena to sit.

"Father got my letter," Maddalena says. "He heard my news."

"Yes, and he's sent a response for you." Beneto holds the envelope just out of Maddalena's reach, raising it higher when she leans for it. "And I'm here on behalf of the rest of us. To explain his response."

"He sent you?" Maddalena's hand darts out, but Beneto is faster.

"No. I sent myself."

"Give it here." Having said his piece, Beneto hands over the letter. Maddalena tears through it, which doesn't take long, as there are only a few dashed-off sentences. Very sad, ultimately for the best, she can come home and then take three months to find another husband. When and if she fails they'll find a comfortable nunnery and the priesthood for Beneto, perhaps, he'll have to learn to like the hats. Much love and has she seen the current show at Teatro San Cassiano, what a travesty— when she gets home they will go.

"You see now," Beneto says, "why I came."

Maddalena stares at him, expressionless. Have they both been written off? After years of swearing their legitimacy, does Marcantonio give up on them?

"He's caged it in, who knows what, the theater, but he's really quite serious. Things don't look good for any of us, I'm afraid."

"You think I can't do it," Maddalena says slowly. "I can find a husband. I told him that I'm going to find a husband."

"I think too much depends on the whims of a girl."

"It's not my fault Maffeo Celsi liked Luisa." Maddalena can feel herself confirming his assertion, yet can't keep her tone from thinning to petulance. Beneto isn't much older than she is. What is he doing to help?

"You could have done more. Nicolò said you barely spoke to the Celsis at Mira."

Maddalena has no answer. She'd been too distracted to play her assigned role at the Grimani party, which in retrospect she thinks was deliberate. The gondolier said he was called by the music—wouldn't he also be called by her desperation? If the thing in the water feeds on her need, how better to serve it than by sabotaging Nicolò's effort? Now Maddalena has three months to find a husband, her only prospects the water and a wish.

"I promise you I'm going to fix this." Maddalena reaches across the table. "I'll get a proposal that Father and Nicolò approve of, someone so well regarded that there won't be any question of our parentage. Someone wealthy and old and boring, and so important that it will be easy for you, then, to have anyone you please."

"You're giving up on love?"

"On love in marriage," Maddalena says. "Like most girls must and do. Never on love."

Beneto smiles at this, a rueful laugh of admiration. "I'll wish you luck, of course. And love, where you can find it."

She already has both. She taps his wrist. "Just get me out of here."

Beneto leaves once his wineglass is empty, fortifying himself for a meeting with the Priora to begin negotiations. They'll pay through the year, of course, but he agrees that Maddalena's chances are better if she can move without the Pietà's leash. She's had a good four months of tutelage. If she so chooses, she can continue her musical training with weekly private lessons. She's always welcome to join the figlie at prayer. Nicolò and her father will write to confirm Beneto's position, and as soon as all is sorted, she'll be back at Palazzo Grimani as if nothing ever happened. As if the many weeks of a hard bed and dry food and constant church bells were a dream. A dream that will guarantee her humility and good faith and obedience for all her time as a wife, of course, et cetera—in public, this past spring and summer will not go to waste. "And to think," the ladies will say over faro, "she did it all in the city, in the heat!" Now that she's remembered the game, Maddalena will play it for sympathy, but this doesn't disguise the fact that she hasn't really changed. She still both blames and needs her mother. She still hates Latin. Her discipline leaves much to be desired.

It's all a show—a puppet booth in the Piazza San Marco during Carnival—but instead of Pulcinella they have a little Maddalena bobbing about. Behind the curtain are the gondolier and the hand in the water. Tucked away in a corner, behind a pillar or against a wall, Luisa.

A show, a game. Each move among the patriciate is carefully calculated: every marriage in service of the family, every family in service of the republic. The republic, Maddalena supposes, in service of everyone, but mostly its well-established men.

Consider, Nicolò has demanded more than once at family dinner, what happens when the doge dies. Perhaps he is old, or catches fever, or he stumbles and suffers a fall. In Venice's early days, he would retire to a monastery once his political prowess veered toward impotence. This is less common today, where even in La Serenissima—a republic without despots, a place where all coups fail—men cling to power. Still, however it occurs, the doge will die or abscond, and the Great Council must choose his successor. What do they do? This part feels like a test, Nicolò waiting expectantly, Maddalena yawning, finally parroting an answer. Naturally they go to San Marco and find a ballot boy—any boy will do, preferably the first in line of sight, and young enough to be innocuous. A boy, though, who will then draw lots to choose thirty electorates from the Great Council. Of those thirty, now choose nine, who then nominate forty, who must have the approval of at least seven to succeed. A lottery makes those forty into twelve, and those twelve nominate a different twenty-five. Prune those to nine, who will choose yet another forty-five, each with enough electors in agreement to move them on to the next round. Cull the forty-five to eleven. Those choose the final forty-one, who will each nominate a candidate for the actual position of doge. They'll vote, raising a hand for any candidate they'll accept, and if the man with the most votes exceeds a total of twenty-five, he is elected with a festival to welcome him, a coronation and procession through the streets. Fair, Nicolò says. Nothing impulsive or self-serving. An infallible system—if followed—that harkens back to the glory days of Venice, when mirrors were the special provenance of Muranese glassmakers and naval champions swept through pirate fleets, et cetera, et cetera, how Nicolò drones on. Heaven forbid some new blood comes to disrupt these traditions. Heaven forbid a woman take power, or a craftsman, or the poor. Good thing these men spend their days investigating every aspect of a patriciate marriage and how it appears. Maddalena pictures ants moving crumbs from one small pile to another, the same boot coming to crush them regardless of where they choose to build.

She watches Beneto exit the Pietà, trepidatious but with a slight jaunt to his step that she would like to think is hope. She waits until he's vanished into the crowds along the Riva degli Schiavoni. Then she ties on her apron and repins her hair and wipes the wine from her mouth. She takes the stairs down to the lower floors two at a time, ignoring the afternoon traffic. Thanks to the thing in the water, the figlie rarely pay her notice when she's not with the rest of the girls, and now that she knows she'll be gone soon, she abandons all caution. She sprints past the dormitories and through the courtyard, turning toward the practice rooms that face the lagoon, where she stops short. The enchantment lets her escape notice, but it doesn't let her move through solid matter, and a group of girls carrying several large baskets of laundry plod under the weight of their cargo, fully blocking the hall. Maddalena steps into an empty practice room to give them a wider berth. As she does, she glances out the window, which looks down onto one of the lesser-used doors of the church. A figure is just leaving, taking off his hat and putting it back on, fingering the collar of his cloak. She wouldn't give it any thought, but she knows the tilted way he holds his shoulders.

"Nicolò?" Of course he can't hear her through the stone walls and the music stands and chatter all across the fondamenta. But when he turns to take the bridge east, she sees it is indeed Nicolò. How strange that he would be here and not tell her. If Beneto had known Nicolò was in town, much less in the same building, he would have shunted the bulk of his discussion with the Priora. He must have come to hear the music at Mass. Perhaps he's stewing over the failed proposal. Perhaps his visit was unplanned and he has somewhere else pressing to be— though if he was in a hurry he wouldn't be so lackadaisical, drifting across the bridge and down the promenade, jostled by the crowds and apparently unbothered. His presence is strange, and it irks her. But the laundry is gone and the hall is clear and she has only three months before they send her to a nunnery, and she loses Luisa forever.

The gondolier waits at the water gate. He welcomes her into the boat as he has always done, a steadying hand as she finds her footing. They row out in silence past crowds still thinned by summer's heat, fishermen skeining their nets, boys setting paper-wrapped entrails down for dogs, whores plying their trade, a medico carrying a sheaf of paper, a guild musician hauling a double bass. When they are out in the lagoon, Maddalena leans out from under the felze for the gondolier's attention. He nods, and she sits against the prow so she can see him while he rows, gripping the sides of the boat for balance, feeling her delinquency as a fizz in the back of her chest.

"I was wondering," she says, loud so he can hear her from where he stands, paddling. *I was wondering*. It's an empty phrase, a way to tread water.

"Yes?"

"How to know what to give." Maddalena understands she isn't eloquent, but she imagines he'll know what she means. "Does it take promises? A firstborn child, or something similar? Something traditional?"

"How much would that mean to you?" The gondolier swerves them around a shoal, and Maddalena jolts forward.

"A child?" She laughs. She's never seriously thought about having her own child, but surely a child is meaningful. What could be more meaningful than the fruit of the body? Women die birthing their children; surely the risk is the gift.

"A prospective child. A child that might never be, so really what you're offering is your motherhood."

"Motherhood means nothing," says Maddalena. Nursemaids offered the most childhood affection, and she was twelve when her mother disappeared. A lamb—a poor, lost child. If her mother could leave her, leave her brothers, knowing what was said about that Austrian soldier, knowing how harsh Venetian society would be to those who disobeyed its rules, then what was motherhood, really? Luisa's mother left her at the Pietà, as did Adriana's, Chiara's, Orsetta's. Motherhood seems like a tenuous bond, at best.

"Well, you could offer," says the gondolier.

They reach the shrine. The wood looks shabbier than Maddalena remembers it, salt bleached and splintering. The metal chains holding the poles together flake with age and wear, and the flowers draped across the little pediment are dead, the crusty, crumbling brown of an insect's shell.

Maddalena turns. "Is this the right place?"

"Would you like me to take you farther?"

"Not if it doesn't matter."

She's nervous, but that won't change. He could sail her across the Adriatic, and she still wouldn't feel ready. "There isn't a way you can give me some privacy?" The gondolier nods and turns his back. Maddalena tries to remember the feeling of Ascension Day, the way the mist rode the water, the way her desperation tightened her chest until she thought she might break. She leans over, trailing two fingers in the water of the lagoon. It's brackish. She can feel her own desiccation, imagines her flesh sucked away by salt and chewed by fish until only bones remain.

"I need—" she whispers. There has always been a thing to give, a coin to drop and wish on. She has a little cloth in her pocket, the one she used to wipe the timpani clean. She has her cap, her slippers. "In a week or so I can bring you jewels. A necklace." But Maddalena suspects they'd mean only as much to the creature in the water as they mean to Maddalena herself, and though she appreciates luxury, it isn't essential. She can't bring herself to offer a speculative child. "What do I have that you want?" She's barely speaking the words, afraid the gondolier will hear and interfere, worse yet, make fun.

The answer comes immediately, revolting in its simplicity. First the crown of the head, rising as if the body stands on an erupting pedestal. A garland of red-orange flowers braided into white-gold hair. Water streams down the face, which is frozen in an expression of awe: wide eyes with clumped wet lashes, snub nose, sweet pursed mouth. Luisa as a doll, Luisa as a vision. She raises her arm, cutting smoothly through the pressure of the water, until she has raised her violin and is exactly who she was when Maddalena first saw her at Lido.

Maddalena is young enough to feel ownership over the object of her love. She takes the sea's request as literal. Having previously given up physical objects, she can see no way forward but a tangible sacrifice. She imagines an ocean of girls with blank faces, sawing away at their strings for an audience of mollusks. The orchestra will have built up over the centuries, ranks swelling with new members. She will not add Luisa to it.

Everything Maddalena has done is for Luisa. She'll forever be in search of the feeling Luisa gives her—that sense of possibility, as if life is showing her the cracks where light seeps through, and if she pries it open wide enough, she'll one day be engulfed by the sun. Even in the beginning, when Maddalena offered herself in exchange for what the water could give her, it was seeing what she now knows as Luisa that stirred her.

There must be another way forward, one that doesn't mean losing Luisa. Maddalena wants Luisa in such a way that no one else can have her. She wants to be the only one she speaks to, the one to whom she bares her soul. When Luisa is ill, Maddalena will tend to her; when Luisa is hungry, Maddalena will help her eat. There isn't room for any sort of giving up, any shared custody. If the thing in the water will offer its help only in exchange for Luisa, Maddalena will make other plans. She shifts away from the side of the boat.

"Let's go," she says brusquely to the gondolier. In silence, he returns her to the Pietà for the last time. The fishermen have cast their nets for mussels. The gondoliers-for-hire whistle for customers. The sun begins to sink against San Giorgio Maggiore, sky blinding.

When she steps out of the gondola, already searching the canal for a new savior—might it be the bespectacled gentleman on the bridge? The caped man, that one there in the ridiculous hat?—she looks down for a moment to get her bearings. By the time she turns back to the water, her gondolier is gone. She doesn't take this to mean that he and his patron have finished with her, now that her life moves back to the palazzo. She knows she has a debt still owed.

Within the week, Maddalena goes home. Her real home, the palace in which she was raised. Palazzo Grimani is like a wrapped present with its gaping mascarons, its pillars and its balconies, its studies and vast stairwells and ballroom, its painted library and her own cano-pied bed. She doesn't return to the Pietà for private music lessons; she doesn't have the inclination or the time. But after a week away—a week in which she writes Luisa daily, sometimes multiple times a day, with instructions on how to ready her trousseau, what to expect from her betrothed, what she should call his sister and how she should greet his aunt—she goes to Sunday vespers for Luisa's final performance.

It's surreal to enter through the main doors of the church and slide with Nicolò into a back pew. The Pietà girls haven't arrived, but atten-dants are shooing visitors to their seats, more concert ushers than altar boys. Maddalena looks up at the balcony, only a few flickering candles behind its dark grate. Luisa should have a true stage as her last. All of Venice should see the way she races her fingers down the violin's neck, the way her teeth clench at a particularly tricky set of measures, the way her head shakes almost imperceptibly with every vibrato. Or maybe they shouldn't—perhaps it's for the best that she stays hidden, just a glimpse of her white dress, her pomegranate flowers, the dark wood of the violin patterned in the shadow of the grate. To hear Luisa play is tantamount to confession, the way the feelings you'd thought safely suppressed begin to shake the hinges of their locked chests, the way you spill out of yourself. Grown men have cried. Maffeo Celsi proposed. Better to hide her now, have her remain Maddalena's.

Here she comes.

It is the full orchestra, really, entering the choir lofts, the singers settling by the organ and the instrumentalists filling the side balconies. The violinists sit near the nave, and Luisa sits in the first chair, her gleaming hair announcing her location. All through the preces Maddalena watches her, stumbling through the Our Father, biting back a smile as she hears Nicolò bungle it as well. Then the oratorio, for which Luisa comes forward. She's incandescent. Even Nicolò clenches his hand against the pew when she begins.

The crowd knows Luisa's leaving. Venice is a small town, and word has spread. The rarity makes what is already magic into something sacred. They lean toward her, drinking each note. When the full orchestra comes in, the congregation seems to wake, only to fall immediately into an enchanted dream when Luisa solos. Sweet, as Maddalena hears it. Honey dripping from the violin. Her warm, wet depths unfolded, tenderly.

And then it is finished, and the priest gives the benediction. The Coro files out—no applause, no final bows. The loft again empty of all but a few flickering candles.

Luisa

Soon, Luisa is married. This shouldn't come as a surprise; she did accept the marriage proposal, she did sleep alone in a room above the dormitory once the marriage contract was confirmed, she did take gifts of lace from the other girls and a respectable dowry from the Pietà, she did write to Maddalena for advice. And yet the wedding and the vows feel as if they are happening to someone else. She imagines herself underwater, looking up at a different version of Luisa who takes the host and kneels before the priest, who leaves the church on the arm of her new husband and sits at a table with his family and select guests and bows her head modestly as they toast her health and good fortune.

The feast is like nothing Luisa has seen. Sixteen courses, footmen at every shoulder, a quartet—not Ospedale quality, but still rather impressive—to play through dinner, and then a full ensemble in the ballroom. Luisa watches a woman with a towering hive of a hairdo and a smeared black beauty spot spit a half-chewed sea urchin back onto her plate, watches a man whose wig is so powdered he leaves a slight film on anyone who stands in his vicinity spill two glasses of wine within ten minutes. Maffeo's aunt chews with her mouth open, and no one says anything because she's in her late fifties and mostly responsible for the family's rise.

"We bought our way into the nobility three years ago," Maffeo's cousin Cattina admits immediately. "We have since bought our way into the hearts of several prominent families." Cattina, who drips with jewels, takes Luisa's arm and leads her over to a curvature in the ballroom, from which they can survey the crowd. "That's a Contarini over there, and Andrea Memmo. Even the Dandolos have come. It's an honor, especially given your background. When the Great Council opened up the offer of nobility to merchants who could pay, only the Celsis and a few others were sufficiently stupid and snobbish to give coin. But they've been warm enough. They like our food."

"The food is good," says Luisa, who's had very little of it. Her nerves won't let her take more than the slightest taste, which is likely for the best, as it's all cream and waxy meats and glistening cuts of fish that would sit heavy in her stomach after the simplicity of meals at the Pietà. She wonders where the unfinished food goes—not a single guest completes each course, not even Pietro Morosini, who hovers over the rest like a giant, though Luisa does watch Cattina down at least ten prawns in very quick succession. She pulls Luisa down to meet the stream of well-wishers who want to kiss her hand and invite her to their salons and fawn over her final performance as first violinist.

"What is it like to be adored?" asks a woman with a pointed nose and a diamond ring the size of Luisa's front tooth.

Luisa looks to Cattina, unsure how to answer. For the millionth time that day she wishes Maddalena was invited to the banquet—either more awkwardness remains between the Celsis and Grimanis than Luisa realized, or else her friend's fate as socially undesirable has already been sealed.

"The mother ran off with an Austrian soldier," Cattina said when Luisa asked after the family, by far the bluntest assessment of Maddalena's history that she has heard. "And there was some scandal years ago that led to talk the youngest aren't true Grimanis, if you see what I mean."

Cattina is useful for gossip. She knows which of the guests appreciate their wives, and which would rather hear compliments directed toward their mistresses. She knows whose Stradivari is in hock and who has bolstered their fortune at the Ridotto; who goes to church to pray and who solicits at the nunneries. As guides to society go, Luisa could ask for no better. But when the dancing dies down and Maffeo comes to take his wife out to the gondola that will carry them to her new home, Cattina is useless. She pats Luisa's bottom with a cheeky and, given how long they've been acquainted, entirely inappropriate smirk, and takes her leave of the newlyweds.

"Well," Maffeo says, blushing.

"Well," Luisa repeats.

They go to the Celsi house, not a palazzo by name but certainly palatial in practice, and retire to their separate sets of rooms. Luisa sits at the edge of her new bed, wondering if Maffeo will come and be her husband. She has decided that if he does come, she will think of Nicolò, how pure he is, how perfect—she'll envision him glowing, that afternoon by the Brenta. If Maddalena were here, she could ask what to expect. Will it hurt? Will it be quick?

Maddalena, of course, is not here. But Maffeo has also not appeared. Luisa sits and she waits and she anticipates, and finally, when the last candle has tapered down, she climbs between the silk sheets and lies supine and alone, staring up at the unfamiliar brocade canopy.

Carnival season, in which the city goes masked, begins in October. The city squares fill with carpenters constructing booths and stages, and Venice pulses with pleasure. Carnival itself is the pinnacle, but the days leading up to it are equally titillating. Luisa watches from the window of her bedchamber, the breakfast room, the Celsi balcony, as preparations commence. Boatmen rush bolts of cloth from skiff to water gate, seamstresses tripping behind. Arrangements of fresh flowers appear in the campi, to be replaced by different arrangements after several clever rodents make a meal. Luisa wonders if Maffeo is waiting to consummate the marriage until the festivities begin in earnest. She wonders if Nicolò will come to her in a full black cloak and bauta, how she'll feel when she finally sees him among the crowds. The first year of marriage for a Venetian noblewoman is a sober one—a black dress and a pearl necklace instead of the usual silks and jewels in private ballrooms, prudent behavior at the Ridotto, a modest cicisbeo, if any. This won't be difficult for Luisa, who already feels gluttonous. She doesn't pray before bed, or upon waking. She eats pastry for breakfast.

Maffeo spends most of his time at work for his uncle, or petitioning for the library he wants to build out on Giudecca. She sees him twice in the first week of their marriage, and both times he's awkward, stumbling over his words, unsure how or if he should touch her. When Cattina asks about their wedding night, Luisa mumbles vague assurances and blushes, which she hopes will be taken as proof.

"Do you mind where I go?" she asks Maffeo when she sees him again at dinner. They are dining in the piano nobile with the rest of the family, seated next to each other so they have some room for private conversation.

"Where you go?" The tips of Maffeo's ears are prone to reddening, which somehow clashes with the red of his hair.

"Can I go out to visit friends, I mean?" Luisa whispers so that the other Celsis don't hear and involve themselves. They're a rambunctious clan, prone to knowing one another's business, especially Cattina, who lives across the Grand Canal but dines most nights at the main residence.

"Of course!" Maffeo laughs with relief, placing a gentle hand over her own. "You're free from all that now." He must mean the Ospedale. He likes to think of himself as her savior; perhaps this is why they remain chaste. "Take the gondola, go wherever you like. Within reason."

"Within reason," Luisa agrees. She writes to Maddalena that night, and by morning has a response, and by midafternoon is instructing a gondolier in Celsi livery to take her to Palazzo Grimani.

It's the first night of Carnival, or will be, when the sun sets, and though it's not yet three o'clock, already revelers are crowding into the Piazzetta, flooding the campi, shaking out tapestries and flags to hang from balconies. Fortune-tellers' booths are draped with canvas and lined with lanterns; wires have been strung across the square for acrobats and tumblers. A group of serious men sand boards that will be used to support human pyramids, hefted on shoulders as platforms for rival clans competing for dexterity and height. Some large, putrid animal growls from within its wooden cage, unhappy to be taken from its menagerie and brought to Campo Santa Maria Formosa. A little boy scatters straw where presumably the beast will soon emerge.

At Palazzo Grimani, a motley crew of servants are tying together a group of boats, ribbing one another, making as if they're going to push a gangly boy into the canal, then jumping aside at the last minute. One of them moves to help Luisa off the gondola with a pert little bow, walking her through the archway and into a large courtyard made up of rosy brick and Corinthian columns. A white stone staircase runs down the side of one wall, and from that stair comes Maddalena.

When she hugs Luisa, Maddalena's grip seems stronger than it was at the Pietà. She beams as she threads her fingers through Luisa's and pulls her past the carved white fountain—a woman wearing a crown of stars, seated next to two small lions—and through one of the lower doors. From outside, the palazzo looks narrow, but as Luisa moves through, she sees its depth. Every surface is carved or painted, often both. Chandeliers hang like intricate icicles; mirrors span entire walls. Furniture is made of gold or velvet, and the ceilings are all frescoed. Maddalena brings them into a room painted robin's-egg blue, with wide windows looking out on the canal and plaster vines crawling the molding. A pianoforte at one side of the room holds court to a carved urn and several sofas. Maddalena sits on a settee strewn with gold-tasseled pillows and motions Luisa to join her.

"What is marriage like?" Maddalena leans in so Luisa can feel her breath, which is sweet with the hot chocolate that's laid out for them. Luisa nestles next to Maddalena, considering her answer. Maddalena waits, running a finger across the lace cuff of Luisa's sleeve.

A voice rises outside their window, followed by jeers and laughter. Maddalena doesn't stir. Luisa turns so they are facing each other on the settee. "He hasn't…" She licks her lips. "…*come* to me." The last she says in a whisper. She can tell Maddalena is trying not to laugh, eyes registering both her surprise and her good humor.

"He's an idiot." Maddalena squeezes Luisa's hand.

"I'm not unhappy about it… at least, not yet." Again, Luisa blushes.

She's certainly not going to tell Maddalena about her nightly ritual—picturing Nicolò across the city, or wherever he may be, preparing herself to impose him on Maffeo, if Maffeo does come. It's profane no matter how she explains it to herself, an actual lover or a dream one, a man in her bed.

"Nobody came the night after the wedding for the sheet with the blood?"

Luisa shakes her head.

"Of course they didn't." Maddalena says this mostly to herself, and Luisa senses she's remembering something, likely a conversation about propriety, perhaps about her mother. "Well." Maddalena leans over for a cup of chocolate each, clinks hers with Luisa's. "To marriage, then. May it remain nonintrusive." The drink has cooled, and is overly rich.

"Any progress with yours?"

"There will be." Maddalena winks. Luisa assumes that Maddalena means this to impart confidence, but instead she feels her stomach sink. "Speaking of." Maddalena stands. "I've a dress fitting for tonight's celebrations. The dressmaker should be quick, just a few pins, she says—she's already here with my aunt—but it must be within the hour, before she goes. Do you want to come with me?"

Luisa has sat through enough fittings these past weeks. Besides, as a new wife she won't be going to this ball; her social circle will be small for this first year of marriage. What she wants is to play the pianoforte. She has Nicolò's violin at the Celsis, but she's been afraid of how it will sound in their grand rooms filled with ornaments and filigreed new wealth, afraid of how she will feel when she plays it. She misses the violin. Of all the things she's left behind—Maddalena, the liturgy, Vivaldi, and the rows of red-dressed girls—it is the violin she thinks of most. Playing piano feels like a compromise, a middle ground, a way that she might ease back into music.

Maddalena sees her looking. "Stay and play." She smiles. "I'll be back soon."

Luisa walks toward the instrument, one she knows, but not well. The keybed is black, and it stands on spindly legs, painted gold around the edges with a geometric design. The underside of the lid has been painted the red of Venice, with a stand shaped like a golden heart to hold sheet music just above the keys. Luisa taps out a quick melody. She's had a little training on the harpsichord, but nothing so ornate, or capable of such dynamics. Luckily, the piano lets her play very quietly, and she eases into her own imagined rhythms with the idea that no one in the household knows she's here.

"You can play louder. The walls are thick. They're making too much of a ruckus out on the canal for anyone to hear you." Nicolò steps into the room, and at first Luisa thinks she'll die of embarrassment, but as he comes closer, it's all she can do not to leap from the bench into his arms. He is smiling again, and so she smiles, and now they are two smiling fools at the center of a city on the brink of celebration, a small quiet place in a world soon to explode. This is his family's house, a portrait of his great-grand-somebody, a doge, on the wall, and Nicolò could lock the doors and have his way with her.

"I'm here," she says.

Nicolò joins her at the piano—he takes up the melody, Luisa the bass. Every so often he jumps down an octave and their hands brush. Still very soft, still very gentle. Nicolò is gentle where Maffeo is fumbling, and when Nicolò turns suddenly and kisses her—the curtains pulled open, all of Venice out on the water and no one looking in—it is, at first, like roses. Like being kissed by blooms, until she, too, is blooming. He's clean-shaven and he smells like charred wood and something sour but still quite pleasant, something entirely his own. His hands on her cheeks. His tongue.

She pulls back, finally, not because she wants to pull back but because she is afraid of Maddalena. "I'll be back soon" might mean an hour, or ten minutes. She can't have Maddalena walking in on them together like this, after already stealing the Celsis, writing letter after letter about how she doesn't love Maffeo, how she doesn't know what it feels like to be in love with a man. After lying.

She does plan to tell Maddalena the truth, eventually. Soon! Soon she'll have some system by which to see Nicolò, and once they're settled and she knows it is worth mentioning—not a quickly spent passion, not a lark—she can include Maddalena. Who wants to hear that their closest friend has married their expected fiancé and now moves in to take another of their men? It's too much. It's too soon. Luisa's too much of a coward.

"I'm sorry," Nicolò says at once. "Did you not—"

"I just want to be careful." Luisa puts a hand on his wrist. "Somewhere more private..." She blushes, but he doesn't. "If we could plan..."

The smile again; across his face, such joy. She wants to cry with her good fortune. They have so many days. Now that she's free of the Pietà, they have the world.

"Tonight?" Nicolò asks. It can't be tonight. If—when—Luisa breaks her sworn sobriety, it can't be at the start of Carnival, when the city releases the breath it's been holding since May in a great gust of impropriety. Tonight will be debaucherous and lewd to an extent they will not see until Advent, when Carnival pauses for Christmas and its citizens once again purge themselves in a great excess that will leave them spent and open to the Holy Spirit, a city of pronounced ascetics with their sanctimony and their plans to carouse yet again at Epiphany. The Pietà girls watch this cycle through their slitted windows, listen to the nightly rabble from their cots.

It isn't just propriety that makes Luisa fear what the city will become tonight, after she's returned to the Celsi house and is safely on her balcony, listening to the barcaroles shouted drunkenly across the canals. Even if she weren't the new wife of a new nobleman, with all the expectations that go with that, Luisa would ensconce herself at home. Carnival is frightening. A person is capable of anything when they can hide behind anonymity. The streets become not people interacting with other people but a swarm of egocentrics, each choosing only for themself. Supposedly the masks promote equality, but to Luisa all this means is that everyone can be equally rude, equally ruthless.

So she will not see Nicolò tonight. Next month, perhaps; in a few weeks. Luisa spares not a thought for Maffeo. Maffeo will go out tonight among the rousing throng; he'll watch the fireworks from the square, maybe sate himself with a courtesan. To Luisa's mind, this is the best scenario: Maffeo kind and comforting and finding comfort elsewhere. She does consider her vows—what she's sworn before God and what it means to disappoint Him—but only briefly. She's distracted by the flutter of her heart, the way her hands tingle, how Nicolò is looking at her, how she wishes he would look at her forever.

"I'll write to you," Luisa says to Nicolò. "By way of someone we can trust. One of your servants? There must be someone." Her hand travels his wrist, fingers sliding along the veins, down to his palm. His thigh brushes hers at the piano bench. He nods. "Imagine," she whispers, "I can write to you at breakfast and by noon you can respond." It's beyond what she ever imagined at the Pietà, exactly what she'd hoped for when accepting Maffeo's proposal.

Nicolò closes his fist over her fingers, brings her hand to his heart.

"We'll find a room," he says. "We'll make a plan." He is about to move the hand to his lips when they hear a rattling sound, someone coming through the anteroom. They jump apart, Nicolò at the high keys and Luisa at the low, almost falling off the bench in her effort to increase the space between them. She's afraid it will be Maddalena, but it's only a girl coming to refresh the chocolate tray. Luisa and Nicolò watch in silence as the used cups are gathered, a plate of nuts and cheese set down.

Luisa recognizes her anxiety as what it is—guilt. There is enough to keep in mind with Nicolò: Maffeo's anger, the Grimani family's scorn, a spurning from society, which has miraculously welcomed her, an unnamed orphan with a bourgeois husband and nothing to recommend her now that she cannot play her violin publicly. There's no reason to add fear of a friend. She'll tell Maddalena about Nicolò as soon as it makes sense, as soon as they're alone together. Probably. Most likely.

"Should you go before your sister returns?" Luisa can't help but ask. It hurts to sit so close and still so far from him, to want to put her fingers in his hair and to hold back. If he's here when Maddalena returns, surely she'll see the way Luisa's body turns itself inside out, the way her voice cracks with desire. Nicolò agrees, but he is slow to go, just sitting there at the piano, looking at her. Finally, he tears himself away. He's going out for Carnival, to the ball that Maddalena's being dressed for. He, too, should dress. He'll write to her.

Luisa downs a glass of wine from a crystal carafe. She plinks out a tune on the piano. Outside, the canal is crowded with traders running last-minute wares, mask makers and tailors and those attempting to get home before the revelry begins. It's strange not to be bound by attendance at chapel. What should she do with her time, now that she has it?

Maddalena returns, her hair loose and her expression foul.

"You don't like the dress?" Luisa asks. Maddalena scowls. "You could wear something else?"

Maddalena stands behind Luisa at the piano, makes three clanging minor chords. She grips Luisa's shoulders, her bony hands surprisingly spry, clawing into the flesh under the new black silk dress. It hurts. Maddalena is hurting her. Then the grip eases and Maddalena is massaging, moving toward Luisa's neck in such a way that Luisa can't help but relax into the rub of fingers against tightly wound flesh. She leans back so that her head rests against Maddalena's stomach, the ends of Maddalena's hair brushing her cheek.

"The dress will be fine." Maddalena takes deep, calming breaths that Luisa can feel through her body. Calm begets calm, the tension ebbs.

"You'll be beautiful," says Luisa, and the words are trite even as she speaks them. Maddalena says nothing, just continues the dull pressure. Tell her, thinks Luisa. Get it over with. Instead she says, "I mean, any man would be foolish not to fall to pieces over you in a ball gown." What is she saying? What is coming from her mouth? Maddalena doesn't falter, but she also doesn't laugh the way she might have laughed, back in the dormitory bed when Luisa said something silly. Out on the canal, another shout. It's getting late. If Luisa is to be home by evening meal, she should go. "Enjoy tonight," she says to Maddalena. She stands, straightens her skirts, and kisses her friend's cheek. "If you can."

"I will," says Maddalena, with a grim sort of smile.

Maddalena

Palazzo Grimani. In the future it will be a museum, and tourists will flock to see its carved fireplaces and frescoed ceilings, its collections of antiquities and unparalleled art. Absurd, that this belongs to one family. Absurd, that the family is hers. Such a house doesn't suit Maddalena—she'd prefer something more vibrant, more personal, the sort of trinkets and keepsakes that make a house a home. As is, it's ostentatious yet tasteful, if having money for quality versions of what's gaudy when done cheaply defines taste. Maddalena does enjoy the courtyard. She's missed the garden on the roof.

Her brothers all still live here, and her father. Growing up, she could usually find him in the sala d'oro or reading in the library, but these days he deliberately avoids her, heavy footsteps preceding her entrance into rooms with half-drunk coffee and hastily piled papers. This, more than anything, feels like her condemnation. If he could say, *I do believe I'm not your father*—with that expression of genuine surprise that comes so naturally to his overly round face, the pleasant crinkle to his bright-blue eyes—they could dispense with the pretense that he's too busy to properly greet her. But if he could say, *I'm not your father*, her whole childhood would be different. Because what has truly changed, other than the spotlight of public opinion? Society saw the Grimanis try to woo the Celsis, and society saw them fail.

"Is he like this with you?" she asks Beneto after a blustery encounter with Marcantonio in the main hall that ends with some excuse about the Palazzo Ducale. "So obviously ashamed of you?"

"He's ashamed of himself," Beneto says, plucking a grape from the sideboard.

"For being a cuckold?"

"I don't think that's it."

Beneto is still sent on family errands; he's still polished and presented to society as if his parentage is assured. Maddalena supposes she is, too—having demonstrated modesty and deference as a ward of the Pietà, she's now allowed out of the house under proper supervision. She goes to the modistes, where she is given new dresses, gets a dedicated hairdresser, as if the perfect teased coif will mean the difference between failure and success. She misses Luisa. For the first time in months she goes to bed without the prospect of another body joining her. She takes her meals without the furtive whispering that undercuts the constant drone of the Priora's lectures. She has no mandated prayer.

Daily, hourly, almost by the minute, Maddalena considers what she can give to the water in exchange for a husband. Surrounded by luxury, she realizes how little she actually values. She could cut her hair, she could pry off a fingernail, but short of gouging out her eyes, she doesn't think that a gift of her physical self would do. All Maddalena has that matters are Luisa's letters, which now come in a steady stream from Ca'Celsi. Maddalena keeps even the most innocuous tied with ribbon in a trick compartment at the back of the writing desk in her apartment. They smell like nothing, like paper and ink. Before she sends her own responses, Maddalena presses the envelopes to her lips.

Her aunt—her father's sister—is in residence. Aunt Antonia is a wealthy widow, with one grown son and three grown daughters all scattered across the Veneto in either convents or profitable marriages, and now she's here to instruct Maddalena into a marriage of her own. She's simple enough to avoid. She isn't an especially large woman, but she moves with the affected air of one who must haul her flesh through passages, out of chairs, into gondolas. This to say she often sits, and is easily escaped with a simple quickening of Maddalena's pace. Aunt Antonia will be Maddalena's chaperone tonight at the Contarini ball that marks the start of Carnival, and given her disposition it will be fairly easy for

Maddalena to become unchaperoned, whether to slip out with Andrea to see the acrobats at the Piazza San Marco, to make eyes at a potential suitor, or to find her gondolier.

First, Luisa will visit. At breakfast comes the news that Luisa has finally found the gumption to leave her new house. Maddalena knows it's unkind to view things thus. Luisa's reticence and slowness—exactly the opposite of Aunt Antonia's: cautious, not lazy—is a part of what makes her so wonderful. Maddalena watches the canal for the Celsi colors as she paces the music room—of course the place to bring Luisa, with the new pianoforte from Florence and the warm blue walls, the wide view of the water. She orders a tray of snacks and the hot chocolate that Luisa loved at Mira, and she paces until she sees the blue and gold of the Celsi gondolier, rounding a curve in the canal and approaching the house.

She races through the hallway, takes the stairs down to the courtyard two, then three at a time. There is Luisa. Framed by the stone archway, the sunlight at her back so her hair positively glows. She's dressed in the chic and simple black of the nobility, Celsi's wealth flaunted with flourishes of black embroidered flowers and black lace—but underneath she's the girl from the Pietà, the vision Maddalena saw at Lido with her fine bright hair and her serious eyes and the smile that churns Maddalena until her innards are cream.

Maddalena can't help but touch her, initiating a hug meant to fuse their two bodies, holding on longer than propriety allows. She strokes Luisa's wrist, interweaves their two sets of fingers. Luisa stumbles happily after her, and when they reach the music room she pivots to take it all in, just as Maddalena had imagined. The piano. The refreshments. The tapestries on the walls and floors, the paintings. The curtains are pulled wide to show La Serenissima preparing for her festival, the maids in the house across the canal shaking their linens and the boys below tying boats together to make a barge of private felzes for her brothers and their guests. From the piano they can see the campo, crowded with expectation. A glass vase of white lilies. A complicated urn.

It's strange to share something that both does and drastically doesn't belong to her, this house that might be fully hers if only her mother had practiced discretion. But Luisa seems awed, and Maddalena brings them to the settee by the chocolate tray with a sense of having performed well by her friend. She sees herself as a capable provider. She's surprised by how important it suddenly seems that she should be able to take care of Luisa, how much joy she now receives from giving joy.

"What is marriage like?" Maddalena sits close, only half resisting the urge to nuzzle Luisa's skin. She isn't really worried about the answer— there's no way that Luisa is as happy with Celsi as she is here in this room with Maddalena, as they were together in their little dormitory cot, as they will be once the boundaries of their new life in Venice are established and Maddalena has placated the water. Still, it's lovely to hear that marriage is nothing, that Maffeo keeps his wife intact, that he is proving himself to be the idiot Maddalena suspected.

From across the canal, the muffled bells of Chiesa di San Lorenzo pronounce the hour. The tailor has come to pin and snip in preparation for tonight. Of course Maddalena wants Luisa to join her, and of course she encourages Luisa to stay and play the new piano. When else will she have the opportunity? There's sheet music on the bookshelf, and wine in the carafe. Maddalena will only be gone a few minutes.

She makes sure it is only a few minutes, standing so still and silent that the seamstress can't help but work quickly. In the mirror she watches herself become a mèlange of brocade and embroidery, her skirt wine red, her hips pronounced with a hoop, little seed pearls running up and down her bodice. The Venetian style is simpler than the French—this, Aunt Antonia bemoans as she observes Maddalena, who feels extravagant enough without poufing her hair and painting her face and putting on platform shoes so high that she can hardly walk in, let alone dance. She agrees that they are finished at the seamstress's first suggestion, and almost rips the dress taking it off.

Luisa is here, and likely playing the piano. Maddalena's close to skipping. She feels ten years old, in love with anything beautiful. For a moment she considers tamping herself down, putting on the mask and corset and showing a more calculated face. But it's Luisa. Luisa knows her. If Maddalena can't be authentic in her greed and her pleasure, if she can't come to Luisa with her body burst open and her tender flesh bared, when will she ever? She's going to let herself cry with the relief of being known. She's going to take Luisa in her arms and find a way to keep her.

Strange, not to hear the piano. The walls are thick, but by the time Maddalena reaches the third-floor hall, she should hear something. The little clicking sounds the keys make, the rippling bass notes, the brightness that reminds Maddalena of metal. What is Luisa doing, she wonders? And then she knows.

At the piano bench, turned toward one another, sit Luisa and Nicolò. He moves his hand from the keys to her cheek. He leans forward.

At first Maddalena means to burst into the room and throw her brother off Luisa. She's mortified by his behavior—Nicolò has always gone for what he wants, but she never imagined he would force himself on a girl, what, ten years younger, with no experience and no one to defend her honor. Except that isn't entirely true, because Luisa has Maffeo Celsi to defend her honor. It is suddenly unclear if Luisa's honor needs defending. The way she looks at Nicolò—like she has never seen a man before, like he is more than tired eyes and undone shirt cuffs and unpowdered hair. Like he is more than Maddalena's meddling older brother. Nicolò leans in, and Luisa leans with him. When their lips touch, Maddalena recoils.

She can feel herself beginning to cry, and she pats at her cheeks to try to stop the tears. She'd rather vomit onto the boys at the water gate, still fiddling with the boats for this evening. She'd rather scream until her father comes running from wherever he's hidden himself, finally forced to reckon with the girl he has raised as a daughter. Instead she stands here, in the doorway.

There's a sound behind her, the serving maid coming to refresh the tray of drinks. Her feet on the stairs push Maddalena to action, and she slips into the library across the hall, buries herself in a large armchair facing the unlit fire. She isn't sure that she won't be sick, and she gags over a book of poetry that someone has left out on the ottoman. She wants to be sick, to remove the knowledge from her body, to make herself clean.

Luisa and Nicolò. Of course. It's all so obvious, now that she has the pieces. She's an idiot. Her heart—oh, the absurd cliché, the brutal baseness of even thinking it in jest, this empty aphorism that at its core means nothing because it has meant everything to too many people— Maddalena's heart is broken. Her idea of herself is collapsing, the farthest stone of a bridge crumbling with rot that moves through its foundation, until the keystone falls, and with it anyone who stood atop and waved out at the water.

The water. The letters. Luisa.

Oh God, Luisa, laughing with Nicolò at Maddalena's ignorance. Luisa cringing at her touch, Luisa putting up with things because she hadn't known there was another way to live. Luisa pretending affection: a calculated tilt of the head, a stroke of the wrist. And could she still be pretending? Could Nicolò have pressured her until she had no choice? She is susceptible, Luisa. She is—Maddalena has always known it— weak.

She wipes her eyes. She pinches her cheeks for color. Pats her skirts and leaves the library. By the time she crosses the hall and walks into the music room, Maddalena has convinced herself Luisa won't see anything amiss. She smiles with her teeth, expecting Nicolò, but Luisa sits alone at the piano, making a lazy, lovesick tune.

The anger that rises in Maddalena is unexpected, and unmanageable. It comes from her chest—strange how they say the heart is for love, it can break and it can mourn and it can hunger, but it can also blaze and send the pulse of anger through the body. Maddalena's hands are small, but strong. She takes them to Luisa's neck. She imagines herself pressing until Luisa pops like a currant, until she is nothing but a pulpy mess of what Maddalena once imagined she wanted. Until she's spent. Until she's ruined.

"You don't like the dress?" Stupid Luisa. Simple and cruel.

How is it possible to share so much and see it all so differently? All the time Maddalena was holding her, all the plans they were making, meant nothing. Maddalena never imagined that Luisa told her everything. Maddalena herself kept secrets. But they weren't secrets about

Luisa; they didn't fundamentally change the way things were between the two of them. She'd never pretended her devotion.

Luisa leaves without a mention of Nicolò or what she's done with him, and Maddalena says nothing of what she has seen. Everything seems to be happening in slow motion; just walking back up the stairs after seeing Luisa off feels like wading through mud. She supposes she'll get dressed for the Contarini ball. It's early, but her lady's maids don't comment on the hour. Aunt Antonia is having her hair done, demanding this unguent or other, so they're eager to have Maddalena settled, and no one notices or minds that when they finish, she slips down to the main floor and walks out onto the fondamenta. The sun inches down, the buildings wearing autumnal gold in honor of Carnival, the tension of the night soon to break but still building. Every corner, every campo, feels like an unresolved chord.

There's a moment during which Maddalena wonders if the gondolier will know her, here in her rust-colored gown, the colombina mask across her eyes painted black with swirls of gold. She wonders if she will know him, among the many gondoliers, already masked and assembled, ready to take their patricians to cavort in anonymity in the Piazza San Marco, or at one or several of the evening's masked balls. But she spots him immediately in his impeccable black gondola. In the midst of the revelers, the gondolier remains unmasked. He holds his hand out to her, and she moves down the fondamenta to where he is docked.

Into the boat. Away from the campo, from the palazzo and her brothers and her aunt. Surely they will miss her, and surely the water will help them to forgive her absence, which will be lengthy. She has asked the gondolier to take her to Lido. They move through the Grand Canal and out into the lagoon, the sounds of Carnival funneled through the raised felze so Maddalena hears a snatch of laughter, the swooping jeer of a dare, the thin complaints of a small child being shooed indoors before the night takes hold.

Tonight, it has to be Lido. Maddalena wants the sea. She wants the foam against the rocks, she wants the depths. It's easier to imagine an escape into the impossible darkness of an endless drop, to see herself trawling the soft bottoms with those monstrous deep-sea creatures who only wash up on the beach when they're struck by disease. Fish with sharp teeth. Eels with flattened eyes on the tops of their heads, the gummy pink of an undercooked baby, all loose skin and brittle bones. The shrine in the lagoon has been useful, but Lido is where it began.

They reach the sea, the wind chopping the waves and churning the salt spray. The marriage of the sea is deliberately scheduled for spring, when the water is calm and the sky flawless blue. The sort of wedding young girls dream of, with soft bells and carefully planned flower arrangements. At least Maddalena still gets to wear the fancy dress.

She has Luisa's letters in her cloak, and before throwing them into the water Maddalena removes the special ribbon, the one Luisa wore at Mira—it had tied back her hair that day they picnicked across from the barchessa and the little goat came and rested its head in Luisa's lap, looking for food—and releases it to the wind. Off it goes, into a sky like bruised fruit. Maddalena takes the first letter and rips it in half cleanly down the fold, and when she lets the pieces go, they blow toward the beach.

Before they reach the shore, a shadowy hand comes up from the water—sure of itself, attached to an arm. A wrist, an elbow. It doesn't flail. It isn't drowning or in need. The hand waits, and when the time is right, it grabs the pieces of the note and pulls it under. So simply and easily and entirely, Maddalena's bond with Luisa—her understanding of her own place in the world—breaks.

She wants to scream. Why shouldn't she? She does scream—a chesty, snarling cry that grows stronger as she rips the other letters, crumpling them and releasing them into the sea in the hope that she can empty herself of Luisa.

"Take this as a promissory note," Maddalena says to the water. "You can have her. I'll give you all of her, and in return you will give me a husband."

The words are sour in her mouth, but not unpleasant. After all, this is inevitable. She has been thinking and thinking her way around this moment, the way she could avoid this acquiescence. Now the worst has happened, and she doesn't have to fear what it will be. The paper dissolves as it is eaten by the Adriatic. The bargain has been made. The gondolier whistles the same barcarole Maddalena sang at Mira, hitting every note with ease. He doesn't say anything, for which Maddalena is grateful, just turns them back toward the main island, moves them closer to the crowds.

Maddalena feels herself reassemble, layer after layer, until her pulp becomes papier-mâché. By the time they enter the Grand Canal, her eyes are dry. *What's done is done is done is done*, rows the gondolier's oar. Fire-eaters blaze their trade in the campi, acrobats fly across the water on their lines. The Palazzo Ducale is bedecked in paper lanterns, San Marco filled with flowers. Groups in their bautas and medico della peste and arlecchino costumes hurry along, knocking into others paused at stalls to finger pretty bits of glass, or looking on as charlatans defend their unctions, faces red with faux sincerity, voices rising. Fluttering skirts. Drunken laughter. Color everywhere, despite the dark and the late hour. Card tricks on corners, tonight no worry for the law. The world upturned, and all of Venice shaken and set down unexpectedly—the perfect night to disappear, to try one's luck. The Ridotto will swarm with gamblers, both men and women pressed together at the tables in hope of harnessing this first night's good fortune.

The gondolier takes Maddalena to Ca'd'Oro, where the Contarini ball drips with masked revelers and vibrates with music. It's an old palazzo, a massive Gothic punch bowl of eligible bachelors. A group of musicians adorns the courtyard, and the guests lean out from both the middle and upper balconies to hear. No one she recognizes, not from this distance, not in masks. She isn't worried. She steps off the gondola and takes the attendant's hand with the unshakable confidence of the arm in the water at Lido. Back straight, colombina tied, jeweled bodice refracting the light. By the time Maddalena walks through the gate, the first fireworks have begun.

Winter

Luisa

He has a friend who lets them use a room in his palazzo. On Tuesday and occasionally Friday afternoons, Luisa goes to Ca'Dandolo to "play cards and take the air with the young women of the family," which Cattina Celsi says is quite the coup. The Dandolos are an old Venetian family, and while their fortunes—like the fortunes of all other old Venetian families, barring perhaps the Contarinis—have ridden the waves, they are worth knowing. For a newer class of nobles like the Celsis, an invitation into the bosom of one of the twelve founding families is notable indeed, and proves Maffeo's good taste and better judgment.

Cattina says that being married in Venice is the only way to live as a woman—it allows exponentially more freedom than as a chick under a chaperone's wing, or in a nunnery. Luisa can go to the coffee shops and read the latest pamphlets, visit the Ridotto and put sequins down at the gaming tables, picnic on the isle of Sant'Erasmo. She is expected to dress modestly until she reaches her first anniversary, but she can buy any style of gown she can afford. She can take walks along the fondamenta, and visit with friends. She can say that she's off to the Dandolo library and instead meet Nicolò in a room with a large carved bed and a view of San Giorgio Maggiore across the water.

Luisa does preserve her modesty, at first. At first they simply talk, which makes her feel respectable, and useful. Nicolò has many people who will listen, but few who seem to actually hear his ideas about how Venice should function and what La Serenissima should be.

"As a city we've gotten lazy, and indulgent." He speaks with his hands, so every time she rests her palm atop his lower arm, he brings her along for the oration. "Look at what we once did, what we were known for. The lords of the Adriatic! A hub for trade! A republic that the rest of the world listened to and turned to for advice. A military power. Now, we welcome princes and ambassadors in style, but care little for actual policy. If we continue as we are, we'll just be known for hedging bets and spending money. And of course, fornication."

Of course, fornication. Luisa was deceiving herself to think that she would not succumb. They are in a room, alone. They are young, and they desire each other. Nicolò is inexperienced, but not entirely new to the passions they follow. For Luisa, it's an entirely different act than what she now does with Maffeo, who finally came to her one night after too much wine, and then again the next night to make up for his previous failure. With Maffeo it is blunt and quick, like bathing when the water won't warm but the next girl is waiting. A cursory evaluation of their bodies, often a sort of grunt as he releases, and then a moment when he turns his back and wipes himself before he is gone. Once he patted her on the head.

Luisa might mind the flatness of the consummation, if she didn't have Nicolò. Or else she would think that intercourse was simply an act of procreation, a duty akin to sitting with Maffeo when the Celsis host a banquet, to crossing herself when she prays. Like thinking food was merely the polenta that they served to the foundlings at the Pietà, when in fact there are oysters and truffles. In fact there is Nicolò, moving down to taste her, looking up to make sure this is what she wants, and grinning so wide when she nods that she can feel the joy moving up through her body, the crest of a wave. When he has finished he stays inside her and holds her to him. Sometimes his sweat pools in the valley of his chest and she wears it like perfume. Sometimes he says her name, and she can't believe that there was ever a time when she could see a life without him.

Even naked, with the sun glinting in through the Dandolo balcony and her hair splayed across the Dandolo sheets, Nicolò's talk turns to his future, which both does and does not include Luisa. First, he will be a junior commissioner, as is common for all young patricians moving into state service. He will work his way through various councils, eventually taking his father's place in the Senate. Venice frowns upon ambition, and Nicolò doesn't aspire to leadership for its own sake; he doesn't want to be the doge. He wants the power to sow the garden, to reinstitute the laws that might make innovation more desirable, to shake the noble families from their casinos like blossoms from a tree.

"It doesn't do to let pleasure rule," says Nicolò, even as he lies here with Luisa. She supposes he's right, because eventually they must dress and set their hair and return—separately, of course—to the library or the sitting room, where Giacomo Dandolo and his sister are waiting for them, excited to be involved in intrigue. Nicolò swears they can be trusted, and so far this has proven true. When Cattina Celsi saw Tonina Dandolo at some soiree or another and remarked upon the time she had spent with Cattina's new cousin, Tonina spun a story that convinced her.

Often, Luisa thinks of the girls at the Pietà and how they'd fit into Venetian high society. Orsetta and her mouth, Chiara's craftiness. She isn't sure if she misses them. She knows she misses the music, not just playing the violin but being part of an orchestra.

"What would happen if I played music in public?" Luisa asks Nicolò.

"The Celsi family would be fined." Nicolò takes his thumb to her nipple, which means he is not taking her seriously. Why would he, Luisa wonders, when she's posed the question such. "You'd be subject to censure. They wouldn't throw you in prison or cut off your hands—Venice is much more civilized now than we used to be."

"Yes." Luisa catches his fingers in hers. "You've implied that this is part of our larger dilemma."

Nicolò laughs. He's always warm, and he welcomes her teasing. He's aware of his own contradictions—the struggle to behave as he wishes his compatriots would behave. Maddalena always made Nicolò seem fastidious; she thinks him idealistic and demanding. But Luisa's Nicolò is compassionate. After all, he's here with her, loving her.

"I don't know," he says now, with the clear implication that he does

know, "if a concert would be worth it. You can always play at home. And
for me." He straddles her. In certain lights, he looks so young.

When Luisa does come to Palazzo Grimani to visit Maddalena, Nicolò
makes sure he's not at home. He's no good at hiding his emotions, and
what his face doesn't show, the rest of him will surely make obvious.
He'll go off on an errand or visit a friend, perhaps take a walk if the
weather allows. Even being in his apartments is too much temptation,
too much risk. Because despite her intentions, Luisa has yet to tell
Maddalena about Nicolò. She plans to begin gently, a mention of the
fact that she's been thinking of him, something about how she ran into
him at the Piazzetta and they spoke. Then she can gradually work her
way to mention of flirtation, and eventually, if Maddalena seems re-
ceptive, tell a version of the truth. In theory, it's a decent plan, as long
as she can balance all the lies. It does require beginning, which Luisa
has not.

Meanwhile, Maddalena's been at work seducing half the Venetian
population, and she is often tired and irritable, though she attempts to
hide her moods, plastering on a smile or clenching an anxious hand
when Luisa glances at the way it taps the table. Although she's advanced
past Maddalena—she is a married woman, after all—Luisa always feels
a step behind.

"That's a nice dress," Maddalena says.

Luisa thanks her. "I suppose it is, Cattina picked it."

"So you like it?" By now Maddalena is engaged in some menial
activity that she's performing with the utmost focus: wiping a ring of
condensation from the table where she set down her glass, or picking
a bit of fluff off a pillow. Luisa isn't sure what she's expected to say.
She doesn't care much about dresses, and doesn't trust her own taste.
She's reminded of conversations that she witnessed at the Pietà between
Chiara and whoever was that week's unwitting victim. *You thought you
played well?* There was no right answer—a yes would earn an incredulous
laugh and something cutting about getting ahead of yourself, while a no

meant a condescending shake of the head and a scoffed comment that you really should value your work.

"I think so?" Luisa hates herself for the questioning lilt, for her own indecision. Once, Luisa hadn't minded how much she didn't know. Maddalena never made her feel silly for asking, or responding with awe.

"Hmmm." Maddalena looks at her, refusing to offer anything else. Luisa pats her skirt and arranges the frills of her sleeves. She pinches the skin at her neck, just above where the Celsi pearls take pride of place whenever she goes out in public. She wants to be here with Maddalena. Doesn't she?

"Was there anyone promising at the Memmo party?" Maddalena's days are spent writing letters to suitors, and her evenings are a juggler's dream of keeping the group of them balanced. She details her escapades for Luisa as if recounting a shipping manifesto.

"The Barbarigo uncle remains old." When Luisa laughs, Maddalena allows herself a smile. She lifts an arm, lets it wander toward Luisa across the divan. Luisa takes the opening and moves closer, so that her leg brushes against Maddalena's leg in its own, apparently much more fashionable, dress.

"You're going to find someone," Luisa says, assuring herself just as much as Maddalena. She has the feeling Maddalena can tell that her encouragement is based in her own selfishness. If she hadn't stolen Maffeo, Maddalena wouldn't have to put in all this work. She wouldn't be entertaining the thought of marriage with a sixty-five-year-old patrician whose first two wives both died in childbirth, or a pimply fifteen-year-old whose father has racked up severe gambling debts. Maddalena hasn't mentioned any ill will. When Luisa describes her brief encounters with Maffeo, Maddalena shudders in solidarity, and pats Luisa's hand, and shows no jealousy. "Someone much better."

"We'll have everything we wanted," says Maddalena. Luisa's mouth turns down. Sometimes Maddalena will say things that make her wonder if she's gotten it all wrong. Maddalena sees everything, knows everything. But Luisa and Nicolò have been so careful. She can't know.

"Everything but the violin," Luisa says, unable to hide the note of yearning. Here, at least, is authenticity. Not a day passes without the thought of what the Coro at the Pietà is doing. Maddalena stands, leaving Luisa to wonder if the physical distance between them is calculated. "Of course, I've played at Ca'Celsi. It's not like I'm entirely bereft. I did a little concert for the family, and they were all very appreciative."

"That's not the same as a real concert." Maddalena moves over to the window that looks out on the courtyard, where the household staff is lining chairs and propping music stands, preparing to welcome a group of Andrea's friends.

"It's not," Luisa agrees.

"You know the rules are antiquated, don't you? No one is actually going to strike you down for playing on a stage."

"They'll issue a fine," Luisa reminds her.

"Says who?" She can't tell Maddalena who's assured her, not without telling Maddalena everything. "They let you marry into nobility, didn't they? Things are changing. There's no reason they should care."

There is a reason, and Luisa understands it well. If she takes the training she's had at the Pietà and uses it to play in public, to gain acclaim and even fortune, it will be on the backs of those who taught her. Why shouldn't any girl use the Pietà as a launching pad, parlaying her training to a career on the stage? The Ospedali Grandi survive because they offer the best, and if the best scatters across Europe, from whence would come the donations that allow them to remain so?

"Or you could play masked," says Maddalena. "If you play at Carnival, no one would bat an eye. They'd all still clap for you, not knowing it was you, of course, and you'd have proper accompaniment. It wouldn't feel the same, but it would be closer than what you have now."

"I couldn't."

Maddalena mouths a mimicry that's not unkind, nor entirely resigned. "*I couldn't.*" Then she leans back over the balcony to listen to the musicians in the courtyard, who have gathered to tune.

As Luisa is leaving the Palazzo Grimani, a footman races up to her. She recognizes him as the one who brings Nicolò's correspondence to

Ca'Celsi, so when he slips her a note, she's unfazed. On the gondola ride home, she unfolds and reads the letter, in Nicolò's hand, written with uncharacteristic urgency. He's asking her to meet his friend, a flautist, the following evening. Wear a mask—it is the season, after all—and come to the side entrance of a particular establishment in Dorsoduro, where the friend will be waiting with a violin even finer than the one Nicolò has given her. Don't worry about Maffeo, he'll be at the state banquet in honor of some visiting Russian prince, which is where Nicolò will be as well, until he's able to slip away and join her.

Tomorrow night. With all his love.

Maddalena

Even with the promise she has drawn from the water, Maddalena's matrimonial choices are constrained to a select group of gentlemen. Nicolò chose Maffeo Celsi perfectly. He comes from a noble family, but newly so—hardly in need of purification, and unlikely to seek a high office, not important enough to warrant a detailed investigation into where Elisabetta Grimani has gone. And, of course, he is young. Maddalena doesn't understand what a prize this is until she tallies up the others, a group of mostly septuagenarian letches, some with gout, all long past both their financial and physical primes.

Beneto pretends not to understand Maddalena's distaste, though he has seen her choices. "You find an old one and you marry him and live a few years at the teat. Then when he dies, you get to be a widow."

"I'm not saying I won't." They're in a sitting room at Palazzo Grimani, Maddalena at the writing desk. She stretches her neck one way, then the other, and flexes her hands to crack her back. "Just that it's not pleasurable."

"No," says Beneto. "Not everything is."

"It could be." Maddalena takes up her pen and dashes off a quick missive about her heart and how it pines for Alvise Tron, who's nearing seventy-three and missing most of his teeth. Once that is stuffed and sealed, a little sonnet for Pietro Querini—sickly, with three amputated toes and eyes that continuously water. Giacomo Cornaro is younger and still handsome—his brother and sister-in-law died suddenly last year, propelling him into the responsibility of wedlocked reproduction—but several families are vying for his attention, and he seems rather enamored with Contarina Memmo.

Still, a letter declaring her devotion. Hopefully all this attention will sway these men from considering marriage to offering it. Hopefully someone will respond and take her to the theater tonight—Nicolò and Beneto are both going, but Aunt Antonia won't chaperone unless there's a suitor.

Maddalena gives her letters to the footman, who will distribute them throughout the city. Beneto goes to dress for his evening's escapade, which will end at Teatro San Angelo, but begins with full costume and a gathering at Ponte dei Tre Archi, where a chase is planned, the men against the ladies.

Maddalena leans back. She looks out at the canal, already teeming with celebrants, their gondolas bumping each other good-naturedly. In the desk she has a letter that Nicolò sent Beneto from Padua. She holds her breath as she copies the lettering, the little swoops at the top of his *d*'s, the way ink blots on his accents. *Tomorrow night. With all my love.* She practices his signature until she feels she has a good approximation. She melts the wax and stamps the paper with his seal.

Yes, Maddalena feels guilty. She also feels good. She's flexing power, as if in stretching this one muscle, she'll be able to carry the rest of her fate. The world has conspired against her. For the most part there's nothing to do for it, but sometimes, just occasionally, an opportunity reaches from the water and says, *Take me.*

When ice melts, it shifts worlds. Such a slow, small thing—the way the heat will find what's been invisible. Enough melted ice becomes water, and enough water becomes a flood. Here is a letter, by Maddalena in Nicolò's hand, that could become a flood. To see what's coming and still make the decision to precipitate the damage might be an act of supreme selfishness, or else supreme self-love. For what has Luisa done for Maddalena, that she should be Luisa's floodgate? What has Luisa done, other than twist Maddalena and tie strings to her and play her for a fool?

Why shouldn't Maddalena take and take and take what she can?

That afternoon Luisa comes, and they pretend to be the girls they were six months ago, which is not the comfort Maddalena imagined it would be. She'd thought a retreat to her previous self would at least feel warm and welcoming. In reality, it's more akin to hiding in a foxhole: crowded and effortful, with every strained piece of small talk bringing knowledge of her real self walking closer to the sky.

Maddalena tells Luisa about her prospects, her time at masquerade balls and fancy dinners, her glimpses of the chaos of true Carnival: the little monkey perched atop a wire, frowning as he sucks a slice of lemon, the giddy men on wooden horseback booing passing Pantalones, the circle dances of the teeming bell-clad crowd. She describes the music at Palazzo Morosini with as much detail as she can summon, but as her life inside the mathematical intricacies of musical theory recedes, so does her language for it, and Luisa is left with a plate of disparate flavors that don't make a solid meal. Again, Maddalena stokes Luisa's hunger, a deliberate wafting of the music, of the idea that Luisa might play. Why should the Council care? Oh, you must miss it so terribly. Little seeds, little dangers.

And still there are moments when Maddalena can't help but reach for Luisa, looking for the easy intimacy if not the shared passion. She has to squeeze her hand shut, has to summon the image of that letter waiting in the top drawer of the desk, soon to tilt their axis further. The decision has already been made.

When Luisa leaves, Maddalena sends the footman after her. She watches Luisa look around to see who noticed the exchange, noting the way Luisa tucks the letter tenderly to her breast, and feeling her own resolve harden. No matter how Luisa presents herself, she is duplicitous. Maddalena now knows she always has been. This knowledge is comforting.

A response comes first from Giacomo Cornaro, and then another from Querini, both requesting Maddalena's company tonight at the opera house. It doesn't really matter which she accepts. Querini is the easier choice, less likely to take offense when she converses with others, and so absorbed in the minutia of the performance that he won't interfere.

But Cornaro is handsome, and to be seen on his arm raises her personal stock. She reasons that Nicolò will be more inclined to take her seriously if she comes with Cornaro. Nicolò has been avoiding her ever since she moved back to the house, but he can't skirt her if she greets him out in public with Cornaro without adding fuel to the rumors surrounding her birth. This is also true of Querini. Still, Maddalena dashes off a note telling Cornaro to meet her tonight in the Grimani box.

The Venetian opera house is a place to see and be seen—also to see life-size elephants and living camels, hundreds of costumed extras attending the divas and castrati, crafted machines that fly the singers to and from the heavens, dancing horses, rooms that turn into ships that then turn into fountains. Tonight is another Neapolitan libretto, and by Andrea's account it has not been well received. This suits Maddalena's purposes. She doesn't want to be hushed.

The theater's warm with bodies and the secondary tenor already halfway through his first recitativo when Maddalena and Aunt Antonia arrive. Maddalena settles into the back of the empty box, facing the stage. Aunt Antonia takes a plate of cicchetti and then promptly falls asleep, leaving Maddalena alone to consider her strategy for the evening.

The first tap at the door is a servant with another tray of refreshments. The second is Nicolò. He's surprised to see Maddalena, less so Aunt Antonia, who slouches snoring with her mouth open, unmoved by the intensity of whatever is happening to the soprano onstage.

"How is it so far?" Nicolò removes his mask and joins Maddalena at her little table.

"I think they're goddesses?" She shrugs. "Or else ladies in Rome. It isn't clear."

"Hmm." Nicolò watches the stage. "I didn't expect to see you here."

"We're hosting Cornaro."

"Claudio?"

"Giacomo."

At this Nicolò turns to face her, eyebrows lifted. "Really?"

"Yes, really. For God's sake, don't you think anything of me?" Good to get Nicolò feeling penitent; this will make him more susceptible. "You've been avoiding me," she says.

"I haven't." The response is immediate, which proves her point. "I've been busy."

"With Luisa." Maddalena doesn't make this a question, just a statement of fact. She watches Nicolò's eyes flutter with the knowledge he's discovered. It's just the eyes that move, at first, and then a quickening of his breath. On stage two women are duetting, by far the sweetest moment of the evening. The soprano is unknown, but she's quite good. Maddalena thinks she sings of unrequited love, or else her brother, possibly both. Although the box is dimly lit, Maddalena can see Nicolò's face losing color, a slow seeping until he is so white that when Giacomo Cornaro walks in, he asks at first if Nicolò has seen a ghost.

"I'd heard this wasn't one of Santurini's better productions, but that bad? Should I even sit down?" Cornaro's timing couldn't be better. Nicolò gapes, trying to compose himself. He reminds Maddalena of a beached fish, mouth opening and closing, finally stuck in his own pose of rigor mortis: a little pout to the lip, frown lines pronounced. Cornaro bows to Maddalena and kisses her hand. How nice to have the knowledge, to finally be the puppeteer. She bats her eyes and tries to look becoming.

While she makes small talk with Cornaro, Nicolò sits in silence. Three times Cornaro asks Maddalena what is wrong with her brother, and after a bit of pointed equivocation she finally says, "I think he's unlucky in love." This leads to a long account of Cornaro's own romantic travails, which include modest courtesans and impudent nuns and, alas, his recent directive to get married. Cornaro amuses himself easily. He has a chesty laugh and seems indifferent to the amusement of his company. Maddalena grows less enamored by the minute, but he's a good foil to Nicolò, who's barely spoken since he heard Luisa's name.

Act 1 is coming to its close, and when the curtain falls, Maddalena's fairly sure she will lose him. It's easy enough for him to slip out at the intermission and make some excuse to Cornaro before she's had her chance to act. Beneto saves her. He and his friends enter with no care for the performance, a raucous band discussing their footrace and the minstrels they disrupted, and did you see the stilt walker try to back into the piazza by the campanile, my God. There are a few ladies, though none Maddalena recognizes immediately in mask. Mostly these are gentlemen wearing the costumes of Carnival: Pantalone and Arlecchino and some foreign-looking king. She spots a Dandolo and a Farini, and yes, here is Claudio Cornaro, Giacomo's cousin, whom he greets with a great thump to the back. Finally, as Maddalena had hoped, Maffeo Celsi.

She knows him first by his shoes, great golden buckles adorned with the newly minted Celsi crest. Then there is his hair, that dull shade of red, which escapes from his hat. And of course the way he holds himself, a step back from the group, as if he still can't believe he is one of them.

"Signore Celsi." Maddalena turns. "You've met Signore Cornaro, I'm sure?" It's an easy enough introduction to explain, as Maffeo's least connected of the group, and there is every reason to suspect that with his black domino mask he'd be unknown to Giacomo Cornaro. She watches Nicolò, who's barefaced—the bauta mask sitting on the table in front of him like a splintered oar—as he recognizes who has come into their box with Beneto.

Onstage an entire army appears for the act 1 finale. Nicolò is surrounded on all sides.

"Are you well?" Beneto turns to his brother, his voice loud with drink.

"A love affair gone wrong." Cornaro rubs his hands together. He's older than the rest of the men, but not so much that they will look to him for wisdom. He relishes not knowledge but purveying it. Without realizing it, Maddalena has made the perfect choice for her evening accompaniment. All she has to do now is observe.

"A love affair!" Beneto laughs and chuffs Nicolò on the arm. "Who might the poor girl be?"

"Tell us!" says a man dressed as Pantalone in red trousers and a long-beaked black mask. He keeps tugging at the false beard, which looks to have absorbed a good amount of his wine.

"Nicolò, the chaste!" This comes from Enzo Dandolo, one of Nicolò's closer friends. "Finally moored."

"A toast, to whoever she is!" says the disheveled Arlecchino. They realize their hands are empty, and a servant is sent for a round, and Nicolò's chance at slipping out of the box is infinitesimal. The group floats possibilities for his conquest: the pretty Barbarigo girl who has recently come of age, one of the nuns at Santa Maria degli Angeli, someone in Padua. The drinks come and they raise their cups, and still Nicolò sits silent and pale.

"I think it must be a musician," says Maddalena, sipping prettily. "He gave her his Amati."

"He didn't!" Beneto chokes on his drink. "Tell me you didn't."

Nicolò's eyes flash, but he says nothing. His refusal to engage is not surprising, but it is becoming tedious.

"And you, too, Signore Celsi, have recently married a musician." Maddalena turns to Maffeo, who sits with his back to the stage.

"Oh yes." Here's Cornaro again, eager to explain. "That girl from the Pietà. Enough gossip from that match to last my nieces through the season. Apparently she plays the violin well, but she isn't all that pretty."

"She's beautiful," says Maddalena. Cornaro doesn't seem to hear, or if he does, he deliberately ignores her.

"A natural blonde, eh, Celsi?" says the Arlecchino. One of the women giggles and swats at his hand. "So they say—I suppose only you can prove it."

Maffeo blushes, fumbling with his shirtsleeves.

"She is his wife." Nicolò's voice is ice. He pushes back his chair and stalks toward the front of the box. Onstage some hired hands are piecing together a wooden set, the centerpiece for act 2. The general audience call out to one another jovially, and the denizens of other nobly owned boxes lean out to see who else is in attendance, sometimes waving an arm, other times turning abrupt face.

Maddalena raises her voice, ostensibly to be heard over the house.

"Luisa was a friend of mine." Both Maffeo and Nicolò flinch, though Nicolò's reaction is more obvious, and obviously the more painful. "Don't worry," Maddalena says to Maffeo. "I don't hold it against you that you chose her over me. She's truly a talent. And you've left me free here for Signore Cornaro. Imagine me newly married, enamored of dear Giacomo, with nothing to be done about it."

"A loss for us all," Cornaro murmurs, and Maddalena must forcibly stop herself from rolling her eyes.

"Was a friend?" Beneto knows his sister, and Maddalena is glad of it, because he's moved the pawn that clears way for her queen.

"She was my dearest friend." Maddalena doesn't have to pretend. She doesn't mean to let her voice crack, but it does, and she embraces it, pausing and swallowing and dabbing the corner of an eye. "Recently she's proved herself not who I thought she was. I hate to give credence to rumor"—at this she looks around the group, daring them to mention her mother, hoping her own situation will engender their sympathy— "but I've heard that she's sneaking about."

Dandolo coughs. Nicolò faces the stage, where a woman on a daybed sings about her own death.

"Sneaking about?" Maffeo has never seemed more of a child.

"Someone saw her busking with a flautist in Dorsoduro. Even masked, she's easy to spot. You know, that hair."

"In Dorsoduro?" asks Maffeo, unsure of what to do with this new information.

"It doesn't really surprise me." Maddalena sighs dramatically, and the group leans toward her, bees to nectar. An appropriate swelling in the music onstage welcomes a regiment of musical soldiers to replace the lovesick soprano. "She was always a diva. Always promiscuous."

"At the Pietà?" Beneto scoffs. If anyone is to call Maddalena's bluff tonight, it will be Beneto. She meets his eyes through his bauta, willing him to play along.

"She fooled us all," says Maddalena, letting her lip tremble. "Why do you think they let her leave the Coro so easily?" Before Beneto can speak, she knocks her elbow against a tray of scallops. "Oh!"

Maffeo jumps up, and Maddalena apologizes profusely as a servant comes to tidy her mess. "I'm very sorry. For the spill, but also for relaying the rumors. They could be just rumors." She can see Maffeo trying to strategize, the friction of misplaced gears as he assesses what she's said. He was already awkward, and now he seems like he might faint. What a weak man, if Maddalena can call him that. "I spoke out of turn."

"No," Maffeo says. "No, I'm glad that you told me. She shouldn't be so brazen in her first year of marriage. As a woman, unknown, she shouldn't... To play publicly, for profit... Better to address things quickly."

"Address things?" Beneto scoffs. "Whatever is there to address?"

"This opera's awful," says one of the masked women. "We should go to the Ridotto. Who wants to take me to the Ridotto?" Cornaro is the first to volunteer, patting Maddalena's hand as he flirts with his next.

"I'll help, of course," says Maddalena to Maffeo as the group discusses their new plan. "I'll write tonight to my source, and then I'll write to you tomorrow with more information. They'll know where to find her, tell you where you should go."

Maffeo thanks her, and he leaves before the others, his hat in his hand, tripping down the steps. Maddalena gathers herself and makes to follow Beneto and the rest to the night's next entertainment, but Nicolò holds her back.

Aunt Antonia snores in the corner, her commitment to ignoring the ruckus onstage more impressive by the minute. Nicolò's mouth is set, and his eyes are somehow both desperately sad and filled with rage, a flicker of the stage lights between one feeling and the other. He waits to speak until the sound of the group has gone.

"Why?" His voice a rasp.

"I should ask that of you," says Maddalena. "You have to break with her. This will ruin us."

"I know."

"Will you speak to her tomorrow?" She doesn't want him to say yes. If Nicolò talks to Luisa tomorrow, she'll know the note was forged, and she will not go out to play. But Maddalena knows her brother well enough to realize that in this mood he will push back at her suggestion, if only because she's been the one to give it voice.

"I'm in Santa Croce tomorrow. I'll speak to her when I can."

"When you return, then."

"When I can."

Maddalena didn't expect his agreement to be this easy. All enjoyment of the past hour's intrigue seeps out of her. She tries not to imagine Luisa's face when Nicolò has finished with her. What good is naming the fish you've caught to eat?

Luisa

Luisa goes. She debates the journey to Dorsoduro only in that she turns the decision over with each flip of her pillow as she struggles to sleep; all the time she knows that the mix of Nicolò and music is too potent to resist. How meaningless that silly phrase, *I couldn't*. Nicolò knows she's missed music, he has made her these arrangements, so she will play. She imagines him on his errand in Santa Croce, imagining her, and what they'll do once she has played. All day Luisa debates what she'll wear, and by evening has settled on blue satin with little white rosettes across the waist and skirt. Technically she should wear black, the color of Venetian nobility venturing out among the rabble. But it is Carnival. Luisa has so many pretty dresses that have only seen the inside of Ca'Celsi, and besides, she'll have the mask.

Luisa hadn't realized that the bauta was part of her trousseau, yet here it is, the full costume embroidered with gold thread, at once delicate and sumptuous. She puts on the black cloak and dons the accompanying black hat, carrying the mask so she'll complete her transformation once she's found herself a gondola. She doesn't often go out in the evenings—when she leaves Ca'Celsi after dark it has been with Cattina, or Maffeo's aunt or mother, and as her mask she has worn the moretta, which is held at the mouth by the lips. With the bauta she can speak. She thinks it makes her look dangerous, here in the mirror of her boudoir in the Ca'Celsi apartment. The outfit gives her a surge of confidence, such that she hardly worries about eyes in the corridors, eyes on the canal when she walks down to hail a gondola. She does consider doubling back, telling the gondolier to take a less predictable route so they can lose any imaginary tail. Then she reminds herself she's no one, there's no profit in blackmail, and technically she's doing nothing wrong.

And the mask. She's far enough from Ca'Celsi that once she puts on the mask, she could be anyone. The thought is both a curse and a comfort. When you can wipe the slate each morning so only your gambling debts remain, everything presents as a beginning. And while freedom is delicious in theory, in practice it means floating with no way to tie down. It's as if all of Venice is orphaned and told to imagine its own history, which paves the way to any future imaginable.

Luisa is glad to have Nicolò and his instructions. She wishes Maddalena were here to lend her courage. If this were anyone but Nicolò, Luisa would have written Maddalena immediately, might even have her here, where the gondola docks by an unfamiliar building, walking up to the side entrance and lending her arm. As is, Luisa goes alone, fiddling with her mask and pulling at her stomacher. Her heel catches a cobblestone, and she falls, scraping her palms. Her knee burns; she can feel the blood trickling. An ominous beginning, but she tells herself to wipe the slate clean.

When she knocks, the door opens immediately, and a masked woman brings her through a series of what seem to be storerooms, poorly lit and lined with sacks and barrels. Eventually they emerge from the maze, and Luisa steps back in surprise. She's in a vast room, crowded with people, in every corner a table of card players or those throwing dice. Smoky, dark enough that it's difficult to make out a distinct figure until you've come close to them. At least two dozen men in bautas, and women as well, in hooped skirts that take the place of other patrons at the seats next to them, which Luisa imagines as a strategy, though she has no experience gambling. She isn't sure how she's to find Nicolò's friend. The room buzzes with a quiet energy, so much attention paid to an individual hand, a growing murmur as someone loses half their annual income in a poor roll of the dice or makes an unexpected profit. Although everyone wears masks—it's a requirement during Carnival, at this establishment—Luisa can read their eyes enough to understand their addiction. Like playing a particular run of notes until your fingers blister and your elbow creaks, in the hope that this next time you'll finally get the measure right.

"Signora Celsi?"

It takes a moment for Luisa to realize he is speaking to her. How odd, to go from no surname to one that a strange gentleman will use to call her from her thoughts at a casino. She nods, and he kisses her hand. "If I might ask you to come with me."

She doesn't wonder how he recognized her, here among the masked. She thinks of Nicolò, who's going to join her after the banquet, and she follows. They weave through the crowd and pass through a velvet curtain into a small enclave, an inner sanctum populated by only the most important patrons—at least this is Luisa's guess, based on the ermine and the jewels and the obscene amount of sequins a woman has just promised at the card table. In one corner stands a man holding a flute.

"Nicolò's friend!" Luisa curtsies. He chuckles behind his mask, not the bauta common among the patricians, but a gnaga—the cat mask, which is supposed to be worn by men costumed as women, though this man wears just a black velvet coat and breeches. No wig, his own unpowdered dark hair. Luisa senses something familiar about him, but she's met so many men these past few months that she imagines he must have been a well-wisher at her wedding, or an admirer of her violin when she played with the Coro. If he's a musician himself, this would make sense.

"Signora Celsi." He bows deeply. His voice—Luisa knows she has heard it before. But before she can place it, he's giving her a violin, and all else becomes irrelevant. Reddish wood, beautifully varnished, smaller than what she usually plays, though full-size. From somewhere emerges the bow, and she can't help but raise the instrument up. Her face is covered by the mask. There's no way to play a violin in bauta. The porcelain juts out just where she'd rest her chin, and she realizes she's been foolish to use this as her armor.

"I—" She isn't sure what to say. The man lifts his flute and plays a few quick notes, grinning under the half-mask of the gnaga. The flute is not a sensual instrument—it involves such strained expressions, a bizarre blend of pursed lips and spurtive fingers, and often the flautist will dive with the note so the whole body contorts. In a little girl, it can be sweet. In a grown woman, Luisa often finds it irritating, and would much prefer to look away and experience the sound without seeing how it's made. This flautist, though—Nicolò's friend—is worth watching. He has thin, firm lips, and his eyes glow in the candlelight, two orbs. He's taunting her. Beckoning. The violin in her hand is warm with her own need.

She pulls off the mask and sets it down beside her, and she plays.

A small group gathers to watch, and the audience fuels their duet, which swells the crowd. By the end Luisa's sweating, beads between her breasts, the hair slick at her temples, her palm sticky against the violin's neck. She barely notices, so rapt in making music with someone else who shares her passion and, surprisingly, her skill. When she finally sets down her instrument, she realizes her face is bare, and as she fumbles with the bauta's ties, murmuring general apologies, she considers the absurdity of what she's supposed to be sorry for. Being good at violin? Taking pleasure in performing? The flautist lifts her hand in his, and together they bow, applause on all sides, the crowd buoying them until they reach the fondamenta.

Luisa built the wave that the crowd rode so joyfully, and she still feels that power within her, marking her as so much more than the timid wife pacing the piano nobile, waiting for word from her husband or lover. Playing with the flautist gives her all the thrill of her clandestine meetings with Nicolò, and this time she's guaranteed satisfaction. No coming close, and then just watching as at the last minute Nicolò shudders and closes the gates.

What she could do with an orchestra. What she could do with a crowd. She buzzes with the thought of it, already itching for her next attempt, jittery and giggling. No thought to punishment. This is Carnival, and she could be anyone. She has learned from Maddalena that the risk amplifies the reward. Luisa stands by the hidden entrance, waiting for Nicolò. The canal sloshes. From a nearby campo, voices float like smoke.

Here is the flautist, beside her. He exudes cold, and it's familiar, although again she can't say why. He still wears his mask, and now a cloak that makes him even more unknowable.

"You'll come again?" he asks. Why does she think now of the Pietà? Perhaps because in playing publicly, she betrays them. The Celsis as well, and while the consequence of that breach would be much more significant, she finds she doesn't feel it so sharply in her breast. But the Pietà—the Priora, Maestra Vittoria and Maestra Simona, Adriana, Orsetta, even Chiara, Maestro Vivaldi—now that she's lonely in the Celsi halls, they're even more her family.

"I don't know," Luisa says, chewing her lip behind the bauta.

"You're afraid?" She can't tell if he's taunting her. "Afraid of beauty." He must be taunting her.

"It's not allowed," Luisa says.

The flautist laughs. "Then why did you come tonight?"

"Because Nicolò..." Luisa trails off. That isn't right. Nicolò was the impetus, the easy excuse, but she came because she wanted to come. In the distance, dawn is a purplish-gray haze, a berry soon to burst. It's late, or else quite early. Nicolò has been waylaid, and she should leave to get back to Ca'Celsi before someone remarks on her absence.

"Good night," she says.

The flautist laughs again. "Good morning."

She leaves him to his shining black gondola while she goes off in search of her own. Boats are moored all along the riva, and Luisa quickly finds one for hire. She instructs the gondolier to double back and around, on the slim chance that someone might try to follow her. She commends herself on this bit of good sense. Yet as she's ducking into the felze, Luisa notices a flash of blue and gold, three yellow flowers. A gondolier in Celsi livery pushes off from the dock. The figure in the boat turns Luisa's stomach, the residual glee of her performance sloughing off to leave her fully exposed. Tallish, thinnish, with dullish red hair. Maffeo wears a domino mask, which marks him against the slew of bautas on the docks and in the other boats around him. Luisa sees enough to identify him, but not enough to read his expression, and she feels a chill even deeper than the flautist's cold hands, a creeping sense of foreboding.

As her gondola embarks, she keeps her eye on Maffeo's, her body clenched until they've turned and she can be sure that she hasn't been seen. Luisa settles herself, then immediately jumps back. The cushion where she sits is damp, its fringed edges dripping a subtle beat against the bottom of the boat. Water pools on the gondola floor at her feet, a small, insistent puddle.

Maffeo couldn't have been in the casino while she played, because he was with Nicolò at the state banquet. She removed the bauta, yes, but who would know her? At the Pietà she only played up in the balcony, behind a grate, high above the congregation. She'd spoken to visitors in the parlatorio, but always with the grille between them. She'd played for a small crowd at Mira. Her hair is bright and distinctive, her playing recently renowned. She is the new wife of new nobility, a foundling raised above her station, a success story, a warning, a light at which the moths will gather. She removed her mask. She pinches the soft skin of her wrist as she moves farther from, then closer to Ca'Celsi, twisting until she's left little rosettes of regret to match the embroidery on the skirt of her dress.

Still, as she climbs out of the gondola and slips into the house—thankfully unseen or at least unremarked upon—she thinks of how she might play again. A little hole in her seawall, a little trickle of want. She tries to plug it, bucket it back.

Through the front hall. Up the courtyard stairs, then around to her apartment. No one calls out to her, not even the shadow of a servant passing through. But when she goes to her room, as there was in the gondola, there's water. A small condensation on the legs of an armchair, and an odd little stream along the polished stone floor. The edges of a rug have darkened, but the water stays mostly on its particular path, as if it's begun to carve a canyon that leads to the bed. Luisa's too physically exhausted to do more than toss a blanket that might absorb some of the wet. She certainly can't call a servant to handle it, not at this hour, still in the dress she wore in public while she played the violin. She should get rid of the dress. She tears herself out of it and scrunches up the skirt and sleeves, tucking them under her pillow for safekeeping. Then, naked, her hair still half pinned, she tries to sleep.

Maddalena

Maffeo is an easy mark. The morning after the opera he reads Maddalena's forged letters, and by evening there's no doubt in his mind that her anonymous source saw Luisa play the violin at the casino, no question that this spy would be concerned for his welfare and would want to write to warn him, to protect him. How wonderful to be a man, moving through the world with the implicit understanding that it will shelter you. Of course he has come now to Dorsoduro, to settle his affairs.

"And you're certain no one has reported her?" Maffeo itches at his cheek beneath the domino mask.

Were Luisa actually performing nightly in Dorsoduro, there'd be no possible way for Maddalena to know if anyone had slipped a note to the Council with word of her misdeeds. But Luisa spends her nights alone at Ca'Celsi, and Maddalena can say with utter confidence that no one is coming to collect on the Celsis for breaking their contract with the Pietà. Tonight is the first and only night that Luisa will play. Maffeo will be there to see her, if only Maddalena can get him off this boat and through the door. "They could call in your debt at any moment." She taps her fan against the hull. "Which is why you must act first."

They're in the Celsi gondola, idling beside a bridge. Aunt Antonia is asleep at Palazzo Grimani, exhausted after a brief stint at the Ridotto in which she was fed malmsey by the bottle and encouraged to try her hand at baccarat. Maddalena faked a yawn, kissed her aunt's cheek, and then snuck out to meet Maffeo. It was embarrassingly easy to avoid the servants, to duck out of her father's way, and to go down this time to

the Celsi craft instead of her own gondolier. She would have preferred
Maffeo make this trek without her, but apparently he needs his hand
held. Maddalena can see what he'd be like in the right marriage: pliable,
cheerful. He would go to bed early, and be always a beat behind the joke,
and his wife would have access to everything.

"You could come in with me," Maffeo says. He is afraid someone will
see him and connect him to Luisa and laugh. Or else he is afraid that
once he enters the casino he'll be forced by his own honor to defend her,
or whisk her away, or challenge her partner—*They've been playing together
for weeks, I heard*—to a duel. Most likely, Maffeo is a boy brought up on
goodwill and favors who's never had to dive headfirst into a situation
that he knows he will not like. Maddalena doesn't want to go in with
him. She didn't want to come out tonight at all. But the bells have struck
eleven, and she isn't sure how long the gondolier will be able to keep
Luisa playing, and so she agrees.

Maddalena straightens her mask. They disembark and weave their
way through the casino, which is like the Ridotto but unsanctioned—less
gilt, with lower hairstyles and smaller skirts—and through the curtain to
the farthest room at its back. They have to elbow and squeeze, and Maffeo
is good for gallantry, clearing his throat when a man backs into Maddalena, and regularly proffering his hand so she can be the first to pass.

The crowd has come for the music. It sounds small in these low-
ceilinged rooms, but no less mystical. The gondolier wears a cat mask,
which leaves his lips and chin open for his flute. He's a very good player,
but Luisa's still the star. Luckily she's gone ahead without Nicolò, probably
asleep in his own bed by now, oblivious. That is, if he is able to sleep, the
knowledge of what he has to do a vise turned ever tighter. There's a lovely
symmetry to the way the Grimani children will carve up Luisa and eat her.

And Maddalena is hungry. The room is packed with bodies, but
there's a moat around where Luisa stands, her bauta pushed up atop
her head, the violin to her chin. She's lit by a chandelier the twin of all
the others, but she seems celestial, her hair aglow, her eyes closed as she
plays. Maddalena's breath catches. This is Luisa at her purest.

"She doesn't even try to hide it." Maffeo sounds incredulous, clutching Maddalena's wrist, his grip tightening with every stroke of Luisa's bow. She expects him to stand captured like the rest of them, but for once he finds his gumption and stalks back through the curtain, walking over to demand a drink from a passing server. They find a dark corner—an easy feat—and Maffeo nurses something bitter, strong enough that Maddalena coughs when she catches its scent. She sits with her back to the crowd, waiting for him to speak. Surely he'll blame himself, his impulsivity in marrying a girl he hardly knew, who had no family to vouch for her. Instead, he scowls, eyes fired at the curtain, ready for when Luisa walks through. "She bewitched me. She cast some spell. She isn't truly my wife."

Maddalena can't argue with the first—they had cast a spell, or something like it, and it's commendable of Maffeo to notice. Luisa is, however, his wife.

"She doesn't have to be," says Maddalena. "You can file for an annulment and say you never consummated the marriage. You can declare her infertile, and be done with her without involving the Ten or tarnishing the Celsi name."

Maffeo doesn't ask her how she's come to be so ready with these answers. Maddalena supposes this is for the best. Why bring up the fact that this was what her father's friends suggested that he do to her mother, after Elisabetta left? Make it look as if it was your decision, they said. Don't let her write the story. Maddalena's father grumbled, and he mentioned how unlikely it would be to successfully declare a wife infertile once she'd born four living children, and he'd cried at the loss of his wife and good name. The advice sat dormant for three years, but here it is now, reborn in his daughter at a casino in Dorsoduro.

"I should go back in there and get her." Maffeo is drunk, which is annoying. Maddalena sighs.

"You should have a doctor declare that she can't give you children, and the Council will look favorably on an annulment." The doctor, of course, will be the gondolier, and no one will doubt him.

"I'm going to—" Maffeo rises, and Maddalena yanks him back down, because here comes Luisa, in her bauta again but so clearly herself, with a trail of admirers behind her. Maddalena keeps her grip on Maffeo, and Luisa and the gondolier pass through.

"Easy," Maddalena says. Maffeo's anger seems like transmuted embarrassment, though she imagines this is the case for most men, when they are angered. She can also sense that fear: of losing his new social standing, of the money his family will owe if Luisa is discovered. Fear, Maddalena can use. "Don't be afraid," she says, and is relieved to see that this was the right direction in which to take him. Everything in Maffeo settles, if only slightly. His shoulders slacken, and his jaw unclenches. "You have the upper hand," Maddalena says, and Maffeo finishes his drink. "You will be a man of action." This, too, is the right thing, Maffeo the sort who wants to imagine himself a man of action from his comfortable seat in the parlor.

They leave the casino with a plan for Maddalena to contact her dear friend the doctor—again, Maffeo does not question—and for Maffeo to approach Luisa subtly with his decision. The victory feels hollow. All is going exactly to plan, but every pinch of pride fades in the time it would take Maddalena's reddened skin to return to its usual color. Should she press harder? Maddalena decides it must be because she is still lining up the dominoes. The final prize will be a pleasure that outlasts these small moments of accomplishment. The culmination of her plans will be the death of a star. She will live on in its light for centuries.

Luisa

Luisa wakes late, to a letter from Nicolò. Someone has left it on the table in her room, and also folded up the blanket that she used to clean the floor. The crinkly edges of her dress peek out from under her, a reminder of how much she must rely on this unknown messenger's discretion.

Nicolò asks her to meet him at the Dandolos, and as Luisa cleans and dresses, it's with the understanding that her burden is soon to be shared. After all, Nicolò invited her to play with his friend at the casino. He's the sort to think things through—he must have a plan. At very least he will help her sort through to the best course of action, and when he holds her, she'll let go of her dread, if only for a moment.

After a quick meal, a brief gondola ride, and a bit of logistical orchestration, Luisa finds herself at Ca'Dandolo, led through the public areas to the ladies' apartments. Nicolò stands at a window that looks out onto the courtyard. His tawny hair curls against the collar of his shirt, and his back is narrow, shoulders tense. Luisa goes to massage them, but he turns before she reaches him, his face equally tight. Again she feels that surge of dread. She reaches for his hand, and he snaps it away.

"I can't." Nicolò stalks to a chair and stands behind it, his hands clenching its plush, cushioned back. Luisa tries to steady her breathing, tries to staunch the rising panic. She has a mental flash of how he put his mouth on her, the way he pressed his cheek to her breasts.

"I don't understand." She truly doesn't. It would be one thing if he'd just discovered last night's negligence, but he was the conductor. The whole night was his plan. The previous letter she received from him had been heady with infatuation and desire, and their last afternoon together the stuff of dreams.

His hands dig into the fabric of the chair, his fingernails marring the velvet. "There's too much at stake," he says, though it seems like every word is pried open and pushed out like a mollusk. Slippery, salty, distasteful. "If your husband discovers us, it will ruin you."

"I don't care!" Luisa gushes, moving toward him, kneeling on the seat of the chair and taking his arms at the elbow, pulling his hands to her cheeks. He remains stiff, pulling away and stepping back so he's pressed against the wall, scratching stone rather than let himself be close to her.

"It will ruin me."

Luisa exhales. He has talked about his political career, his plans to introduce a new progressivism to the Council and the Senate that could rescue the republic from its current inertia. She knows she'll never have him publicly, not even as a cicisbeo, and she's fine with that; she's made her peace. She needs him privately. He is the reason for every decision, the blade that came between Luisa and his sister, the chain that bound her to Maffeo. She needs him, however she can have him. For God's sake, he's been *inside* her.

"We'll be more cautious. My darling, I—"

"It will ruin my family." Here, Nicolò's breath hitches.

Luisa wants to hold his head, to comfort him, and in doing so begin to comfort herself. Because he's right—of course he's right. Luisa has already stepped in Maddalena's way, a stone on her dearest friend's path to legitimacy. A scandal with Nicolò will topple everything they've built, not just Nicolò and his father, but Maddalena and Beneto and even Andrea. She wonders how they've been so blind to the obvious, all these afternoons together, all these letters between them, and realizes it has been a willful blindness. They chose themselves. But now that Nicolò has said it out loud, there's no pretending away the seismic impact of their damage.

For the second time in fewer than twenty-four hours, Luisa realizes how naive she has been. An utter fool. A love-blinded idiot.

"There must be a way," she says, but even to her own ears she sounds weak and disbelieving. She can feel the itchy salt of tears from eyes to cheeks to lips, the effort of holding in a full-out moan. She shakes her head. "I'm sorry." But why should she be sorry? Nicolò is the one who has shattered her. Did he not think what this would do to her? Did he not care where she would end, what she would sacrifice for a few months in bed with him? She sinks down, on her knees, her elbows on the chair and her hands clasped in a mockery of prayer. Then she lets her head drop and she sobs.

She hears him move away from the window, hears him come close. She thinks he will at least put a hand on her back, but he just stands there, the heat of him, watching her. Nicolò is a good man—she still believes this, that he is gentle and kind and good, and that is why he loved her and also why he's leaving her—yet he stands and holds his hands tight to his sides and he says nothing.

Nicolò's mouth puckers with the effort he makes to hold himself away from her. His knuckles are white, and his eyes deep with feeling. At least there is this. At least he struggles, which feels to Luisa like a strange thing to appreciate, because she doesn't want him to struggle. She wants to stroke his hair. She wants to kiss him warm and willing. Even now he stirs her.

But she rubs her eyes with the heels of her palms, and she stands and smooths her skirt. The first fifteen years of her life have been spent excising all desire but for music; she's expert in self-denial. She raises her chin, and she can see the recognition in his eyes, almost a panic as he realizes she isn't going to fight him. She is going to turn around and make her way through Ca'Dandolo, back out onto the street, where she will walk until she's left him, where she will handle the residual toxins of last night alone, where she will bleed Nicolò out of her and tamp herself down and be a wife to Maffeo, because that's the choice she made, and now she'll live with it. She'll dream of him, of course, and of the music. But Luisa is a good girl, and she's going to be a good woman. *Walk away now*, she instructs herself. And she does.

Maddalena

Nicolò leaves Palazzo Grimani before Maddalena wakes the morning after Dorsoduro, but when he returns she is waiting for him. She sits in the window, drinking strong coffee and watching the traffic on Rio de San Severo, as he comes walking up the fondamenta, unmasked and unwigged. He looks like a soldier, his shoulders straight and stiff and his usually open expression shadowed by both the angle of the cloud-filtered light and his despondence. A strong, wet wind blows in from the direction of the lagoon, and Nicolò's loose hair tangles. He's walking quickly across the bridge, and Maddalena abandons her cup to slip down to the calle entrance and intercept him.

She doesn't bother making their run-in seem casual. They haven't spoken since the opera, but both know what Nicolò has promised to do, or—from the pink rims of his eyes, the purposefully vacant expression that threatens every second to reveal his inner self-flagellation—what he has already done.

"Well?" says Maddalena. "Have you broken her heart?" She means this to be callous, but she hears the quaver in her voice and tries to hide it with an expression of pity. Maddalena has learned that pity is the purest poison: it goes quickest to the bloodstream and works in all manner of ways. No one can accuse it of violence, though it's often a barb.

"It's done," Nicolò says. "I've ended it." Maddalena follows him down the hall, through to the courtyard with the fountain of the lady and her lions. In her haste, she has come out without a cloak. Nicolò sees her shiver, does nothing.

Should she comfort him? Truly she hasn't done anything Andrea would not have, though she's done it with more malice than she thinks her brother capable of. She does feel for Nicolò. She, too, has fallen prey to Luisa. She, too, wants more. But when she reaches to put a hand on Nicolò's forearm, he shrugs her away, and with her arm goes her sympathy.

"It was the right choice," she says, her voice sharp, "but it was still a choice." Nicolò could have abandoned the political career. He could have said to hell with his family. He didn't. He made one choice, then another, and nobody forced his hand. Maddalena herself did no more than point out the obvious. There are a million other girls, and he could have any of them.

Nicolò gives her a look of utter and complete disappointment, a twist of the lips and a cast to the eye that make Maddalena feel like a selfish child. How many times has he explained that she doesn't understand the way society functions? Here she is, winding its gears, a connoisseur of its most intimate and sordid details, and now he asks for her humanity? She can't help herself. She lets out a huff of air and smacks his shoulder. When he simply stands there, she hits him fully, her two fists against his chest, and then when all he does is look at her, exhausted, she reels back and shoves him. Nicolò leans down, bracing against the stone of the fountain. He doesn't seem angry, simply tired.

A group of servants gather on the stair, open-mouthed, arms full of the washing and the silver. All wait to see what Nicolò will do. He could whip her, have her locked inside her room. Instead he straightens his coat and tucks his hair back.

"We sent you to the Pietà to learn modesty and manners. What a shame to have spent all that money, and have it come to nothing." There's regret in how he looks at her, still not anger precisely, but a growing blot of hate. Nicolò has been distant, he's been exacting and insufferable, but he has never before treated her with such unabashed disdain. Maddalena wants to howl. She wants to hug him, but she's too old for his arms, and frightened by the chance he wouldn't have her.

So she smiles—a cruel smile, sharpened to kill, not a sign of how effortfully she wields it.

"I'm sorry you had to lose your little lover." Maddalena doesn't want to use Luisa to rip down his final sails, but she will. Their course is set, and there is nothing Nicolò can do about it. "Although now that you've spoiled her, it should be all the easier for her when she goes to the brothel."

"She's married." Is that panic? Does he know how he's misjudged her?

"Ah." Maddalena makes that harpoon smile. "But not for long."

Nicolò isn't one to beg for information, not of her, not after all that's just happened between them. His eyes widen, and his thoughts turn inward, and Maddalena can see him calculating risk. Later, she will not be sure if she wanted to hurt him, or simply herself. The beauty of the trap she's set for Luisa is that Maddalena can step decidedly out of it. No one has to know she wrote that letter, that she prodded Maffeo and pushed Nicolò to sense.

But Maddalena has never been one for anonymity. She wants Nicolò to know. She wants to break him the way she has broken Luisa, let him see what she does and will do to those who betray her. "The Celsis aren't happy that she played last night in Dorsoduro. Imagine what they'll do if they find out that it was at your behest. Your signature on that letter, indisputably clear."

"At my . . . ? I never wrote a letter."

"Of course you didn't." Maddalena leans closer, on the chance that the servants are still listening. She doesn't want all Venice to hear her, just Nicolò. She has him pressed against the fountain, both hands back behind him and clutching the stone. "But I did."

If she could, Maddalena would rise up above the open courtyard, arms spread wide, her black skirts swelling. She would look down on Nicolò, the devastation she's wreaked clear across his face, his smallest finger twitching, his breathing labored, as if the air refuses to come.

Maybe from on high, he would seem awed, not disgusted. Maybe from on high she would feel powerful and happy, not bereft.

Luisa

Luisa hurries down the waterfront, tying on a little half-mask so she'll blend with the eternal crowd of Carnival: the hawkers with their tonics and tapestries and grease-glistened foods, the jostling children and the booths of puppeteers. She rubs her thumb against the blisters that have formed along her fingers, the calluses beginning to bloom after a long night of violin. Just last night, though it already seems years ago. Was that why Nicolò sent her to Dorsoduro? Because he knew he must be finished with her, and wanted her to have some small happiness? Or was he destroying her, ruining her so fully that he knew he wouldn't give in to temptation and take up with her again? She never even got to play for him, never showed him her soul.

She's glad of the oblivious crowds in which to be alone, and yet surrounded. She considers what remains to her: an unnurtured talent, a bland husband, though undoubtedly kind. The possibility of children, noble children who will be educated and well dressed, who will have all avenues open to them. They'll have a future in Nicolò's future Venice—again a global power, cleansed of the lethargy and excess that now builds like algae on a pond.

Boats pass one another, gondoliers whistling. Somehow a wave jumps up and wets her hemline—she's standing far from the water, she can't explain how it has found her. Yet it has, and she shakes her foot to dispel some of what's pooled in her shoe. As she's bracing herself against a pillar, a hand grabs her elbow from behind, and she lets out a little scream.

"Don't be frightened," says Maffeo. He wears the full bauta—large white mask and black cloak and hat—but she knows him immediately by his voice, which is a comfort. However little she engages with him, Maffeo's still her husband.

"What are you doing here?" The damp from Luisa's slipper crawls up her stockings.

"What are *you* doing here?" Maffeo's tone is rougher than she's ever heard it, as is his grip as he pulls her through to a little courtyard off the main promenade.

"I was just visiting—"

"The Dandolos?" He looks around, sees that they are mostly alone, then lifts his mask and spits onto the ground. "Just as last night you were just *visiting* the casino." He still holds her at the elbow, his fingers digging ever deeper.

"I didn't—"

"I was *there*. I *heard* you. Everyone heard you."

"It was the first time," Luisa whimpers. "The only time, I promise."

"What good is your promise?" Maffeo practically growls. "You promised to cherish and obey. You promised to be faithful. You are a fickle, foolish girl."

"Yes," says Luisa, weeping despite her strident efforts. "I am."

"I'm inclined to show mercy," says Maffeo. "I've said nothing to my uncle, who stuck out his neck for us, who cared for you. An annulment, of course. A doctor will examine you and conclude you are infertile, and then it will all be done."

"Surely—" Her head is spinning, she can't keep pace. "You must—"

"You had us all under your spell," Maffeo says. "But now it's broken, and we'll be lucky to come away mostly unharmed."

"I—"

"I'll see you at home. You will say nothing." Maffeo pulls down the mask, and with a flip of his cloak he is gone. Luisa inhales, then immediately vomits. What comes out of her is brackish, endless, a veritable ocean, and when she's empty she does not feel clean.

She wanders, untethered in disbelief, out of the courtyard, down the riva. She finds herself back at the Pietà.

Once a year the Coro and its initiates travel the short distance from the Pietà to the Piazzetta, to perform for the doge upon raised platforms set up in the little square off the Piazza San Marco. The risers are angled, so the boats that collect in the Molo to hear the music can perchance catch a glimpse of the musicians, framed by the columns of San Marco and San Teodoro, between which Venice used to execute her traitors. The sculpted patrons sit atop their marble pillars in judgment; the Campanile rises lean and sharp behind. This is one of the largest public venues for the Coro, and all involved are anxiously hoping their recital will surpass whatever the Incurabli or Mendicanti have recently bestowed upon the crowd.

Outside the Ospedale della Pietà, the girls line up in their white dresses and red cloaks, smaller instrument cases in hand, the larger already assembled and hauled the short way down the Riva degli Schiavoni. Maestra Simona stands at the front of the group, her arms raised to conduct the Coro's passage, and several young men have been hired to clear the crowd so they can walk undisturbed. Luisa stands back, watching. Less than three months ago, she was one of them.

There is Orsetta, whispering in Adriana's ear, a wrinkle of distaste across her nose and then a little swallowed giggle. Betta with her clarinet. Chiara stands at the front with shining eyes, already living her performance. They peel away from the Pietà, walking in two straight lines with ushers alongside them, and the last one out the door is Don Antonio himself, done up in a red jacket, his wig long. He wheezes a bit, and pauses to clear his throat. The others look straight ahead as they walk, but he gazes up, at the clouds, at the looming facade of the church they leave behind them. Luisa slips after him, watching the way he taps along in his low-heeled shoes.

The walk to the piazza is brief, and soon the girls are mulling around the platform as their handlers try to settle the crowd. A drunken Pantalone holds court at the top of the wooden stage, and Vivaldi comes to hiss at him. Most of the girls Luisa knows well are either watching the row, open-mouthed, or whispering about it behind their hands. One stands apart, already stretching her fingers and circling her wrist.

"Chiara!" Luisa beckons, surprised at the comfort she feels in her former rival's company. Chiara, at least, is the same.

"Luisa?" Chiara squints, trying to make out Luisa's features behind the half-mask. She looks from the ruckus—the Pantalone has removed his black cloak and seems ready to unbutton the red doublet, no intention of vacating the stage as he motions other costumed drunks to join him—to the chittering jumble of musicians. Luisa watches her calculus, and shudders with relief when Chiara tucks her violin case next to the maestra and steps to the side. They walk to the library's loggia without speaking and stand in its shadows.

"Well?" says Chiara, when they are hidden enough that they won't attract undue attention. Luisa isn't sure what to say. Part of her wants to spill all the misfortunes that have overwhelmed her in the past few hours, to fall at Chiara's feet and ask her to use her influence to somehow take Luisa back into the fold of the Coro, impossible as that may be. Another part of Luisa is proud, and will not beg. She thinks this must be Maddalena's impact—how, once you have fallen, will it behoove you to pretend that you haven't? Luisa looks at Chiara, waiting patiently, pure and unmasked among the rabble. She can't prostrate herself.

"I just wanted to say hello." To her own ears, Luisa's cheerfulness sounds forced. The lump in her throat—like a mussel swallowed whole and now stuck in her larynx—threatens to bring tears. Chiara flares her lips in an amusement that isn't entirely unsympathetic.

"No, you didn't," she says. "Why are we here?"

"I . . ." Luisa heaves a breath, and finds she can't continue. Nearby, a man ascends the shallow steps of the loggia, dragging a giggling woman by the hand. Her skirts whisk past; Luisa feels their breeze.

"You miss playing," Chiara says simply. "Of course you do. Who wouldn't?" Luisa nods. This is nowhere near the whole of things, but it is true. She opens her mouth to speak but feels that water rising up, and there's no way she can respond without crying. "None of us envy the decision you had to make," Chiara continues. "But you do get to wear silk."

Now Luisa can't help but cry, the lump still firmly lodged in her throat.

"Chin up," says Chiara.

What did Luisa expect? That Chiara would offer Luisa her place as the first violin in an important public concert for which Luisa hasn't studied? That Chiara, who'd never even been a friend, would make some sacrifice to set Luisa's world back on its axis?

"Just tell me this before you go." Chiara twists her mouth. "Does it hurt to lie with a man?"

"What?" Luisa sounds like a bullfrog.

"Does it feel good, or is it painful?" Chiara is asking because she can't know, and even in her current state, Luisa realizes the power in her own knowledge. Chiara will play with the Coro for ten years, possibly longer. She'll teach, and she'll retire to one of the private rooms, where she will die. There is the slimmest chance someone will see her and ask for her hand, and that when her indenture is over, she'll marry him. But by then, she will be old. At least Luisa has had this, while she is fresh: the good and the painful.

"Both," she whispers. Chiara nods. From the Piazzetta comes the flutter of the Coro preparing their instruments. The disturbance has been cleared, and Chiara touches Luisa's shoulder very briefly before dipping back into the crowd. Luisa stands, bracing herself against a pillar, watching as the Coro files onto the stage. The awkward fumbling of the cellos. The oboes long and lean and mournful. The girls on the bassoons flutter their fingers, gulp in and hold the air. The violins.

As they play, Luisa involuntarily moves closer, called by the speed of Chiara's bow, the way Vivaldi beats the time onto the wooden boards. She pushes past vendors, skirts one hawking flowers and another with little vials of tonic. When the violins begin their measured ascent, she shoves a fist into her mouth. A man standing next to her pats her softly on the back, and the compassion is too much. Luisa cries out, coughing through the mass in her chest, expelling more of the brackish water she'd spat out before. The man jumps back, swearing at her. Luisa crouches slowly, bites her knuckles, and closes her eyes. She has nothing to lose. She gives herself fully to the clarinets, the chilly tiles that pave the Piazzetta. The flute seems to be laughing at her.

Luisa imagines how she might play, were she still with the Pietà. She thinks her bariolage would be smoother than Chiara's, her wrist always more dexterous. And the maniera—could anyone deny that Luisa now has the courage with which to imbue the work? Not a simulacrum made from promises and poppets in the night—she can perform fearlessly because anything that can hurt her already has. She sinks from a crouch to sit fully on the ground, among the muddy boots and slippers. Her hands, now free, play a phantom. Here is how she'd end that phrase; here is how she would join the accompaniment. She can see herself, there on the stage in white, the way the setting sun would fire her hair and the people on their boats docked at the Molo would raise their hands in gratitude.

Her skirt is wet. Not just damp, but fully wet, as if she's unknowingly sat down into a puddle. Water inches up her ankles, and she jumps up and opens her eyes. The stage and the musicians are gone. The crowd is gone. The sky is a lavender-tinged gray, and everywhere is dirty gray water. It hits Luisa at the knees, pawing at her like a street dog. A tabletop floats past, and a wicker chair. The Piazzetta is deathly calm, with not a soul in sight, but the music continues, Chiara's notes suddenly mournful. The boats are gone, the Molo empty, the lagoon empty beyond it. Even San Giorgio Maggiore, across the way, seems empty of everything but the water that beats steady, like a heart.

Then, over the flooded square, comes a gondola. It is black, and its gondolier wears black. No recognizable livery. He has a gnaga—fully black, nothing embellished or bejeweled—and as he approaches and holds out his hand, she knows him as the flautist. She turns away, trying to run, but the water is deep, and the best she can do is wade away from him as quickly as possible. Don Antonio's newest concerto continues out over the lagoon, across the Piazzetta, echoing through the loggias.

There has to be someone else, another person she can turn to, a place to escape the water, a way to go inside and rest. Luisa moves toward the piazza itself, but as she does, she trips on something underwater, and she stumbles. Her head under the flood, her eyes open to the detritus—a chair leg, splintered. A large fish with silver scales. A frond of seagrass, dancing.

She sputters as she emerges. Though she's soaking wet, the square, again, is dusty tile and full of people. That same man looking at her with barely disguised disgust. That woman selling flowers. The Coro on their platform, working as one to Don Antonio's conducting staff, which pounds the beat. The sun falls slowly toward the boats, all moored and peopled, and the loggias burst with masked carousers. Luisa shakes her head, feeling the wet hair against her neck. What is happening to her?

She swallows. She brushes the water from her eyes, wrings out what she can of her skirts. She leaves the Piazza San Marco, the figures of her childhood singing behind her, and goes to look for Maddalena.

Maddalena

She dresses in gray damask, vines winding up around her stomacher and silver flowers woven onto her skirt. A fishing boat has overturned somewhere in the lagoon—strange, given the prowess of the fishermen, the calmness of the waves—and the pungent haze of what was left wafts down the canals, interrupting the floral musk of blooming gardens and the heavy oils of festival foods. It's a quick walk to the Piazzetta—winding down calli until she reaches Piazza dei Leoncini and moves past its muscular guardians, past the clock tower with its golden zodiac and sturdy old San Basso. During Carnival, San Marco and the piazza are much the same no matter the hour—the same jugglers and fire-eaters and jostling drunkards, the booths selling impossibly colored feathers and paste jewels and tonics to cure heartbreak and tinctures to smooth the skin or strengthen the teeth, boys calling out for ready victims to come test their wits against the newest card tricks and then abandoning their decks and diving into the crowd when they see someone coming to fine or arrest them. Groups dressed as characters from commedia dell'arte: Pantalone in his red suit, Colombina with her tambourine, Arlecchino with his boil. Men in full bauta, others skirted with their gnaga masks and little baskets of kittens. Maddalena has her colombina tied prettily across her face, one eye framed in glossy black, the other gold. She moves through the crowd alone and unafraid.

When she arrives in the bustling Piazzetta, a grumbling Pantalone is being hauled off the wooden stage, and the extended Coro of the Ospedale della Pietà files on from its other stair, carrying instruments.

Maddalena moves into the loggia of the Biblioteca Marciana, sharing an alcove with a pair of lovers so enraptured that they seem not to notice her. From here she has a good view of the platform, the Coro in their white dresses bright against the geometric pink stone of the Palazzo Ducale. She'd like to have a better angle on the crowd—she sees mostly a jumble of costumes, men and women standing shoulder to shoulder. A mongrel dog sniffing from cloak to cloak. A shattered glass bauble, crunched progressively smaller underfoot.

The oboe plays the A, and the rest of the orchestra tunes around it in a thick fog of sound that quickly dwindles to the last vibrations of a single violin. Vivaldi stands at the side of the platform with his conducting staff, each tap against the stage marking the time.

"You've heard about Lulli?" Without announcement, the gondolier is next to her, watching the composer's nostrils flare with each beat. "Or as the French call him, Lully." A flourish of the hand as he mentions the French.

"The one who wrote the ballets?" Maddalena's eyes remain trained on the Coro, moving into their allegro. Bodies swaying, music floating out over the lagoon.

"Took a conducting staff to his own foot by accident, and then died when it turned gangrenous." The gondolier chuckles, which Maddalena finds unbecoming.

"Couldn't they cut off the leg?" Betta has the solo, and from a distance her pocked face appears smooth, although the strain of controlling her breath is apparent to anyone turned toward the stage. If you close your eyes, the song is effortless.

"He wouldn't let them amputate. He said if he couldn't dance any longer, then what was the point?"

"Such a grave choice to make, for pleasure."

"But not unusual. People choose pleasure all the time." The sun dips, and the lanterns set along the docks and hanging from the gondolas light up in little fairy bursts. Nearby, the nobility drink wine and toss away their money at the gaming tables of the Ridotto. Somewhere within his Gothic palace, the doge looks on.

Maddalena, herself, has chosen pleasure. A palazzo instead of a nunnery. Her own fulfillment instead of Luisa's. Where is Luisa? She must be here; where else would she go? Maddalena searches the crowd for a glimpse of white-gold hair.

"Most people face much graver consequences, or at least set grave things into motion." The gondolier watches Maddalena. "Though if it doesn't impact you, is it a consequence at all?"

"Of course," Maddalena says, automatically.

The gondolier just looks at her.

"Do you see Luisa?" Maddalena asks. "Where is she?" The gondolier holds up a finger, testing the direction of the wind. He reaches out and takes Maddalena's hand.

The Piazzetta changes suddenly. It's still filled with music, but the people are gone, replaced by water that climbs the docks and infiltrates the loggias, water that seems to darken the sky. What looks like a table, perhaps the cushion of a chair, sweeps toward the Palazzo Ducale. And there, the only body above water, is Luisa. She looks up at her surroundings, too far away for Maddalena to see her expression; besides, she is masked.

The gondolier releases Maddalena, yet his vision remains. Something bumps against the back of her leg, which is now submerged in water to the knee, though strangely she doesn't feel the wet, only the cold, the same cold she felt holding the gondolier's hand. She turns to see his gondola, black and slippery, floating past the library steps. He offers to lift her in, but she shakes her head. Instead she watches as he hops atop the prow and pushes off with his long oar. Will he take Luisa now? He can't. Maddalena isn't ready to give her.

"Stop!" she cries. The gondolier looks back at her, and this pause seems to give Luisa the courage to run. She goes as quickly as she can through the water, splashing heavily and tripping over stones. The gondolier steers back toward Maddalena, his expression patronizing, unsurprised.

"Soon," says Maddalena. "Soon, I swear it. Just not yet."

Luisa

She goes first to Palazzo Grimani, and is told that Maddalena is not in. No one seems to know immediately where she's gone, and Luisa doesn't wait around for conjecture. A shadow passes by the window of the second-floor balcony, and she imagines it is Nicolò, looking down on the street. Luisa will not beg, not even after all that has transpired with Maffeo, and she's mortified to think of him seeing her here, expecting her to fall at his feet in some show of hysterics. Better Nicolò remember Luisa as she left him at Ca'Dandolo, her shoulders held straight enough, her head still high.

Now her wet dress clings to her legs, her bright hair is tangled. She remembers Maddalena, months ago in the lagoon, shining at the prow of the boat that carried them to the shrine. They must be related, the shrine and the water in the Piazzetta. Maddalena will know how. Maddalena will know what to do.

Luisa retraces her steps, weaving down ruge and through corti and calli. The dark is coming fast, the last soft pinks and oranges leaching from the sky, and the palazzi rise like fortresses, narrowing the back roads and the bridges. Night makes an already boisterous city even wilder. Luisa comes out onto Campo Santa Marina, which is ablaze with torches and packed with masked revelers. A wire has been strung across two adjacent roofs, and two men in motley swing outrageously low, the crowd egging them on. Luisa stops to watch the one, and then yelps in surprise as the second comes down right in front of her. She steps back into a group of powdered ladies—a gelatinous mass of fans and perfume laughing at hysterical pitch—that deflects her entrance and bounces her over to a different group in bautas who are playing at a duel.

"This pretty one goes to the winner," a small man shouts, and his larger friend grasps Luisa's wrist, his face bent down so she can see his red-rimmed eyes beneath the bauta, the point of the chin jutting toward her, the mask's wide nostrils flared. She tries to pull away, but his grip is strong and he squeezes until she thinks he's going to break her right arm. Her bowing arm. She envisions herself hobbling through a broken legato as Vivaldi scowls, ever more irate. She tries not to envision what these men plan to do to her. Fortunately, this is a public square, and eyes are everywhere. The large one presses harder, then laughs and releases her with a swat to the behind. "Off you go, then." Luisa scurries away, red-faced, fingering the spot under her sleeve where she is certain that she'll bruise.

She presses between booths, swerving to avoid hawkers. Two masked men argue while a third vomits red wine into a barrel. A woman's cloak brushes dangerously close to a torch, the air foul with its singe. If Luisa moves west, she'll reach the Grand Canal, where she can get her bearings, but when she asks a gentleman dressed as Pierrot—one black tear dripping down his mask, a large white ruff engulfing his neck—which way is west, he merely laughs. Luisa knows she should go home, but can't imagine going home before she's found Maddalena, before Maddalena has solved the problem of how Luisa will live—be it with or without Maffeo—and who will care for her. Maddalena has logistical considerations of her own, but she is both lucky and clever. She is bold, and Luisa needs boldness. She chooses a direction, decides at every fork she will turn left.

By the first left she's uncertain; by the second she is lost, stumbling through an empty alley, the dark arch of the buildings above blocking all light. She launches herself into the narrow darkness before she can lose courage. Something drips down the side of a building, collecting in an echoey trickle. The smell of turned meat, a heady decay. Luisa's heel catches on a cobblestone, and she bends down to remove her shoe, limping through some standing water, the chill creeping up her stocking. Then, at the third left, is Maddalena.

A girl, standing in the shadows at the base of a bridge, her gown ornate and her chin lifted in defiance of the mask she wears, daring anyone who passes not to know that she is Maddalena Grimani, here alone under a window box of night-lit chrysanthemum and iris. She wears her dark hair in a simple knot, loose curls framing her face. She doesn't seem surprised to see Luisa.

"I've been looking for you!" Luisa stumbles toward the bridge, catching herself on Maddalena's arm. Is it her imagination, or does Maddalena flinch? Maddalena takes a step back, toward the water. Most of Venice's bridges have no rails, just wide steps of stone and wood that lead from one side of a canal to the other. It is easy to imagine—and not fully uncommon to see—a person go over.

"And I you." Maddalena regains her balance, her composure. "What are you doing out here alone?" Luisa could say the same to Maddalena, but it would ring false. They both know that Maddalena is often out here alone.

"I have so much to tell you," says Luisa. So much to tell, but how to tell it? Must they discuss Nicolò? Even now, she hedges her bet. She set out in search of both Maddalena and utter transparency, but having found one, the other seems less appealing.

"If you're out, let's go to Lido." Maddalena takes Luisa's hand, laces their fingers. Such a familiar gesture, one that brings back the sticky warmth of the June dormitory, the sweet, grassy scent of Mira. For the first time since leaving Nicolò, Luisa has the sense that things might come out right. "The city's mad with St. Cecilia's Day. No one will ever know."

"Yes," says Luisa, grip tight. "Yes, let's just go."

Maddalena smiles. She's lovely in lantern light, all shimmering skin and darkness. A gondolier whistles down the canal, about to pass under the bridge on which they linger, and Maddalena hails him. She helps Luisa in, then climbs in after. "To pay—" Lido is far, and Luisa isn't sure how much money she has in her pocket.

"I've paid already."

They pass under Ponte di Rialto, the white stone monolith still teeming with people despite the late hour. The banks of the Grand Canal pulse, light and music spilling out from the palazzi, gondolas plentiful, keeping pace with their own. The proprietor of Luisa and Maddalena's particular boat wears a bauta, just the white mask, not the full ensemble. Luisa's relieved—she keeps an eye out for the black gnaga of the gondolier in the Piazzetta, but luckily the nearby traffic seems innocuous. She thinks she might tell Maddalena about the flooding, the way the square was cleared of people. If anyone would understand what happened, it's Maddalena with her shrine.

Easier to begin there, rather than with Dorsoduro and the flautist. A vision, a fantasy—these are surmountable problems. After all, what else is music?

"I—" says Luisa.

At the same time, Maddalena begins, "It's been a—" They both laugh. "You go first," says Maddalena. They're moving out into the eerie edges of the lagoon, past San Giorgio Maggiore, its church glowing white in the distance.

"I was at the Piazzetta, to hear the Coro," Luisa begins. "I had ... I don't know what I had. Like a dream, but awake. It was so strange, as if the whole square had been swallowed by the lagoon."

"The heat," Maddalena says at once.

"It's freezing."

"But when you're bundled up, I mean. The crowds and the wool cloak." Maddalena waves her hand. "I'm sure you overheated."

"Maybe." It's an inauspicious beginning. Luisa bites her lip. The lagoon is still, La Serenissima indeed. The gondola slices through the water with barely a wake.

"Is that all you had to tell me?" Maddalena turns in the felze so she's facing Luisa directly. "That you saw the Piazzetta falling into the lagoon?" Her tone is light, but her eyes are dark mirrors. She doesn't seem right.

"All?" says Luisa, a mimic. They're moving through the open water: marsh grass and shoals. Their gondolier has made quick work.

"That you had to tell me," Maddalena repeats. She blinks patiently, her hands spread open on her lap.

"It isn't good," Luisa bursts, sudden and strong. "I've been so foolish. He's going to annul our marriage and say I'm infertile, and send me away." She feels like she's describing someone else's life. There's no way that Maffeo meant her, Luisa the obedient, Luisa the careful.

"Why?" Maddalena asks simply, and Luisa feels again that shiver of unease. Surely Maddalena should immediately curse Maffeo's name, promise revenge and swear she'll stand by Luisa, her sister. Reasons should be secondary, no match for their bond. "Why would he say so?"

"Because I played the violin at a casino in Dorsoduro last night, and he knows, and he's afraid of what will happen."

They've reached Lido, their gondolier steering them into the canal that will move them toward the stony shore that faces the sea. No one but the three of them, no light but the half-moon and prickling stars and the little lantern that dangles from the prow of their boat. Luisa looks down at her feet, one stocking still damp.

"Why?"

"What do you mean? What does it matter why? I did it." Luisa feels the tears gathering, that cinch in her throat. She'd had such expectations for Maddalena, what she could do in response to Luisa's predicament, whether it be extorting the Celsis with some prize bit of intimate knowledge or convincing Luisa that Maffeo's storm would pass. If Maddalena is the edge of the world, and Maddalena has nothing to offer, Luisa's descent is all but assured. She tugs on her cloak, takes in the air in ragged gulps. Maddalena puts an arm across Luisa's shoulder and tucks Luisa's head to her breasts, murmuring something nonsensical and soothing. Luisa lets herself be held.

When she looks up, the gondola has moored. Rocks of all size stretch out before them, holding back the sea, lining the chilly, untouched beach. She can hear the waves, the roll of them like massive gears grinding. From here there is no view of the main island, no rose-quartz city twinkling beyond the quay. Only the long stretch of beach, salt water lengthening toward invisible Dalmatia.

"What are we doing here?" Luisa whispers. Maddalena, who is climbing out of the gondola, then over the rocks, seems not to hear. She takes a few steps in the sand, her low heels making divots that disappear before Luisa's eyes: like watching a flower bloom, impossible to parse or deny. After a moment, Maddalena crouches to take off her shoes. Luisa lets the gondolier help her from the boat and follows suit. Two pairs of shoes in the sand. Maddalena's are yellow.

The gondolier gives them a single-fingered salute.

"Will he stay?" asks Luisa. "Will we be stuck here?" But Maddalena is too far ahead, sidestepping sharp bits of seashell as she walks over the beach, toward the water. She must have some ritual in mind, something to do with the waves, something that wouldn't work were they to stay in the lagoon. It stands to reason that the sea would have a stronger hold on Maddalena's imagination. Luisa turns back to the gondolier.

"We won't be too long," she says. "Will you stay?"

"Of course."

She knows that voice. She knows this man. A sinking, the sand to silt and then to water; the nauseous drop of her heart. The gondolier takes off his bauta, and of course he is the flautist, and of course the flautist is Maddalena's gondolier. She couldn't place him masked at the casino, but she knows him now, here in his boat in the dark. How can that be? What does that mean?

The gondolier sets down the bauta, and from somewhere in his jacket comes the black gnaga. He doesn't tie it on, just holds it up to his face, and then away. He looks at her, and she can't read his expression, though he's lit by the boat's lantern, his smooth cheeks and his salted hair, handsome in an otherworldly way, as if he's come to Venice from somewhere very far away, like Constantinople or Vienna. How ridiculous to think that she was safe, simply because when they boarded his boat he had a different face. You can't live here in Venice and not understand innately that a mask is interchangeable. She hurries after Maddalena, to warn her of the gondolier's disguise.

Maddalena stands in the water, the tide licking the hems of her skirts. The moon is perfectly bisected by the night, a glowing semicircle casting its reflected glory down onto the sea. Maddalena wears a gray dress, with silver flowers twining the waist and sleeves and skirt. She's still wearing her half-mask, and Luisa has the urge to tug at its ribbon. Funny, how little Maddalena looks like Nicolò, although they share at least a mother. Where he is sweet and transparent, Maddalena is sharp, shining surfaces. Luisa wants to take a hammer to her, crack until she's broken through the glass. She reaches the water, puts her own skirts in the waves. She removes her own mask and tosses it onto the sand, where it sits, never truly a part of her. "Did you know that it's your boy from the Pietà who's brought us here?"

A crash: a wave against a far-off pier. Maddalena nods. She says nothing.

"I didn't know until now," Luisa says. "He's the one from Dorsoduro who encouraged me to play." More silence, still the mask. If only Maddalena would remove it, then they could speak freely. Dread weighs Luisa's limbs, her bones all turned iron. "I have to tell you why I went," Luisa says, voice raised to counter the surf, "why I was there in Dorsoduro, and why I trusted him." The water in, the water out. White foam reaching its greedy fingers. "Nicolò sent me."

"Oh," says Maddalena, her voice flat. Luisa knows this voice; she's heard Maddalena use it on Chiara, on her brothers. It's the voice that comes ahead of the kill, the voice that pretends a retreat, before ravaging.

Maddalena knows. Maddalena has known. The knowledge hits Luisa physically, sending her stumbling. "I was trying to tell you," she says, stepping closer. She's near enough that she can see Maddalena's breath as a small mist against the dark, smoke from the fire that says, *Look, I am still here, against the elements*. "I tried so many times to tell you."

"And yet." Maddalena with that same even tone, although she's quieter now than she has been. She moves her mouth toward Luisa's mouth, a lover's prelude.

"How did you know?" Luisa's voice is so soft that she can barely hear herself against the relentless rhythm of the water.

"I saw you," says Maddalena. A little flash of tongue against the teeth, wetting the lips. Too dark to read much else.

"I'm sorry." And Luisa truly is. Regret has gutted her, deboned her like a market fish. She guides Maddalena's hands to her own shoulders, presses her palms against them as if touch is absolution.

"I loved you," says Maddalena, leaning in, letting her hands move closer, press tighter.

"And I love you." Luisa melts with relief. She takes Maddalena's waist, closes the small remaining distance between them. Sand scratches against her stockings, one foot atop some broken shell, but she ignores it, inhaling Maddalena, loving her.

"You don't understand." Maddalena's hands climb closer to Luisa's throat. "I *loved* you." She's strong for one so slight. "I loved you, and then there you were, with *him.*"

"You're hurting me." Luisa lifts her hands, trying to pull Maddalena's away. Maddalena presses harder.

"I want you to know that it was me," Maddalena says. "I was the one who sent the letter telling you to play in Dorsoduro, and I was the one who told Maffeo to be there to see you. I was the one who reminded my brother of his duty to his family and the republic. I am the one here now."

Now is nothing. Now is exploding, exponential stars; the water and the water and the water. Wind rising to turn the sand to shards of glass, and from somewhere—could it be?—a mournful cello. Luisa collapses. Maddalena's hands are finally off her throat. Luisa is too swollen, too shocked, to apologize further. But there is time. They will have time. They will return to the gondolier, and Luisa will hold Maddalena while she cries, or perhaps they will both cry. Perhaps it will rain.

The rush of body against body, long starved and gritty with sand. Maddalena kisses Luisa's neck, where her fingers have surely left bruises. She straddles Luisa, licks Luisa's ear, a little nibble on the lobe. The two of them roll into the surf. Luisa thinks of the puppies in the kitchens at Ca'Celsi, at play, most likely, but always that thrill of aggression. She lifts herself to Maddalena, who is still wearing the mask.

Why is she still wearing the mask?

Another roll, both bodies into the water, which buoys them as they clutch each other, teasing their hair from their coiffures, weighing their dresses. Luisa first on top, and then below. Too long below. Again, her hands scratch at Maddalena, asking for air, asking for mercy. Luisa thinks if she can only get the mask, if she can find Maddalena beneath it. To the last she is reaching, squeezing flesh.

The last comes in a great inhalation of salt water, burning Luisa's lungs, creeping in through the corners of her eyes. It is a long shadowy hand, guiding her out past the pebbly bottom to where the sand is sleek. The promise of a symphony, the first breath before the music begins, when everything is possibility. Girls in white, with pomegranate flowers in their hair. A church, musky with incense, lit with candles. And then the sweetest violin, emerging from the ensemble like a bird, like a murmuring spring.

Maddalena

Two set out for Lido and only one returns, *Maddalena trium-phans*. She would like to think that they are both gone, that the girl who crawls from the beach with her arms scratched red and the ribbon of her mask dripping wet down her back is someone born from that last moment, a trick of alchemy that builds a new person in place of the old. She feels like if she raises an arm, the water will come in a great tide to do her bidding. She feels like she has swallowed the night.

While they were rowed out to Lido, she'd been afraid of herself. She'd been afraid she'd not be capable, that at the final moment some part of her would crack, first a small fracture, then a breaking of the berg. But in that moment, with Luisa in the waves, there was no break-ing. She did what she must. Maddalena is her mother's daughter, and she acts for herself.

The gondolier sees her, a wet dog climbing the rocks, the salty shake of her hair, the drag of her skirts. In her hand is a small lock of white-gold hair, which she will keep in a sapphire locket shaped like a tear that hangs down between her breasts, mostly unseen and unremarked on. That is later. Now she wraps it around an index finger so tightly that the blood divides. The gondolier sees her, and he holds out a hand. His skin, usually so cold, is smooth and warm.

The city seems particularly quiet. Of course it is late, but she ex-pected the roar of Carnival, at least its embers: the hiss of a drunkard pissing over a bridge or the squeal of a whore faking pleasure. Right-fully, Maddalena would be ushered back to the Rialto with the tremble of a master's violin. Music should bow to her, its sovereign. If she opens her mouth, will the darkness and the way Luisa sputtered and the reel of the stars all pour out of her? She says nothing to the gondolier. He rows.

Home is silent, lamps put out and the household abed. The gondolier presses her hand in his. She thinks he might kiss it, but he doesn't. *When will I see you again?* She cannot speak—the night not yet digested. He makes a one-fingered salute and rows away.

Sleep comes easily. Maddalena lets her lids fall, lets the sway of it overtake her without fear. Dreamless and black, the bed speckled with sand and smelling of the marsh, her hair matted when she wakes. In the morning there are letters: from Giacomo Cornaro, from Pietro Querini, from Alvise Tron. Here is one from Marco Zanni, who is all but engaged, and another from the doge's nephew, Paulo Mocenigo. All express their undying devotion. All wonder what she has planned for this evening: Does she fancy a trip to the Ridotto, a visit to the theater, a stroll through Castello? When I get permission from your father, each man says, we will write up the marriage contract. Say the word, and I'll meet with my lawyers. What do you want? I'll give you anything. I will make your life a pleasure garden.

A scratch across her jaw, fingernails scarring the backs of her hands. Maddalena brushes out her hair without washing it, and salt christens the floor. She calls for a breakfast tray. Drinks chocolate in the window, looking out toward the sea.

With Luisa gone, things are easy. Nicolò assumes her disappearance is his fault—he doesn't say as much but he mourns guiltily, jowls thickening, a drooping dog who skulks about the house. Maffeo assumes it is his fault, and takes pride. He writes to Maddalena: little love sonnets and sketches of himself at her feet, little apologies. She's going to marry him. Even Nicolò knows that with Luisa disappeared and the unfortunate marriage annulled, a Celsi alliance is inevitable.

"When I am married," Maddalena whispers to herself, sorting her

letters. The admirers continue, a plethora from which to choose a cicisbeo. When she is married she will wear pearls for a year, then take
a lover. She'll develop a gambling habit; it will be good that she has
married into money, however new. Pleasure, always. Feasts and regattas
and sumptuous concerts, the Ospedali Grandi hired out to play at private palazzi, although she will never hire the Pietà. It will be pleasure,
ever more aggressive, ever more stifling. At the end of the century, the
republic will fall to Napoleon with *vive le plaisir* on its lips.

Her children will be citizens of an unknown nation, but Maddalena
will have pleasure. Her city will age to obsolescence; so will she. Her skin
chiffoning, crepey at the elbows, her locket hanging down her sagging
chest. She will powder her wig and paint on her beauty mark, and she'll
sit with a long cigarette, a half-mask, and a grin, and roll her dice. She'll
never wear a moretta; she'll never hold anything in her mouth that's not
deliberate and by choice.

Luisa tasted exactly as Maddalena had imagined. Luisa took off her
mask, and her skin glowed transparent in the moonlight and her braid
fell from its coil.

"I love you," she said, and Maddalena felt the impossibility of this
night-blooming moment, the impermanence of her world and its shores.
Maybe if she had been born on terra firma. Maybe if she'd had no pride.
But the waves flowed and ebbed, and they beat *traitor* with each slap
against the legs of the girls in the water.

"I *loved* you." The words burned Maddalena's throat. To be so vul-
nerable, there in the little bed with Luisa. To open endlessly, and let
herself be seen. It wasn't the promise to the thing in the water, or the
intrusion of Nicolò, or the clock counting down on her father's desk,
that sent Maddalena's hands to Luisa's hair, then to Luisa's throat. This
was Maddalena herself.

She had been perfectly content—the lacing shadows of the leaves
on Luisa's body in repose, the slow trickle of the fountain at Mira—and
it had all been an illusion. Enough to whet the appetite, but nothing to

fill her. Isn't it difficult enough to be a girl coming to womanhood, to be eternally penitent for your mother's sin? Maddalena had pushed back at every warning, every truth about the world, for the chance at those clouds and that thick summer sky. She pressed against Luisa, wanting, hating. She was a hissing cat in heat. She was a storm.

The space between submission and loss is so small. In the water they held each other, two girls, then one. Maddalena thought of the Coro, up in the balcony, the way the separate instruments emerged to tell their story, then slipped back into the whole. She thought of the long summer, the burning fall. When Luisa played her violin, and it was just for Maddalena, those improvised cadenzas in the small practice room at the back of the sala. When they sat arm in arm at chapel. When Maddalena took off her dress at Mira and waited and waited, and Luisa did nothing. Now Luisa's mouth gasping, Maddalena's tongue in her ear. So primal and so beautiful, the warmth within them steaming the winter water.

She'd thought this was a way to say goodbye to Maddalena of old. That Maddalena who wanted so nakedly, who exposed such tender flesh. What better farewell than this, a kiss and then a long, slow baptism? There might have been a better way, a way that would absolve her. Had she been twenty-five, not fifteen. Had there been another boat in the canal, another body on the beach. Had the moon been gone that night, had Luisa been more penitent, had the thing in the water done more, or been greedier. There might have been a better way, but if there was, she'd never know.

Acknowledgments

Thank you, always, to Stephanie Delman. Your insight and friendship are unparalleled, and it is such a joy to be your client. Thank you to Khalid McCalla and the rest of the coven at Trellis—Michelle Brower, Allison Hunter, and team—what a home you've made. May every author find such support and community.

Thank you, Caroline Bleeke, for seeing what this book could be and guiding it gently and thoughtfully to the best version of itself. Your encouragement has strengthened me since 2016, and I still can't believe the stars aligned for us. To everyone at Flatiron: Sydney Jeon, Keith Hayes, Mumtaz Mustafa, Kelly Gatesman, Megan Lynch, Malati Chavali, Donna S. Noetzel, Emily Walters, Morgan Mitchell, Eva Diaz, Claire McLaughlin, Erin Kibby—you are the real deal. Thank you for your patience, for making me feel heard, for going all in on this book. I couldn't ask for a better group of advocates and artists.

To Miranda Ottewell, who has traveled with me through gothic fairy tales and 1940s New York: thank you for making eighteenth-century Venice so perfect.

To my early readers and dear friends, without whom this would be a much lesser book: Isle McElroy, Katie Gutierrez, Amy Jo Burns, and Sophie Brochu. I tell my students that their first readers are vital to a project's success, and you four have proved my point a hundredfold.

To Brian Cavanagh-Strong, A. Natasha Joukovsky, and Mara Winston Grigg: thank you for making a wildly mediocre musician sound like a pro. Truly, you are superheroes.

This book is partially a love letter to Venice and its history. Thank you to the vaporetto, every aperol spritz, and the perfection of the city in early spring. To the Chiesa della Pietà, and the lovely volunteers who helped me dig through time. To the front desk staff at Hotel Metropole, who humored my strange requests, and the team at the Ruzzini Palace Hotel, for flexibility in an age of pandemics, and impeccable hospitality and care.

I am forever indebted to *Vivaldi's Ring of Mystery*, the 1991 cassette tape from Classical Kids that began my lifelong interest in the Pietà. Thanks also to Vanessa Tonelli's "Women and Music in the Venetian Ospedali," Patrick Barbier's *Vivaldi's Venice*, H. C. Robbins Landon's *Vivaldi*, and John Julius Norwich's *A History of Venice*. Without such rich scholarship, I could never have written this novel.

To my musical inspirations: Kirill Troussov, Midori, Katariina Maria Kits, Anne-Sophie Mutter, and, of course, Olivia Rodrigo.

To Dick and Denise Berdelle for childcare, a quiet place to edit with the world's best fireplace, and so much love and support. To Michael Fine, for conversation and enthusiasm and lifelong encouragement. To Susan Fine, for being my favorite travel companion and very best friend.

And to Rick, Elliott, and Margot: you let me be and do so many things. I love you.

About the Author

Julia Fine is the author of *The Upstairs House*, winner of the Chicago Review of Books Award for Fiction, and *What Should Be Wild*, which was short-listed for the Bram Stoker Award for Superior Achievement in a First Novel. She teaches writing in Chicago, where she lives with her husband and children.

Recommend
Maddalena and the Dark
for your next book club!

Reading Group Guide available at
flatironbooks.com/reading-group-guides